KINGPIN WIFEYS

K. ELLIOTT

CONTENTS

PART 5:
LANI'S DILEMMA

PART 6:
A STARR IS BORN

PART 7:
WHO DO YOU LOVE?

PART 5:
LANI'S DILEMMA

CHAPTER 1

"You sold my goddamned car!" Craig stood up from the sofa, his demeanor cold. He very much wanted to smack the fuck out of her, but he didn't want to have to explain to his wife how he'd gotten locked up for beating this crazy black bitch. Besides, Anne didn't know about the other Maserati.

"I didn't sell the car," Jada said.

Craig presented her with the paperwork stating that the Maserati would be Joey Turch's in the event that she didn't pay the legal fees. She'd left the paperwork on the kitchen table.

"Did you even read the damn paper? Where is my car?" yelled Craig.

"The attorney's got it until I give him five grand."

"What is this all about?"

Jada hid her eyes. She couldn't look him. She was very ashamed.

"Jada, what the hell is this about?"

She sat on an armchair across from the sofa, still avoiding his eyes, gathering her thoughts, trying to think of half-truths, but there was nothing she could say to pacify him.

"Is this about that drug-dealing thug of yours?"

She met his eyes, a single tear rolled down her cheek. "Yeah, he got into a little bit of trouble."

"And he didn't have the money to get himself out?"

"No."

"That's hard to believe."

"Why?"

"I have counted thousands of dollars in my office—money that you got from him."

"Look, motherfucker, people go through hard times."

"Okay, you're cursing me out. After you spent my money on him! *You* people, I tell you."

"What the fuck is that supposed to mean?"

He stood and paced. "I can't believe you sold or pawned my goddamn car and now you're talking shit to me."

"Look I'm sorry. I'm going to get the car back, and I'll sign it back over to you."

"You damn well better!"

His angry tone was pissing her the fuck off.

"What?" said Jada.

He walked over to her and said, "I said you damn well better."

She pushed him back a little and said, "Can you get the hell out of my personal space?"

He eased back a little. "I want my car back."

"You're going to get your car."

"You're such a disrespectful little bitch."

She stood and placed her pointing finger on the tip of his nose and said, "I ain't going to be too many more bitches."

"Jada, you need to leave. This is not working out."

"Fine." Then she thought, where in the hell would she go? The house that she lived in with Shamari was months behind in the rent and she didn't want to go back to Louise's house. There was no way in hell she could survive in that dysfunctional situation.

She eased up to Craig and wrapped her arms around him and said, "I'm truly sorry. I was wrong for doing this to you."

He hugged her back and said, "Jada, you really, really, let me down."

She looked him in the eyes and said, "I know I let you down, and I want to make it up to you."

"I don't want no goddamned oral sex! I want my car."

"I'm going to get the car back."

"Tell me what happened."

"Shamari got locked up."

"The Feds again?"

"No."

"What happened?"

"A long story but basically he got set up. It was a deal gone bad, and this attorney, Joey Turch, needed the money right away."

"Is that why you had me sign the car over in your name?"

"No...I mean, yes."

"Yes or no."

"Well, I was hoping I didn't have to sign the car over, but I wanted it in my name just in case I needed the money."

"You're so loyal to him?"

"I am, just like you're loyal to your wife."

He pushed her away. "Leave my wife out of this."

"I'm sorry."

"Look, I think you need to leave."

She stared at him but didn't say anything. She didn't have anything so say. She gathered her things and left for Skyy's house.

CHAPTER 2

Mike called Lani. She answered on the second ring.

"Hello...Hello?"

There was a sniffling sound like he was trying to get his thoughts together. Lani realized Mike was crying.

"Mike?"

No answer. She glanced at her phone, she could see the call was still connected and she had a very good signal.

"Mike? You there?"

"Yeah."

"What's wrong?"

"It's Chris."

"What's wrong with Chris?"

"Chris's body was found in the trunk of an old Lincoln out in the country. Burned."

"You're kidding me, right?"

He took a deep breath. "I wish I was. I really wish I was, but my brother is dead and whoever did it, shot him in the head."

"How did they know it was him?"

"Dental records."

Lani sobbed, "Please, Mike, tell me this is a bad joke."

"No, I wish it was."

"I'm so sorry. Who could have done some shit like this?" Then she thought about Black.

Mike said, "I don't know, we're still trying to figure everything out."

Lani said, "Me and Chris weren't on good terms, but I still cared."

"I know you did. I'll talk to you later."

"Please do, and let me know when the memorial service is."

"I will."

Lani hung the phone up. She started to call Chris's mother, but she didn't know what to say. She called Black right away.

"Hello?" Black said.

"Chris is dead."

"Who?"

"My ex."

"Damn, that's fucked up. I'm sorry to hear that."

"I'm sure."

"No seriously, I don't wish death upon nobody."

"Okay, when can I see you?"

"Anytime, I can come by tonight if you want me to."

There was no way she wanted Black to come to her house at night. She didn't want him to think they'd be having sex. She said, "Can you come in the morning?"

"I'll be busy all day tomorrow."

"Come by tonight."

"Okay, I'll hit you up around eleven."

"That's too late."

"Ten?"

"Okay."

Black called at 11:45 pm, Lani was in bed, but still not asleep. She was awake thinking about Chris. She knew there would be no way she would get any sleep for the next couple of weeks. Black said he was around the corner. This would be the first visitor Lani had since she moved into her loft.

"The code to the building is 618."

Black stepped into her place five minutes later without crutches, but with some old school walking cane. He looked like a pimp from the seventies. He eyed Lani completely, she was wearing a t-shirt and some pink boy-shorts that gripped her ass wonderfully, her legs glistened and she wore a vanilla scent. Black wanted to lay her right down on the floor and fuck her like an animal.

"Nice place. Where is the furniture?"

"Don't have the money for it right now."

"Should have told me."

"Well, I'm telling you."

"I'll send Kyrie over here tomorrow with some money."

"Look, Black, you don't have to do that. You've done more than enough."

"I know I don't have to do that. I wanna do it."

"Okay, in the meantime, let's go to the bedroom."

Black smiled, "Exactly where I wanna go."

"I don't know why. Ain't shit going down."

He laughed and followed her to the bedroom. She sat on the bed. He tried to sit beside her and she directed him to a chair across from the bed.

She looked him in his eyes to see if he was hiding something. Same ol' Black.

"So I can't get on the bed with you?"

"Not right now."

"Wassup?"

"Well you know Chris got murdered."

"Good."

"On the phone you said you were sorry to hear that, and that you wouldn't wish that on anyone."

"Look, that nigga tried to kill me! He shot up your mama's house! Anybody could've gotten killed in there."

"Did you kill Chris?"

"No."

"Did you have him killed."

"Look," he paused then he said, "No."

"That's all I wanted to ask."

"But was I gonna kill his punk ass? Yes."

"That's a whole different matter."

"Look, when you're heavy in the drug game, anything can and will happen." Black looked away for a brief second.

"I understand that. But I just wanted to make sure you didn't have nothing to do with it."

"Why?"

"Because if you did it, it indirectly links it to me."

"Listen, I'll never let you go down for anything. I'm a mother-fuckin' man. I can do time."

"It's not being a man. This is a man that I lived with, I slept with, I loved. Now he's dead. I don't want that on my conscience."

"And it shouldn't be on your conscience."

Black sat on the bed beside her. He put his hand on her thigh and she pushed it away. "Look, I'm not in the mood tonight. Somebody that was very close to me got killed. Try to understand."

"I understand."

He leaned into her and kissed her jaw. Then he stood and grabbed his walking cane that was still lying next to the chair. He headed to the front door and she trailed after him. When he opened the door, he turned and kissed her, his arm on the small of her back. She didn't resist him. He gripped her ass and she began to kiss him back until she stopped and said, "Black, please go."

He smiled and said, "I'll send Kyrie over with the money for the furniture."

"You don't have to do that."

"I want to do that."

When the door closed, she lay back against the door until finally she was on the floor sobbing. Damn, she missed Chris. And she hated to admit it, but she wanted Black back. She wanted very much to believe that he didn't have anything to do with Chris's death. Time would tell.

CHAPTER 3

Chris's memorial service was held in the back on his mother's church—his ashes in an urn. The service was small, mostly made up of his college basketball teammates and a few hustlers he'd done business with. Lani, Starr, and Jada arrived at the service about five minutes late. Jada and Starr were there to support Lani, although they hated each other's guts.

They sat in the very last row. The first person Lani saw was Tika, Chris's make-believe cousin, seated in the front row with Chris's mother, Mattie, and Chris's stepfather, an old white man named Jack. Tika hugged Chris's mother and patted her as Mattie wept for her son. The service was short. Chris's college coach said a few nice words and a couple of his teammates did the same. Lani cried silently as Starr and Jada supported her. She didn't really think she would take it so hard, but this whole thing made her realize death was so final and to hold onto the things you loved. Lani and the girls headed to the parking lot before the service was over. They were about to get into Lani's car when Mike walked up to them.

"Lani?" called out Mike.

"Yeah, Mike."

"Can I holla at you for a second?"

Lani said, "Of course." She handed Starr the keys to the car. Starr and Jada walked to the BMW and got inside.

She hugged Mike and said, "I'm sorry."

"Really?"

"Why wouldn't I be?"

"Well, I think your boy got something to do with this."

"What boy?"

"Black."

"No. I asked him."

"Of course he said he didn't."

This conversation was getting uncomfortable for her. She felt like she was being interrogated.

"Look, I asked him did he know about it. He said he didn't and I believe him."

Mike said, "Whoa!" You don't have to get upset. It's not like I'm going to call the police on him. That is not the way my brother would want this shit handled."

"What are you talking about?"

"I really hope Black don't get caught. I can't let that ride. I cannot let a nigga get away with killing my brother, seeing my mother mourn like that. I've never seen my mama cry like that."

A single tear rolled down Lani's cheek. She removed some sunglasses from her clutch. She wanted to hide behind them, so she sat them on the edge of her nose

"Can you imagine what it would be like to see your mom mourn?"

"Yeah, my mama buried my brother," Lani said, thinking about the time her brother had gotten murdered and Black shelled out the money to bury him because her brother didn't have life insurance. Black was good when he wanted to be. That was why it was so hard for her to believe that he had anything to do with Chris's murder.

"I didn't know you lost a brother. So, you know exactly what I'm going through then?"

"I do."

Mike hugged her and said, "If you know anything, let me know. Don't say a word to the police. Let me handle it my way."

Lani didn't respond, she just said, "Send your mother my condolences."

"I will."

Lani headed to the car.

Trey had found Shantelle Parker on Facebook. Shantelle was the woman that Monte had alleged talked to the Feds about him. Shantelle was beautiful and was very much into herself. Trey could tell by all the selfies on her Facebook page. She was tall, thin, and brown with perfect teeth. Trey remembered the police report that alluded to the fact that Shantelle had given Monte head. This was not the type of woman who would never deal with a loser like Monte. Her page said she was from Seattle and had gone to Georgia State. Something wasn't adding up. Trey was staring at one of her three thousand pictures, a pic of Shantelle leaning up against a BMW 325. She was wearing workout clothes, her hair shoulder length. This bitch looked amazing—there was no way she gave Monte head. Trey recognized the background of the photo. Atlantic Station. Trey called a private investigator that worked for his lawyer's law firm and got Shantelle's exact address. He hung out around Atlantic Station watching her house from a distance for about three days until one day he spotted her coming back from a jog wearing some ridiculously tight black yoga pants, a sports bra, and her hair in a pony-tail. Trey approached her.

"Hi," he said.

She looked at him but kept walking.

Stuck-up bitch. How in the hell was she going to talk to Monte but not even say hi to him?

"Hello"

Again, she didn't respond then Trey realized that she had her earbuds in. He waved his arm to get her attention and she removed the earbuds.

"Hi."

He extended his hand. "I'm Trey."

"Good."

"Can I buy you some coffee or an energy drink, a Gatorade, anything?"

"An energy drink or a Gatorade, that's original."

Trey gave her the once-over and said, "Well, you look like the type that would wanna keep her electrolyte intake up."

She giggled and said, "My apartment is within walking distance. So, no thank you." She smiled politely.

"Shantelle, I know you don't know me, but I'm Trey."

"How do you know me?"

"Look, do you know Monte?"

Now there was a huge frown on her face.

"Unfortunately, yes."

"Can we go somewhere and talk for a few moments. It don't have to be your home."

"Let's go to Cheesecake Bistro. It's right across the street."

They sat at a table in the back of the restaurant. Trey ordered a strawberry cheesecake and a glass of water, Shantelle just ordered a glass of water. After the waitress left, Trey said, "So, did Monte ever say something to you about me?"

"Before I answer these questions, what's going on? I mean, I've never met you and all of sudden you're over here where I live. How did you find out where I live and what do you want with me?"

Trey bit into his cheesecake and said, "You're name was on Monte's paperwork."

"Okay. And how did you find me."

"Facebook."

"Facebook told you that I lived at Atlantic Station

"You just told me you did."

"That's before I knew you knew Monte, I thought you were just some guy trying to hit on me. But this is scary, you tracked me down."

Trey smiled, "I did, didn't I?"

"What do you want?"

"I just want the truth about what happened the day you got busted."

"And you're Trey?"

"Yeah, did Monte ever mention me?"

"Yeah, I'd been with him a few times when he called you."

"What did he say 'bout me?"

"He said that you were his partner."

"Okay. So what happened?"

"I thought you saw the police report."

"I did."

"What did it say?"

"It said your hair was disheveled."

She laughed. "Yeah, it was."

"You went down on Monte?"

"Are you out of your goddamn mind? Hell, no! Did you ever look at that dude?"

"Hey! I'm just repeating what the police report said."

"Look, Monte saw the police and got nervous. He said, 'look you need to pretend to be giving me head, so the police can let us go.'"

"What sense did that make?"

"Well his thinking was when the police pulled us over, he would beg the cop to let us go saying that he was cheating on his wife. Monte thought this would deflect from the fact that we were riding so much cocaine."

"I see."

She sipped her water again and said, "You know it would have worked if…." She stopped.

"If what?"

"If the police didn't smell the weed."

"What weed?"

"Monte had been smoking weed earlier."

Trey bit into his cheesecake. "What the hell?"

"Yeah, your boy is a genius. But thank God he did what he said he was going to do."

"What was that?"

"Well Monte always said if things went wrong, he would take the blame and for me not to worry."

"But I don't remember reading about no weed on the police report."

"That police report was fake. Monte knew you would go the fuck off if you knew he'd been smoking weed."

Trey, now with a mouthful of cheesecake, washed it down with some water. He was trying to get a feel for this woman, but so far, she had been difficult to read. He'd never imagined that she would be the type of woman that would be down with a drug operation. He sat his fork down on the saucer. She was staring at him. He avoided her eyes but got a glimpse of her incredibly nice thighs.

"Shantelle, can I ask you a question?"

"Sure."

"Don't take this the wrong way, but you don't seem like the kind of woman that would go on a—"

"A drug run?"

"Yeah."

"Well, I'm no angel, but I've dated D Boys before when I was younger. Everybody did."

"Dating a dope boy is different than making a run."

"I know, I'm ashamed to be doing some shit like that at thirty too. I'm too old for that."

"Why'd you do it?"

"Needed the money."

"And you don't need it now?"

"Well, not really."

"What changed?"

She huffed, she was uncomfortable answering the question, plus he kept looking at her thighs.

"Look, I was just trying to get some money to start my business." She flipped her hair and said. "You know, I was just like every other pretty girl in Atlanta—doing videos and the modeling thing, but it wasn't getting me anything."

"Your Facebook page said you went to Georgia State."

"Damn! You're a real live stalker," she laughed.

Trey said, "The Feds asked about me, did they?'

She flicked her hair again and smiled, "Oh I see. Is this what this is about? It's not about me, it's about you?"

"Answer the question."

"Look, nobody asked about you. Nobody knew about you. Monte wanted to extort you. You know, make you believe the Feds were after you, and he'd be the only one that could set you free by not cooperating. He wanted me to pretend like I was going to cooperate unless you gave us some money."

"That motherfucker!" Trey said.

"The truth is, nobody asked me anything after Monte claimed the drugs."

"Really?"

"I swear to God."

Trey believed her. He wanted to find bitch-assed Monte and fuck him up, but he had to let it go. Monte would be going to prison soon.

Trey stood up and threw a twenty dollar bill on the table.

Shantelle stood up from the table and placed her earbuds back in.

They shook hands and Shantelle said, "Call me if you ever need anything."

"Like what?"

"A favor. Anything I can do to help. It's hard out here for a girl."

"What's your number?

"404-567-0987."

Trey punched it into his iPhone.

CHAPTER 4

Jada had asked Skyy if she could crash at her place for a few days. Jada was standing in front of the full length mirror, applying lotion to her body when Skyy barged in. Skyy didn't say nothing, she just stared. She was staring so hard that it made Jada uncomfortable. She was hoping that the threesome with Craig didn't give Skyy the idea that she would be fucking her during her stay.

Jada applied lotion to her ankle and said, "What the hell are you looking at?"

"Just admiring your body. It's damn near perfect. This is the first time I really got to see it."

"Well, I spent a lot of money getting this way."

"Well, I knew you had gotten your boobs done, but is that ass all yours? I've always wanted to know but didn't know how to ask you?"

"Yeah it's mine, I paid for it."

They both laughed. Though Jada didn't want to admit to having a butt augmentation with most of her friends, she would admit it to Skyy since she was a dancer and most of the dancers in Atlanta have fake body parts. It was no big deal to them, but the minute she admitted it to a civilian, they'd be acting like her ass was fake. She didn't have time for that foolishness, debating over whether her ass was real or not. There were more important things in the world.

Skyy said, "I know that's right."

Jada said, "Craig performed all my procedures."

"Really? So they were free?"

"No, I had to pay for them, but that's how we met."

"Oh, okay I see. I'm thinking of getting my boobs done. You know I wanna take them up a cup size."

"What are you now, a B cup?"

"An A."

"So you wanna go up to a B? Who in the fuck does that? You need to take them things up to a C and get your grown woman on."

Skyy laughed. "I guess you're right. I've been saving."

"Let Craig do it. One thing I gotta admit, he is good at what he does."

"So have you spoken with him?"

"He called, but I sent him to voice mail."

"Wait a minute! You wronged him, but you sent him to voice mail?"

Jada placed the towel on the guest bed and sat down on it. "Look, I know I wronged him, and I'm going to get that money back and get that car back. I got a few watches worth close to twenty grand. I'll sell them and get him his car back, even though he signed it over to me."

Jada stood up and slid into a yellow g-string that contrasted wonderfully with her skin. Her ass cheeks swallowed the g-string. "With the rest of the money, I'm going to get an apartment. Jada Simone will be back on top—you can believe that."

"With that body of yours, you should be stripping. You'll make so much money, bitch."

"I can't deal with that. All those niggas touching you and dis-respecting you all night. I'm not cut out for that."

"Not everybody is."

"How do you do it?"

"I just toot my powder and I'm good."

"That's something I couldn't do either."

"Well, if I had rich men throwing themselves at me, I wouldn't have to do it neither."

Jada ignored Skyy because now the bitch sounded like she was hating. Jada put on a pair of tight skinny jeans and some wedges. She grabbed her bag and said, "I'll talk to you later. I'm going to see Shamari."

"See you later."

CHAPTER 5

Trey was driving down Auburn Avenue when he noticed a white Toyota Prius hatchback flashing its lights behind him, trying to get his attention. He pulled over at a B.P. Gas Station. A blond white lady jumped out of the car and was walking toward him when he realized it was his baby mama, Jessica.

"What the fuck does this bitch want?" he mumbled.

He put his Range Rover in park and hopped out of the car. "Wassup?"

"Wassup my ass! You move and don't let your son know where you live?"

"Tell me what you want?"

"I don't want shit from you Trey. I just want you to do right by your son."

"Well, let me get him every weekend. I've told you I want joint custody."

"And what about the money?"

"I was giving you close to three grand a month, and you went and took out some child support on me."

"Trey, I'm the mother of your son. I'm riding around in this piece of shit, Toyota Prius, when you got this other bitch with the ghetto-ass name living better than me and T.J. You're going to rot in hell, Trey."

"And you tried to put me in jail. Actually tried to send me to prison! How would you explain that to our son?"

"You goddamned right! You wanna act like I don't exist. I'm going to show you that I do."

"What is that supposed to mean?"

"Whatever you want it to mean."

"Well, I've been locked up for child support. I'll see you in court."

"See, you ain't no real man. A real man would take care of his son up until the time he goes to court."

"Whatever."

"Trey, you need to pay me or I'm going to make your life a living hell. You know I know all you're goddamned secrets. And I'll tell them to Starr."

"What are you talking about?"

"I'm talking about those two abortions you paid for. Starr don't know the half."

Trey walked back toward the Range Rover and jumped in and drove off. Seconds later he got a text from Jessica: *How are you enjoying the floor to ceiling glass condo?*

"Trey said, "Fuck, this bitch knows where I live."

Trey received a text: *Hey Trey. This is Shantelle.*

Trey: *Hey*

Shantelle: *Do you have anything for me to do yet?*

Trey: *Not really.*

Shantelle: *Well I need to make some extra money. If something comes up, keep me in mind.*

Trey: *I know you said you didn't like to do videos anymore, but would you consider doing one more for me, please?*

Shantelle: *Huh, I didn't know you were a rapper.*

Trey: *I'm not a rapper, but I own a label.*

Shantelle: *Like every other dude in Atlanta.*

Trey: *I guess so.*

Shantelle: *How much does the video pay?*

Trey: *A thousand bucks, but I'll throw in a bonus.*

Shantelle: *Just let me know when. I'm down.*

Trey: *Actually I think they're shooting it tomorrow. I will call my guy and find out more details.*

Shantelle: *Let me know. I'm there. I need the money baby.:-)*

Trey: *I will.*

She was calling him baby. He wondered if that meant anything or if that was what she called everybody. Trey was definitely attracted to Shantelle and he figured that she was probably attracted to him as well, but he had to be careful.

CHAPTER 6

Mike called Lani and wanted to meet her right away. Lani agreed and they met at Chris's mother's house. Lani had wanted to see Chris's mother, but she wasn't home. Mike led Lani into the den. Two goons were already there. Lani recognized one of the men, she'd seen him with Chris a few times. His name was Tater.

"Hey, Lani," Tater said. Tater was an average sized man with a huge head shaped like Mr. Potato Head. He'd been in and out of prison his whole life.

"Hey, Tater."

"You member' Kenny-Boo don't you?" Tater asked, acknowledging the other man

Kenny-Boo was fat and had a round baby face. He had crossed eyes, red lips and the nappiest hair Lani had ever seen in her life. Kenny-Boo wasn't smiling, he just nodded his head.

"You want something to drink?" Mike asked.

"No."

"I'm going to cut to the chase. I know for a fact that Black killed my brother."

"How?" Lani felt uncomfortable. Ugly-ass Kenny-Boo stared at her with those big eyes and those chapped lips. Yuck!

Mike said, "There is this dude named Twan on the west side selling weed cheap."

Lani said, "I don't get it."

"Look, whoever killed Chris robbed us. Took over a thousand pounds of weed and now I have a debt with the Mexicans."

"Okay, but where does Black come in?" Lani said.

"Black and Twan are friends," Mike said.

"I've never heard of Twan," Lani said.

"Look, I know niggas that know these dudes be together," Mike said.

Lani said, "I was with Black for years and I've never heard of nobody named Twan."

Mike's eyes became serious. "Look, I need you to tell me how to get in contact with Black."

She avoided his eyes.

"Mike, I can't do that."

"You said you loved my brother. If you really loved him, you would let me know where the fuck Black is."

Still looking away from Mike, she said, "Look, I did love your brother and I loved Black too. You have to look at it from my point of view. This shit is putting me in a very fucked up position."

"I understand that," Mike said.

Kenny-Boo said, "I'm sure Chris was in a fucked up position too—think about that. They shot him in his motherfuckin' head and threw him in the trunk and burned that man up like he was some old-ass trash."

Lani didn't want to think about it. She didn't want to imagine what had happened, and she wished Kenny-Boo would shut the fuck up. She would have told him that but he looked like the type of nigga that might punch a girl.

"Look, I can't help you, and like I said, I don't know Twan."

"My cousin said this nigga named Twan was over in his hood with pounds of weed on the low, tombout how they'd stuck this nigga for over a thousand pounds," Kenny-Boo said.

"So we know Twan is Black's friend. It's just a matter of time before we catch him slipping," Mike said.

"So if you know all that, what in the hell do you need me for?" Lani asked.

"We don't need you. We just thought you would help."

Kenny-Boo leaned toward her and said, "Since you swear you loved him so much." His breath smelled like hot shit. It was time for Lani to go. There was no way in hell she was going to let this ugly-ass man with his horrendous breath keep getting all in her face. She stood and said, "Mike, I have to be going."

CHAPTER 7

Jada sold two watches to a drug dealer on the south side of Atlanta. He'd given her fifteen thousand dollars instead of the twenty she'd asked for, but it would have to do because she didn't have any money. She needed to get out of Skyy's apartment as fast as she could. She paid Joey Turch five thousand dollars to repossess the car and drove it back to the townhouse. She was hoping that Craig would be happy when he saw the car because she needed him now. She didn't really want him to cut her off. Hopefully they could resume their arrangement. She really didn't want to have to find another dope boy to support her lifestyle. She entered the townhouse from the garage. She planned to grab a pair of earrings on the dresser and she would leave the car keys there as well. They'd be in plain view where he would see them. She spotted her earrings lying on the floor. She picked them up and put them in her purse and was about to drop the keys on the dresser when she noticed a small, powdery pile beside a tiny straw. What the fuck was this? It couldn't be what she thought it was.

She scooped the substance up and placed a little on her tongue. It numbed her tongue and after she smelled it, she knew it was coke. But whose was it? She had never seen Craig use coke or any drugs for that matter. She wanted to call him and ask him, but she figured if this was something he wanted her to know, he would've told her. She called Lani and asked to be picked up. Lani arrived fifteen minutes later.

When she got in the car, Lani asked, "So I see you and Dr. Handsome still at it."

"Not really, I don't live here anymore."

"I didn't know that."

"I know, I couldn't tell you with all the shit you had going on with Chris's funeral."

"What happened?"

"I had to pay for Shamari's lawyer."

"I know."

"Well, I signed over one of Craig's Maseratis to the attorney until I could come up with the rest of the money."

"You scandalous bitch."

"What was I supposed to do? I couldn't let my nigga go to court and get railroaded. Fuck Craig! Shamari is my dude."

"I feel you. You did the right thing." Lani laughed and then said, "But you gotta admit, that was some scandalous-ass shit."

"Hey, it's an arrangement. I think we just forgot what it was. He's using me and I'm using him, but I do care for him."

"Well, nobody wants to admit when they have an arrangement."

"I know, but I think when you admit it, everybody will be a lot better off."

"But who wants to admit that they're getting played."

"You're right."

There was a long silence. Finally Lani turned into the parking deck of a high-rise building.

"Where are we going?"

"Starr's house. I promised I would come check out her new place."

Jada said, "Sheesh."

Lani laughed, "I thought you two got along well at the memorial service."

"Well, that wasn't the time or the place for beefs, and we both are grown women."

"I was glad ya'll were making small talk."

"Hey, I don't have shit against her. She's the one with the problem with me."

"Be nice today, okay?"

"Hey, I ain't saying shit."

When Starr opened the door, she gave Lani two air kisses and she even air kissed Jada. "Take your shoes off, divas."

The women slipped out of their heels and Starr gave them a tour of the place.

Starr showed them the impressive banisters and the spiral staircase that led to a massive bedroom. In the bedroom there were huge Jack and Jill vanities, and a sauna, but what the women were most impressed with were the floor to ceiling glass windows.

"I would love getting fucked from behind, hands on the glass, looking out at the city of Atlanta," Jada said.

Starr laughed and said, "Girl, don't give me no ideas."

"Why did you move?"

Starr sighed and said, "I didn't wanna move. Trey got a crazy-ass baby mama that was basically making our life a living hell."

"She'd been calling me, hanging up, and even sent the police to our home."

"Damn," Jada said.

"I loved my life and loved my neighborhood, but after we went to jail, I didn't want to be there anymore."

"I know the feeling."

"How is Shamari doing?"

Jada assumed Lani had told her about Shamari's situation.

"He's good. He won't do too much time. He was set up, and his best friend, Duke, did most of the talking to the informant."

"That's good."

Lani was happy that Starr and Jada were being civil to one another. They were her two best friends.

"I'm happy for you, Starr. This is a nice place. Very nice, very classy, and I like what you've done to the place. Love the Tiffany Blue that you have going on in here. Who did your decorating?"

"You are looking at the decorator."

"What? No way?'

"I love decorating."

"I wish I had your talent. I would get paid," Jada said.

"I've always told her that she has an eye for this kind of shit," Lani said.

"Okay, bitches. Get the business and I'll do the work."

"Don't say that unless you mean it," Jada said. "I'm low on money too."

"Maybe we should all do a business together."

'I'd like that," Jada said.

Starr led her to the kitchen and the three women sipped champagne while they caught up on each other's life. This was the first time they had all spoken for a while.

CHAPTER 8

Shantelle called Trey. He picked it up on the second ring.
"Hello."

"Bad news."

Trey thought about Monte. He wondered what was going on now. Did his name come up in the investigation?

"Let's meet and talk."

She laughed, "Hey, I'm referring to the video. I showed up for the video and the director told me the artist was in a car wreck."

"Really? That's my artist. Why haven't I heard anything about it?" Then Trey remembered that Derringer's baby mama had called him twice, but he wasn't able to answer the phone.

"The director told me that he broke his collar bone, but he was doing okay."

"Damn, I guess I need to call his baby mama back."

"Yeah, I hate that it happened. I needed that money."

"Where are you now?"

"I'm at Piedmont Park on my way back home."

"Why don't you just meet me at Houston's across from Lennox? Let's get some lunch and I'll just advance the money."

"Hey, I'm not in any shape to turn any money down or a free meal. I'll be there in fifteen."

"Me too."

Trey was waiting in the lobby of Houston's when he saw her black BMW drive up. It was the same car from the Facebook page. She gave the key to the valet. She was wearing a short red skirt that was shellacked on her ass and those six inch heels made her calves look amazing.

They sat in a booth in the back of the restaurant. When they were seated, the waiter appeared. She ordered a Cobb salad and he had a steak medium well.

"Do you mind if I have a drink?" Shantelle asked.

"Order what you want."

"I'll have a martini," she told the waitress.

"Water for me."

The waitress disappeared and came back with the drinks. After she left, Trey passed Shantelle two thousand dollars.

She smiled brightly. "What's the extra thousand dollars for?"

"You seem pretty cool, and you seem like you're hurting for money."

"Seem like I'm broke."

"What did you go to school for?"

"Business."

"And you can't get a job?"

"I don't want a job, I want a business."

"Oh yeah?"

She folded the money and placed it in her purse. "Maybe you can invest in my business?"

"Maybe."

"No, I'm serious."

"Let's hear the business plan."

"Business plan?" she giggled.

"Why are you laughing? What am I supposed to do—just hand my money over? The white man wouldn't do it."

"That's fair."

"Well it's simple and it's not like it hasn't been done before, but I know a lot of designers here in Atlanta and in L.A that don't have a platform to sell their stuff, so I wanna build that platform."

"E-commerce site?"

"Yeah"

"So, why do you think you can succeed?"

"Well, that's where my branding expertise comes in."

"And your brand is?"

"Thrill Gal."

"I like that."

"Thank you."

"I would have to see some of the stuff you'd be selling."

"Of course."

There was an awkward silence. She flipped her hair off her shoulder and he was staring at her lips wondering if they were as soft as they looked.

She said, "So where is your woman, Trey?"

He laughed. "How'd you know I had a woman?"

"You have a lot of money, and the way these thirsty-ass chicks are in the A, there is no way in the hell a man like you is single, besides Monte told me."

"He did?"

"And he showed me where you lived"

"Really?"

"Yeah." She sipped her martini then said, "At first, he was pretending that the house was his. But he wouldn't let me see the inside, and then I told him I thought he was lying. He admitted it and told me it was your house."

"Damn," Trey laughed.

She laughed and said, "Monte is a trip." She paused then said, "You know he going to prison on Monday?"

"I'd forgotten."

"But yeah, I know you got a girl."

"I do."

"You happy?"

"I am."

She licked her lips and said, "Well, every successful man needs somewhere he can go when things aren't going right at home." She took a quick sip from her drink. "You know, kind of a stress reliever."

"Like a massage?"

"If that's what you wanna call it." She laughed and said, "I can give you a good massage."

"Is that so?"

The waitress appeared with the food. Trey looked into Shantelle's eyes and wondered if she could really keep a secret, because right about now those damn runner's calves were looking damn good to him.

CHAPTER 9

Around ten p.m. Lani met Black at the Waffle House in Alpharetta, about thirty minutes outside of Atlanta. When she pulled into the Waffle House, she spotted Black's Porsche, the one that had gotten shot up. It had been repaired and there was no sign of damage. He lowered his window.

"Follow me."

"Where we going?"

"Surprise."

"I like surprises."

"What woman don't?"

Lani followed Black's Porsche closely, and they drove about ten more minutes until finally he turned into a sub-division of mansions. Black turned into the winding driveway of a cobble-stone mansion. He hopped out of his car and opened her door.

"Whose house?"

"It's my house, I mean our house."

"Our house?"

He removed the keys from his pocket and tried to hand them to her, but she wouldn't take them.

"Take the keys."

"Seriously, whose house is this?"

"This is our house."

"What the fuck are you talking about?"

Black headed to the front door with Lani right behind him.

When he opened the door, the first things she noticed were the two chandeliers, the huge foyers, the impressive staircase, and the marble floors.

"What the hell."

"Are you ready to be treated like a queen?"

Lani couldn't help but gush as she eased into the mansion. Her heels clacking as she admired the massive place. "Let me give you a tour."

She blushed. "I guess I'm here now, so why not?"

Black showed her the twelve bedrooms, the theatre room, and the bowling alley. The huge mansion also came with eight bathrooms and six kitchens.

"Who in the hell is going to live here?"

Black smiled. "The king and queen."

For a moment Lani wanted to ask him if he was buying or renting, but she knew there was no way in the hell Black could verify his income. "How much is this place a month."

"Twelve thousand."

"Okay. Lemme get this straight. You're going to pay twelve thousand dollars a month for something you don't own?"

"Rent with an option to buy."

"Look, as much as I love this house, this makes no goddamned sense."

"I'm a multi-millionaire and not on paper. I got this baby!"

"So you think you're going to always have it like this?"

Black smiled as he sat behind a baby grand piano, toyed with a few keys. "When have you known me to be without? Even when I was in State Prison, I always had more money than the next nigga."

She sat on top of the piano and she felt like she was in a movie. She loved this home. She wanted to live in it, but she wasn't sure how long this would last."

Black said, "I see a look of concern on your face."

"Of course, do you know how motherfuckin' nervous I would be in this place?"

"Why?"

"We'd probably be the only blacks in the neighborhood."

"Now that's where you're wrong. There are a couple of dudes that play for the Falcons here and a couple of Atlanta Hawks ball players."

"Pro athletes."

"And who's to say I'm not a pro athlete."

"Get serious."

"Okay, you know that but our neighbors don't have to know, plus, this is not the kind of neighborhood where the houses are all on top of each other. The next neighbor is like one hundred yards away."

"I noticed that."

Black stood up from the piano and picked her up. She felt protected in his arms. She looked up at her and he kissed her.

"Put me down."

When he sat her down, she looked sad. She walked to the door and looked out at the night sky. She thought about Chris and how she had loved that man. She thought about the feud that he'd had with Black, and though Chris had put her out and she'd known Black longer, she felt guilty about being with Black.

She turned to Black and said, "Do you know somebody named Twan?"

"I know a lot of niggas named Twan. You know just like there's a lot of dudes that go by the nickname Black. There is probably just as many that go by the name Twan."

"True, but do you hang with a Twan and do you have any close friends named Twan."

"No. Why?"

"Well, they're saying a dude named Twan killed Chris."

"Who is they?"

"Chris's brother, Mike, and this dude Tater and some ugly-ass nigga named Kenny-Boo."

"Why do they think this Twan dude had something to do with it?" Black asked. He was careful not to sound too interested. He didn't want her to get suspicious.

"Well, they said this Twan dude was over off Bankhead, bragging that they had hit a lick for close to two thousand pounds."

"Damn," Black said then he turned from her gaze briefly before resuming eye contact. "Now I wish I would have came up like that. That's damn near a million dollars worth of weed."

"So you don't know this Twan dude?"

Black looked her straight in the eyes and said, "No."

CHAPTER 10

Trey was in the penthouse suite of the Four Seasons hotel. He called Shantelle and asked her to come right over. An hour later she arrived, wearing a black body suit and heels, with her hair pulled back in a ponytail giving her an innocent look. Those thighs were looking absolutely delicious, but Trey couldn't keep his eyes off her hard nipples. He invited her in.

"You want a drink?"

"What you got?"

"What you want?"

She smiled then said, "I don't wanna be the only one drinking. Are you drinking?"

"Maybe." He sat on the bed and she sat in an armchair across from the bed.

"I don't wanna drink, because if I drink, I might be a bad girl."

Trey blushed, "Being a bad girl ain't a bad thing."

"Oh really?"

"I like bad girls."

"Is that so?"

"I want some vodka, you got Patron."

"I saw some Grey Goose. I don't know if there is any Patron." When he opened the bar, he saw a bottle of Patron. "You're in luck."

"Whoa. How much do the hotel charge for that stuff?"

"I don't know. I don't give a fuck."

She laughed and said, "Excuse me, you fancy, huh?"

"Money is never a problem"

"Bashful too."

"No, didn't mean it like that."

He poured the Patron in a glass and she said, "Will you add some coke to that?"

"Of course."

He poured the coke and passed her the drink. She sipped it and said, "So, Trey, what did you call me over for?"

"Well, I like you."

"Really?"

"Yup."

He sat down on the bed and said, "I just wanna clear something up."

She stirred the drink and said, "What you wanna clear up?"

"I love my girl, been with her for a long-ass time and I ain't been perfect."

"Hey, I'm not here to judge and I damn sure ain't perfect."

Trey continued, "I fucked up a few years ago and got this other chick pregnant and hid the baby for over five years."

"Damn."

"I didn't know how to tell her, I mean it was one of those situations where every time I wanted to tell her, I just couldn't."

"How did she find out?"

"Baby mama."

She took another sip from her drink. "I should have known."

"Yeah, I had to beg her to get her to forgive me."

She laughed and said, "I bet it cost you a pretty penny too."

"Well, my girl is not like that. She likes nice shit but she can't be bought. Part of the reason I love her."

"I see." She finished her drink and then said, "So what the hell does all this have to do with me?"

"I'm just saying I wanna fuck with you."

She laughed and said, "Can you fix me another drink."

"Sure." He stood up from the bed and made her another drink and handed it to her.

"Thank you." She stirred it and said, "You don't want me to blow your spot up?"

"Exactly."

"That's not me at all." She finished the rest of her drink then sat on the bed beside him.

"Everybody says they can keep a secret then they get whipped."

"Is that so?" She rubbed his dick. "Impressive."

Trey eyes were now on her nipples and those sexy-ass lips.

She loosened his belt and said, "If I'm taken care of, you won't hear a word from me. Not a damn word." She blew in his ear.

Trey took a deep breath. "Good. I don't need nobody—"

"Shhhhhhhh." She placed her finger over his lips. "Let's talk about something else."

She unleashed his penis. Thick and veiny, and beautiful to her. She wanted to lick that motherfucker like a popsicle.

He tried to say something but she hushed him again and said, "I don't wanna talk about nothing but this dick going inside my pussy."

She licked the head of his cock as Trey sat back, a pillow propped behind his head, and watched her pretty ass go to work.

Jada received a call from a number she'd never seen before. She decided to answer. "Hello?"

"Hey, babe, it's Shamari. I'm out."

"What do you mean, you're out?"

"Joey Turch got all the charges dropped on a technicality."

"You're lying."

"I'm serious. Turns out the coke they charged us with was fake. It was a sting operation set up by the police. I never talked on the phone to the informant and the one person who could testify about my involvement was Duke and he's dead."

"That's wonderful, baby. I'm so fuckin' happy for you."

"I'm happy for myself."

"Where are you?"

"I'm outside the jail. I literally just got out. I'm on this guy's phone. I have to give it back to him. Can you pick me up?"

"You're on Rice Street right?"

"Exactly."

"Okay, to be honest with you, Shamari, it's going to take me at least an hour, maybe longer. I haven't showered or anything."

"It's cool, baby. I'm just so happy to have my goddamned freedom back."

"Okay see you in an hour."

An hour and a half later, Jada picked Shamari up in front of the county jail on Rice Street. She greeted him with a big hug when he hopped in the car. They made eye contact for a few minutes, things seemed very awkward, until she gave him a kiss.

"Damn, I missed you."

"I missed you too."

She drove away. Shamari avoided looking back in the direction of the jail. He hated every part of that experience. When the jail was out of sight, he asked, "Where are we going?"

"That's a good question. You know we don't have a house. They padlocked the place since we didn't pay the rent. I was able to get a few of your things. I put them in storage along with some of my stuff."

"I know it's been rough on you, babe."

"I can't explain to you how rough."

Another awkward silence.

"So what's up with your sugar daddy?"

"I don't wanna talk about that shit right now! Will you just chill the fuck out!" she yelled.

There was another awkward silence in the car. He did want to talk about her sugar daddy, but she did do the right thing and paid for his attorney, and he would be forever grateful to her for that.

"But seriously, I'm living with my girlfriend right now."

"Lani?"

"No, a girl named Skyy. I don't think you know her." She turned to Shamari. "Lani's man got murdered."

"What?"

"Yeah."

"Chris, right? The basketball playing nigga?"

"Yeah."

"Who did it?"

"Nobody knows right now, but I think Black had something to do with it."

"Which Black?"

"The one that did state time with you."

"Tyrann. Man, he must've done something to Black. Black is cool as hell."

"I know he seemed pretty cool. He gave me five grand to help with your lawyer fee."

"For real? I have to pay him back, when I get on my feet."

"So, where do you wanna go?"

"Well, first take me to Popeye's and then you can drop me off over at my sister's house."

"You going to that ratchet-ass neighborhood? I could go stay with my mom, but her house too small and plus I can't stand her boyfriend."

After Shamari got his two piece snack with dirty rice, Jada drove to his sister Tangie's house, on the West Side of Atlanta. When he pulled up, he noticed somebody was peeking out of the window.

Shamari called Tangie from Jada's cell phone. "Sis, it me, Mari. I'm gonna need to crash at your spot for a few days."

"Wait a minute, Mari, there is some motherfuckers out in front of the crib in a BMW."

"That's me, sis, me and Jada."

"Oh you still with that hoe."

"Look Im'ma need to crash your crib for a few days. Till I get on my feet."

"How the fuck did you get outta jail?"

"Beat my charge."

"Come on in, you know I got room for you"

Shamari kissed Jada on the cheek and grabbed his box of chicken and disappeared inside the house.

CHAPTER 11

Black slapped the fuck out of Twan with his walking cane. Twan stumbled to the ground and bounced back up holding his jaw, and Black was about to strike him again when Kyrie and K.B. got between the two men.

Twan spat two of his teeth and said, "What the fuck is your problem, nigga?"

"What the fuck you think is my problem? You down in the fuckin' hood running your mouth about what happened! You gonna get all of us locked the fuck up!"

"Man, I ain't said shit to nobody." Twan spat out more blood.'

"Niggas saying you were on Bankhead tombout how much work you got."

"Who said it?"

"It don't matter who said it."

"Ain't nobody said shit, dude. You just think everything is about you."

Black presented his 9mm and cocked the hammer and aimed it. "I'll kill you, nigga."

Kyrie said, "Chill, Black. Man, it ain't worth it."

K.B. said, "Me and Twan been together, and he hasn't even been on Bankhead."

Black said, "So you been with him 24-7?"

"No."

"Well then you don't know what he said. My sources are reliable. Twan's name came from somewhere. Motherfuckers ain't just pull his name out of a hat."

Black looked Twan in the eyes. "Just want you to know that niggas are looking for you."

"I'm not afraid of no niggas."

Black said, "Nobody is going to fuck with you as long as we're around. We'll go to war for you." Black put his gun on his waist.

K.B. said, "We're all in this together."

Kyrie said, "I wasn't even there, but I'll die for anybody in this room."

Twan, nursing his jaw, blood oozing from his mouth, looked at Black and said, "I'll die for you, Big Bruh. I swear to God, I ain't tell nobody shit, especially no niggas on Bankhead.

Black took a deep breath and then smacked the fuck out of Twan with the cane again. Twan fell again and Black stood over him and said, "If you get picked up by the police, you're on your own, nigga. Don't you call my motherfuckin' name."

CHAPTER 12

Shamari's sister, Tangie, was brown skinned. She had a different father than Shamari. Her father was a guy named Nat, who had been sentenced to twenty-five years, and was murdered in prison after his thirteenth year. Tangie never got to know her father—she was only four years old when he got sentenced. Everything she knew about him, she'd learned from Shamari because Shamari was eight when Nat got sentenced. Shamari remembered riding around with Nat when he was a kid, going to different "aunties' houses." He later learned those aunties were Nat's other women.

Shamari believed that his sister always needed a man to be around because she never had a man in her life when she was younger. She had abandonment issues. Tangie's boyfriend was a nigga named Hunch. Hunch was a tall black dude and was slightly humpbacked. This is where the name Hunch derived from. Hunch was in the kitchen, dressed only in his drawers, eating some toast and drinking orange juice when Shamari woke up.

"Mari, wassup?" Hunch smiled and revealed gold teeth.

"Wassup, bruh?"

"Want some toast?"

"No, I'm good. Where is sis?"

"She had to go to work, they called her in"

Tangie worked as a dental hygienist.

"Wanna play Madden?"

"Hunch, how old are you?"

"Thirty-four."

"Damn, you older than me."

"Yeah, what are you? Thirty-two?"

"Exactly. What time do you go to work?"

Hunch spread some grape jelly on his toast and said, "I ain't got no job, bruh. I got laid off a few months ago."

"So lemme get this straight. My sister is working all god-damned day while you sitting at home playing Madden?"

Hunch bit into his toast. "Wait a minute, bruh. You need to direct your anger somewhere else."

"No, I'm directing my anger at the right motherfucker."

"Nigga, you act like I ain't bringing shit to the table."

"I see you brought your goddamned ugly-ass face."

"You can get the fuck out of my house."

"My sister's house you mean?"

"I pay bills in this motherfucker."

Shamari removed his t-shirt, preparing for a scuffle. Hunch was a few inches taller than Shamari but Shamari was ripped and he'd been exercising day and night during his brief stint in the county jail.

"I fuck you up, clown!" Shamari shouted.

Hunch set his toast down on the table, eying Shamari's muscles thinking, he would have to stab this motherfucker. There was no way he could beat Shamari in a fist fight, plus he didn't have the energy to fight him anyway. Hell, he smoked two packs of Newports a day.

Just as Hunch stood up from the table, the front door opened. Hunch called out, "Tangie, you better get your brother before I fuck him up."

Tangie said, "What the fuck is going on in here?"

Shamari turned to Tangie and said, "I just don't like nobody using you, that's all."

"What are you talking about?"

"I'm talking about this nigga playing PlayStation while you at work."

Hunch said, "Nigga, mind yo' goddamn business."

"My sister is my business."

Tangie said, "Both of ya'll shut the fuck up." Then, she turned to Shamari, "Mari, you know I love you, bruh, but Hunch is my man, and I don't want you disrespecting him. He helps me out, believe me, he helps out."

Hunch laughed and said, "I told this clown to mind his own business."

Shamari slid back into his shirt. He wanted to bust Hunch upside his motherfuckin' head, but he didn't want to disrespect Tangie. He just stared at him without saying a word.

Tangie turned to Hunch, "My brother ain't no motherfuckin' clown either. Just like I will put him out for disrespecting you, I'll put yo ass out for disrespecting him. There is nothing to tie us together, we ain't got no kids."

Hunch offered Shamari his hand and said, "Look, I'm sorry if I pissed you off, bruh. I love the hell out of your sister, so you know I gotta have love for you."

Shamari shook Hunch's hand then he disappeared into the back room, thinking he had to get the fuck out of there and fast.

CHAPTER 13

Jada startled Craig when she entered the townhome. He frowned and said, "I wish you would call before you just pop up over here."

"I'm sorry, but I have some clothes over here that I need.

"When are you going to get the rest of your things?"

"Why are you in such a motherfuckin' hurry for me to leave?"

"I trusted you and you disrespected me. I thought you were better than that."

Jada rolled her eyes. "Ok, I see where this is going Mr. White Man. You meant to say you thought I was better than the rest of them, as in black people."

"Don't try to make this a race issue."

"What else could it be?"

"Will you stop the bullshit? You know goddamned well I'm the last person that is racist."

"You just used the word nigga the other day and you're always mocking slang."

"Let's stay on subject. You sold my car."

"I didn't sell your car."

"There no point in arguing with somebody like you."

"What did I do? I signed over a car that was technically mine. Remember, you gave me the car."

"But I didn't know it was going to be some goddamned collateral for some goddamned drug dealer."

Jada wanted to slap the fuck out of his punk ass but she knew that even though he was far softer than Shamari, he was still a man.

He headed to the kitchen and she was right behind him. He poured a glass of orange juice. He sat at the bar. "I can't believe that you have the nerve to say the car was yours?"

"It was mine. You gave it to me."

"Think about it. How would you feel if somebody gave away something that you'd given them?"

"I didn't give it away."

He sipped his juice and said, "Listen, Jada, I'm not in the business of helping drug dealers."

"I can't tell. You damn sure helped some drug dealer when you bought that package you had in your drawer the other day."

"What the hell are you talking about?"

"I'm talking about that coke that was in your dresser the other day."

"That wasn't mine." He stood and looked at her for a split second, then he looked away, then he looked back at her for a second time and said, "You know what? You need to give me my goddamned key back."

"Give you your key back because I found out that you're a fuckin' coke head?"

"I'm not a coke head. Give me my key and my gate FOB back."

"I won't."

"You will. Don't make me call the police on you."

"You better make sure your house is clean then."

"Jada, give me my goddamned key back."

"I will not."

"Fine, I'll change the locks."

Jada eased over toward him and got in his face. They were nose to nose. "You change the goddamned locks and I swear to God, Anne will know about every motherfuckin' item you've ever bought me. You hear me, white boy?"

"You're blackmailing me?"

"Take it how you wanna take it."

He walked back to the fridge. This time he got a bottle of water, twisted the top off and drank some before saying, "You're nothing but a user."

Jada said, "Motherfucker, you're married. How am I using you? If it's anything we're using each other."

"Whatever."

"Okay, so now you mad cuz I know you like to use a little nose candy?"

"Hey! That wasn't my coke! Can you just give me my key back, please?"

"You'll get your key back as soon as I move into an apartment. I have nowhere to go, remember? You put me out."

There was an awkward silence. Damn he wanted this woman out of his life. She had turned into nothing but trouble. She started walking toward the bedroom.

"Where are you going?"

She turned to face him, "I have things here, you know. I need to get some of my clothes."

"Can you just get all your stuff and put it in storage? I will pay the storage fee for a year."

"I don't want my stuff in storage."

"Why not?"

"Because before you asked me to come over here, I had a place for my things. Don't worry, I'm not going to go looking for your nose candy." She laughed and then said, "You know it's always the motherfuckers that think they're better than everybody else.

When she entered the bedroom, he was right behind her. She stepped into the walk-in closet and as soon as she entered, she noticed a pair of purple boy shorts lying on the floor. She scooped them up and examined them. "So you've been having company."

"I don't know what you're talking about."

She slung the underwear at him. "I'm talking about somebody leaving their stinking-ass drawers here."

"Huh?"

"You know goddamned well those aren't my underwear, motherfucker!"

Craig stood there, looking dumb as hell, before she approached and backhanded his ass.

He grabbed her hand. "What the fuck did you do that for?"

"You ain't shit, motherfucker." Tears rolled down her face.

"This is not what you think?"

She laughed and said, "That's what every motherfuckin' man says when they get caught doing something, First it was cocaine, now it's thirsty bitches. Fucking with you is just like fucking with a dope boy."

He was sweating and visibly nervous. Finally, he said, "For all I know, these could be your friend's underwear."

"What fucking friend?"

"The girl you brought over here. What's her name? Skyy?"

"Those are not Skyy's?"

"How do you know?"

"Because these panties were not here when I left, and they weren't here the other day when I found your little nose candy."

He sat on the bed, his head in his hands. "I don't know where that underwear came from."

"I'm sure you don't, just like you don't know where the coke came from."

"Why am I explaining myself? You're not my lady and I'm not your man."

She slapped him again and he yanked her arm.

She said, "Motherfucker, you better let me go. You ain't even seen the ghetto side of me. I will turn this bitch out. I will burn this motherfucker down. Let me go."

He pulled her to him. "I think you better leave," he said. They were nose to nose. She could smell the orange juice on his breath.

"You can't make me go nowhere."

He released her from his grip.

She grabbed a towel and picked up the boy-shorts. "I would never wear some bullshit like this. This ain't even sexy, motherfucker."

"I've never seen them before today."

Jada said, "Just tell me one thing and be honest with me."

"What?"

"Is she black or white?"

"What? There is nobody!"

"Tell the goddamned truth."

"Give me my key and FOB back."

Jada dug into her purse and pulled out the key and FOB and said. "Take it, motherfucker". She didn't care about giving him his goddamned key back because she had an extra key that had been on the keychain of the Maserati.

She headed to the door and before she exited, he asked, "When are you coming to get the rest of you things?"

She turned and said, "Whenever I motherfuckin' feel like it." She slammed the door hard, vibrating the windows.

K.B. called Black and said he needed to see him right away. They agreed to meet at the Flying Biscuit restaurant in Little Five Points. Black and Kyrie arrived five minutes before K.B. When K.B. arrived, he dapped up with Black and Kyrie before ordering pancakes. Black had the same, and Kyrie had eggs and salmon. After their water glasses were filled, K.B., who was visibly jittery, said, "Man, I got some bad news."

"What?" Black said.

"Me and Twan were on the news last night."

"For what?"

"When we snatched Chris from the Cactus Car Wash, the security camera caught us.

Black said, "What? The Car Wash? What the fuck are you talking about?"

K.B. avoided Black's eyes and said, "Yeah, that's where we caught up with Chris at."

"What the fuck?" Black said.

The waitress came and dropped plates before disappearing to the back. Black poured some syrup on his pancakes, while eyeballing the waitress. Trying to make sure nobody could hear the conversation. When the waitress was gone, he said, "So let me get this shit straight! You snatched the nigga up in broad motherfuckin' daylight?

"Yeah."

Black bit into his pancake. Kyrie grabbed a forkful of eggs. "So what the fuck were ya'll thinking?"

K.B. said, "Yeah, Twan smashed one of the security cameras with a baseball bat."

Black said, "But there were witnesses, right?"

"Yeah."

Black set his fork down and said, "You know, this has got to be some of the dumbest shit I've ever heard of."

K.B. dropped his head for a second and then said, "But they still managed to get us on camera." Black wanted to beat him across the head with his cane and if it wasn't for the twenty white patrons, he would have done exactly that. K.B. knew that which was why he wanted to go to a public place.

Kyrie said, "But you smashed the camera."

"Obviously there were more."

Black said, "Nowadays these cameras are so goddamned small. I'm sure you smashed a dummy camera. Dummy!"

K.B. said, "My homie said they were showing pictures of me and Twan on the news all day yesterday, asking if anybody had any information about us to let them know."

Black said, "Motherfucker, I'm telling you right now. Don't mention my goddamn name. Is that understood?"

"Black, I would never say nothing about you. Ever."

"If you do, I hope you plan to move your whole family out of Georgia. Is that understood?"

"Black, you ain't got shit to worry about. This is on me and Twan."

Black stood and tossed a hundred dollar bill on the table and said, "I gotta get the fuck away from you, nigga. You're a wanted man."

CHAPTER 14

Lani sent Black a text which read, *come over*. As soon as she sent it, she began to have reservations about him coming over for a couple of reasons. The first reason was that she knew he was bad for her and they really weren't in the same place. The second reason was that she wasn't sure he was telling the truth about his involvement with Chris's murder. But she was feeling lonely, and she needed to be held. It was 12:32 a.m. when Black walked into her home. She was wearing a t-shirt with a thong underneath. When Black hugged her, he held onto her ass cheeks. She shoved him a little.

"What's wrong, baby?"

She placed her head on his chest and said, "I just wanna be held tonight."

Black placed his hand on the small of her back and kissed her forehead. She headed to the bedroom with him behind her. She sat on the edge of the bed and Black said, "I'm gonna take a shower if you don't mind."

She led him to the shower and ten minutes later he came out with an erection that was so hard that she thought about fucking him for a brief second then she said, "Will you put your underwear on. I'm not feeling like sex tonight."

"So what you call me over for?"

"I told you, I just wanna be held. There is just too much going on now."

Black slid into a pair of white boxers, his erection still very much ready for action though he didn't feel like he would see any.

She said, "Nothing has happened except I lost my boyfriend."

"You weren't seeing him before he died."

"True, but that don't make it better, I loved that man."

He sat on the bed beside her and massaged her back before wrapping his arms around her and sucked gently on her earlobe before whispering, "You know I got you no matter what."

They made eye contact and she said, "I know that, that's why I called you."

Black, now holding her hand said, "I love you, Lani. I know you loved Chris, but I loved you first, and I'll always love you."

She believed him. She knew that if there was one person who had her back, it was him, but she also knew that he was bad for her. Black wasn't capable of loving one woman. He was a whore and no matter what he told her, she knew that's what he would always be. This was the price you had to pay when you were with Black.

Black slid his hand underneath her t-shirt and grabbed her breast. She wanted to tell him to stop but couldn't bring herself to say it. He felt so goddamned good, his dick now poking her in the back

He kissed her neck and she said, "Can you just hold me please. I need to be held."

He removed her t-shirt and kept massaging her breasts. He knew exactly where her spot was, and she hated that he knew that. She turned and kissed him, now his hands were on her ass cheeks, seconds later, he was yanking that tiny-ass thong down to her ankles.

Lani grabbed Black's dick and something about those big ass veins made her pussy wet as hell. She continued to stroke his dick and was about to go down on him when he said, "Stop"

She looked confused.

"I wanna pleasure you."

He spread her legs like a pair of scissors and with his finger, toyed with her clit for a moment. She could feel herself getting wet. He kissed her inner thighs while he moved in and out of her pussy with his finger, and finally, he put his mouth on her clit. He sucked her lips and began to move in and out of her pussy with his tongue. Then, he flipped her over on her back and ate her from behind and licked the crease of her ass.

"Goddamned, baby, you feel so good," she said.

He continued gnawing her pussy. The vacuum sound was turning her the fuck on.

She finally said, "I want you inside of me."

But he ignored her and continued the foreplay. When he licked her asshole, she said, "Goddamn, Black, you feel so fuckin' good. Why do you do me like this?"

He pulled her hair and stopped sucking for a moment and said, "Like what?"

"You gonna make me beg for this dick?"

"Tell me you want it."

"Please, please put it inside of me."

Black smacked her ass and watching it jiggle made his dick extra hard. Finally, he penetrated her. Fucking her hard, doggy style, and smacking her ass at the same time. Black was inside her for about eight minutes, before she had multiple orgasms. She hopped up on top of him and rode him until he exploded inside of him. Moments later, he fell asleep. She scooted her ass up beside him and wrapped his arms around her. Then she heard her phone rang. She didn't feel like hopping out of bed but since it was damn near one o'clock, it must be her mom, or somebody important. She hopped out of the bed and eased over to the dresser, picking up the phone. It was Nana. What in the hell was that woman up for? Nana usually went to bed at around nine o'clock.

"Hello?"

"Is Tyrann with you?"

"Yeah. How did you know?"

"He called me and told me he was on his way to see you."

"Is there something wrong, Nana?"

"Well, tell Tyrann his friend, Twan, has came by here twice looking for him. He just left."

"He left your house at one o'clock in the morning."

"Chile, you know I cussed his ass out. Gonna have to ask the lord to forgive me about that one, but I was mad as hell."

"I bet." Lani shook Black to wake him up.

"What? What the fuck is going on."

Lani said, "It's Nana. She wants to talk to you."

He sat up on the bed and she passed him the phone.

Nana said, "Twan been over here twice looking for you, and he woke me up."

"I'm sorry he's been bugging you. I will take care that."

Nana said, "I cussed his ass out."

"Ok, Nana, I will take care of it."

"Oh wait a minute, nigga, don't be rushing me off the phone. You think you getting off the hook like that?"

"What you tombout?"

"I'm tombout you having all these niggas running over my house looking for you in the middle of the night."

"All of what niggas? You said it was just one."

"There was another big, tall, stupid-ass looking nigga with him."

"Okay, I'll handle it."

"Tyrann, what the hell is going on? I know if somebody is looking for your ass in the middle of the night, nothing good is gonna come out of this. I gotta feeling you done got yourself in some more shit."

"I haven't done anything."

"Tyrann, don't lie to me."

"I'm not lying to you. Look I gotta go. Im'ma call you back later." He ended the call.

Lani said, "What did Nana want?"

"One of my friends came over looking for me."

"Who? Twan?"

Black met Lani's eyes. She knew he'd been lying to him. How would he justify his lies? He was trying to think of a way to smooth it over.

"Why the fuck did you lie to me, man?"

Black handed her the cell phone then turned from her gaze.

"Why did you lie to me?" she repeated.

"Look, I knew how you felt about the nigga, but the motherfucker was no good." He paused and reflected, "He wasn't a good person."

"You murdered Chris!"

"Look, I didn't kill nobody."

"But you had him murdered. Didn't you?"

"I might know something about it."

"I'm sure you might know something about it, because you're the one that did it!"

He met her eyes and then said, "Ok. This dude shot up Miss Carolyn's house and you're defending him?"

"You leave my mama the fuck out of this. This had nothing to do with her. You did this because you wanted to do this! Just admit it."

"Ok, I lied, and I had something to do with the murder but don't make me out to be the bad guy." He sat on the edge of the bed for a second then he disappeared into the bathroom for a moment. When he came back out, he was dressed.

"I'm getting the fuck out of here."

Lani was sitting on the bed, tears coming down her face. She said, "Go! Please just fuckin' go!"

He leaned over and attempted to kiss her, but she shoved him and then slapped the hell out of him.

He held his jaw. "So, you were really in love with this clown."

She stood up. She was still butt-ass naked so she slipped on a pair of shorts. "Please, go."

Black said, "Look, I'm sorry."

"Sorry. So you admit you did it?"

"I didn't admit shit."

"Look, I'm not the police, but you better believe they will know."

Black thought back to what K.B. said about the news showing mug shots of him and Twan. Thinking he should have killed K.B. and Twan. Idiots.

"Are you planning on going to the cops?"

"I'm not going to the cops, but I don't know what I will say if they ever question me."

Black sighed and said, "So you don't know what you're going to say?"

"I have a goddamned conscience, man."

Black walked toward the door. Before he let himself out, he turned to make eye contact with her and said, "Lani, I love you and I always will."

She didn't respond, but the truth was she loved him and she always would love him too and she hated that fact.

CHAPTER 15

It was 6:13 a.m. when Starr scooted her butt against Trey's erect dick, which she felt poking her ass involuntarily. She took hold of it through the hole in his underwear. She stroked it. He was asleep, but his man was wide awake and it was hard and firm, just how she liked it and she wanted that big motherfucker inside of her. Now. Not tomorrow. Not an hour from now, but right motherfuckin' now. She took him in her mouth. He woke up when he felt her warm mouth. He stared at her as she sucked and hummed on his balls. He ran his fingers through her hair. She stopped and moved up to the head of the bed, her hand still wrapped firmly around his dick and kissed him then she whispered, "I want you inside of me."

"Not now."

"Why not?"

"It's six in the morning."

She stared at him and said, "What the fuck does that mean?"

"It's too early."

"It's too early for me to get some dick?"

"I'm tired, baby. I'm really tired."

"Now it's been almost two weeks since I've had some. It's always, I'm tired, or I don't feel like it. Trey what the fuck is going on?"

"Nothing"

"I know nothing is going on, that's the motherfucking problem!"

"Just been stressing lately."

She stood up from the bed, wearing a tiny red g-string with a crystal heart. holding the strings together. Trey eyeballed her ass until it disappeared into the kitchen and returned with a bottled water. She popped the top and said, "Trey, are you trying to make me cheat on you?"

He sat up on the edge of the bed. "Why would you even talk like that?"

She sipped her water. "You know damn well I ain't going nowhere, but you making me think you been dipping out again."

"Fuck no!" Trey said with a straight face, but the truth was Shantelle was draining him. He'd fucked her six times in the last four days.

"What's going on, Trey? Why can't I get some dick? And I don't wanna hear that lame-ass I'm tired bullshit."

"You know all the shit with Monte."

"Monte is gone and you don't know that girl he was talking about. So who gives a fuck what she tells the Feds. You've never met her."

"You're right."

"So why can't I get some dick?"

He said, "Come here."

She came over and stood in front of him. He tried to yank her g-string down. She stopped him.

"What you do that for?" he asked.

"Look, I don't want you to do something that you don't wanna do. I want my man to wanna fuck me."

"Sheesh. Ok, I can't win for losing. I wanna fuck, now you don't wanna fuck."

"You know why, Trey?"

"Why?"

"Because I can feel when something ain't right, and I gotta feeling you been fucking with that goddamned baby mama again."

"Hell the fuck no!"

Starr finished her water and headed to the kitchen. Before she left the room, she looked back at him and said, "Time will tell, motherfucker. Time will tell."

It was 8:30 a.m. and fat-assed Hunch was lying on the sofa in a toddler t-shirt and a pair of boxer briefs that looked like they were about to bust at the seams. Hunch was eating a jelly sandwich and watching Sports Center when Shamari entered the room.

Hunch turned the volume down. "Morning, brother-in-law."

Shamari wanted to drag his fat ass off the sofa and kick him in the face. Instead he just threw up a peace sign.

Hunch said, "Can I talk to you for a moment?" He bit into his jelly sandwich and took a swig of water.

Shamari sat in a chair across from Hunch. "Wassup?"

"Look, man, I got something I wanna discuss with you, but I don't want you to say anything to Tangie.

Shamari just nodded his head, but he wasn't about to promise this clown shit. His loyalty was with his sister and if what he was about to disclose to him was going to be harmful to his sister, he would surely tell her.

"There is some Mexicans on Bankhead. They big-time, bruh, big-time."

"What the fuck does this have to do with me, and how do you know them?"

"I buy a little shit from them, but they don't never cut me no deal. They always trying to tax a motherfucker."

Shamari laughed, "What are you buying?"

"A couple of ounces, here and there. You know I ain't big-time like you."

"They getting big loads, bruh." Hunch's eyes expanded. "I've seen hundreds of bricks."

Shamari was getting upset. Why was Hunch telling him this? What was he supposed to do, jump up and down because he's seen hundreds of bricks. This shit didn't impress him. He was nobody's dick rider. He stared at Hunch with a 'get to the point' look on his face.

Hunch finished his jelly sandwich. Then he drank some water and said, "We should get them, bruh. Think about it. If we get a hundred ki's, we will be set."

Shamari ordinarily wouldn't even entertain this buffoon, but he was broke and he needed some money quick. But, he didn't want to go to jail or hell trying to get it. "What makes you think we can pull it off?"

"I don't know if we can, but it's something to think about."

"How would we do it?"

"They don't have anything right now, but they always call me when they re-up."

"Why do they call you, nigga? You buying ounces."

"Well, because I bug the hell out them. I call them so much that I keep myself on their radar."

"They trust you?"

"Yeah."

"Why?"

"I've known them for years."

Shamari headed to the kitchen thinking of everything that could go wrong if he tried to rob the Mexicans. Would he put his sister in danger if he did something like this? Was Hunch telling the truth? Had he seen hundreds of ki's like he said? He didn't know if he believed Hunch, and he didn't know if he would go through with it but one thing he did know—he was broke as fuck.

CHAPTER 16

Jada moved into the Four Seasons hotel. She would stay there for a month until she got herself together. She had paid for her room upfront with the leftover money she had after she paid Joey Turch, but her money was getting low and she knew she had to come up with some more money and fast. There was a fat, ugly dope boy named Ty that had been trying to get in her panties for months. He'd been texting her for months saying thing like, '*Let me take you to the South of France*'; '*I'm at the Gucci store. What do you want?*' He'd sent her pictures of Loubintins that he wanted to see her walk in. She would respond to his texts from time to time but never took him up on his offers. Jada thought now was a good time to call him. He was listed as "Big Papa" in her phone. She shot him a text: *Hey Boo.*

Big Papa: *My wife* :-)

Jada: *This is your wife.*

Big Papa: *Where you been?*

Jada: *No. The question is, where you been?*

Big Papa: *I thought you didn't love me, I been busy you know, doing what I do.*

Jada: *I think we should do lunch.*

Big Papa: *Let me know when and I'm there.*

Jada: *Tomorrow at 1:30, meet me @ Houston's across from Lennox*

Big Papa: *Let's do it.*

Jada watched as Big Papa drove up in a White Bentley with cream colored seats. The motherfucking car looked amazing. Big Papa jumped out wearing some old school Gazelles, a t-shirt, a pair of Levis that didn't cover his fat ass and a pair of scuffed up Adidas. Jada thought how could a man with so much money have such bad taste. She would have to work on that. He was smiling hard as hell when he saw her.

They hugged. When he released her, he said, "Goddamn! You fine as fuck."

She blushed and said, "You always say that."

"It's the truth."

"Give us a booth," Big Papa told the host.

"There's a wait for booths. You want a table?"

Big Papa looked at Jada to see what she preferred. She thought about his fat ass not being able to fit on the tiny-ass chairs in the dining room and possibly exposing the crack of his ass. Eeew!

She said, "I can wait."

Big Papa dug into his pocket, removed a wad of hundred dollar bills, and handed some to the young host. "Put us at the front of the line."

The young woman smiled and said, "Soon as the busboy cleans the table, I'll take you to the booth in the back."

Three minutes later they were seated.

Big Papa looked uncomfortable as hell in the booth. Jada should've known that he would be more uncomfortable in a booth. He looked almost in pain with part of his belly overlapping onto the table. Finally, he turned sideways, so he could fit better.

Big Papa stared and was smiling at Jada like she was a three piece of Popeye's chicken. Finally she asked, "What you looking at?"

"You, sexy ass. I meant to tell you, that dress is motherfucking amazing on you."

Jada smiled. She had worn the form fitting light blue dress because it made her waist look extra tiny and her ass pop-out.

The waitress came. Jada ordered salmon, rice and a diet coke. Big Papa ordered a burger, some fries and a coke.

After the waitress came back with the food, Jada said, "So where you been? What's been up? What's new?"

"You tell me? You still got that problem?"

"What problem?"

"Your boyfriend," he said, dipping a french fry in a pool of ketchup then devouring it.

"No, we broke up."

"I'm so sorry." He made a sad face being sarcastic.

"I'm sure you are."

"But don't worry. I'm here to save the day."

She bit into her salmon and took a swig of water. "Is that so?"

"Hell to the yeah."

She laughed. "How many women do you have? You seem like you gotta lot of women."

Jada wanted to laugh after she said that, but he probably did take care of a lot of women,

Big Papa said, "I ain't gone lie." He bit his burger and was about to speak again—

She cut him off, "Don't talk with your mouth full."

Big Papa chomped down the burger quickly and said, "I use to have a lot of bitches."

Jada wanted to laugh in this man's face because she knew his fat ass probably thought he was really a player.

"What changed?"

"Well, just got a little bit older, and I want a family one day."

"Really? You don't have any kids?"

Big Papa laughed, "Now, I didn't say all of that."

"How many kids you got?"

"Well one and a possible. I have a son and maybe a little girl—the jury is still out on that."

"Well, you know you can do an over-the-counter DNA test."

"She's eight now, and I'm the only daddy she knows."

"So you don't wanna know?"

"It's really no point now. I love her and she loves me."

Jada bit into her salmon. She felt sorry for Big Papa. He seemed like a really good dude with a few insecurities, but he seemed to have a good heart. She really didn't want to take advantage of him, but she was in a big-time jam. She had to put her feelings aside. For now.

"So you have two kids."

"Yeah."

"And you want more."

He grinned. "Lots more. You gonna help me?"

She laughed and said, "I wanna settle down too."

"What are we waiting for?"

She caught him staring at her breasts. She glanced down at them to let him know she saw him looking and he said, "My bad, I couldn't help myself."

She smiled, "It's okay."

"So what are we waiting for?"

She sipped her water then she toyed with her hair like a little girl.

"So what's the hold up, Jada. I been trying to get at you for a long time."

"I know."

"Just say you don't like me."

"Look, I've always liked you. I just don't know if you can handle a girl like me."

"What is that supposed to mean?"

"I require a lot. I demand a lot. I can be needy. I'm emotional, you know I'm very much a girl and sometimes I'm moody as fuck and I'm high maintenance. I demand the best."

"Look, one thing about me. I know women and high maintenance, that's nothing. I got plenty of bread. I can handle you, believe me. If you were with me you'd be in a new Benz, not last years."

"How do you know what I drive?"

"You remember I saw you at Cheetah's parking lot? You were valeting your car."

"Damn. I forgot about that. That was about six months ago."

"Yup."

"So you think you can handle me."

"I know I can."

Jada smiled then licked her lips seductively.

Later that night Jada texted Big Papa.

Jada: *Hey Boo WYD?*

Big Papa: *Thinking about you.*

Jada :-) :-):-)

Big Papa: *Really I was.*

Jada: *What were you thinking about?*

Big Papa: *Just thinking about us starting a family*

Jada: *I think I would be a good mommy, what you think?*

Big Papa: *I think so.*

Jada: *I have a little problem. I really hate to bother you with it.*

Big Papa. *Tell me, Princess.*

Jada: *I'm ashamed to tell you this.*

Big Papa: *Come on, tell me.*

Jada: *Well I've been staying at the Four Seasons ever since I broke up with my boyfriend and the month is almost over. I have to pay them for another month. They been letting me stay here at a discounted rate of 7500 per month. And I don't have it all.*

Big Papa: *How much do you have?*

Jada: *Well, I got about a thousand dollars.*

Big Papa: *LOL, meet me tomorrow and I'll take of that for you.*

Jada: *You sure?*

Big Papa: *I told you I was gonna take care of you, Princess :-):-)*

Jada: *I missed you today.*

Twan was coming out of his baby mama's house in some run-down apartments off Bankhead when Kenny-Boo smacked him with his 9mm. Twan tried to run, but Tater grabbed him and slammed him on his goddamned head. Twan fell, so they picked his ass up and tossed him into the back of a Black Escalade. They put the child locks on, and Kenny-Boo sat beside him. Mike was driving the Escalade. Mike drove Twan to a condo he had downtown.

Mike grabbed Twan around his throat and choked the fuck out him and then said, "Motherfucker, you killed my goddamned brother and you thought you were going to get away with it?"

"I ain't killed nobody. What you talking about?"

"You know what the fuck I'm talking about. Nigga, don't play dumb."

Kenny-Boo slapped him again with the gun then put the barrel against his nose. "Where the fuck is Black?"

"Who?"

"Tell us where Black is, and I promise not to kill you."

"I don't know no Black."

Mike said, "Quit playing dumb, motherfucker." Then he spit in Twan's face.

With spit rolling down his face and ugly-ass Kenny-Boo looking at him, Twan knew they were going to kill him. He needed to tell them something fast. There was no use in lying like he didn't know what the fuck was going on.

"I know where his grandma lives."

"Where?"

"The West Side. I don't know the name of the community, but I can show you."

"What the fuck you mean you don't know the name of the community?" Tater asked.

"Man, I'm from Alabama. I'm not from here. Besides, I'm gonna have to show you the house. I mean it's not like I got the address memorized.

Mike said, "I don't wanna know about where his Grandma lives. It's not like I'm going to do something to her old ass."

Twan said, "But you can find Black over there sometimes. He loves his grandma."

Mike thought about how his brother must have been suffering and begging for his life. He grabbed Twan and began choking the hell out him. He picked Twan up and slammed his ass to the floor.

Twan tried to sit up but Kenny-Boo kicked him in the face.

Mike said, "We gotta kill him, man. There ain't no another way around it. These motherfuckers got me owing the Mexicans damn near a million dollars with all the work they stole."

Tater said, "I forgot about that." Then he kicked Twan in the ribs. Kenny-Boo kept kicking Twan in the back of the head. Twan lay on the floor trying his damnedest to cover his face.

Trey and Shantelle lay on her sofa, naked. They'd finished having sex and Shantelle wanted more but Trey said, "No I can't." He was adamant that he wasn't having sex again. He stood and put his boxers back on.

She made a sad face. Then she stood across the room from the sofa, Trey was looking at her ass, her pussy lips hanging from the back, and he thought 'damn this sexy-ass bitch is draining me every day.' He'd thought he'd be used to fucking her by now, but he still loved her.

Trey said, "Come on, baby. You know I got a lady."

"I know, but I can't help it. I want you."

"I haven't had sex with my girl in a very long time and she's accusing me of fuckin' somebody else. I mean it's like she's sensing it and it has me nervous."

"Female intuition, Trey. You know how that goes."

"I'm starting to believe in that shit and I know I can't keep avoiding sex with her."

"We all have intuition."

Trey sat on the sofa."

Shantelle looked sad and Trey asked, "What's wrong?"

"Nothing is wrong."

"Come on. You just said, 'we all have intuition'. I can sense something is wrong with you.

She put her knees up to her chin, her T-shirt covering her knees but still giving Trey an excellent view of her V-J. He was careful not to stare. He had to stay focused and not give in. "What's wrong?"

"Look, I tried to see you without involving my feelings, and I know I agreed to play my role, but I want you, Trey. You're a good man, and I want you for myself. I think I'm falling for you."

Trey looked at her. He didn't know how to respond to that. He didn't want his life to be more complicated than it already was. This was not what he wanted to hear. Though he enjoyed being around her, there was no way he could offer her more.

"Look, you don't have to say anything."

"I don't know what to say."

She stood and said, "There is nothing to say." She walked into the kitchen, Trey still not sure what to say or do, just eyed her ass and kitty, knowing damn well he wasn't ready to give that up. Not just yet.

Mike, Kenny-Boo and Tater drove Twan to a wooded area about forty-five minutes outside of Atlanta to a town called Newnan. There Kenny-Boo and Tater tied Twan to a tree and at point blank range the three men fired eighty-three shots into Twan's chest and dome. Hunters would find him two day later. His body, still tied to the tree had been half eaten by coyotes.

CHAPTER 17

Hunch, Shamari, and one of Hunch's friends, a tall goofy ass nigga with big ears named Jace, staked out the warehouse belonging to the Mexicans. They were across the street from the warehouse in a wooded area at the top of the hill.

This was day three of the stakeout.

Every time somebody would come by to make a transaction, Jesus, a short Mexican in his early forties, would run out to the red Dodge Durango located in the back of the warehouse behind the dock and get the drugs. He would then run back into the warehouse where the transaction would go down.

Hunch said, "I'm telling you, bruh. There is ki's in the trunk of that car, and I ain't talking about no motherfucking car keys."

Shamari said, "Well he's ran out there six times already. They gotta be getting low."

"Doesn't matter. Hector told me that just got a shipment in the other day and these motherfuckers are getting hundreds."

Jace lit a Newport and said, "Look, we need to make a move and fast. I can't be out here all motherfucking night again."

Shamari stared at Jace, he wanted to slap the fuck out of him. For the past three days all he'd been doing was bitching and complaining.

Shamari said, "Look, man, I'm not doing anything half-assed, and I'm not going to get killed out here fucking with you dudes. We gotta make sure we got all bases covered."

Jace blew a smoke ring and said, "Man, we've been over the game plan about six times now. Now it's time to put it in motion."

Shamari said to Jace, "We gotta be careful. I ain't tryna get killed out here." He turned to Hunch. "If what brother-in-law say is true, you better believe they gonna protect their shit. We ain't the only ones with guns."

Jace said, "Man, we been watching this one simple-ass Mexican run back and forth to the car for three days. Let's just go down there and get the shit."

Shamari said to Hunch, "I'm about to leave man. I don't wanna be a part of no dumb-ass plan. I'd rather be broke than get killed fuckin with this clown-ass dude."

Jace became angry. "Who the fuck is this nigga calling a clown? I'll fuck your bitch-ass up."

Hunch got between the two men. He didn't want to see Shamari beat the fuck out of his childhood friend. He looked at his watch and said, "Let's get the fuck out of here."

"Why?" Jace complained.

"Because I said so."

Jace said, "I'll go rob the Mexican by my goddamned self. All I need is one of ya'll to drive the car."

Shamari said, "I ain't doing shit for you." Then he exited the woods and headed toward the car that was waiting at the bottom of the hill. Hunch followed and Jace stood there for a few moments looking dumb as hell, before finally leaving.

K.B. was driving down Interstate 485 about to get off on the Perimeter exit when he noticed cop lights flashing. The Georgia State Patrol. He had his brother Kevin's driver's license. They looked identical, only an inch shorter. He put a half smoked blunt in the bottom of his shoe. Maybe he'd swerved or forgot to give a signal. He would present his license and the officer would write him a ticket then he'd be well on his way. Well, he thought that, until he spotted three more state patrolmen and two unmarked cars.

He remembered the gun that was underneath the seat. He wanted to hide it but when he reached underneath the seat, he couldn't feel it. He knew he was fucked. He dialed Black's number and just as Black answered the phone, the patrolman called out. "Kelvin Bryant! Put your goddamned hands up where I can see them!"

K.B. dropped the phone to the floorboards, the phone still on. He wanted Black to hear the conversation between him and the officer, just in case he got locked up.

"What's the problem, officer?"

A plainclothes cop that had been riding in the unmarked car said, "You just shut the fuck up! We'll ask the questions!"

K.B. stared at the man, wanting to tell him to go to hell, but he didn't say anything.

The patrolman said, "Are there any drugs or weapons in the car?"

"No."

"Okay, hands on top of your head."

K.B. placed his hands on top of his head and the patrolman opened the door.

The cop pulled K.B. out of the car and they searched the car, along with the K9 Unit. They found the phone, the gun underneath the seat, and some marijuana residue.

When the cop showed K.B. the gun, he knew he was fucked. He wondered what else they had on him. K.B. said, "What about my Miranda rights."

A short, stocky, bald, black cop with shitty breath stood in front of him and said, "Fuck your rights, nigga. Where you going, you ain't gonna have no motherfuckin' rights."

CHAPTER 18

Shamari snatched the short-ass Mexican by the collar, covered his mouth, frisked him and found a nine millimeter handgun on the man's waist. He placed the gun to the man's temple and said, "Make a sound and I'm blowing your motherfucking brains out." He stared the man in the eyes and said, "Is that understood?"

The man nodded, and then attempted to put up a struggle until Shamari smacked him in the back of the head with his pistol. "Where is the motherfuckin' dope."

The man pointed to the Dodge Durango.

"Okay, Im'ma take my hand off your mouth, but I swear if you scream, it will be the last time you scream."

The man felt the cold steel on the back of his head. He'd never thought about dying, but the thought of death had become very real to him. He didn't want to leave his two-month-old son and his new wife. He would cooperate.

"Where's the work?" Shamari asked again.

The man opened the back door and retrieved a small, green duffle bag and passed it to Shamari.

Shamari opened the duffle bag and spotted three bricks wrapped in brown tape. "Where the fuck is the rest of it?"

"My friend, my friend. This is all I have. There is not anymore."

"I'm not your motherfucking friend."

Shamari slapped man in the mouth, knocking out four front teeth then sprinted into the woods.

Thirty minutes later, Shamari stepped into his sister's living room. Hunch was in his usual spot on the couch watching TV.

Tangie was in her bedroom watching reality TV.

Shamari said, "Hunch, I wanna see you for a second." Hunch followed him back to the guest bedroom—the room where Shamari had been sleeping. When they were in the room, Shamari locked the door and said, "I got him."

"What you talking about, brother-in-law?"

Shamari dumped the three kilos on the bed.

Hunch was smiling and looking dumb as hell at the same damn time.

Shamari handed Hunch one of the bricks. "Yeah, I wanted to do it by myself."

"Why?"

"I just didn't like ya boy. I thought he would fuck things up, and I'd rather do it by myself. I knew that if I had to run, I could. I'm in shape. Ya'll ain't in no shape to run.

'You right about that." He examined the brick before saying. "There was only three?"

"That's all he had."

"I think we waited too late. We could've got at least twenty."

"Yeah, but the point is we got away with it, and it was free."

"You got away with it, you mean."

"But you're going to benefit."

"What about Jace?"

"I don't give a fuck about Jace. I only care about you and my sister."

Big Papa was wearing some jeans that was clearly too small for his fifty-six inch waist, so the crack of his ass was showing. Yuck. Jada stepped inside his midtown condo, which was exquisitely decorated. Jada assumed he'd hired a decorator because although Papa had money, he clearly lacked class. Jada wanted to throw up as she stared at Big Papa's ass crack. A remnant of toilet paper dangling from his cheeks. Disgusting.

She smiled brightly when he tossed her an envelope with fifty one hundred dollar bills. She counted the money and said, "Thank you, daddy."

Big Papa smiled, revealing brownish yellow teeth. She'd been seeing him a total of two weeks and he'd already given her over fifteen thousand dollars.

Papa sat on the Italian leather sofa, Jada sat on the sectional across from him.

"If you want, you can turn on the television."

Jada really did want to turn on the television and avoid talking to him at all cost, but hell, the man did just hand her five thousand dollars. She would have to pretend that she was really into him.

He aimed the remote at the TV before she said, "No, leave it off."

"Why?"

"I wanna talk to you." She gave him a fake smile.

"Really?"

"Yes, really."

"Well, why don't you come over here? Quit acting all high-class."

She laughed, "I am high-class."

Big Papa said, "With your boushee ass?"

"Boughetto. I'm boushee, but I'm from the ghetto."

"You coming over?"

She stood and he was staring at her from the waist down. She was wearing a green skirt that was shellacked on her ass and made it look extra pronounced. She called that skirt her money skirt. The last time she'd worn that skirt she'd gotten a Fendi bag from Craig and the time before that, Shamari had agreed to pay for her boob job.

Jada stood and walked over and sat beside Papa. He placed his arm around her then he said, "Damn, you smell amazing."

She was wearing Love in White by Creed. She loved it, but the affect it had on men was unreal. She smiled and said, "Well, how is a lady supposed to smell?"

He said, "Like you."

She wished she could say the same thing about him, but the fact of the matter was he smelled like he'd just taken a shit.

Big Papa said, "Jada, you know I have a hard time reading you."

"I don't understand."

"Well, most of the time I call you, you're busy or you rush me off the phone. Sometimes, I text you and you don't text back until the next day."

"Yeah, I'm bad about that."

"Are you really bad about that, or are you bad about getting back to me?"

"It's not you."

"But I do so much for you, and there is nothing I wouldn't do for you."

"I believe that." She wanted to tell him to shut the fuck up. He was making her feel guilty and she didn't like feeling like that.

"I guess what I'm trying to say is, I just don't think you like me like I like you."

"What are you talking about? If I didn't like you, I wouldn't be here."

"You're here because I told you I had a surprise for you."

"I didn't know that surprise was money."

"Yeah, but you know I'm very generous to you."

"You are." She gave him a fake smile wondering where he was going with this.

Big Papa leaned in, attempting to kiss her, and she pushed him away.

"See what I mean?" he frowned.

"I just ate a sandwich with onions on it."

"Really?"

"Yes." She rubbed his chest and his little pecker got hard. She could see the tiny motherfucker pointing at her through his pants.

She said, "Look, baby, I like you a lot. Can I say I love you? I can't say that, but I like you a lot, maybe what we have will grow into love."

Big Papa stood up strolling to the other side of the room, the piece of toilet paper still dangling from his ass crack. Jada turned her head refusing to look at it again.

Big Papa said, "Look, baby. This is ATL and I'm rich. I don't have to give my money away."

Jada said, "Do you want your gift back?" She offered him the envelope, hoping like hell that his pride would make him refuse the money. He refused it.

"Listen, I don't want the money. It's not about the money."

She stood and walked up behind him before noticing that annoying piece of toilet paper. She stepped back and said, "Daddy must have sat on a piece of toilet paper somewhere. There is a piece stuck to your butt."

He looked behind him and when he noticed the toilet paper he looked embarrassed and excused himself. He disappeared into the bathroom and came back five minutes later.

"I'm so embarrassed."

"Don't be."

"But like I was saying—"

She cut him off. "Look, I think I know where you're going. You feel like you're not getting anything for what you do for me."

"Exactly."

"Look I want you…but I'm not a touchy-feely type of girl. I wanna kiss you, but I don't like kissing."

"You don't like having sex either, huh?"

"I love having sex."

"But not with me because I'm fat."

She rubbed his fat-assed stomach again. "No, it's just right now I can't."

"I'm horny."

"I'm on my cycle." She knew it sounded like a lie, but she really was on her period.

He made a sad face and she wanted to offer him oral sex but there was no way in the hell she wanted her head anywhere near his stinking ass. Maybe if he showered first.

He tried to embrace her again and she pushed him away.

He said, "See! That's exactly what I'm talking about."

"So, you're mad cuz I'm on my cycle?"

"I don't believe you."

She removed her skirt and he saw the pad through her underwear.

He said, "I don't mind having you on your cycle."

"I'm not having sex on my period."

He dug into his pocket and handed her fifty more one hundred dollar bills. She tried to give it back to him but he wouldn't take it. She sat on the sofa with her bare ass. He got on his knees right in front of her and pried her legs open.

Big Papa said, "I just wanna taste you."

"Are you serious?" asked Jada.

There was no way this man wanted to taste her bloody-ass vagina. This was sick, but he'd just given her ten thousand dollars. She removed the pad and Big Papa licked her thighs. He was indeed disgusting as fuck.

CHAPTER 19

Black received a phone call from an unknown number—he usually didn't answer those kinds of calls, but he answered the phone on the second ring. "Hello?"

A woman was screaming and hollering. Black could hear others in the background crying as well. "Who is this?" he asked.

No answer, only more hollering and screaming.

Black said, "Who the fuck is this?"

"Black, this is Tameeka."

"Tameeka who?"

"Twan's baby mama."

"Oh hey, Tameeka, what's up?"

"Twan got murdered execution style last night. His body was found in South East Atlanta.

"What?"

Tameeka was screaming and whimpering.

Black said, "Calm down, Tameeka."

"Yeah, I'm calling you because he told me that if anything happened to him that you would know what to do. I swear, Black, it's like he sensed that something was going to happen to him."

"Are you sure it was Twan.

"I'm positive. This is bad. This is real bad, Black. I got all these goddamned chaps to raise without a daddy."

"Tameeka, I'm going to help you all I can." Black said as he thought about Twan's three kids by Tameeka, and another three by Tameeka's cousin, Latrica, and his own five kids. He now had a goddamned soccer team.

"I know you will, Black. I think that's why Twan told me to contact you."

Black held the phone, thinking about all that had transpired since he first saw Chris with Lani. This shit had gone too far but he was in it now, and there was no way he could let Twan die in vain.

Another unfamiliar number showed up on his caller ID. "Tameeka, I need to take this call."

"Hello."

"Black, this is Kelvin's baby mama, Danielle. He told me to tell you he's in jail."

"I know. I was on the other end of the phone when they arrested him."

"You know what? I'm tired of this motherfucker. It's like every fuckin' six months this dumb-ass nigga is in jail. Every motherfuckin' six months! I'm sick of this bullshit! I can't take this dumb shit!"

"What's his bond?"

"He ain't got no bond and I'm glad. Black, you just don't know what I go through with this motherfucker. He ain't did shit for his son in two years and soon as he go to jail, I'm the first motherfucker he called."

"What are his charges?"

"I don't know and I don't give a flying fuck. He told me to call you and I did. Don't expect to hear shit else from me cuz I ain't accepting no jail calls! I ain't getting the block off my house phone! I ain't sending no prison pictures! I ain't visiting him! I really wish they throw the goddamn book at him."

Black removed the phone from his ear and put her on speaker phone as she went off for the next five minutes.

"Hello, Hello?"

Black placed the phone back up to his ear. "Hello."

"Well, I told you what he told me to tell you."

"Thanks, Danielle."

Black terminated the call and as soon as he did, his phone rang again.

The caller ID said, "Sis." It was Black's sister Rashida and she was calling him on his other phone. What the fuck was she calling him on that phone for and how did she get the number?

"Hello?"

"Boy, what the fuck have you gotten yourself into?"

"What are you talking about?"

"I need to see you."

"Okay, let's meet at Nana's house."

"We can't go there."

"Why not?"

"It's just not a good idea right now. Let's meet at Gladys Knight's Chicken and Waffles."

"How long will it take you to get there?"

"I'll be there in fifteen."

"See you then."

Black's sister Rashida was almost forty but didn't look a day over thirty. She was short and curvy with perfect teeth. Her slightly graying hair was in a short twist and she looked very professional. She was the only one of his siblings who had gone to school and was doing well for herself. Rashida was a physician's assistant in Southwest Atlanta.

Rashida was sitting in a booth at the back of the restaurant when Black entered the restaurant twenty minutes late. Rashida was already eating fried chicken and waffles when he walked in. When she laid eyes on her younger brother she completely forgot about how dignified she looked and said, "Motherfucker, what the fuck have you gotten yourself into?"

Black examined his sister's face and he saw she was clearly upset with him. He'd seen that look on her face plenty of times. He sat into the booth and Rashida was still staring at his ass coldly.

"So you're not going to say 'hello, little brother' and give me a hug or nothing. You just going to light in on my ass, huh."

Rashida dropped her fork on the plate, scanned the restaurant and said, "What the fuck have you done, Tyrann?"

"What are you talking about?"

"I'm talking about why the hell did the homicide detectives come to my job asking about who owns my cell phone?"

Black was looking puzzled as hell.

"Huh?"

"Yeah, the goddamned phone I got for you in my name. They knew I was the owner of the phone."

"Huh?"

"What have you done, Tyrann?"

'I ain't do shit." Black lied.

"Well, they said that my cell phone signal was in the vicinity where a homicide took place on the night of a murder."

"Are you serious?"

She looked pissed when he asked that dumb a question.

"What else did they ask?"

"They asked me who owned the cell phone. They said they didn't think it was me."

"What did you tell them?"

"I ain't tell them shit. I asked them was I under arrest and they said no and I went back inside to work."

"Good. Don't worry, I'll get you a lawyer."

She bit down into a drumstick and said with her mouth full, "What the hell do I have to worry about. I ain't done shit."

Black said, "Will you calm the fuck down!"

"You telling me to calm down and I got the police coming to my job, got these white folks looking at me like I'm from the goddamn ghetto or something."

"Hell, you are from the ghetto. That's your motherfuckin' problem. You done forgot where you came from."

Rashida said, "I know you ain't talking shit to me."

Black could sense the conversation going in the wrong direction. His big sister was getting emotional and he needed her to be calm so he could find out what the fuck was going on. "Look, Sis, I'm sorry."

Rashida sipped her water and said, "Man, what have you done?"

"It's a long story."

"Tyrann, did you kill somebody?"

"No."

"Look me in my eye, Tyrann, I'm your sister, you can tell me anything."

"Some things you don't need to know about."

Rashida said, "Where the hell is that phone? You know if you got that phone on you, they know you're here and they know I'm here."

"I didn't bring it. When you called me on the other phone, I knew something was up with the phone."

"Good."

"How did you get the number?"

"Nana."

Black looked confused. He didn't know Nana had his phone number.

"I think one of your kids gave it to her. Man-Man, I think." Man-Man was Black's oldest son.

"Oh, okay."

"So you don't wanna tell me what happened?"

"Sis, I don't want you to get in any trouble."

A tear rolled down Rashida's face. She'd seen her brother go in and out of the penitentiary since he was fourteen years old. She'd seen him do what he had to do to make sure his family ate. Though he was younger than her, he'd given her large sums of money to help her get on her feet when she was fresh out of school.

Black grabbed her hand from across the table and said, "Don't you start crying and whatever you do don't tell Nana."

Rashida sniffled and said, "I just don't want nothing to happen to you."

Black said, "Nothing is going to happen to me that I can't handle. Trust me, sis, I'll be fine."

He stood up and threw a hundred dollar bill on the table.

"What is this for?"

'The food."

"I can pay for my own food, Tyrann."

"I know that, but I'm the man."

He headed to the door and Rashida watched her brother as he left the restaurant. He was indeed the man, he'd been the man of the house every since he was fourteen years old. Though her brother was respected in the street and she loved him and everything he stood for, she'd never thought he could kill anybody. But maybe she was wrong.

CHAPTER 20

Starr poured Lani a cup of green tea. They sat outside on the balcony looking at the Atlanta skyline. Starr sipped her tea and said, "I think Trey is fucking somebody else."

Lani stared at Starr. She remembered what Starr's sister had told her about Trey having a child that Starr had just found out about. She chose not to comment.

Starr continued, "He don't want to touch me most of the time."

"Huh?"

"Yeah, I haven't been fucked in a very long time."

"Maybe he's tired."

"Look, it's been a month. I know my man and he loves pussy and especially head, but now he hasn't touched me. Something is wrong."

"I can't see Trey cheating on you. He's such a good man."

Starr said, "Trey's just like any other nigga."

"But you have no proof that he cheated."

"Well I have no physical proof, but I could have sworn that I smelled some perfume on his clothes."

"What do you mean. Either you did or you didn't."

"Well, it wasn't poignant enough for me to really say it was a woman's perfume."

"Like I said you don't have proof."

Starr said, "Well I didn't tell you, but Trey has a child."

Lani had to pretend she didn't know. Starr's sister Meeka had initially told Lani about Trey's child, but once Meeka realized that Lani hadn't known about it, she made Lani promise not to say a word to anybody.

Lani looked surprised.

"Yeah Mr. Fucking Perfect Trey has a five year old."

"Well ain't no nigga perfect."

"And Trey damn sure ain't."

Lani sipped her tea and said, "I'm sorry to hear that."

"That's not the worst part. His baby's mama is white."

Lani spit her tea out. "What?"

"Yeah, she's white."

"Damn."

"So how did you learn this?"

"Well, you remember those anonymous calls that I'd been receiving?"

"Yeah."

"Those were from the baby mama."

"Get the fuck out of here."

"I'm serious. So one day she shows up at the old place with little T.J. while Trey was gone."

"T.J.?"

"Trey Junior, chile."

"Oh, okay."

"Yeah, girl, I'm been going through it. I even left Trey for a couple of days, checked into a hotel room and then his ass come showing up with a goddamned engagement ring begging and pleading for me to come back."

"So, ya'll getting married?"

"Hell, no! I ain't marrying no man that don't really want to marry me. The only reason he showed up with the ring is because he'd been caught."

"I feel ya," Lani said then sipped her tea. "So you think he fucking the baby mama?"

"Now that I don't believe because that bitch is crazy. Trey really can't handle crazy chicks. He can barely handle me when I'm going HAM on his ass.

"So who do you think it is?"

Starr looked pensive as she thought about the possibility of Trey being with another woman. Why the fuck would he do this to her again? Why would he tear down what they built up? She loved him but all he seemed to care about was fucking other women and breaking her heart over and over again. She had no proof, but her gut was telling her something wasn't right. She made eye contact with Lani. "I don't know. That's just it, I have no idea."

There was a knock at the door. Starr looked at Lani and said, "I wonder who in the fuck that could be?"

"Maybe you ordered something. Maybe it's UPS."

"No, I didn't order anything." She stood and stepped back inside the house and opened the door. A thin white man with skinny jeans and a t-shirt and designer eyeglasses stood in front of her. "Hey, honey, I'm Mike from across the hall. Can I use your phone?"

Starr invited him in. Mike said, "I'm really sorry. I locked my keys and phone in my house and my partner is at—." Mike stopped in mid-sentence as he looked around the gorgeous apartment. "Oh... My ... God! This place is amazing! Who decorated?"

Starr said, "You're looking at the decorator."

Lani said, "It's stunning, right?"

Mike said, "Me and my partner were just thinking of hiring a decorator, but hell we might need to hire you, what are your prices?"

Starr said, "I don't know what to charge. I've never done anything like this for anybody else. This is more of a hobby."

Mike said, "Well, honey, you need to start charging."

He sounded just like a woman and Lani and Starr looked at each other, they both had figured out that Mike was indeed gay by the use of the word partner and what straight man would care that much about decorating.

Starr passed Mike her cell phone and he called his partner to tell him that he was locked out and then passed the phone back to Starr. Then he asked, "Can I walk around?"

Starr said, "Yeah, you can go everywhere except my main bedroom."

Trey sometimes left wads of money on the dresser and the last thing she needed was the white people in the building whispering that they thought Trey was a drug dealer.

When Mike came back into the living room, he said, "You are so creative and I love this Tiffany Blue theme in the living room."

Starr said, "My girlfriends was just telling me that I needed to be a interior decorator."

"They are right. Honey, you have an eye for this. Thanks for allowing me to use the phone," Mike said.

Starr said, "Where are you going? You can't get in."

"Well, I didn't want to wear my welcome out."

Starr said, "Come out on the balcony with us and have some green tea."

Mike smiled and said, "I don't mind if I do."

CHAPTER 21

Nosey-ass Luke, the neighbor from across the street, was sitting on his porch eating sunflower seeds when Jada pulled up to her old residence to check the mailbox. When she opened the mailbox, there was a red envelope with no return address. It simply said, *For Shamari.* Jada assumed somebody dropped it off. There were a few bills but nothing else. When she was about to get in the car, Luke approached her. "Good evening, ma'am."

"Hey. How are you?" Jada asked, though she really didn't give a fuck about how he was doing. It just seemed like the right thing to do.

"A couple of mornings ago, this house was surrounded my U.S. Marshals and ATF. I told them that nobody lived here. I don't know what or who they were looking for."

"Really?"

" Me and my wife was headed to work when we noticed them. They were all over the place, even in the back yard. The rental company showed up and let them search the garage."

Jada was thinking, goddamn this man is nosey. He was able to see the rental company arriving. Who the fuck does that? Only a nosey motherfucker.

He spat some sunflower seeds on the ground then poured more into his mouth.

"Did you find out anything else?"

"No, they didn't tell me anything. They just asked me how long had the house been empty, and I told them a few weeks. One of the Marshals gave me a card to give you if you showed up." Luke handed her the card.

The card read, U.S. Marshal Tommy Blair. 770-568-9087.

"They didn't tell you to call them if you saw us?" Jada wanted to know exactly what Luke knew. She wanted to gauge the situation, to see exactly how bad things were.

"No, they actually told me to tell y'all to get in touch with them. Nobody told me to call them."

Jada said, "Thank you for letting me know this."

Jada wanted Luke to get the hell out of her face but he was still standing there looking stupid as hell and Jada said, "Did you want to tell me something else?"

Luke said, "As a matter a fact I do."

"Okay," Jada said, staring at Luke wishing he would say whatever the fuck he had to say.

"Hey, I don't know what the Feds were doing at your house and I don't care to be honest with you."

"Really? You don't care?"

"Why should I care?"

Jada said, "Well, you shouldn't care, but I think you do."

Luke looked confused, "Why did you say that?"

"Well I heard you were the one that always complained to the HOA about us."

Luke folded the pack of sunflower seeds and put them in his pocket then turned away from Jada's gaze. "Well, you're right, I do care. I care about the neighborhood and I care about you. I don't know you, but this is the second time that the Law Enforcement have came to your home in the past month." Luke paused and spit more seeds on the ground then said, "I don't know what you're into, but I suggest you stop. You have your whole life ahead of you."

Jada stared at Luke. He was no longer the nosey-ass neighbor from across the street but a concerned person with empathy.

"You're young. There is a better life out there for you. Just something to think about," Luke said.

Jada said, "Well, thank you, Luke."

"How did you know my name?"

"The whole neighborhood knows your name."

"That's true."

Luke turned to walk back across the street but before he got to the other side of the rode he said, "Think about what I said."

"I will," Jada said, and she drove away.

Hunch eye's zoomed right in on Jada's boobs and decided that they looked down right delicious, bursting out of the wife-beater. It was a ponytail kind of day today but she still looked amazing in her tank and tight jeans and stilettos. Hunch kept looking with a silly-ass grin on his face. Jada noticed him staring. Jada said, "What the fuck are you looking at?"

"My bad," Hunch said.

"Can you go get Shamari please?"

"Come on in and have a seat?"

Hunch disappeared and seconds later he emerged with Shamari standing behind him.

"Hey, baby." Shamari hugged Jada.

"Can you give us a moment alone," Shamari said to Hunch who was still standing there stealing looks at Jada's ass and boobs.

"For sure, brother-in-law."

When Hunch was gone, Shamari said, "Damn, I know we ain't kicking it. You just forgot about a nigga."

"No, I've been trying to get somewhere to live. And since you didn't have no phone, I didn't know how to get in touch without driving over here."

"I got one today and I called you, but you didn't answer."

"You know I don't answer numbers that I don't know. Why didn't you text?"

"I did."

Jada glanced down at her iPhone, there were seventy-eight unread messages. She was sure Shamari's messages were among them.

"So you didn't want to come over here?"

"You know your sister don't like me."

"I know, but I fucks with you Jada. I know we had our ups and downs, but what you did for me—nobody would have done that. I mean, you were really down for me."

"I know and I always will be," Jada said. She didn't really know what to make of their relationship. Though she knew she didn't want to be with him, she still had a lot of feelings for him.

Shamari said, "Look, I'm going to pay you back"

Jada said, "You don't have to pay me back. Man, just get yourself together. I know it's rough for you right now."

Shamari pulled her into his arms. He hated to admit it, but he still loved this goddamned woman.

They kissed briefly then Shamari said, "I'm gonna pay you."

"You don't have too."

He kissed her again. This time his hand was on her ass and she felt his dick throbbing, now she wanted him inside of her but it would be too much work. They'd have to go back to the hotel and she'd have to bring him home. She couldn't fuck him in his sister's house.

He whispered in her ear, "Baby, I hit a lick and we're going to be alright."

"What in the hell are you talking about?"

Shamari lowered his voice and told her about the robbery and how it went down.

"So you got three kilos?"

"Well, I gave one to Hunch. But that ain't all. I learned yesterday one of them was a kilo of heroin."

"What does that mean?"

"Mean that I can make at least three hundred thousand off of it."

Jada smiled. She was happy for Shamari and she knew that he would take care of her, but she became sad suddenly and he wanted to know why.

"I went to check the mail and I seen nosey-ass Luke. He told me that the Feds had been by the house a couple of days ago."

"What? For what?"

"I don't know."

She handed him the card from the U.S. Marshall.

"What else did Luke say?"

"He said they told him to tell one of us to get in touch with them, and he said that they searched the house."

"Fuck."

"I know, babe, if it ain't one thing, it's another."

Shamari said, "I need to make some money, I gotta have lawyer fees if it's something serious."

Jada handed him the envelope she had gotten out of the mailbox.

"What the fuck is this?"

"I don't know. I started to open it but since it had your name on it, I didn't bother."

He tore into it and there was a piece of paper inside that read, *Call Zandra ASAP. 770-223-9087*

"Who is Zandra."

Shamari was thinking hard. I don't know babe.

"Look, you don't have to lie to me. You know I've done my dirt, so don't lie, Shamari. That's where I went wrong."

"I really don't know."

There was an awkward silence in the room then Shamari said. "You know what? Zandra is one of Tony's baby's mothers."

"Tony?"

"Yeah."

"Oh fuck." Jada thought back to the day when she heard Tony, Shamari and Duke plotting to kill an informant named Don.

Shamari pulled out the iPhone he'd just bought and dialed the number on the paper: *Hey, this is Z leave a message at the tone.*

He looked at Jada and said, "Straight to voicemail."

"Try again."

"I'll call her later. Probably Tony's lawyer needs more money."

"But what about the visit from the Feds?"

Shamari said, "Look, I'll call them later. I have money to make."

"You better be careful. I mean, what if they pull you over and you have a warrant on you?"

"I'll cross that bridge when I get to it." He pulled her into him and kissed her again, his hand palming her ass. Damn, he didn't know why he loved this woman so much.

CHAPTER 22

Lani wondered who in the fuck was knocking at her door and ringing the doorbell at the same time and how had they been able to get into the building. She looked through the peephole; the only thing she could see was Kenny-Boo's red and chapped lips and crossed eyes. She wanted to vomit. She wasn't going to open the door until she realized that Mike was standing behind him. She opened the door and led them to the living room.

When they were all seated, Mike said. "Have the police been in touch with you?"

"No. Why? Why would they be in touch with me?"

"I saw on the news that they picked up one of Black's friends."

"I didn't know that."

"Yeah, the car wash where my brother was abducted had hidden video cameras."

"I still don't understand why they would contact me?"

Kenny-Boo said, "Look, bitch, you got a lot more do with this than you think."

Lani said, "First of all, motherfucker, I ain't nobody's bitch and secondly, you can get the fuck out of my house."

Mike said, "Chill, Kenny-Boo."

"I don't like this ho, man. I'm telling you, she had something do with this shit."

Mike said, "Listen, the police are obviously investigating and they are going to realize sooner or later that the common link between Black and Chris is you."

"Yeah, you bitch," Kenny-Boo said looking at her with one eye and that lazy eye pointed toward the kitchen.

Lani stood up and said, "I want this clown out of my house right now."

Mike grabbed Lani's hand and said, "Have a seat. Calm down, Lani." Then he turned to Kenny-Boo and said, "Will you shut the fuck up."

"Okay, bruh. I'm just saying, man."

Mike said, "Don't say shit. I will do all the talking."

When Lani was calm, she said, "Mike, I loved your brother. I loved Chris."

"You loved Black too."

"I did."

"Are you in love with Black?"

"At this point no, but I have been in love with Black."

Mike said, "We're getting off subject. The point is, I don't need you communicating with the police. I don't need you telling them shit."

Lani looked at Mike and said, "Nobody has asked me shit."

"They're coming eventually. You can believe that."

Lani knew what Mike was saying was right. She knew they were coming to talk to her. She didn't want to think about it, but there was no way that they were going to leave her out of it. What would she say? What would she do?

Mike said, "I guess you heard about Twan?"

"Who?"

"Black's homeboy bitch," Kenny-Boo said, that ugly-ass eye staring right at her. She wanted to puke.

Lani looked at Mike and said, "I don't know Twan."

"Well, somebody murdered him."

"Damn."

"Black ain't tell you?"

"I hardly talk to Black."

Mike stood up. Kenny-Boo was still seated and Lani said, "You can stand your ugly-ass up too because you're getting the fuck out of here, bruh."

Kenny-Boo finally stood and they walked toward the door. Before they left Kenny-Boo said, "I'm not like other niggas. I'll fuck a girl up. So just remember that if you wanna go running your motherfuckin' mouth."

"Whatever, nigga," Lani said and she slammed the door shut.

Jada was getting ready for dinner with Big Papa when she got a call from Shamari.

"Hey, I'm downstairs in the hotel lobby. What room are you in?"

"Fuck." Jada said. She wanted to lie and tell him she wasn't there but she'd asked the valet to bring her car and she was sure it was parked out front. She knew damn well he'd seen it.

"I'm in 2501."

She dialed Big Papa. His phone was going straight to voice mail. She mumbled, "Answer the goddamned phone, you fat mother fucker." She called two more times, still no answer. She was about to text him when Shamari knocked on the door.

She opened the door and hugged him. He passed a Neiman Marcus shopping bag to her. When she looked inside, there was a Celine handbag she'd been eyeing the last time they'd gone shopping together. She hugged him and said, "Goddamn, baby, you didn't have to do that."

He grinned. "I know I didn't have to, but I wanted to. You've done so much for me. Look in the interior pockets."

When she opened the interior pockets, she found two bundles of one hundred dollar bills. She could feel more bills in the other interior pocket.

Jada said, "Goddamn, baby, how much is this?"

"This is forty thousand dollars. The heroin I had was pure, which means that I'm going to make at least three hundred thousand off it."

She smiled and hugged him and said, "I didn't pay your legal fees cuz I wanted it back, I paid it because I'm down with you."

"I know and that's why I had to give you your money back."

"But you didn't have to."

"Yes I did. I'm a man and I had to do what was right."

There was a knock at the door.

Shamari said, "You expecting someone?"

"No."

"It might be room service."

Jada said, "Who is it?"

"It's me."

Jada recognized the voice then peeked through the peephole. She saw Big Papa with his fat ass standing there grinning. What the fuck? Who told him to bring his big ass up to her room? How did he even remember her room number? How the fuck did he get on the elevator without a room card?

Jada said, "Hey, can you come back?" Hoping Shamari would think it was room service or house cleaning.

Instead he eased his way toward the door and said, "Open the door."

"I don't want to."

"Whoever that is on the other side of the door said, 'It's me.' That means they know you."

Jada was leaning up against the door blocking it. Shamari picked her up and moved her aside then opened the door. "Can I help you, bruh?"

Big Papa said, "I'm here to see Jada."

"What?"

"I need to see Jada."

"Who the fuck are you?" Shamari asked

"Who the hell are you?"

Jada said. "Shamari, this is my friend—"

Shamari said, "Friend? What the fuck is he doing coming up to your room?"

Big Papa said, "Jada, what's going on?"

Jada hugged Shamari from behind and said, "This is my boyfriend, Shamari." Even though he wasn't her boyfriend, she wanted to show Shamari some respect. Her loyalty was with him.

Big Papa said, "It's like that?"

Shamari said, "It's like that, motherfucker."

Jada stepped in between the two men and said to Big Papa, "I'm sorry. We're going to try to work things out."

Big Papa turned to walk away and Jada watched him stroll toward the elevator.

Shamari yelled, "Take a hike, fat boy."

Jada stepped back inside the room and Shamari said, "What the fuck was that all about?"

Jada said, "Look I needed some help and he helped me."

"So you're fuckin' fat disgusting motherfuckers for money?"

Jada punched Shamari in his goddamned mouth. "First of all, I ain't fuckin' him," Jada said because technically she hadn't fucked him. She'd only let him go down on her, but Shamari didn't need to know that.

Shamari grabbed his jaw and said, "So, why did he think he could come to the room?"

"Well, he's been helping me out."

"How did he know where your room was?"

"He'd been up here before," Jada said. Then she sat on the edge of the bed before saying, "Look, motherfucker, you went to jail. You didn't leave me no money out here, and I had to hustle up money to pay for your attorney. It left me broke. I had to do what I had to do."

Shamari sat down beside her and thought about the sacrifices that Jada had made to make sure he didn't go to prison. He knew that she'd gone broke and had to beg and steal to get him an attorney. There was no doubt in his mind that if it wasn't for Jada, he'd still be in jail.

"Look, babe, I'm sorry," Shamari said to Jada.

"It's okay."

There was a long silence before Shamari said, "I really do love you Jada. I don't know why, but I love you."

Jada said, "I love you too. It's dysfunctional as hell."

They locked lips before he removed her robe and subsequently a pair of boy shorts that had been fighting hard to contain her amazing ass.

CHAPTER 23

There was a suitcase at the foot of the bed that Trey had left for Starr to count. Starr popped it and dumped the money on the bed. A black, female blouse fell from the suitcase. It smelled like fresh perfume. Starr examined the shirt. It had come from Zara.

What the fuck was this shirt doing in Trey's bag? She called him and he picked up on the second ring. "Trey, you need to come home right now."

"What's wrong?"

"Nothing's wrong. Come home."

"I will be there in twenty minutes."

"Okay."

Starr was fuming. She couldn't believe this motherfucker had begged her to come back home after she'd learned about T.J. and she had been stupid enough to come home. Now this nigga was back up to his same old tricks. She would have to admit to herself, one woman would never be enough for Trey.

Twenty minutes later Trey entered the house. "What's up baby?"

Starr held up a black shirt. "What the fuck is this?"

"It's a shirt."

"Yeah, but it's not my motherfuckin' shirt."

Trey stood there looking confused.

Starr said, "This shirt fell out of the suitcase you left."

"Okay, and what do you want me to do about it?"

"Whose goddamn shirt is this?'"

"How am I supposed to know that? Kenny gave me this suit-case." Kenny was one of Trey's lieutenants.

"Whatever." Starr said then flung the shirt at Trey. He ducked then punched in a number on his phone and put it on speaker. It went straight to voicemail.

"Who the fuck are you calling?"

"Calling Kenny. Asking him whose shirt it is?"

"Trey. All I gotta say is 'I'm not stupid.'"

"I swear, baby, this shirt is probably one of Kenny's bitches."

Starr said, "I would believe you, but the shirt has perfume on it. This is the same scent I thought I smelled about a week ago on your clothes."

"So the department store sold only one bottle of that kind of perfume?"

"You know what, Trey. You're fucking pathetic. You are a piece of shit and I wish I wouldn't have never came back."

Trey said, "Look, you're tripping. I'm getting out of here. I don't feel like arguing."

"When you come back, motherfucker, I might be gone."

When Starr heard the door shut, she flopped on the bed and began to cry.

Shamari called Zandra, Tony's baby mother, and she told him that she would prefer to talk to him in person. She'd given him an address in Lithonia. Zandra was a thick Georgia girl, brown skin with a baby face. She looked much younger than thirty-four. She invited Shamari into the townhome. When they were seated she said, "Look, Shamari, I probably shouldn't be telling you this. Tony is trying to save his ass."

"Huh?"

"The U.S. attorney said they were going to pursue the death penalty or at best a supermax prison. You know the kind where you are locked down for twenty three hours a day and you read your mail on a computer screen?"

"What does this have to do with me?"

"Tony is going to give you up to save his own ass."

"How do you know?"

Zandra looked away and said, "His other baby mama told me."

"Really?"

"Yes. Look, Tony is one bitch-assed nigga. I wished you would have talked to me before you hired him for this."

"I didn't hire him."

Zandra lifted her shirt and laughed, "Look. I'm not wired. I have nothing to gain. I'm not in trouble, but like I said, Tony is pathetic." She paused, "How do you think I know that you hired him." She giggled. "I'll tell you how? He told me. He runs his mouth like a bitch."

Shamari looked away, trying to take it all in, wondering why Zandra was telling him this.

Zandra said, "Look, Shamari, I know about everything, I know how you paid him and I know you gave him money that was supposedly to take care of his kids because he knew he was going to do time. I'm telling you, Tony is going to save his own ass, if he hasn't already."

"His other baby mama told you this?"

"Yeah."

Shamari looked at Zandra, she seemed like an honest person, for the most part. Zandra was a typical hood chick who wanted to do better for herself and her kids. She'd worked mostly in the fast food industry until a few years ago when she went back to school to become a medical assistant. She got a job in a doctor's office and now she was making what she considered good money. She was so glad she'd been able to find a decent place to live that wasn't section eight.

"I have nothing to gain."

"So, why are you doing this?"

"Doing what?"

"Telling me what you think Tony is going to do?"

"Think? What part of what I just said don't you understand? Tony is going to tell on you. Tony is a bitch."

"Okay. Why are you telling me this? What do you have against Tony?"

Zandra made eye contact with Shamari and said, "Tony has made me and my kid's life a living hell."

"Okay."

"Tony has two kids by my goddamned sister, Shamari. Do you know how fuckin' embarrassing that is? My kids' first cousins are there brother and sister."

Zandra broke her nail on the arm of the sofa as she sat down. "Damn it! I just got a fuckin' fill-in today. Now I gotta go give them fuckin' Chinesses more of my money."

Shamari wanted to say that the nail techs were probably Vietnamese but he knew Zandra didn't give a fuck. They would always be Chinesses to her.

"Fucked up my champagne glass too."

"Huh? Champagne glass?"

Zandra showed Shamari the champagne glass made of rhinestones that were on her nails."

Shamari handed Zandra a hundred dollar bill, "Get your nails done again."

Zandra passed the money back to him. "I can pay for my own nails. I work every motherfuckin' day."

Shamari folded the money and put it back in his pocket.

Zandra said, "But that's the deal. He told Shareese that his lawyer said if he was convicted, that the prosecutor was going to seek the death penalty or at the least send him to some supermax prison in Colorado."

"Who's Shareese?"

"My sister, aka baby mama three."

"He told Shareese all of this?"

"And he told her he wasn't going to go down by himself."

"Really?"

Zandra stood up from the sofa still nursing her jagged nail. She made eye contact with Shamari and said, "You better take heed to what I say and prepare yourself for the worse."

Shamari thanked Zandra and walked out of the door. When he was outside he said, "Fuck." He damn well hated that he'd trusted bitch-assed Tony. He dialed his attorney, Joey Turch, and told him that the U.S. Marshals were looking for him. He gave Joey the man's name and number on the card. Joey assured him he would look into it the first thing in the morning.

CHAPTER 24

Lani's clock read 1:07 a.m. when she got a call from Black. She looked at her iPhone hard and contemplated not answering the phone before deciding to pick it up on the very last ring before the call would have gone to voicemail. "Hey."

"I'm downstairs, can you let me in?"

"The code to the building is 618. I told you that before"

"I punched it in. It's not working."

"Look for my name on the keypad and then hit pound."

"Okay."

She ended the call. Seconds later she got a call from Black. She pressed 9 to let him in the building.

She stood up from the bed. She was naked, so she slid into a pair of running shorts and a wife beater T-shirt, grabbed her robe that was hanging on the door, and she opened the door.

Black kissed her on the forehead. He looked worried. "What the fuck is going on?" she asked.

"A whole lot."

"Come on, are you going to tell me or am I going to have to guess."

Black looked at her with serious eyes, but he didn't say anything. There was a long awkward silence before Lani said, "What the fuck you gotta tell me?"

"Look, I killed Chris." He paused and then said, "Well I didn't kill him. Twan shot him."

Lani had already known that Black had something to do with Chris's murder. Hell a six year old could have figured that out, but to hear him admit it made her feel really fucked up inside.

Black began to pace and was popping his knuckles then he removed a blunt from his shirt pocket and said "Do you mind if I light up?"

"Since when did you start smoking, Tyrann?"

"I'm not a smoker, but I've been stressed the fuck out."

He lit the blunt and said, "Look, I didn't want to involve you in this because if the police asked you something, you could really say that you didn't know what the fuck went on."

Lani sat on the sofa and rested her face in the palm of her hands. "I don't know if I can take much more of this bullshit," she said.

Black sat on the chair beside her. "What bullshit?" he asked.

"So what happened to Twan?"

"Twan is dead, and K.B. is in jail."

"K.B.?"

"He was with me and Twan."

"So how did he get locked up?"

"Well, a security camera showed him and Twan throwing Chris in the back of a SUV."

"Geniuses."

"I know."

There was another awkward silence. Black blew a perfect smoke ring and said, "Lani, I'm sorry."

"Sorry my ass. This shit didn't have to go like this. You didn't have to kill Chris."

Black eased over to the sofa and sat beside her and tried to rub her back. She removed his hand and said, "You get the fuck away from me."

Black moved to the other chair. He was looking for an ashtray but there wasn't one. There was an incense holder on the table, so he dumped his ashes there.

Lani looked up at Black and said, "So what made you tell me this shit now? You been denying this shit the whole god-damned time."

Black said, "Well, you're the only person that I can tell. You're the only one I trust."

"Don't you see this shit puts me in a fucked-up position?"

"I know." Black's puffed the blunt again and made eye contact with her. His eyes looked sad.

"So, why did you tell me this shit again?"

"You're the only one I trust."

"Who else knows"

"Only Twan and K.B. and I'm assuming one of Chris's friends had Twan killed."

Black finished the blunt and rolled another one. Then he made eye contact with Lani again, and said, "I don't know what to do."

"You've done enough." She turned from his gaze. A single tear rolled down her cheek. She hoped he wouldn't see it, but he did.

"What's wrong?"

"I was just thinking about Chris."

"Chris deserved what he got."

She turned and met his eyes. She fanned the funky-ass cigarette smoke away from her face and said, "I'm going to bed."

Black put the blunt out in the incense holder and said, "I wanna spend the night."

Lani said, "Please take a shower. I don't want weed smoke in my bedroom. There are extra toothbrushes under the sink."

After Black showered, he got in the bed. Lani was butt ass naked under the cover but was asleep and she was snoring slightly. He scooted next to her. His dick was rock solid as it pressed against her ass but he wasn't in the mood for sex and he was sure she wasn't either. He wrapped his arm around her as his mind raced. He knew the police was after him. He thought about Twan and how he would be responsible for Twan's kids along with all of his kids. Damn.

Then his mind drifted to K.B. and how he'd been appre-hended. Would he rat? How the fuck could these clowns be so stupid? Then there was the matter of his cell phone being tracked near the site of the crime. How would he get out of this shit? He finally drifted off to sleep.

Lani woke up the next morning and Black was still resting. She didn't know if he was asleep or not. He'd tossed all night. She was in the kitchen microwaving some oatmeal when she heard somebody knocking on the door. The first things she thought about was ugly-ass Kenny-Boo and Mike. She tiptoed over to the peephole. The goddamn police.

Two black detectives. What the fuck would she do? She wanted to go warn Black but she was afraid they would hear her. She stood still for a moment before the microwave bell sounded. Right after that, Black's cell phone on the coffee table started ringing. Damn.

One of the detectives said, "Somebody is in there."

Lani opened the door. As soon as she opened the door, she remembered Black was lying in the bed. There was no way to warn him now.

The taller of the two black detectives had dreadlocks and was wearing jeans and a polo shirt. Looked to be in his thirties, intro-duced himself as Officer Thomas Kearns.

The shorter one said his name was Officer Mike Williams.

Lani said, "Can I help you?"

"Can we come in?" Kearns asked.

"For what?" Lani asked.

"Just need to ask you a few questions."

"About what?"

Kearns said, "Your ex-boyfriend, Chris Jones"

"Okay."

"How can I help you?"

"Can we come in?"

Lani said, "Why do you want to come in?" Lani said it loud enough for Black to hear. Then she asked, "Am I under arrest?"

"No."

Mike Williams said, "You seem kind of nervous Ms. Miller."

"No, not at all. I was about to eat. My oatmeal is getting cold."

Finally, Lani invited them in. She didn't want to, but she was sure that she did seem kind of nervous. Now, she wanted to convince them that she was in fact relaxed even though she wasn't. Truth was, she wanted them to get the fuck out of her house.

Mike Williams said, "You can go get your oatmeal"

Lani gave him a fake smile and said, "I will just make another pack when you leave."

Kearns said, "Your boyfriend got murdered."

"Okay."

"Do you know anything about it?"

"How would I know anything about it?"

Mike Williams was staring between Lani's legs at her camel toe. When she caught him looking, he immediately made eye contact with her and said, "Do you know Black?"

"I know lots of Blacks."

"This Black's name is Tyrann Massey"

"Yes, that's my ex-boyfriend."

"We know."

"Okay, if you know, why are you asking me some dumb shit like that?"

Mike Williams was now looking at her nipples.

Kearns said, "Word on the street is that you had Chris set up."

"Set up how?"

"You told Black where Chris kept his stash, and you had him robbed."

"Oh no the fuck I didn't!" Lani said. Then she stared at Mike Williams and said, "Will you keep your goddamned eyes off by fucking breasts, you pervert."

Mike Williams laughed and said, "I like how you're trying to get off the subject."

Lani stood and said, "Am I under arrest?"

Kearns said, "No."

"Well, you need to get the fuck out of my house."

Kearns said, 'Do you mind if we look around before we leave?"

Lani said, "Do you have a warrant?"

Mike Williams said, "Actually we do." He glanced over at the blunt that was lying on top of the incense holder.

CHAPTER 25

It was eight a.m. when Jada left the meeting with the owner of a townhome near Lennox Mall. She wasn't one for early meetings, but the owner insisted that the meeting take place in the a.m. He lived in Phoenix and he was only in town for one day. Jada loved everything about the townhome except for the pile of gravel that was next door in an unfinished lot. She still would have taken the place if the owner would have come down a couple of hundred dollars a month on the rent. The owner said there was no way he could do it, and Jada said there was no way she was going to pay three thousand dollars a month to live next to a pile of rocks, so no deal was made.

Jada was pissed as fuck because she could have still been asleep. She drove past the gated community where Craig's townhome was and decided to turn around. She still had the set of keys that Joey Turch had given her when he'd given the keys to the Maserati back to her, but she didn't have a key FOB.

As soon as she pulled up to the gate, a white Bentley was pulling into the gate so she followed. She didn't really like sneaking into the home, but she still had things there, and now was as good a time as any to repossess them.

She entered the town home through the front door, since she didn't have the garage door opener. Two beeps sounded as she punched in 5684 # to disarm the alarm and headed to the bedroom.

A trail of women's lingerie led her to the bedroom. A red thong. A pair of turquoise boy shorts. There were bitches in the house. She could smell the cheap watermelon flavored Bath and Body scent. The nerve of this motherfucker, not only did he have bitches entertaining him, but they were cheap ass hoes at that. She tried to open the door.

Jada heard one of the girls say, "Craig, somebody is at the door."

"What?"

"What, my ass! This is Jada!"

"Huh?"

Jada pounded on the door. "Open this goddamned door, motherfucker."

"You get the hell out of my house or I'm calling the police."

Jada could hear someone scrambling as if they were putting on clothes.

"Open the goddamn door!"

"Get the hell out of here!"

Jada kicked the goddamned door off its hinges and when the door fell, Jada entered. She saw a tall black woman with a tiny ass waist and a long weave. "Who the fuck is this bitch?"

The woman said, "Who the hell are you calling bitch?"

"I'm calling you a bitch, you Amazon-looking ho. I will fuck you up."

The woman swung at Jada, but missed.

Jada removed her six inch stiletto and charged the Amazon and slapped the fuck out her with the heel, gashing her head. The Amazon fell on the floor and Jada got on top of her.

Another woman appeared from the closet. Jada recognized her immediately.

Skyy was standing there with a new boob job.

Jada said, "So, Skyy. You fucking for boobs now?"

"Jada, it's not what you think!"

The Amazon tried to get back up and Jada kicked her in the face and then rushed Skyy and grabbed her by the neck. Jada began to choke the fuck out of Skyy. "Bitch, I will kill your dirtbag ass." She slung Skyy into the Amazon and pulled out her pink 380. "I will kill every motherfucker in here."

Craig said, "You get the fuck out here. I swear I'm calling the police."

"Call the motherfuckin' police," Jada said, as she pointed to a pile of coke on the dresser.

Craig said, "What do you want?"

"I came to get my things."

"Get your things and leave."

"And if I don't want to?"

"You're going to leave."

"No, motherfucker, you're going to pay me or your wife is going to learn that you're a goddamn coke head that likes to trick on black girls."

"What do you want?"

"I want twenty-five grand in my account by the end of the day."

"Fuck you."

"No, fuck you"

Craig stood there looking stupid, butt-ass naked.

Jada pointed at the Amazon. "You two bum bitches get over and stand beside that small dick cracker."

And when they were all standing beside each other, Jada snapped two pictures with her iPhone. "The money by the end of the day or else."

"Or else what?"

"You're going to be ruined, motherfucker."

* * *

It was 10:30 in the morning when the FedEx man buzzed. He said he had a package and Starr let him in the building. She wasn't expecting anything. She hadn't ordered anything online.

He handed her a package and asked her to sign for it and he disappeared. She tore into the envelope to see a picture of Trey and a beautiful black girl holding hands. The next picture had Trey kissing her on the jaw. And the third and final picture was of Trey palming the girl's ass. Star frantically searched inside the package for the any clues as to who may have sent it. There was no return address, but there was a note inside and it read: *I guess you know now that that nigga ain't shit. Signed J.*

She dialed Trey's phone three times before he picked up. "Bring yo ass home right motherfucking now. We got something to discuss."

* * *

Joey Turch called Shamari and he answered on the second ring.

"Got some good news and bad news. What do you want to hear first?" asked Turch.

"Bad news."

"The bad news is the Feds have an indictment out on you. Murder for hire on a government informant and drug conspiracy."

"What the fuck is the good news?"

"The good news is you know Joey Turch"

"What is that supposed to mean?"

"I'm the best attorney in Atlanta. I've already shown you that. Don't get discouraged. I can help...for a fee."

"What's your fee?"

"A hundred thousand dollars and it needs to be paid in full."

There was a long silence. "Why paid in full?"

"Shamari, with your record and the seriousness of the charges, I don't think you will get a bond."

"This is just fucking great."

"Come by my office, and we will arrange for you to turn yourself in."

* * *

To be continued

PART 6:
A STARR IS BORN

CHAPTER 1

Starr's mind raced as she paced the room. Who in the fuck was this girl in the pictures with Trey? The package was signed J, she figured it was Trey's baby's mother, Jessica, but how did she send a package from FedEx with no return address? FedEx required a return address, she knew this much for a fact. Why did she send it with no return address? Where the hell was Trey? She had called him over an hour ago and he hadn't arrived. She dialed his number again. He needed to answer the phone and he needed to come home and explain this bullshit to her. They needed to talk and talk right away. How could he do her like this again? How could he just rip her heart apart again? She didn't deserve this. Trey, please answer the phone. She felt herself becoming undone. She'd never in her short life felt this hurt. He answered the phone.

"Hey, babe."

"Trey, where the hell are you?"

"I had to take care of something, be there in a few minutes."

"How long is it going to take you?"

"What's wrong, Bae. Why can't you just tell me what the fuck is going on?"

"I'll talk to you when you get here."

"Gimme forty-five minutes."

She terminated the call and dialed the last known number she had for Jessica.

"Hello?"

"Hey, this is Starr."

"You must have gotten the package?"

Starr didn't answer. What was Jessica's point? What did she want? Why did she want to destroy what she and Trey had? But she couldn't blame Jessica for Trey's bullshit. Clearly this nigga was out of control.

There was an awkward silence before Jessica said, "I'm really sorry, Starr. You seem like a really good person and I just wanted to let you about the *real* Trey."

"What the fuck is your point tho'? You want me to team up with you against Trey?"

"Look, Starr, I'm not the enemy here…I mean we women gotta stick together, we can't continue to go at each other's throats when it's the man that's fucking up."

Starr said, "So you act like you're the other woman. Trey hasn't dealt with you for years."

Jessica sighed and said, "You're so naïve. Let's meet up and talk face to face."

"Not a good idea."

"Trey is not the man that you think he is."

"I know Trey better than you do."

"True, but there are sides of Trey that you don't know about."

Starr stared at the pictures. "Obviously."

Trey burst through the door. Starr said, "I'll call you back."

Trey said, "Who was that?"

"My friend, Shari. Why?"

"Why did you rush off the phone?"

"Cut the bullshit, Trey. What I got to discuss with you is way more important than a conversation with Shari."

"I rushed home to see what's bothering you."

Starr glanced at her watch and said, "I called you almost an hour ago so you didn't rush no motherfuckin' where!" Starr said and flung the pictures at Trey. They were now scattered all over the floor.

Trey scooped up one of the pictures and looked at it. It showed the palm of his hand clutching Shantelle's ass.

"Trey, how could you do this to me? Again!"

Trey wondered who in the hell sent these pictures. Who hated him that much?

"Answer me?!" Starr shouted.

Trey picked up the other pictures still not believing this was real. It felt like a horrible nightmare. Damn, he didn't know what to do or say. He hated making Starr feel so bad. He wondered if Shantelle sent the pictures because she did say that she wanted more from him the other day.

"So, you don't have shit to say?"

"What do you wanna hear?"

Starr approached Trey and began pounding on his chest. "I hate you! Goddamn it, Trey! I hate you so much!" She flopped to the floor, dropped her head between her legs, and sobbed.

Trey sat beside her and tried to rub her back.

Starr shoved Trey's hand and said, "Don't touch me!"

"I'm sorry and I know I fucked up bad this time."

She looked him in the eyes and said, "Trey, sorry doesn't repair my heart. You can't even imagine how I feel right now."

"Look, babe, I don't love her. I love you."

Starr made eye contact with him, her eyes now the color of tomatoes. "Trey, it feels like somebody just ripped my heart from my chest. Trey, you're my heart. Well you were my heart. You can't be trusted!"

A tear rolled down Trey's face. He wondered if the sex from Shantelle was worth it. He was going to lose something real for something not real at all. Shantelle, just like most of the women he'd been with, wanted him for his money. He knew Starr would be there for him, even if he didn't have a cent.

Starr stood up and said, "Trey, I'm going to get my things out by the end of the week.

"You don't have to go. I don't want you to leave."

Starr disappeared into the bathroom and came back with a Kleenex. She wiped her eyes and said, "Trey, I have to go. I can't put up with this bullshit. I gotta leave."

Trey stood and attempted to hug her again but she pushed him away. "Stop trying to hug me."

Trey stood there looking at Starr for a long time and then he glanced at the picture with his hand on Shantelle's ass. With Shantelle it was clearly lust but things were different with Starr. This was the woman he loved and he wanted to spend the rest of his life with, but it appeared that it was too late. Starr said she was going to leave and Trey knew her well enough to know that she was going to do exactly what she said she was going to do.

Lani said to the cops, "Lemme see the warrant?"

Mike Williams said, "The fact that you got marijuana out in plain view gives us the authority to look around. We're not going to search, but we're going to look around. If you ain't hiding anything, you won't have nothing to worry about."

Thomas Kearns made his way into the kitchen and scanned the laundry room.

Mike Williams asked, "Where's the bathroom?"

Lani said, "I'll show you." She led him to the bathroom. Mike Williams was staring at her ass thinking what it would feel like to fuck her from behind. Damn those shorts were gripping.

Then they went to Lani's bedroom and Lani followed thinking it was about to be all over for Black if they had an arrest warrant for him. Mike Williams looked inside her walk in closet then he opened her dresser drawer and retrieved a pair of black laced panties.

"Close my goddamned drawer!"

"I bet your ass look amazing in this."

"What the fuck does this have to do with you 'Looking around'?" Lani snatched her panties away from Williams and said, "You can get the hell out of my house! You see ain't nobody in here!"

Thomas Kearns appeared and Lani said, "Please get this sex offender out of my house!"

Thomas Kearns passed her a card. "If you speak to Tyrann tell him to give me a call and we'll probably be back in touch with you." The two detectives left.

Seconds after the door closed, Black tip-toed into the living room.

"Where the fuck were you?"

"Under the bed praying that motherfucker didn't look under the bed."

"They couldn't have arrested you unless they had an arrest warrant, right?"

Black held up his hand and signaled for Lani to follow him to the bedroom. He closed the door behind her.

"Who knows? We have to be careful, babe. Those sneaky motherfuckers probably outside listening."

"Right."

"Yeah, I was under the bed listening to that Lame. What was he trying to do?"

"Looking at my lingerie."

"Damn, if he wasn't so perverted he would have found me." Black paused then said, "I don't know if they have an arrest warrant for me or not, but I wasn't trying to find out."

"I think they would have said it if they did."

"No, they think you would tell me and I'm sure they know I'll run. I never turn myself in, that's in my file I'm sure."

"What?'"

"Yeah I've never turned myself in except for one time, when Nana begged me to.

"Tyrann, I'm afraid."

He knew from the way she sounded that she was really afraid. He held her in his arms and kissed her forehead and told her it was going to be okay. She didn't believe him though.

CHAPTER 2

Shamari sat across from Joey Turch, nervous as hell. He was thinking that he should be trying to get the hell out of town. He didn't even know why he was entertaining the thought of getting an attorney, the charges that he was facing were real serious and he actually should be running instead of trying to fight this case.

A Mont Blanc pen dangled from Joey Turch's mouth as he read Shamari's indictment.

"This guy Tony Greer that you allegedly hired to commit the hit, how well do you know him?"

"I met him in prison years ago."

"His record shows he's career criminal."

There was a long silence and Shamari wondered what his fate would be given that he would have to hustle up a great deal of money to fight this case. He'd made some money but he simply didn't have the kind of money that Joey Turch would charge.

"Well, I'm not really worried about what he's going to say, he's a habitual offender facing serious charges. He'll do anything to save his ass. I'll destroy him in cross examination. But...." Joey Turch looked pensive.

"What's the problem?"

"The man Tony tried to kill."

"What about him?"

"Well he's a snitch and a credible one at that."

"What the hell is a credible snitch?"

"Hey, I agree, man. These guys will do anything to save their ass. I see it every day."

"Listen, I don't wanna hear all of that. Can you make this go away?"

"I can't say. I don't know all the facts."

"What happened to all that bravado you had on the phone and when you came to see me in the county jail? All that shit about it being good news that I hired Joey Turch."

"Listen, Shamari, if there is anybody that can help you, it's me, but a federal case is a hell of a lot different than state and you know that."

"Have you won in Federal Court?"

"Yes, and I've lost, but I've won more than I've lost."

"Who is the best lawyer?"

"You're looking at him."

"But you've lost."

"Every attorney has lost before. If any lawyer that says that he can get you off before he sees the facts, you need to run away from him as fast as you can."

"So what's the next step?"

"I need a hundred thousand dollars."

"A hundred thousand dollars?! Are you serious?"

"Very."

"I guess somebody has to pay for those thousand dollar custom suits and this expensive office."

Joey Turch straightened his suit collar. "I work very hard for everything that I have."

"A hundred and you might lose or we might plea?"

"If you plea, you'll get at least half of that back."

"Look, I'll get the money to you." Shamari stood up. "You just better make this shit go away."

Joey Turch stared at Shamari as he stormed out of the office. There was no way he could make promises about this case. He was a damn good lawyer but he wasn't Jesus Christ.

Shamari left Joey's Turch's office and was about to step into the elevator when he heard someone say, "Mari?"

When Shamari turned, he locked eyes with Black, a man he'd met in state prison and occasionally gambled with. He was glad to see him. He'd been meaning to get in touch with him to thank him for the help he'd provided Jada.

"What's up, homie?"

The two men shook hands and Black said, "Jada told me about the little situation you were in a few months ago."

"Yeah, it worked out great and I appreciate you help, bruh, and I wanna pay you back."

"No sweat, homie. I mean I wish I could've done more, but I'm glad I could help out." Black glanced at his watch. "So what have you been up to?"

Shamari took a deep breath. "I'm in some more shit, homie. Well it's some old shit that's come up."

"Really?"

Ordinarily Shamari wouldn't dare let a man know what was going on about a criminal case, but Black was as real as they came and his street cred was known all over Atlanta.

Shamari said, "I've been indicted."

"You're indicted and you're on the streets?"

"More like on the run."

"Damn."

"I know, but I gotta make some money before I turn myself in."

Black looked confused. "Turn yourself in. Why would you do that?"

Shamari shrugged.

Black said, "You got serious ass charges. No way in the hell I would turn myself in. I think the cops are looking for me too, but I'm not gonna turn myself in."

Shamari said, "Where are you going?"

"Go see my lawyer, Joey Turch. That man is a magician if anybody can make a case go away it's him."

"Yeah, but that motherfucker wants a hundred thousand dollars from me and I ain't got it right now."

"I feel ya."

Shamari said, "What's your number."

Black said. "I don't know my number. I just got a new phone today, but tell me yours and I'll call you right now."

"404-787-0987."

Black dialed Shamari's number and saved it.

CHAPTER 3

At ten a.m. Starr called Trey's baby mother, Jessica, and they decided to meet at Shout restaurant at 1 p.m.

Jessica ordered a Mediterranean pizza and Starr just ordered a Patron and Coke. It was early but she preferred to be fucked up in order to handle the bullshit Trey had put her through.

"Thanks for agreeing to meet me."

"Not a problem." Jessica bit into her pizza.

Starr examined her. She was much more put together today. The first time they met, Starr thought she was cute, but dressed a hot-ass mess. Today she was dressed nicely in a pair of skinny jeans and heels, her blonde hair pulled back in a ponytail which made Starr notice her sparkling blue eyes. Starr thought back to the picture of the other woman. She didn't look nothing like Jessica or Starr, the only thing that the trio had in common was they all had a vagina. Well, Starr wasn't exactly sure if the third woman had a vagina, as muscular as her goddamned legs were. If she didn't know Trey so well, she would've thought that woman was a tranny.

Starr downed her drink, and flagged the waitress for another. She wanted to be loose when she spoke to Jessica. She took another sip and said, "So what do you wanna tell me 'bout Trey?"

"What do you wanna know?"

"Whatever you wanna tell me? You sure seemed to have a lot to say over the phone."

Jessica said, "I'm not the enemy, honey"

"Look, I'm sorry. I know you're not the enemy."

"I was in love with Trey."

"But you knew he had a girl at home."

Jessica bit into her pizza again, then dabbed her mouth with the napkin. "I knew he had a girl, but he made me feel absolutely amazing when I was with him and then there was the fact that he said...."

"What'd he say?"

"I don't wanna get into what he said. The bottom line is he is a lying, cheating dog."

Jessica's blue eyes suddenly looked sad. Eyes of a woman who had been broken, she called the waitress and ordered two more drinks.

The waitress dropped the drinks in front of Starr. She slid them to Jessica's side of the table.

"I didn't ask for anything."

"I know you didn't, but I'm going to need for you to get loose."

Jessica smiled and sipped her drink." Her smile was perfect. Starr figured Jessica must have had braces.

"Tell me, Jessica."

"Tell you what?"

"What did Trey say to you?" Starr took another sip.

Jessica said, "Trey said that you guys weren't in a good space at the time and that he was trying to figure out a way to leave you."

"What the fuck?" Starr spat out her liquor

"He told me a lot of shit."

"Like?"

"He loved me."

"Really?"

"Yes." Jessica downed her drink."

"What else?"

Jessica chomped her pizza hard trying to decide what was worth divulging to Starr. Of course, she would embellish a little. She wanted Trey's life ruined, just like he'd ruined her life.

"Jessica, are you going to tell me or not?"

Jessica sat the pizza end on the saucer and asked, "Why do you wanna know?"

Starr was getting pissed. Was this little skinny, white bitch trying to get smart mouthed? Starr wanted to yank her little skinny ass across the table and that's exactly what she would've done if they were alone.

Starr said, "Are you gonna tell me what went on or not? I have no time to play these silly-assed games with you. I'm a grown motherfuckin' woman!"

"And I'm a grown woman too," Jessica said. The liquor was getting the best of her. She finished the rest of her liquor then flashed a blinging-ass diamond ring. "Do you know what this is?"

"An engagement ring?"

"No."

"What is it?"

"Trey gave me this. It's a promise ring. He gave me this right after he told me that he was leaving you. Two years. No three years ago because T. J. was two I think.

"Lemme see."

Starr examined the massive diamond ring and said, "Impressive."

"I know I like it. Actually, I'm thinking of taking this ring back to Jesus to see what I can't get for it. I'm broke as hell. Like really broke."

"Take it back to who?"

"Jesus."

"You know Trey's jeweler in New York?"

"Yeah, I met him almost four years ago. Trey bought me a presidential Rolex."

"What?" Starr was getting furious. Not because she wanted jewelry—she could care less about material things—but the fact that her man had splurged so much on another woman was pissing her the fuck off.

"Yeah, I know I've gotten at least a hundred thousand dollars worth of jewels over the last few years, most of which I've pawned over the last year or so because he cut me and T. J. off."

"Now wait a minute, I know Trey hasn't cut his son off!"

"Well, he's paying the minimum required by the courts. You and I know Trey has lots of cash."

"That doesn't mean you deserve it."

Jessica toyed with her blond locks. She sipped the second glass of liquor and said, "I see where this is going. You think I'm a god-damn gold-digger."

"You said it, not me."

"Look, Trey was the one that wanted to put a two-year-old kid in private school, not me."

"What are you talking about? T. J. is not two."

"But T. J. had been going to private school since he was two and when Trey cut the money off, I had to enroll my son in public school. Can you imagine?"

"Hey, there are worst things in the world."

"Would you kill the goddamn sarcasm? It's just that T. J. is still friends with the kids that he went to private school with and some of them tell him things like, 'You don't go to our school anymore because you couldn't afford it.'"

"Poor kid."

"Do you know how frustrating it is because I can't afford to give T. J. the things that all his friends have?"

'I understand," Starr said. The waitress came and Starr asked for two more drinks.

"So what happened between you and Trey?"

"Nothing happened. I just couldn't take the lies anymore." She paused then said, "How old are you?"

"Twenty-eight."

"I'm twenty-nine."

"Good to know." Starr wanted to say what the fuck is the point.

"Trey is ten years older than you and nine years older than me and he's never going to stop playing these silly-ass games."

She knew exactly what Jessica meant. He'd been saying that they were going to marry and have children for a very long time.

"Trey's never going to settle down and he's never going to stop dealing." Jessica paused. "Starr, leave him alone, not because I want him, but because this man will drive you over the edge like he did me."

"Over the edge?"

"I had a nervous breakdown about a year ago."

"Why? What happened?"

"I don't know. I just couldn't get over the fact that this man just used me and manipulated me and he had no intention of leaving you and no intention of getting married to me and I've done a lot for him, things for him that nobody knows about."

Starr pushed the other drink over to Jessica's side of the table. She wanted her to drink up and furthermore she wanted the bitch to keep talking.

"What have you done?"

"Well, a couple of years ago, Trey lost a hundred kilos coming out of Houston."

"I remember."

"Well he owed his supplier for half of that and he didn't have the money to cover it."

Starr stared at her as she thought back. She remembered when Trey had lost that load. Monte and Trey had fallen out and Trey found a dude from Tennessee to bring his drugs back to Atlanta.

"How did you help him?"

"Trey said the supplier would kill him if he found out that he'd lost that load."

"Really?"

"Well, you know how the load got lost right?"

"No."

"Back in those days, a dude named Gene from Tennessee was driving the load back to Georgia. Well, he went missing with all the product. He just up and left Trey in a really fucked up position. Trey called me crying that night, not knowing what the hell he was going to do, saying they were going to kill him."

"And you helped?"

"Well, I didn't have a choice. As fucked up of a person as he is, he is my son's father."

"How'd you help?"

"We knew the supplier had an upholstery company. I called the supplier, pretending I was the DEA and I told him that his business card was found in Gene's car."

"And what happened next?"

"He hung up and turned his goddamned phone off. What most black dudes in the game would do, if they heard a white woman's voice on the other end of the phone."

"Damn."

"I saved his ass because the supplier didn't charge him for the product since he thought the police had confiscated the drugs."

"Look, I don't have all day to tell you all the things Trey has done to me and how I've helped him but the bottom line is the man drove me insane. He knew I am manic depressive already and he played on that."

"You're manic depressive?" Starr felt stupid for even asking her this. She'd known this bitch wasn't wrapped too tight ever since she started calling her from anonymous numbers.

"I'm on Lithium."

Starr felt bad for Jessica.

Starr said, "Two more questions?"

"Okay."

"How in the hell did you send a FedEx box with no-return address?"

Jessica smiled, "The man that delivered the box wasn't really a FedEx man. I just put the pictures in a FedEx box. I figured if you'd seen my name, you would have been afraid to open it, but I'm glad you did."

Starr said, "That brings me to the second question. Why?"

"Why what?"

"Well, if you say you don't want Trey, why are you telling me all of this shit?"

"Look, Trey is not a good person and I wanted you to know that. I know you've known Trey longer than I have, but there were some things that you didn't know about Trey. His brother Troy tried to warn me and I didn't listen."

"You met his brother?"

"Yes. Troy is such as sweetheart. He comes and picks up T. J. from time to time when he's not working."

"I've met Troy on a couple of occasions, but Trey really don't like Troy."

"Because he always does the right thing and Trey doesn't know what the right thing is."

The waitress dropped the check and Starr paid the bill and the two ladies hugged.

* * *

Craig texted Jada: *Listen, bitch, if you extort me I'm going to the police. I'm not giving you one red penny.*

Jada texted: *Is Anne's number still 770-987-8789.*

Craig: *How did you get my wife's number?*

Jada: :-)

Craig: *I will send you fifteen.*

Jada: *Damn, I didn't realize your dick was so small. Well, I guess it looks small standing next to two thick ass black women.* There was an attachment of the picture Jada had taken of Skyy, Craig, and the Amazon.

Craig: *Who is to say that if I give you the money that you won't extort me again?*

Jada: *Extort, don't say extort. Extort is a bad word.*

Craig: *What would you call it then?*

Jada: *I just call it the price of doing business with a real bitch.*

Craig: *Really?*

Jada: *Yes really, sweetheart.*

Craig: *I'm not your goddamned sweetheart.*

Jada: *Don't be so angry with me, honey-bunny.*

Craig: *Fuck you.*

Jada: *The money better be in my account by tomorrow or everybody in Atlanta is going to know about its famous plastic surgeon and his fetish for black vagina.* kissyface emoji

CHAPTER 4

Tangie said, "Bruh, I love you, but you gotta get the fuck out of here."

"What you tombout?"

Hunch entered the living room, wearing what appeared to be a toddler t-shirt, and eating a peanut butter sandwich. He said, "Brother-in-law, Feds had this motherfucker surrounded this morning."

"What?"

"Feds came here with a picture of you and an arrest warrant."

Tangie said, "Mari, you need to find somewhere to go. You know I love you but this is just too much. Besides, if you stay here, they are going to find you. You need to either turn yourself in or find somewhere to lay low, but that somewhere can't be here because they said that they're going to come back."

Shamari embraced his sister and said, "I understand, I'm going to get a few of my things and I'm leaving."

Where would he go? Where had the Feds been? How long can he hide and how was he going to make the money he needed to pay his attorney, Joey Turch.

Hunch said, "Bruh, you need to go out west. They'll never catch you out there. I'm telling you, bruh. I got a homie that's been running for 9 and a half years."

Tangie said, "Why are they looking for you, bruh? What did you do?"

"I'm telling ya, go to L.A.," Hunch said.

Shamari stared at his baby sister wanting to tell her the whole story, but he knew that he couldn't tell her the whole story with dumb-ass Hunch in the room.

Hunch said, "Brother-in-law, I can get in touch with my homeboy and he can tell me where to get the fake ID's and all."

Fed up with Hunch, Shamari said, "Will you shut the fuck up?"

Tangie said, "Yeah, will you shut the fuck up? As a matter of fact, let me speak to my brother alone."

When Hunch left the room, Shamari said, "It's a long story, but I've been accused of attempted murder on an informant."

"Did you do it?"

"Without going into the details, I had something to do with it." Shamari knew he could tell his sister anything. She was the one person that he would bet his life that she wouldn't cross him.

Tangie hugged her big brother, not wanting to let him go but wanting to protect him like he'd protected her when they were growing up in the mean streets of Atlanta.

"I love you, Mari, and no matter what I'll always be here for you."

His kissed her forehead and laughed. "But I can't stay here, right?"

She made a sad face. "Mari, it's not safe."

"I know."

She finally released him and said, "Tell me where in the hell did Hunch get money from?"

"Me. Well, he put me up on a lick and I split it with him." Shamari didn't know whether to tell her that he'd given Hunch product or not. He wasn't sure if she would be pissed if she knew that he'd had drugs in her house.

Shamari gathered a few items of clothing and some shoes, kissed Tangie on the forehead again and said, "I'll be in touch, and don't tell Mama what's going on."

"I promise." She wouldn't tell her mother, but it's not like their mother would be upset. She'd practically disowned Shamari ever since he'd gotten released from state prison and decided that he was going to keep hustling.

Black called Shamari and they met in Alpharetta at the home Black had rented for him and Lani, except she didn't want to go along with the plans.

"This heroin is pure. Where in the hell did you get this from?"

"Mexicans."

Black looked perplexed because this was not the kind of heroin that Mexicans were known for. They were known for black tar.

"You must have gotten a good price."

"You ever had a price better than free?"

"Huh?"

"Jacked them fools."

Black laughed and then said, "Mexicans usually have that brown bullshit. This comes from Afghanistan or somewhere." Though heroin was not his thing, he'd been on the streets since he was a kid and the OGs had taught him about all kinds of drugs, including heroin.

"Honestly, when I took it, I thought I had three bricks of coke but one of them turned out to be heroin."

"You check them all?"

"I did and the others were coke."

"Damn! That was luck, bruh"

"But I don't know what to do with heroin. It's not my business."

"Not mine either, but I can help you get rid of it."

"Now that's what I'm talking about."

"But first we gotta give it a name, so people will know it's ours. Get some baggies and stamp the product."

"What do you wanna call it?"

Black thought for a moment. He didn't know what to call it. He scanned his house and there were two boxes of Girl Scout cookies that he'd bought from some little girls in the Wal-Mart parking lot. He said, "Hell, let's call it Girl Scout cookies."

"Girl Scout cookies? Nigga, you a fool."

"I'll get a stamp. We'll stamp the baggies and I'll drop this shit off to my homie, and he'll move this shit. Trust me, we're going to get paid."

Shamari said, "It's going to have to be fast because I'm on the run."

"I know."

"So what ever happened to your situation?" Shamari asked.

"Joey Turch said there was no warrant for me and the police just probably wanted to talk to me."

"I heard that they trying to tie you in with Chris's murder."

"What the fuck does that have to do with anything?"

"I just don't wanna be in a situation where you get arrested with my shit and I don't have the money to pay for an attorney. You know I gotta give Joey Turch a hundred grand to retain him."

Black wanted to slap the fuck out of Shamari at first but then he realized Shamari was in a really fucked up situation and he understood where he was coming from.

"I'll handle Joey Turch."

"You're going to give him the money?"

"I'll give him fifty thousand and tell him that you're going to pay him the rest."

"He wants it paid in full."

"I know he does, but I've been dealing with him for a while, I'll take care of him. Don't worry."

"Perfect."

Black said, "After I see him, I'm going to need you to hand off the product so we can get to work."

"For sure."

They shook hands.

CHAPTER 5

Trey rested his head on Shantelle's lap. She brushed his hair. She noticed that he'd been quiet since he arrived and his silence was very awkward for her. It was driving her crazy, she wasn't used to this. "What's wrong, Bae?"

He turned over, so now the center of his head was on her lap as he stared up into her eyes. "Starr knows about us."

"How?" Shantelle wanted to know how this was possible. She hadn't said anything to anybody about her and Trey's relationship, not even to her best friend, Alicia, She hadn't told her best friend on purpose because she knew she would have been judgmental.

"My baby mama sent her pics."

"What the fuck? Pics? How?"

"This bitch is crazy, like in a stalker kind of way, so who knows how she got the pics. Maybe she had a P.I. follow us. I don't know, but I've seen the pics and we were at the movies, restaurants, parks."

"What did you say?"

He sat up. "There was nothing I could say. I mean what am I supposed to say? It was clearly me." He remembered the pictures, particularly, the one with his hand gripping her ass. He imagined how Starr must have felt looking at the pictures. He knew he'd hurt her and he felt bad for her but yet he was back at Shantelle's place. And he wasn't even sure if he wanted Shantelle, but he was almost certain that it was over for him and Starr.

"What did she say?"

"She's moving out." Trey looked sad.

Shantelle was now getting pissed. It was clear that he cared very much about Starr and she didn't like it.

"I feel so bad for her," Trey said.

Shantelle crossed her arms. She didn't want to say anything because she knew if she said something to him, it wouldn't be nice.

"We were practically married."

"Trey, do you think I give a fuck about this? I really don't care to hear about this bullshit."

"What the hell are you mad about?" Trey stood up and said, "Look, you know I had a girl and you chose to put yourself in this position. Now you're mad cuz I'm upset that my girl is leaving me."

"How am I supposed to act, Trey? I have feelings too." Shantelle took a deep breath and said, "You love that woman don't you?"

"I do, but you knew that."

"I know you do, Trey, but I've just been thinking that you and I can be together."

"It won't be the same. You know I got history with Starr."

"I don't think you really love her, or else you wouldn't be here."

Trey looked at her and said, "I do love her."

Shantelle said, "I believe you, but if you were in love with her, there would be no way you would put her through what you put her." Shantelle stood and walked across the room, Her grey running shorts giving her a wedgie as Trey watched her ass and for a brief moment he wanted to throw her down and fuck her right on the sofa, but he resisted.

"Trey, you know who you're in love with?"

Trey stared at Shantelle wondering what the fuck she had to say. He surely hoped she didn't think he was in love with her because although he loved sexing her, he definitely didn't love her.

"Who am I in love with?"

"Trey is in love with Trey."

"Huh?"

"You don't care about anybody but yourself."

"What are you talking about? As many people as I help, including you."

"That don't mean you love me because you throw money around and women can detect that. You can get women with you because everybody needs some money in some capacity, but money is not going to make a woman want to stay with you if you disrespect her."

"What are you getting at?"

"Nothing, Trey."

He stood up and he was now face to face with her as she attempted to march past him. He cut her off.

"Get the hell out of my way," she said.

"Talk to me."

"What do you want?"

"Why are you so damn angry with me? You have no reason to be mad."

A river of tears fell down Shantelle's face.

Trey threw up his hands and said, "Oh my God, now you're crying?! What the hell are you crying about?"

With her t-shirt, Shantelle dabbed her eye.

"What's wrong?"

"You're really that goddamned stupid?"

"What?"

"Trey, I love you. I've told you I love you and you're crying about that bitch. I don't want to hear it, Trey. I know I might sound insensitive but I really don't want to hear about her."

Trey made his way over to the sofa. His Nikes were resting underneath the coffee table. He slid his feet into them and laced them up.

"So you're leaving because I told you I don't want to hear that bullshit about Starr."

Trey said, "No, I'm leaving because you knew what you were getting into before you got into it with me."

A heart shaped vase sat on a lamp stand. Shantelle slung the vase at Trey's head, barely missing him and the heart shattered into pieces. It was symbolic to how Shantelle felt. She opened the door of her tiny apartment and said, "Get the fuck out, Trey. I'm so tired of you playing with my goddamned emotions. I know that I can never be with you. I don't even know why I tried. All of you D-boys are the goddamned same."

*   *   *

Black and Lani sat across from Joey Turch. They'd come to get some legal advice for Lani. Just in case she encountered the detectives again.

Joey Turch said, "What the hell are you thinking, Tyrann?"

Black looked confused.

"Did you just pull up in that yellow Lambo outside?"

"Yes, it belongs to a friend of mines." It was one of Kyrie's cars.

"Listen, Tyrann, I've never really asked you any questions about your business dealings but riding around the city in a yellow Lambo without any legitimate income is not a good idea. I don't care who the car belongs to. Give it back to your friend. And you wonder why everybody thinks you're a goddamned drug-dealer."

Lani chuckled, but didn't say anything. She was sure as hell glad the attorney had warned him.

Black said, "I appreciate the concern, but you're not my daddy."

"True." Joey Turch extended his hand to Lani and said, "I'm Joey."

"I'm Lani."

Joey couldn't help but notice her lips. They were so full and voluptuous, He knew that she would give some amazing head, but this would be something he would never experience from her because he knew that if he'd ever tried to make a pass at her,

Tyrann would kill his white ass. For years he'd seen Tyrann march in his office with beautiful women and he wouldn't dare make a pass at any of them.

"Tyrann, what brings you here today?"

"Well, the police have been harassing her, asking her questions about a murder. Shit she don't even know about. I keep telling her that she don't have to say shit and I wanted her to hear it from you."

"Lani, when is the last time they contacted you?"

"A couple of days ago."

"And what did they say?"

"They came by my place again but I didn't let them in this time."

"This time?"

"Yeah the first time I let them in."

Lani's voice was sexy as hell and Joey wondered how she sounded when she was fucking. Was she a screamer or a whiner? Did she spit or swallow? She had small breasts which meant she probably had an amazing ass. He would have to wait until they left to steal a look.

"Listen, don't let them in. If they come back, tell them to call your attorney."

"You?"

"No, I can't represent you because I'm Tyrann's attorney." Joey Turch removed a card from his desk and passed it to her. "Tom Gilliam is a friend of mine. We'll get him to represent you."

Lani smiled and placed the card inside her clutch.

Black turned to Lani. "I just wanted you to hear that."

Joey Turch said, "Don't ever speak to the bad guys."

"The bad guys?"

"Yeah they're the bad guys and Tyrann and I are the good guys. If I can get him to get rid of that goddamned 'Look at me, I'm dealing drugs, Lambo'"

Lani was cracking up. This man was funny as hell and Lani liked his style.

Black said, "Excuse me, baby. I want to talk to Joey for a moment.

"Gimme the keys I'll wait in the car." Lani stood and walked toward the door and those tight jeans gripped her figure superbly and confirmed Joey Turch's suspicions—indeed she had a spectacular ass.

When the door closed behind her, Black said, "I need a favor?"

"Anything."

"It's about Shamari Brooks."

"What about him?"

"He's a close friend of mine."

"I didn't know that."

"I need you to let him retain you for 50 thousand for the time being and we'll get you the other fifty thousand in two weeks."

"Oh, I see. You guys get to ride around in exotic cars and I gotta discount my rates"

"I promise that we'll give you the rest of the money in two weeks."

"So, when am I going to get the fifty thousand?"

"Now." Black opened the briefcase that was stuffed with cash.

Joey Turch said, "Oh brother, give me a break! Last time I got cash from you, you had five thousand dollars in one-dollar bills.

Black laughed, "This time it's only four thousand nine hundred and ninety-nine."

"Is it all there?"

"To the last penny."

Joey pushed the suitcase aside and said, "I don't have time to count it. I'll take your word for it"

The men shook hands and Joey Turch escorted him to the reception area. The first thing Black noticed was an amazing looking black woman wearing a tight pantsuit that made her look curvaceous as hell. The woman was bending over, reaching for a *People* magazine.

Black scanned the room, looking for Lani before remembering that she'd said that she would be waiting for him in the car.

After the woman had the magazine in her possession, she took a seat and smiled. Her smile was even more amazing than her body. Black wanted to ask Joey Turch about her but he simply had too much drama going on in his life, plus she didn't seem like the type of woman that would be into a hood nigga. He smiled politely and headed to the car.

CHAPTER 6

Starr packed her things. She would move back into her parent's home, find a job, save some money then strike out on her own.

Trey walked into the house, Starr kept packing, ignoring his stupid ass. When he saw the boxes stacked, he said, "So you're really leaving?"

She snickered and said, "What do you think this is? A joke, Sir?"

"No."

"Why'd you ask me some dumb shit like that?"

"Well, I don't want you to leave."

"We don't always get what we want, do we?"

There was an awkward silence as Starr placed bathroom towels in the box in front of her. She said, "You know, Trey, there were a lot of things that I wanted. I basically put my life on hold thinking we were working toward that goal, but I guess you had other plans."

"Look, I'm sorry."

"Hmmph! Whatever, Trey."

"I know you don't believe me, but I never meant to hurt you."

"You're right I don't believe you. Would you just shut the fuck up, you're working my nerves right now."

He wedged himself between her and the box of towels and said, "Bae, can you give me one more chance?"

"I don't want to talk about it." She plopped on the sofa and began to cry. "You know what? I do wanna talk about it. Trey, who's the goddamned girl in the pictures?"

Trey sat on the armchair and took a deep breath. His mind raced trying to decide what he would and would not tell her.

"Trey, who is the girl? What is her name?"

"Shantelle."

"Where did you meet her?"

"Atlantic Station."

"So you're just like walking up to random bitches and talking to them?"

"No…I mean, yeah. Well not exactly."

"How'd you meet her?"

"Through Monte."

"Monte's in prison."

"You remember when we met Monte at the IHOP and he told us about the girl that he was with when he got arrested? You remember he told us that she might be snitching?"

Starr laughed, "So you decided that you would fuck the snitch?"

"No."

"What happened?"

"She's not a snitch. Monte wanted her to pretend to be a snitch, so he could try to get some money out of me."

"So you started fucking her. How did that happen?"

"She was making runs with Monte and when Monte went away she didn't have a way to make money. I was trying to keep her employed."

Starr laughed. "So when did it become your job to save hoes?"

Trey said, "You're right, Bae. I shouldn't have went there with her, but I did and there is nothing that I can do about it."

"You're right, Trey, the damage has been done. But you know what the fucked up part about all of this?"

"Huh?"

"Finding out that your man is a hoe and everybody else knew."

Trey dropped his head again. There was nothing he could say. She was absolutely right.

Starr placed a few more towels in the box before taping the box. "Trey, we've been through this before, there is no way in hell I can keep taking you back. "

"I understand."

"Why is this girl so special? What the fuck does she have that I don't have? She's obviously not ambitious. The bitch is making drug runs."

"I don't know. I guess I got caught up in the moment."

"Her legs look so fucking manly. I didn't even think that was your type, but then again, I didn't think your baby's mama was your type. You will fuck anything with a pussy, huh?"

"Hell, no!"

"Trey, she has a cute face but that body, that has to be like fucking a man."

Trey laughed, "That's what you call being in shape."

Starr frowned. "Well I don't wanna be in shape if I have to look like that."

"Babe, there is nothing wrong with you. I love your body. I love your curves."

"I don't know what you like, but if you wanna be with a man. You go right ahead."

"I wanna be with you."

Starr held her hand up as if to tell him to stop.

Trey dropped his head again then he said, "Hey, you don't have to move out, I'll leave."

"I can't afford this place so I'll leave.

Trey said, "I'll give you a year's rent. I mean it's only fair. I was the one that fucked up."

"A year's rent is over sixty grand."

"Hey, I'll pay it."

Starr didn't argue with him. She really did like the new place and she didn't want to leave. She had met a few neighbors and was very comfortable in the building, besides she'd agreed to decorate the neighbor's place. She didn't want to have to explain how she ended back up in the hood.

CHAPTER 7

Black received a call from Joey Turch. He answered it on the first ring. "Hello?"

"Joey Turch here."

"I recognized the number."

"Where is the Lambo?"

"Gave it back."

"Good. By the way, there were over ten thousand dollars in one dollar bills. It took me and my wife all night to count that money."

"Is that what you're calling about?"

"No actually. There are two things I need to talk about."

Black said, "Okay, I'm waiting. I got things to do, bruh."

"Well the first thing is I need you to tell your boy he needs to surrender. He's making it bad for himself."

Black knew that he probably was but there was no way in the hell he would tell Shamari to turn himself.

"Are you listening, Tyrann?"

"I heard you."

"Make sure you tell him that."

"I got a question for you?"

"Shoot."

"If he turns himself in, will he get a bond?"

"Probably not."

"That's exactly what I thought."

"But he needs to do this. He's making the situation worse."

"I don't know how that situation could be any worse than it is."

"Well if we have to make a plea for his life. You never know this situation could be very tricky."

"Okay what else did you want to talk to me about?"

"Well, did you see the woman in the reception area the other day?"

"The one with the ridiculous ass?"

"Boy, that was a nice ass," Joey Turch said. And when he said that, it confirmed Black's suspicions that Joey Turch was lusting after Lani's lips. Up until this point, he didn't think Joey Turch would fuck with a black woman. Black wasn't worried though because he knew that Joey understood that if he made an attempt to flirt with any of his women, he'd fuck him up.

"Okay, what about her?"

"She wanted to know who you were. Said you were very attractive. Especially, after I told her that you were driving the Lamborghini."

"You know that's not my car."

"But you can afford one if you want one."

Black laughed. "Maybe."

"I'll text you her name and number. She wanted your number but you know how often you change your number."

"Okay. Text me the number."

"Before I text you this number I need to tell you something."

"What?"

"Her name is Sasha Anderson."

"Okay."

"But that's not what I had to tell you."

"Tell me."

"She's a he."

"Oh hell the fuck no! I don't want that number!"

Joey Turch was laughing his ass off. Finally he got his composure and then he said. "I'm just kidding."

"Don't play with me like that."

"But seriously, she's the mayor's daughter."

"You're lying?"

"No, I'm serious."

"And she wants to talk to me?"

"Look, I haven't told her anything about you. So you let her know what you want to let her know. I mean if nothing else, she looks like she would be a good lay."

"For sure. I'm going to call her. Are you sure she's a she?"

"Yes, she's a woman." Joey laughed before hanging the phone up.

Little T. J. ran up to Trey and took hold of his leg and didn't want to let go. Trey rubbed his son's hair.

T. J. said, "Daddy, did you come to play catch with me?"

"Not today, but I'll be back to play catch with you."

"You gotta leave again?"

Trey didn't respond and Jessica said, "Why don't you go ahead and tell your son another lie. Lie to him like you always do."

Jessica's mother appeared and Trey said, "Mrs. Turner, will you take T. J. for a walk while I talk to Jessica?"

Jessica's mother grabbed T. J. by the hand and made a beeline for outside.

After they disappeared, Jessica said, "Why do you always lie to your son, Trey? You're a horrible father, just horrible."

"No, the question is why the hell are you always up in my god-damned business?"

"What are you talking about?"

"Those pictures! Don't play stupid, bitch."

Jessica laughed and said, "I should've known that you came over here to talk about the pictures. And I thought you just maybe wanted to see your son."

"You leave my son out of this. You know I love my son."

"You sure as hell have a fucked up way of showing it."

"I'm no deadbeat."

"What the hell is your definition of a deadbeat? You haven't seen your son in two months, Trey. Two goddamned months! You like to think of yourself as a good person, but the truth is you're a horrible person and a terrible father."

Trey wanted to slap the fuck out of this bitch, but he knew that if he did, it would be a big black man's word against a tiny white woman, and he knew whose side the law would be on.

"Who is the new girl?"

"You tell me who she is, private investigator?"

"You just can't keep your dick to yourself. Can you?"

"Why don't you just admit that you're mad because I don't want to fuck you?"

She paced and Trey glanced at her ass for a second and remembered why he started fucking with her in the first place. Though Jessica was much slimmer than Starr, she'd had a very nice ass for a white girl, but she was toxic.

"Trey, the more I think about it, the more I realize that I only wanted what I thought was best for T. J."

"Why the fuck are you trying to ruin my life?"

"Ruin your life? You seem like you got a pretty good fucking life to me. You live in this great high-rise apartment and you have two very attractive women."

"You shut the fuck up!"

"Trey, what did you come over here for?"

"I came over here to tell you to stay the fuck out of my life! Leave me the fuck alone! Can you do me that favor?'

"Trey, I didn't sign up to be a single parent. My mom told me not to fuck with black dudes, but I didn't listen and now, I'm a goddamned single parent."

"What is that supposed to mean?"

"It's easy for you to go out and drop your seed all over the place and go start over." She stopped pacing and stared him straight in his eye. "Do you know how goddamned hard it is for me to get a man now? Dating within my own race is out of the question, no white man is going to deal with me with a biracial child and the black men that I meet, just want me because I'm white."

"So I fucked your life up? It's my fault. So you want to fuck my life up?"

"Trey, you sold me a dream. I believed you. I believed that you were going to leave Starr and be with T. J. and me."

Jessica began to cry and Trey tried to console her. She shoved him and said, "Will you just get the fuck away from me?! I can't stand your ass! You ruined my goddamned life!"

Trey made his way to the other side of the room.

Jessica made eye contact with Trey and said, "I'm sorry for yelling, but I'm going through another bout of depression."

She was very calm and it was scary to Trey because she'd cursed him and was crying a few seconds ago. He remembered that this bitch was loony, which was one of the reasons he'd chosen not to deal with her.

"So what do you want from me?"

"I just want T. J. to have as normal a life as he can. Can he get a fair shot at this?"

"Will you leave me alone?"

"Trey, I promise you won't hear a goddamned word out of me if you do right by your son."

"I can do that." Trey was heading out of the door and Jessica said, "Aren't you going to wait for mom and T. J. to come back?"

Trey said, "I'm going to ride around the neighborhood and find them."

Jessica smiled.

CHAPTER 8

Black and Kyrie sat at the kitchen table, with over a thousand packs of heroin with the word Obamacare stamped on the packets. When Shamari arrived, Black introduced Kyrie to Shamari.

Black said, "This is my best friend since kindergarten."

Shamari was cool with meeting Kyrie. He'd known Black long enough to trust him. He'd heard that Black had done a lot of shady shit in the street, most things he'd also done himself.

Shamari asked, "What happened to Girl Scout Cookies."

Kyrie said, "Obamacare is the best package in the street right now, and we just chose to capitalize off what was already hot instead of trying to establish something."

"Makes sense to me." Shamari paused and said, "So how is it going?"

Black passed Shamari a briefcase and said, "There is a hundred thousand dollars in here, you would've had one-fifty but I gave Joey Turch fifty grand."

"Appreciate you, bruh."

"No problem. Hell, I appreciate you."

"So how much did you make?"

Black didn't answer, he'd made just as much as he'd given Shamari, but there was no way in the hell he was telling him that. He knew from past experience that when suppliers were able to determine what he made, they'd go up on the price.

"Why is that important?" Kyrie said.

"Cuz I wanna know."

"Some things ain't meant for everybody," Kyrie said.

Shamari wanted to backhand Kyrie, and he would have if he wasn't Black's friend.

"I ain't talking to you."

"I'm the one that was responsible for getting rid of the shit, so you are talking to me, nigga."

Shamari glanced at Black and said, "Tell this nigga to shut the fuck up."

Black wedged himself between the two and said, "Chill the fuck out."

Seconds later he pulled Shamari aside.

"We got paid too, that's all Im'ma say."

"I ain't got no problem with that. I just don't wanna get fucked."

"How are you getting fucked? You got this shit for free."

Shamari didn't respond. Black had him in a really fucked up position. Shamari didn't understand the heroin game, so he had to just hope what Black was telling him was the truth. And Black was right. Shamari didn't have anything invested in it so he would have to just take Black's word for it.

Black said, "Look, Mari, man, I'm as real as they come and if I was going to fuck with you, I wouldn't have given your girl the money to help with your attorney. I didn't have to do that. Then, I go to Joey Turch and drop fifty grand for your new case. You my man, I'm not going to fuck you. Am I going to make sure I get something out of the deal? Hell, yeah! I mean if I get caught with the shit, I don't believe you're going to step up and say it was your shit."

Shamari laughed and gave Black a pound. "Hell no, good point. I ain't tripping." He paused then said, "Joey Turch called me today tombout turn myself in."

Black said, "Yeah, he told me to tell you the same thing. Man, I didn't even bother telling you that bullshit."

"I need a million dollars before I even think about that."

"If you get some more of this product I know we can make a million."

"I know that ain't possible. Remember I took this shit by force. But I know a few people out in Cali. I'll reach out to them to see what I can do."

"Dude, make it soon while we got the momentum going. We gonna to take over the city."

*   *   *

The Sundial restaurant was located on the 72nd floor of the Westin Hotel, and it offered a panoramic view of Atlanta. Black had only been there once. He wasn't much of a fine dining type of guy. He'd rather go to a steakhouse. Sasha made reservations and they decided to meet at 8:30. Black arrived at 8:40, very fashionably late. He had dressed casual—a pair of Jordan's, a long sleeved polo shirt, and some jeans. He'd hope she didn't expect him to wear a suit. It wasn't happening. He was a nervous about meeting her. Not because he wasn't comfortable around women. He was raised by his grandmother and big sister and he'd always kept at least two women. But this woman was different. She came from a different background and she was the mayor's daughter. Probably raised in some rich-ass suburb, attended some private school. What the fuck did she want with a nigga like him? He would soon find out. Black approached the maître d'.

"I'm looking for someone. I think they're already seated."

"Describe her?"

Black thought about the correct way to describe a woman without saying an average height black woman with an amazing ass.

Black was about to give his description when Sasha approached.

They hugged and he followed her back to the table. She was even more beautiful than he remembered. Her face was radiant and she had shoulder length hair with bangs. She wore an absurdly tight black dress that made him want to see her naked.

When they were seated, they ordered drinks. He had a Ciroc and cranberry and she had a mojito.

She smiled and he noticed that she had amazing teeth.

"Is this your first time here?" she asked.

"No. I've been here before."

"Yeah, I like this restaurant."

"The first time I was here," Black said, "I was already fucked up and I didn't know that the restaurant rotated. I asked my homie what the fuck was going on and he was like what are you talking about?"

Sasha was laughing her ass off.

Black said, "I'm sorry for cursing so much. I mean I can try to control it if you want me to."

She laughed and said, "No, be yourself, Tyrann."

"You don't mind if I curse?"

"Not at all."

"Yeah, I was like everything is spinning and they were like you're tripping man. Finally, the waitress came over and told me I wasn't tripping."

Sasha said, "I like the view. It's one of Atlanta's gems. I mean there are better restaurants but I just love being this far up looking at the skyline.

There was an awkward silence as they looked at the amazing Atlanta skyline.

The waitress brought the drinks and they ordered entrees. Sasha had a Cobb salad and Black ordered short ribs and sweet potato grits. The waitress disappeared.

"How are sweet potato grits?"

"I don't know but I'm about to find out tho'. I love grits. I'm a Georgia boy born and raised."

"I was born in Florida, but I been here since I was twelve."

"And you're thirty now?"

"How did you know? I never told you my age. Did Joey tell you?"

"Nope, you look younger, but your demeanor is more mature than you look."

"How old are you?"

"I'm in my thirties."

"You got secrets. Ashamed of your age?"

"Not at all. I'll let you know when the time is right."

"Okay, mystery man.'"

He sipped his drink. "Not a mystery man."

There was another awkward silence as both of their eyes drifted out to the Atlanta skyline.

The waitress dropped their food off and disappeared.

Black took a bite of grits. "So tell me. Why do you like me?"

"Who said I liked you."

"You asked for my number."

Sasha took a bite of her salad and said, "I did, didn't I?"

"You sure did."

"Well I wanted to know what you were about."

"Why? Because of the nice car I was driving? That car ain't mine."

"I know. Joey told me." She took a swig of her drink and said, "See, I'm not a gold digger. Besides, I make my own money."

"I never said you were."

She smiled and sipped more of her drink."

"Your daddy is the mayor?"

"He is. But I work. I'm not a spoiled daddy's girl."

"What do you do?"

"Banking executive."

"I'm impressed."

She smiled. "So, what do you do mystery man?"

"Sales."

"What do you sell?"

"Luxury cars."

"Really?"

He could tell that she didn't believe him. Black took another bite of grits and said, "I'm going to be honest with you. I'm not the kind of guy you might want to be involved with."

"I'll be the judge"

"I'm a bad guy."

"Bad is a matter of perspective. Besides, I like bad boys."

She licked the salt from her glass. Black was now rock solid. He hadn't had new pussy in a very long time. The thought of fucking the mayor's daughter intrigued him very much.

"You like thugs?"

"Maybe a little."

"I don't get it?"

"I get bored easy. I like unpredictability."

"I'm as unpredictable as it gets."

The floor of the restaurant had spun around for the third time and Black said, "I notice every time we get to this certain point, you look out at that high-rise." Black pointed.

"You pay attention."

"In my business, you gotta pay attention."

"Car sales?"

They both laughed their asses off.

"I was looking to see if I'd turned off my lights."

"You live in that building?"

Black didn't want to sound impressed because truthfully he wasn't. He could live anywhere in Atlanta. He had the money to do so.

"So, really. What do you want with me? I mean you're the goddamned mayor's daughter."

She said, "Look, Tyrann, I'm not trying to marry you, just calm down a bit. Besides, I have someone that I'm seeing."

"You do?"

"And you do to. Maybe several women."

Black grinned. He wouldn't confirm or deny her assessment.

"So you want a fuck buddy?"

"Maybe."

Black thought damn this chick was a freak.

When they finished their dinner, Black paid the tab and walked her to her car in a parking deck across from Westin.

She drove a white BMW X6. He opened the door for her and when she got inside she lowered the window and they stared at each other for a long time. Then, he finally leaned in and they locked lips. Seconds later Black was on the passenger side of the car and she unzipped his pants and took him in her mouth. Black leaned back as he ran his fingers through her hair. Damn he thought, this sexy motherfucker is actually sucking my dick outside in a parking deck! Oh what a feeling.

CHAPTER 9

Jada took a selfie as she stood in the mirror. She wore an electric blue dress that made her waist appear extra tiny and she looked amazing. She posted a picture for her more than twenty-five thousand Instagram followers, most of which were men wanting to fuck her and women wanting to see what designer clothes she would be rocking with a few haters sprinkled in. She posted the picture with her ass poking out. The comments were hilarious to her.

Sharchild5675 said: *Girl I want my face to be your chair.*

BlackTommy wrote: *Fake but I'd still smash.*

EfromtheA wrote: *How much for a date?*

BlackBeauty wrote: *Girl, you are gorgeous no-homo.*

She posted two more pics before heading to meet Craig. Now that the twenty five grand from Craig was in Jada's account, they agreed to meet at a Starbucks in Buckhead. They sat in the back corner alone, away from the other patrons.

Craig said, "Okay, now you got the money. Now I'm going to need for you to delete the pics. As a matter of fact, just hand me your phone, you can report it lost and get a new one."

Jada removed her phone from her purse and deleted the text exchange between her and Big Papa and handed Craig the phone. She'd already added the pictures of Craig and Skyy to her Dropbox account. Though Craig was a very savvy businessman, he was not savvy at all on the technical side of things. He didn't believe in email and she'd once suggested that Instagram would be good for his practice, showing before and after pictures of his patients but he'd said it was a waste of time. She very seriously doubted that he would realize that she could add the incriminating pictures to her Dropbox account.

"What are you going to do with my phone?"

"Destroy it."

She wanted to laugh, but she said, "Okay."

"How do I know the pictures aren't out there floating around?"

She tried to contain herself but found herself laughing out loud. "I guess it's a chance you gotta take."

"What?" He passed the phone back to her and said, "Just delete the goddamned pictures."

She showed him the pictures and he was so embarrassed that his face turned beet-red.

She said, "I didn't realize your dick was so goddamned tiny."

"Will you just delete the goddamned pictures!"

She deleted the pics.

Craig said, "You know what you did to me is called extortion, right?"

"I call it getting even."

"That could land you in jail."

"And it could land you in the news and embarrass your wife."

"You're so fucking mean."

"Look, you're the one that started fuckin' my friend. So you really just have a black girl fetish and any black vagina will do, huh?"

"I don't have a black girl fetish. I actually liked you."

"I'm supposed to believe that after you fucked my friend? Well, not only did you fuck her, you had a goddamned threesome, a threesome! Makes me think you're some kind of sex addict of something."

"I admit I shouldn't have done that but you shouldn't have pawned my car to get your drug dealer boyfriend out of jail."

"First of all, I didn't pawn your car to get him out of jail. The car was used for collateral to pay the attorney."

"I was a little upset because of that."

"You're doing coke now."

"I'm not an addict. I party a little bit."

She sipped her coffee and said, "There is just so much shit I'm learning about you, that I never knew."

"I'm not a coke head."

"I never said you were."

"You're insinuating it."

"I ain't insinuating shit."

"Look I'm sorry for betraying you with Skyy. Do you think we can start over?"

There was an awkward silence. Jada missed him a little but she would never let him know this. She took another sip of her coffee and then said, "I'll think about it."

*   *   *

Starr, Jada, and Lani met at Benihana. Ordinarily Starr would have declined, not because she thought she was too good to eat at Benihana's, but she just didn't like the food that much. But rather than staying in the house thinking about what went wrong with Trey, she decided that hanging out with friends, with probably just as much drama in their lives as hers, was the way to go and she was actually starting to tolerate Jada. Yes, she was a little whorish, but she felt deep down inside she was a good person. A little damaged, but she had a good heart and was down for people she liked. Starr and Jada ate Hibachi chicken and Lani had the Hibachi steak. They all had Mai Tais to drink. Starr had downed three drinks when Lani said, "You know you gotta drive home, right?"

"I live like five minutes away. I'll be fine."

Jada said, "I was going to say something myself. You really should slow down."

"Ok, Momma," Starr slurred with the look of a dumb alcoholic on her face.

"I've never seen you like this. What's going on?"

"Niggas ain't shit, that's what's going on!"

Lani and Jada looked on as they sipped their drinks. They couldn't believe Starr was almost belligerent. They'd never witnessed her like this before—she was usually so goddamned composed.

Starr continued, "I've given my heart to this man for damn near ten years and the last few months has been hell. First, this mysterious-ass baby shows up with a white baby mama and now he's been fucking some girl with more muscles than he has."

Lani said, "What?"

"Yeah, he moved out today. I guess since he finally left, I'm feeling it."

Jada said, "Baby, I'm so sorry. But you're strong, Starr, and you're a good person, you'll be fine."

Tears rolled down Starr's face. "I know I'll be fine, but it just hurts so goddamned much. When you've put your all into a relationship and this is what you get."

Lani said, "How did you find out about this woman?"

Starr composed herself and then said, "His baby mama had a P. I. trailing his stupid ass and she sent me pics." Starr paused and downed another drink. Then she said, "The motherfucker is so stupid, for all he knows the police could be trailing him. Trey has not been himself. He's always been leery of people trailing him, but that's beside the point. I'm so goddamned hurt right now."

Lani rubbed Starr's back. She felt so bad for Starr, because Starr really was one of the few genuinely good people that she knew.

"But I knew it all along. I mean, I know my man. I told you, Lani, that I had a feeling that his ass was running around.

"You called it," Lani said.

"It was so obvious. He barely touched me. I guess he was so busy screwing that man-looking bitch."

Lani laughed and said, "Cut it out, I know that woman don't look like no man."

Starr presented her one of the pictures.

Lani examined the picture and said, "She's cute, but she needs to stop working out so much."

Jada said, "Ewww. Yuck! Gross. She has a pretty face but I agree she works out too much."

Lani said, "But what ya'll don't understand is men just want variety of pussy. Cheating-ass Black taught me that. You should see all his baby mamas. You tombout a hideous bunch of bitches? Only one that's semi-cute, an Asian looking chick. Black don't care. He just wanna stick his dick in a hole. Any hole as long as it's female."

Starr said, "Men are disgusting. I swear I just want someone to love me. I don't care what he has, I'm so sick of this."

"So, if he moved today, how are you going to pay your bills?"

"Well he gave me the money to pay the rent for the remainder of the lease. I'm just going to have to get me a job. I can do it, I've worked before. I ain't too good to get a job. I've got to decorate the gay couple's condo across the hall. They're going to pay me six grand for that and one of them said they had a couple of friends that they were going to tell about my services, so hopefully I can get more work until I get a job."

Lani said, "You should start your own business."

"With what? I ain't got no money."

Jada said, "Couldn't be me. This nigga would have to pay for his transgressions I'm a good person until you cross me then I'm getting revenge."

Starr said, "I'm going to be okay. I have faith that I'm going to be okay. He can take all his money but he can't take my faith."

Jada said, "I feel you on that, but you know what the bible says—faith without work is fruitless." She rubbed Starr's back.

The bill came and Jada took care of it and had Starr follow her to the Four Seasons and gave her 5k in an envelope. Starr thanked her, this validated what she'd been thinking recently—Jada was really a good person. She just had some problems, like everybody else. Starr vowed she would become less judgmental of people.

CHAPTER 10

Word on the street was there was a nigga named Kenny-Boo was out to get Black. A guy named Spider was raised in the same Projects as Kenny-Boo. Spider was related to Black, but not a blood relative. Spider's mother and Black's Uncle Jabo had been common-law husband and wife for the last nineteen years. Black gave Spider a pound of weed and Spider let Black know exactly where Kenny-Boo lived. Black and Kyrie followed Kenny-Boo to South DeKalb Mall and when he came out of the mall, they followed him to a home in Gwinnett that belonged to his girlfriend. Kyrie wore his Papa John's hat when he rang the doorbell.

"Who the fuck is it?"

"Papa John's."

"Sharika, did you order a pizza?"

"No, I ain't order no pizza."

Kenny-Boo opened the door. "Aye, homie, I think you got the wrong house."

Kyrie said, "My bad."

Kyrie turned to walk away and just as Kenny Boo was about to shut the door, Kyrie presented a nine millimeter and wedged himself between the door. Kenny-Boo tried to force the door shut. Kyrie fired a shot that whisked over Kenny-Boo's head.

Kenny-Boo yelled "Sharika, go get my gun!"

Kenny-Boo and Kyrie struggled before Kyrie fired a shot into Kenny-Boo's groin area and Kenny-Boo stumbled on the floor then howled.

Black sprinted from the car as Kyrie and Black were inside Kenny Boo's house. Sharika was a horse-faced brown woman with braids. She was slim but her body was still curvaceous.

Black aimed his gun at Sharika and said, "Sit yo skinny ass on the floor!" Sharika complied.

Black said, "Who else is in here?"

"Just my two babies," Sharika said.

Kenny-Boo was still flailing around on the floor hollering and holding his groin.

Kyrie searched the whole house before finding two toddlers in one of the upstairs bedrooms. One was asleep and the other was sitting in the floor playing with an action figure. Kyrie made eye contact with the kid, made a funny-face, and closed the door. Then he ran back downstairs and said, "Nobody is here but some small kids."

Kenny-Boo said, "You can kill me but don't hurt those kids."

Black slapped the fuck out of him with his gun and said, "Motherfucker, do I look like I hurt kids?" The thought of him insinuating that he would hurt a kid made Black even more furious and with the butt of his gun, Black slapped the fuck out of him again.

Black said, "What's going on Big Bad Kenny-Boo? I'd been hearing all these words in the street that you're a killer and that you're going to get me? You better ask about me."

Kenny nursed his jaw and said, "I don't even know you."

"I'm Black. You sure got a lot to say about me in the streets. Now your bitch ass pretending that you don't know me?"

Sharika said, "Please don't kill us. I have my babies. I want 'ta raise my babies. Do you want the money?"

Black stared at Kenny-Boo. He never even thought that this bitch-ass nigga had any money.

Kyrie said, "Where the fuck is the money?"

Kenny-Boo stared at Sharika as if he wanted to tell her to keep her goddamned mouth shut.

Black yanked skinny-ass Sharika from the floor and said, "Kyrie, get this simple motherfucker's stash.

Sharika was wearing some skimpy ass pink shorts that were crawling up her ass crack. Kyrie couldn't help but grab her booty.

She turned and looked at him like she wanted to tell him to stop but she didn't as they made their way up to the bedroom. Sharika grabbed a Nike shoe box and gave it to Kyrie. Kyrie opened the box and saw a small wad of cash. "How much is this?"

Sharika said, "I don't know, maybe four or five grand."

"Is this it?"

"That's all we have."

Kyrie said, "This ain't shit." Seconds later they were back downstairs.

Kyrie said, "Black, this nigga ain't got but five stacks."

Black said, "I'm surprised this dusty-ass motherfucker got that much."

Black spotted a lamp with a long cord on a table across the room. Black said, "Cut that cord and tie this skinny-ass hoe up."

Five minutes later Kyrie had Sharika hog-tied and Black made his way over and examined her before saying, "Goddamn, this skinny-ass bitch looks like she gives some amazing head."

"I was just thinking the same thing." Kyrie said and unzipped his pants.

Black backhanded the hell out of Kyrie and said, "Just because I said she had some dick sucking lips, don't mean you need to go get your dick sucked."

Black eased back over to where Kenny-Boo was lying and ordered Kyrie to hold him down. They stripped Kenny-Boo butt-naked, then cut the cord from another lamp and Kyrie held him down as Black whipped the fuck out of him with the drop cord. Kenny-Boo was in so much pain he wanted to cry. The only reason he didn't cry was because his girlfriend was staring at him.

After whipping his ass they tied and picked him up, and threw him in the back of Kyrie's Dodge Charger. They put him out on the middle of Interstate 285 butt-ass naked.

Black drove into Nana's driveway. A detective car blocked him in. Black shoved his gun underneath the passenger's seat. He bounced from his car and started walking toward the house when Officer Williams said, "Black!"

Black turned and said, "Do I know you?" Knowing goddamned well they were the cops. He could play games with them, especially, since Joey Turch told him that they didn't have a warrant for his arrest.

"I'm Officer Mike Williams of APD, and this is my friend Thomas Kearns."

"Okay, you gotta badge?"

The men presented their badges and Black said, "Ok, nobody called you. What can I do to help you?"

"Can we talk for a minute?"

"We're talking."

Thomas Kearns had a smirk on his face and he wanted to make Black shut the fuck up, but he couldn't. He knew if he got into a verbal sparring with him, the little chance that he had of getting information from him would go out the window.

There was an awkward silence. Neither of the officers knew how to address the experienced criminal that clearly knew the law and knew his rights.

Black glanced at his watch and said, "I gotta be going so I'm going to need you to tell me what you want."

Mike Williams said, "We want to ask you about a murder that occurred a few weeks ago."

Black said, "You can stop right now. I don't know nothing 'bout no murder."

Thomas Kearns said, "A cell phone belonging to you was in the vicinity of the murder."

"That's real unfortunate."

Mike Williams stepped right up to Black and stood nose to nose with him. "What's going to be unfortunate is when we put yo' ass away, Tyrann, and with your record you'll be gone for life."

Black took a step back and said, "No, what's unfortunate is that they haven't made a mouthwash for your stankin-ass breath."

"Fuck you!"

Thomas Kearns grabbed Mike Williams by the arm and said, "Will you just chill?" He then apologized to Black and said, "Look, Tyrann, all we want is a few minutes of your time. You know, just to sit down and talk. If you didn't have anything to do with it, we won't bother you again, but we're going to find out, one way or another why your phone was in the area."

Black said, "Do you have an arrest warrant?"

"No."

"Well, get the fuck out of my nana's driveway before I report you for harassing me."

CHAPTER 11

Jada looked sensational in some black tights and the pair of six inch Louboutins she wore lifted her buns to absolute perfection. She glanced in the mirror with her iPhone in hand. She snapped a couple of selfies for her Instagram fans and haters alike. Over twelve hundred likes in ten minutes. She glanced at a few of the comments.

Mikey 808 said: *Yeezus!!! Now that's a bad bitch!!!*

WalesWife said: *That ass is tho!*

Mr.989 said: *Can I take a bite of that apple?*

It was confirmed. She looked damned good, which was just what she needed for Big Papa. She knew she had treated a good guy wrong and she wanted to meet up with him and apologize. But she also knew she had to look damn good and judging by her Instagram fans, she'd overachieved.

Jada met Big Papa at the Cheesecake Bistro in Atlantic Station.

She hadn't seen him since he'd shown up at her hotel room and got into that little verbal altercation with Shamari. They sat at a booth in the back of the restaurant.

Big Papa looked like he'd lost a few pounds but was still big as hell. He sat there with a stupid ass grin on his face.

Jada asked, "Why are you smiling so hard?"

He said, "No matter how hard I try to cut you off, I can't cut your sexy ass off."

Jada made a sad face. "Why would you try to cut me off, baby?"

"What you did to me was so wrong."

Jada made another sad face and said "That's why I felt I needed to apologize." "Look, Ty, you're a good person and what I did to you was totally wrong, and I'm so sorry that happened."

"So why didn't you tell me you still had a man?"

"Well, technically, we aren't together any more but we still have feelings for each other. But it's not going to work."

"Why?"

"We're different people now."

Big Papa said, "Let's not talk about him." There was that stupid grin again. "How do I look?"

Jada said, "Looks like you lost a little weight." His T shirt still looked like it was struggling and that belly was still creeping out underneath but not quite as bad as before.

"Yeah, I've been working out. Trying to lose at least a 100 pounds. You know I want to be around a while."

Jada stared at him thinking if he lost a hundred pounds, he'd still be large—at least he was trying.

Jada presented him with a box.

"What is this?"

"Open it. It's a little token of my appreciation for you." She licked her lips on purpose and Papa's little pecker came alive.

He popped the box open to see a stainless steel watch.

Jada said, "I know this isn't what you're used to, but it's what I can afford."

Big Papa smiled and said, "It's perfect. I love it. Nobody's ever bought me anything, ever."

"I mean I didn't know what to get a man that has everything."

"That's what everybody always says to me and then they end up getting nothing and it shows me what they think of me."

"Well, I think a lot of you."

The waitress came and Big Papa just had a glass of water and Jada got a slice of cheesecake

"Not eating huh?"

"Hired a chef. I'm going to lose a 100 pounds by the summer."

"How much have you lost?"

"Twenty pounds."

"I noticed a difference right away."

Big Papa lifted his shirt, exposing his gut and said, "I'm going to be chiseled."

Jada wanted to throw up when she saw those rolls of fat and cellulite instead she said, "Could you put your shirt down, please."

He laughed and complied.

When Jada was about to bite into her cheesecake, she spotted Trey across the room with the chick she'd seen in Starr's picture. She was cuter in person, but those goddamned calf muscles looked rather mannish. Jada thought this bitch must run marathons. Trey and the new girlfriend sat on the same side of a booth. Trey kissed her on the neck. This infuriated Jada. She couldn't believe she was so mad because only a few months ago, she couldn't stand Starr. But now that they'd grown to understand each other, they had somewhat of a bond.

She dropped her fork onto her plate and was now pissed the fuck off. The nerve of this cheating motherfucker! Starr was a good person she didn't deserve this bullshit at all.

Big Papa said, "I'm sorry, babe. I promise not to lift my shirt up again until I lose the weight."

Jada giggled and said, "I'm not thinking about that at all."

"You look so disgusted."

"I am."

"What's wrong?"

Jada said, "Don't look back, but—"

Stupid-ass Big Papa did exactly what she'd told him not to do and was now staring right in Trey and the new girl's face.

Jada said, "Now why in the fuck did you just do what I told you not to do?"

"My bad." He laughed then took a sip of his water. "Do you know those folks?"

"Yeah, that's my girlfriend's ex-boyfriend. They just broke up and now this nigga got the nerve to be up in here flaunting this basic bitch."

Big Papa said, "I understand you upset, but that woman is far from basic."

"You shut the hell up!" Jada said, before realizing that she was directing her anger at the wrong person. "Look, I'm sorry."

"It's okay, baby, I understand that you're upset."

She made eye contact with Big Papa. "What do you think I should do?"

"What do you mean?" He sipped his water. "Jada, you ain't thinking about starting no bullshit up in here, are you?"

"No."

"Good because while I think I can take old boy, I ain't trying to go to jail."

The thought of fat-assed Big Papa trying to fight Trey was comical. How could he possibly think he could take anybody? Well, maybe if he grabbed Trey and squeezed the hell out of him, but he'd have to catch him first.

"Look, I'm thinking of calling my girlfriend."

"No. Don't do it."

Jada said, "You're right." Then she glanced over at the happy couple. She could see Trey rubbing her thigh under the table.

Jada bit into her cheesecake and then said, "I can't take this bullshit."

She dialed Lani's phone. Lani picked up on the first ring.

"Hello."

"You ain't gonna believe who I see."

"Who?"

"I see Trey and his new chick. That nigga out here flaunting this chick boldly! Being so disrespectful!"

"Really?"

"I swear to you."

"I'm calling Starr and we're coming up there."

"Okay. They just sat down."

Big Papa now had his new watch on this arm trying to set the time.

"I like it on your arm," Jada said.

"Now why did you do that?"

"Do what?"

"Call your friend."

"Because I'd want somebody to tell me if I'm being disrespected."

"Damn! I wish you wouldn't have done that."

Jada looked at Big Papa wanting to curse his fat ass out. Damn. She hadn't realized he was such a pussy.

Big Papa sensed that Jada was not pleased with him. "Baby, thank you for the watch again. I love it."

Jada said, "No problem and if you want to leave, I understand."

Big Papa stood up and threw a hundred dollar bill on the table and said, "I don't want no part of this." He leaned over and kissed Jada. "I'm glad you understand. Call me," he said before leaving the restaurant.

Jada paid the waitress and stood outside the restaurant until Starr and Lani appeared. Jada led them right past the hostess and they stood right in front of Trey and the new girlfriend's table.

Trey looked up and said, "Hey, baby."

"Hey baby, my ass," Starr said.

Shantelle looked at Trey and said, "Who is this?"

Jada said, "No, the question is more like 'Who the fuck are you, bitch?'"

"Bitch?" Shantelle turned to Trey. "Babe, who are these dirtbags?"

Trey stood and tried to grab Starr's arm. He wanted to talk to her outside the restaurant. Starr pounded Trey in the chest and said, "I hate you. Trey, I fucking hate you."

Shantelle tried to scoot out of the booth but Jada grabbed her by the hair and shoved her back down. "Stay where the fuck you're at. Don't make me act a motherfuckin' fool in here."

The manager, a short black man with nappy-ass hair surrounding a bald spot, glasses, and wearing some very cheap-ass brown shoes, came over with a security guard and a police officer.

The police officer grabbed Trey when he saw him yanking Starr's arm.

"What's going on?" the security officer said.

Trey said to the police officer, "Let me go, motherfucker!"

"You need to keep quiet before I take you to jail, young man."

"Take me to jail? Motherfucker, I don't give a damn about going to jail!"

The police officer cuffed Trey and escorted him out of the restaurant.

The manager asked Starr, Lani, and Jada to leave. They left and Shantelle stayed in the restaurant until they were gone. There was no way she could fight three hood boogers.

It was 6:21 in the morning and someone was banging on Jada's door. She thought it was housekeeping.

"Come back about noon," she called out. She'd told those motherfuckers time and time again not to be waking her up at the crack of dawn talking about no goddamned housekeeping. She had to get the fuck out of this place in a hurry. Not only was it expensive but they'd become irritating as hell.

They kept knocking.

Jada stood up and slipped into her house robe. She opened the door to see four U.S. Marshals and two FBI agents. "Looking for Shamari Brooks."

"I don't know where Shamari is."

One of the marshals, a tall black man with a graying beard, presented her with a search warrant. "Well, you don't mind if we look around?"

"This is a hotel room. There is not a whole lot to see." Jada stepped aside.

The six officers entered and swept through the room. When they were done, one of the Marshals handed Jada a card. Jada recognized the name, U.S. Marshal Tommy Blair. It was the same name on the card that her neighbor, Luke, had given her.

As soon as they left, she called Shamari's sister and told her to tell him to get in touch with her as soon as possible. Jada crawled back into the bed. Seconds later she heard another knock at the door. She looked out the peephole, this time it was management. When she opened the door, they asked her to vacate the premises, citing that the search warrant had been bad for their reputation.

Jada closed the door and begin to pack her things. "Fuck," she said. While she was pissed, she should have left the hotel a long time ago.

CHAPTER 12

Black called Shamari and told him to meet him at his house in Lithonia. Shamari arrived an hour later. They headed to the kitchen and they sat at the island counter when Black said, "We got serious problems."

"What kind of problems?"

"The police locked Kyrie up this morning."

"For what?"

"Well his six year old son must have thought the heroin was candy or something because he took some of the packets to school and started to pass it out to his classmates."

"You're lying?"

"I wish I was."

"How the hell did he get it?"

"I don't know but that's what I wanna ask Kyrie."

Shamari stood and began pacing. This was the last mother-fucking thing he needed. He was already wanted. He didn't need this but the heat really wasn't on him. It was on Black because Kyrie was Black's friend, but he didn't need to be worrying about this shit. He turned to Black. "Do you have any beer? I need a motherfuckin' drink."

"Got some Henny."

"Give me a shot of that."

Black poured two shots.

He added coke to his glass but Shamari took his shot straight.

"What are we going to do now?"

Black said, "This is all on me, bruh. Don't worry about this."

"But you got your own shit to worry about."

Black said, "Do I look like I'm worried?"

Though Black had just taken a shot of Henny with him, he had to admit that Black didn't look the least bit worried.

"But what's next?"

"I gotta get him out."

"He has a bond?"

"If that's what you want to call it."

"How much is it."

"A million dollars, but it's not a cash bond, it can be property."

"I can help a little, but I'm really dealing with my own shit."

Black said, "Don't worry. I'm going to put my nana's house up and my sister has a house that's worth about half a mil."

"Damn! You got a good family," Shamari said. He knew that if he had that kind of bond, he'd be fucked. Nobody was in any position to do anything for him. That was one of the reasons he was so grateful for Jada helping him out when he'd gotten that state charge. Though she wasn't faithful, she was all that he had. His sister Tangie would like to help him but she didn't have anything.

Black said, "Yeah, I look out for my family and they look out for me. Gotta look out for your people. You never know when you might need them to help you."

"So you're going to get him out?"

"I'm going to try my damnedest."

Shamari said, "Fuck! I hate that this happened. I got a little bit more of this product. What are we going to do with your boy gone?"

Black stared at Shamari like he was an idiot. "Bruh, we're going to get rid of it. We don't need him. I know a lot of hustlers. I got people that can get rid of it even faster than Kyrie. I've been hustling since I was a kid."

Shamari's cell phone rang. An unfamiliar number on the caller ID. Shamari thought about not answering it but at the last minute he decided to answer it.

"Hello."

"It's Jada."

"Who's phone you calling me from?"

"It's my phone. Picked up a new one today."

"Okay, what's up?"

"Need to see you."

"Okay, I'll head over to your room."

"You don't wanna go nowhere near that room. Trust me, boo."

"Huh?"

"Let's meet up."

"Where?"

"My mama's house."

"Man, the last time I saw your mama she shot at me, remember?"

Jada laughed and said, "It will be okay this time. Trust me."

"Okay I'll see you in an hour." Shamari terminated the call. He wondered what had happened with Jada. Why couldn't he go back to the hotel? Why did she want to meet in person? He was sure something had happened, but what?

Black said, "What's wrong, homie?"

"Damn, is it obvious?"

"Yeah, you were looking spaced and shit."

"It was Jada. She wasn't sounding right. Called me from a new number and said she didn't want to talk on the phone."

Black poured them both a shot of Henny. "You're going to need to calm yourself down."

CHAPTER 13

Louise opened the door. She was wearing a pantsuit, her hair was in a bun and her skin was glowing. She looked so much better than the last time. Louise was never a bad looking woman, but the alcohol had gotten the best of her, but today something seemed different about her. She hugged Shamari and led him to the den.

"Come on in."

Shamari was actually surprised that Jada's mother was greeting him so warmly considering she'd vowed to kill him the last time she saw him. She led him to the den and when they were seated. Shamari asked, "So, where is Charles?"

"I had to make him hit the road."

Shamari said, "But ya'll been together forever."

Louise and, "That was too long."

"What happened?"

"Nothing happened. I've been sober for about two months and I realized that I couldn't co-exist with him if he was still drinking and he didn't want to stop, so I had to kick him about."

Louise stood and made her way the kitchen, came back out with some bottled water and she gave Shamari one. "I'm sorry. I don't have any Henny."

"How do you know I drink Henny?"

"I can smell it on your breath. That's the thing about being sober, you can smell alcohol a mile away. I'd gotten so I couldn't smell it anymore."

Shamari took a sip from his water then he said, "Is it hard being sober?"

"One of the hardest things I ever had to do in my life, but it's so worth it. Shamari, I'm damn near sixty years old. I feel better than I ever did, but I'm so mad that I wasted so much time being a damn fool. Drinking and being in that dysfunctional relationship."

There was an awkward silence as Shamari examined Louise. He liked the new Louise. He wished Jada could have grown up with this woman instead of Louise the terrorist that would shoot at your head and smack the fuck out of you for taking the last beer. The one that paid the cost to be the boss.

"Jada Simone called and said that she was running late as always."

Shamari laughed, "You know your daughter."

"Yes I do, always running late and always wasting time. Which brings me to this point, I wasted a lot of time Shamari. Don't waste your life chasing money to the point that you don't live your life. Money ain't everything and if it means leaving my daughter, you do what you have to do to make your life work for you. You can't get time back."

Louise was right. Shamari knew he couldn't get time back and he wished like hell he could do some things differently. But he couldn't and now the Feds were after him trying to give him a lot of time.

The doorbell rang.

"That's Jada Simone."

Louise opened the door and hugged her daughter. "Mama, you look so good."

"Thank you, baby."

Jada followed her into the den where Shamari was waiting.

Louise said, "You two want something to eat, I fried some chicken and there is some potato salad in the fridge."

"No, I'm good," Jada said.

"Shamari?"

"No, thank you."

Louise said. "Ole red nigga, don't think you too good to eat my cooking."

Shamari was shocked at Louise, she'd been so calm before.

Louise laughed and said, "Just cuz I'm sober, don't mean I won't whip yo ass."

Then she excused herself into her bedroom. When Jada heard the door close she said. "The Feds came by my room this morning with a search warrant looking for your ass."

"Your room? How in the hell did they know I'd been there?"

Jada said, "I didn't say that they knew you'd been there, but it's not hard to find out that I was your girlfriend."

"Right."

"But that's not the point, who gives a damn how they found out? The point is they're looking for your ass and you got to do something and do something fast."

"I know."

"Did you pay your lawyer?"

"Black gave him fifty grand for me. I'm going to have to give the rest of the money to Turch soon, but he wants me to turn myself in, I can't turn myself in."

Jada looked on intently. She didn't want him to be locked up but she knew that he was only making things worse for himself.

Shamari gulped down the water in one swig. Damn he needed more Henny or something! Louise picked a great time to stop drinking.

"Jada, I can't turn myself in. I'm going to have to make some more money. I need more money. I need to make sure I'm okay."

"I don't understand. If you have enough money to pay him, why do you need to make more money?"

Shamari made eye contact and said, "Look, if I turn myself in, they're not giving me a bond and there's a chance I'll be put away for the rest of my life or they might ask for the death penalty. If that's the case, I might want to appeal. That cost money. My sister will need money. My mother will need money and you'll need money. You know my family ain't got shit!"

"You trust them with your money?"

"I trust you, Jada. I trust you with my life."

"So how can I help you, Bae?"

"I'm running out of product. You might have to travel to Cali to get some for me."

"I'll do anything for you, Mari. You've been so good to me."

"If I could go myself, I would, but I don't have an ID and I damn sure can't go. They'll identify me, maybe even in the airport. You know they have that facial recognition software."

"I don't think it's in the airports as of yet."

"That's a chance I can't take. I have to be careful."

Jada was lost in thought thinking that her worst nightmare had become a reality. Shamari was going to prison and there was not a whole lot she could do about.

Jada looked worried and Shamari noticed. "Baby, don't worry. I'm going to be okay.

Jada approached the sofa where Shamari sat and said, "I have an idea."

"I'm almost afraid to ask what it is."

CHAPTER 14

Starr's neighbor's paid her nicely for decorating their home and had gotten her two more decorating gigs from two more gay couples. The money she made from the two gigs would hold her for the next few months, but if she wanted to make this into a career, she needed more clients and she needed a showcase. Maybe Lani and Jada could come up with some extra money and they could be partners. She sat outside on her balcony sipping on a glass of wine, trying her best not to think about Trey and how her life had changed in the last few months.

Her phone rang. It was Trey. She sent him to voicemail. He called again. This time she blocked him from calling. She sipped her wine and peered out into the Atlanta night. She couldn't help but think of the good times that she'd had with Trey. All the promises he'd made. How they would start a family. How she could count on him for anything. Trey said that she completed him and she believed damn near every word he said. He'd said all the right things.

Her doorbell rang. She figured it was Mike from across the hall. He'd started coming over from time to time and while she wasn't one of those girls that liked being around gay men, she enjoyed his company. He was so funny and so goddamned rich and she was convinced that his partner was using him for money. Even Mike thought that. She found it quite amusing that even gay men could be gold-diggers. She walked to the door and looked through the peephole. It was Trey.

She didn't want to open the door but she didn't want him to make a goddamned scene, so she opened and he stepped inside.

"Thank you for allowing me to come in."

"Trey, what the hell do you want?"

"I want to talk. I want you."

Starr didn't want to get upset and she was trying her damnedest not to, but this motherfucker was making it hard. She sipped her wine.

Trey strolled over to an armchair in the living room and sat down then said, "Do you mind if I have a seat?"

"I really want you to leave, Trey. I'm in a good space right now. A very good space and I don't need the bullshit."

"What bullshit?"

"Trey. Please go."

"I wanna talk."

"About what?"

Starr eased over to a chair and sat across from him and propped her feet up on the table.

"The other night was a mistake."

Her eyebrow rose. "Oh really? Why was it a mistake?" She sipped her wine. "Was it a mistake because you weren't supposed to get caught?"

"Hell, no!"

She laughed. "Oh, you weren't?"

"No, that's not what I meant. It was a mistake that I was with her."

"Didn't look like a mistake to me. Looked like you were exactly where you were supposed to be. I mean the both of you sitting on the same side of the booth looked like a pretty cute couple, I mean if that's what you're into."

"What are you talking about?"

"Trey, actually, I should apologize."

Trey looked confused. "Why should you apologize?"

Starr stood up and disappeared onto the balcony then came back with a bottle of wine. She filled her glass up.

Again, Trey asked, "Why should you apologize?"

"You moved out. I said it was over. I shouldn't have gotten mad."

"You got mad because you're human."

"I still love you, Trey."

"Why can't we be together?" His face was sad and he was almost pleading with her.

"I gave you a chance and you fucked up. I can't let you keep breaking my heart over and over again."

"Oh, like you ain't never made a mistake?"

Starr sipped her wine. She was trying her best not to curse this silly motherfucker out. He'd violated her over and over and then had the nerve to be out in public with the skank he'd been cheating with.

Trey eased over behind her chair and began massaging her neck and said. "Come on, baby, let's work it out. "

Starr doused him with wine. "Trey, don't you ever put your goddamned hands on me!" Her face was serious and Trey realized that she meant was she said.

Starr stood up and said, "As a matter of fact, Trey, get the fuck out of here!"

She'd tried to keep her composure but she couldn't help but think of him at the restaurant with that ho and now he had the motherfucking nerve to come back over here like she would welcome him back with open arms.

Starr stood up and set the wine glass on the table. She grabbed Trey by the arm and led him to the door and let him out but before she could close the door, Trey stopped it with his foot.

"I'm gonna call the police"

"You would call the police on me?"

"If you don't leave, I will."

Trey chuckled and said, "Ok, so your daddy was once the biggest dope dealer in Atlanta and now you're calling the police?"

"This is a domestic case, nigga. This ain't no drug conspiracy, so please don't try and use that psychology bullshit on me."

A random white dude walked pass the condo and he glanced over and saw Trey's foot holding the door. He gave them a fake smile and kept walking. Though he appeared to be minding his business, Trey knew the man would possibly call the police.

Trey stared at Starr for thirty more seconds. He could sense the hurt she felt. He finally moved his foot and the door closed in his face.

CHAPTER 15

It was around 7:30 p.m. and Black, along with Kyrie's wife, Melody, were at the bondsman office discussing how much money and property it would take to get Kyrie out of jail. Black received a call from Nana. He answered on the first ring and said, "Let me call you back."

"Tyrann, don't hang up that damn phone. This is important."

Black turned to the bondsman and Melody and said, "I need to take this call." He stepped outside the office.

Nana said, "You damn right you better take this call!"

"What's going on?"

"Somebody snatched up Man-Man!"

Man-Man was Black's nine year old son. He was also Black's oldest. Black knew damn well nobody better put their goddamned hands on Man-Man or any of his kids for matter.

"What do you mean somebody snatched him up?"

"Man-Man was out there skating on the sidewalk and all of a sudden I heard Tierany screaming at the top of her lungs. I came out to see what she was screaming for and she said a blue van pulled up and two men got out and grabbed Man-Man. They put him in the back of the van and drove off."

Black said, "What the fuck?!"

"Tierany tried to get the tag number, but the van didn't have a license plate on it."

Black said calmly, "Look, I'm taking care of something. I will be home in about an hour." He terminated the call.

When Black entered the office, everyone looked at him as if they wanted to know what was going on. Black knew he had to keep his composure. He had to give them the impression that he had everything under control.

Melody said, "Is everything okay?"

Black said, "Yeah, just a little problem with my kids."

After Melody signed the paperwork to free Kyrie, Black dashed to Lani's house.

Lani was surprised to see Black show up unannounced. She had just showered and hadn't had a chance to put her clothes on so she covered herself fully before opening the door. She didn't want Black to think that he was going to get any sex. Though she hadn't cooperated with the police, she wasn't pleased that he'd had Chris murdered. And to make matters worse, he'd lied to her about it.

Black said, "Why haven't you been answering your phone?"

Lani said, "I haven't received any calls from you."

"I've called you like 20 times."

Lani picked up her phone. She had eight missed calls. She stepped into the kitchen and he followed. She grabbed a handful of almonds and a banana. She hadn't eaten anything all day and that would have to hold her until she could grab some lunch.

"Shit has gone from bad to worse."

"What are you talking about now, Tyrann?"

Black grabbed a seat at the barstool. "Man-man got kidnapped and I know that punk ass Kenny-Boo and Chris's brother had something to do with it."

Lani ate the almonds and said, "Why do you say that?"

Black avoided eye contact with her and said, "I know. That's all I'm gonna say."

"How do you know?"

Black picked up a banana and peeled it before stuffing it whole in his mouth and said, "Well, I had a run in with Kenny-Boo."

"What the fuck is a run in?"

"Look, Lani, ain't no time to be judging me now! My goddamned son is gone and I gotta bring him back home!"

"Who's judging you, Tyrann? I just asked you a question. What do you mean by a run in?"

"I'd been hearing about this clown-ass dude Kenny-Boo saying that he was going to get me, so I paid him a visit."

"What happened?"

Black said, "Well nobody got hurt."

"If nobody got hurt, why do you think he kidnapped Man-Man?"

"I just know. I need you to call Chris's brother."

"Look, Black, that man's brother is dead. I hate to say it but I don't think he gives a fuck about your son."

Black ate another banana and he grabbed a bottle of water from the counter, unscrewed it and took a swig.

"Just call him!"

"I'm not going to call him. I feel bad for you, but there is no way I'm bothering him. I don't wanna be in the middle of this shit any longer. I think you need to call the cops."

"That's against everything I stand for."

"What you stand for is stupidity and ignorance. Your son's life is in danger and you don't want to call the police? How long do you think you can live this goddamned renegade lifestyle?"

Black said, "All that I have done for you and your family and you can't do this one thing for me? What the fuck? Goddamned, you are so selfish!"

Black's phone rang. The caller ID said, Baby-Mama #2. Man-Man and Tierany's mama. He thought seriously about not answering it. He didn't want to hear her goddamned mouth.

"What's up, Asia?"

"What's up, my ass! All I know is you need to find out what is going on with my son before I go to the police and tell him all about yo stupid ass."

"Wait a minute. How you figure I got something to do with what happened to him?" Although Black knew damn well Man-Man was abducted because of his beef with Chris and Mike, Asia didn't need to know that.

"Black, I ain't got time for this bullshit. You got five hours to bring my son back or else I'm calling the police. And I'm telling them everything I know about you."

She terminated the call.

Black took another swig of water and then got on his knees and said, "Please call Chris's brother? Please, I need you."

Lani dialed Mike's number and he answered on the third ring and said, "Tell yo boy he needs to give you two hundred and fifty large and everything will be okay."

Lani said to Black, "They want two hundred and fifty thousand."

"What? Those niggas are crazy!"

Mike said to Lani, "Lil' man is okay. He's playing Madden with Tater, eating hot dogs." Then he called Man-Man and he put him on the phone.

"Hey, Miss Lani."

"Hey, Man-Man."

"Tell my daddy and Nana and Tierany that I'm okay."

Mike was back on the phone. "Two hundred and fifty large by the morning." He terminated the call.

Lani said. "Two hundred and fifty grand."

Black looked defeated. "Damn!"

He stood up and said, "I'll go get the money. I need you to take it to them."

"I don't wanna be in the middle of this."

"But you are in the middle of this, whether you like it or not."

"No I'm not!"

"Look, can you take him the money I need my boy back safely."

"Why don't you call the police?"

"I already told you I don't believe in using the police to solve my problems and plus as much shit as I've done in my life, I'm the last one that should be calling the police."

Lani didn't say anything. She ate her banana thinking this had to be the dumbest logic she'd ever heard but it made perfect logic to him.

"Lani?"

"What do you want?"

"What kind of person is Mike?"

"Why?"

"Do you think he would hurt my son?"

"No, but Mike is in debt with the Mexicans because of what you took from Chris."

"I'll be back with the money."

CHAPTER 16

Jada met Craig at his office, it was after hours and the rest of the staff had gone home for the evening. Craig smiled when he saw her. He called her into his office in the back and she sat across from his desk. He said, "Can I get you anything to drink?"

"No."

"So what brings you here?"

"I just thought I'd come by to see you. You know to talk."

"About what?"

"About us."

Craig, now resting his chin in the palm of his hand, figured that she must have blown that twenty-five grand and wanted some more money. That probably explained why her cleavage was so prominently on display.

"I thought about what you'd said about us starting over. I would like for us to start over."

"Me too. I missed you."

"Really?"

"Of course."

"Well, you damn sure don't act like it."

"I know, but I do."

She licked her lips and he realized one of things that he really missed about her was her amazing oral abilities.

She unbuttoned her blouse and those perfect tatas were displayed. He wanted to sandwich his dick between them.

Jada made her way to the other side of the desk when they heard a knock on the door.

He thought about his wife. Maybe she'd been watching him. He dialed her number. "Hello, honey. Just called to let you know I'll be late for dinner."

"Okay, no problem. Just text me when you're on your way."

He ended the call as he wondered who in the hell could be knocking at the door.

Jada buttoned up her blouse.

Craig headed to the door. He saw a man in a custodian uniform. Damn, he'd tell the man that he wouldn't need any cleaning today and could just clean the offices tomorrow. He opened the door and as soon as he was about to speak, the man pulled out a handgun and aimed at him. "Okay, Dr., you need to step back inside."

"What the hell is going on?"

Jada ran out of the office.

Craig yelled, "Dial 911!"

The janitor slapped the fuck out of him with the gun.

Jada said, "Nobody is calling no goddamned police over here, white boy!"

Craig took a closer look and realized it was Jada's drug-dealing boyfriend. He was surely about to get murdered and there was nothing he could do about it. He thought about his wife and how she would react to this and his eight-year-old son who would be without a father.

"What do you want?"

Shamari pushed him back and said, "Let's go to the back and don't say a goddamn thing unless I tell you."

"You know we're on camera, right?"

Shamari smacked Craig in the back of his head with the gun. "Shut the fuck up!"

Jada said, "Those cameras don't work. He's told me this many times."

Craig said, "So, Jada, this is how you repay me for all I've done for you?"

This pissed Shamari off more and he slapped the fuck out of Craig again, this time with his fists. He didn't want to knock him unconscious. He needed him and knocking him out cold would not help his situation.

They entered Craig's office and Shamari sat behind his desk. Opened the drawer and just as he thought, there was a gun there. A chrome 9mm nine millimeter. He unloaded it and asked, "Any more weapons in here?"

Jada buttoned her shirt up as Craig stared but didn't say a thing. There were so many things that he wanted ask her. Why was she doing this to him? What did they want? Did they want more money? Were they going to extort him or worse, rob him? He glanced at Shamari, the gun was still in his hand. He wanted to make a run for it, but there was no way he could outrun Shamari. Was this revenge? He wanted to ask but he didn't want to get the shit slapped out of him again or worse shot.

Jada finished with her blouse and she sat on the desk. Craig sat in the chair that Jada had been sitting in before Shamari showed up.

Shamari said, "We're not going to hurt you, but we need your help."

"Help with what? What do you want? Money? I don't have any cash and the bank is closed."

"I don't need money."

"What do you want?" Craig asked without fear of getting cracked upside his head. Shamari had spoken to him so he assumed it was okay to have a conversation.

"I need a new look."

"What do you mean?"

Jada said, "Look, the police are after him and he needs a new face. I don't know maybe some cheek implants. Chin implants? A new nose?"

Craig laughed and said, "You can't be serious!"

Shamari showed Craig the barrel of the gun. "Do you think I'm playing?"

"N-N-No."

"Okay, do you think you can help me?"

Craig looked at Jada. "You know I deal with mostly boobs and buns. Dr. Phillman does all the facial procedures."

Jada said, "But you've done facial surgeries before?"

Craig nodded. "I have."

Shamari leaned across the desk and snatched Craig up by his collar and pressed the gun against his temple.

Jada said, "Mari, put that gun away!"

She was nervous that the thing would go off. Though she wanted to help Shamari, she still cared a lot about Craig. Even though he had his issues, she thought he was a decent person and she didn't want that gun to go off accidentally and kill him.

Shamari lowered the gun.

Craig said, "Then there's the matter of anesthesia. I'll have to apply anesthesia."

"Can you do it?"

"I can, but I don't usually do this and I'm not the best at it."

"You're going to do it, motherfucker!" Shamari said.

"My wife is going to be calling."

"And we'll let you answer the phone and assure her that nothing is wrong." Shamari said.

"But what will I say?"

"Your motherfuckin' problem, not mine," Shamari said. "If you can do it, I'm going to need you to do it now."

"Right now!"

"Three procedures before morning."

"Morning? I have to be home tonight."

"You're not going home tonight until you do what I need done."

Craig stared at Jada then back at Shamari and realized that they were serious.

"Let me get my scrubs."

Shamari grinned and said, "That a boy."

CHAPTER 17

One of Trey's stash houses was located in Dunwoody. It was an emergency stash house and nobody was supposed to know about it except him, Starr, and his mother. His mother had never been there, but she had the address and he'd given her instructions on where to go to find the money if he was ever locked up. Starr was left in charge of getting him out of jail and getting him an attorney if anything ever went wrong. In case they were both locked up on some serious charges, Trey's mother would be the one that would go retrieve the money and hire the attorneys.

It was 7:13 pm and the sun had just gone down when Starr drove up into the driveway of the Dunwoody home, a regular two story home in a middle class subdivision, nothing extravagant. Trey's home was actually the smallest one on the street and he was the only one that was renting.

A young girl and her teenage boyfriend sat outside on the hood of a blue car making out. The young couple looked to be in their early twenties. Starr got out of the car and approached the doorstep of the house when they came up behind her. The girl said, "Hey, just wanted to tell you those workout tips you gave me really helped."

Starr turned and met the eyes of the young girl. The girl said, "Oh, I thought you were somebody else." The girl blushed as if she was embarrassed. She was a beautiful girl, tall and thin with a flawless complexion, and the cheekbones of a model.

Starr smiled and said, "That's okay."

"Oh I remember you. You were working in L.A., right?"

"Yes, from time to time." When Starr and Trey first began renting the home, they'd told the neighbors that they were in the music business and lived between Atlanta and L.A. They'd been renting the home for almost six years. Starr remembered the young woman when she was a lanky teen wearing braces.

Starr said, "Brooke, right?"

The woman smiled and said, "Yeah. I'm sorry. I don't remember your name."

"Starr."

Brooke's boyfriend stood behind her looking impatient and Starr got the feeling that she was blocking something important to him.

Brooke said, "The other woman that came here must have been your sister."

Starr looked confused as hell.

"The other day, Mr. Trey came here with a woman and she gave me some exercise tips."

"Really?"

The young man said, "Brooke, come on. Let the woman go inside her home."

Brooke said, "Good to see you again."

Starr said, "Likewise." She turned the key to enter the house. When Starr entered the home, it looked exactly as she remembered it. Nothing was out of place. She entered the main bedroom and just as she thought, the bed was unmade. Trey had been here and so had Shantelle according to Brooke. Who else could have given her exercise tips, but she wasn't going to worry about that shit anymore. She entered the bedroom where the safe was located. She entered the combination and counted out five hundred thousand dollars. She wouldn't keep it all, but this was more than enough to pay for a showroom for her design business and get her office supplies. She would return the rest to Trey, but she would make his trifling-ass sweat.

*   *   *

Nana slapped the fuck out of Black as soon as he entered her home.

"What's your problem?" Black said as he held his jaw.

"No, what the hell is wrong with you? Putting that baby's life in jeopardy with your shit, Tyrann. You know it took everything in my power not to call the police?"

Though Nana was in her eighties, 5'4 and weighed only 115 lbs on a good day, she could be mean as a pit bull. She was the only one that would stand up to Black. She was the only one who could hit him and get away with it. He would never raise his hand to her. He had that much respect for the woman that had raised him.

"Tyrann, I want you to bring that baby back home. I don't care how you got to do it." She lit a cigarette. Nana smoked only when she was upset. A pack would last her a month or two.

"I'm already working on it."

"Working on it, my ass! I want that baby home or I'm going to call the police."

"Nobody needs to call the police." He looked his Nana in her eyes and said, "I swear to you he'll be home tomorrow."

Nana grabbed Black by the collar and pounded on his chest. "Now we're going to have to move. We can't live in this house with you out there doing dumb shit and people bringing this bullshit to our house."

"I'll get you a new house. Don't worry."

"No, you need to sit your ass down!"

"Huh?"

"Find something else to do. I'm tired of going through all this bullshit with you, Tyrann. Last time when yo ass was up in that hospital, I spent all day praying over you and the Lord delivered you from this shit. And this is what I get?"

Black said, "This is going to be fixed. Don't worry. Lani spoke to Man-man. He's okay."

"Lani spoke to him?"

"Yeah, I don't want to get all into it."

"Tyrann, what is going on? I know something is going on. Something ain't right. Your friends coming to my house in the middle of the night, and then the police pulling up behind you the other day."

"Huh?"

Nana puffed her cigarette. "Huh, my ass. You think I didn't see you talking to the cops the other day when you came over."

Black didn't think anybody saw him. "You mean they were *trying* to talk to me."

"Whatever! I don't care how you put it. I might be old, but don't nothing get past me."

"I almost forgot about that."

"I'm sure you did." Nana took another drag. "What the hell did they want?"

"They were asking about a shooting that took place on the other end of the street."

"Ain't no damn shooting take place over here, Tyrann. This is a quiet neighborhood. We are the only people here with a lot of drama going on."

The door opened and Black's sister, Rashida, and his children's mother, Asia, barged into the house.

Though Asia's parents were African American, Asia's eyes were slightly slanted which was the reason her mother named her Asia. She was a short, lighter skinned black woman, with thick lips and though she didn't have hips, her body was very satisfying.

Asia spotted Black and attempted to slap him before he caught her hand. He tried to restrain her and Asia kicked him in the shin and right in his groin. He released her.

"Keep your goddamned hands off me!" Black said.

Asia swung at Black again and missed him. Rashida wedged herself between them.

Asia said, "I don't give a fuck about you, nigga. You think I'm going to let you put my son's life in danger and not do nothing? Fuck you!"

"He's my son too."

"I swear to God if I don't get my baby back, you are going down. I can't stand yo' black ass!"

"Fuck you!"

Nana said, "Watch yo mouth!" Though she'd been cussing since Man-Man had gotten abducted, she wasn't about to be disrespected by Black. Asia would get a pass today, only because she was the mother of a child went missing.

Rashida turned to Black and said, "Please tell me this didn't have nothing to do with you?"

"Sis, I don't need you all over my ass too. I'm going to make it right."

Rashida shook her head and dragged Black into the next room. "What the hell happened?" she asked.

"I had some problems with some niggas, but it's gonna be okay. I'm gonna get my son back. I swear."

Rashida stood looking at her brother. She was fed up with his bullshit.

"Look, Tyrann, you need to grow up man. Grow the fuck up!"

"I am grown. I swear, sis, I'm going to make it right."

"Look, I had to convince Asia not to go to the police."

"And tell them what?"

"Tell them that she think that her son has been kidnapped only because the kidnappers were trying to get back at you."

"I can't stand that bitch!"

"You've done lost ya mind. This woman has lost her baby and if she goes to the police, I can't say that I blame her."

"He's my son too."

Rashida saw there was no reasoning with her brother. He was missing the whole point. He would never understand how a mother feels about losing a baby. He couldn't possibly understand. He was a man. "Look, Tyrann, you need to bring that baby back and bring him back safely."

Nana yelled, "Tyrann, come here!"

Seconds later he heard Asia yelling. "Bitch, I'll kill you!"

Black's heart sank as he thought that he would have to fuck this stupid chick up if she laid hands on his grandmother.

Black and Rashida ran into the living room and found Lani and Asia both holding each other's hair.

Asia screamed, "Let my hair go!"

Lani said, "I ain't gonna let a motherfuckin' thing go! You are the one that put your hands on me first!"

Black grabbed Lani and Rashida restrained Asia.

"I don't know what this bitch's problem is," Lani said.

Nana said, "I was telling Asia that Lani had spoken to Man-Man on the phone."

Asia said, "That's all I needed to know, to know that bitch had something to do with it."

Lani said, "I'm going to be the one that gets him back"

Black released Lani and approached Asia who was still being restrained by Rashida and said, "You need to calm the fuck down."

Asia said, "No, you need to bring my goddamned son home or I swear I'm going to the police!"

Nana backhanded Black and said, "I don't wanna see yo black ass again until that baby is home. I swear, Tyrann. You are the reason all this shit is going on. You, Tyrann!" Nana's finger jabbed him in the middle of his chest.

Black said, "I'm leaving."

He headed out the door and Lani trailed him.

CHAPTER 18

Trey called Starr and she sent him straight to voicemail. He called her three more times but she didn't answer then finally he sent her a text.

Trey: *Call me, it's important.*

Starr: *What's wrong?*

Trey: *Call me please.*

Starr: *What do you want?*

Trey: *Did you take my money?*

Starr: *Maybe.*

Trey: *You need to give me my money back now!! And quit playing these silly-ass games.*

Starr: *I'm playing games? LOL whatever.*

Trey called her again. This time she answered. "Hello?"

"I need you to give me my goddamned money, Starr, and quit playing with me."

"Whatever, Trey."

"Starr, that's not your money. It's mine and you need to give me my shit back."

"You know what, Trey? The way I look at it is we were married, you cheated and I'm just getting what was mine."

She laughed and this was pissing him the fuck off, but he knew that he had to play it cool because he didn't want her to do nothing stupid. Right now, he was at her mercy.

"Starr, can we talk about it?"

"There is nothing to talk about. You made your decision."

"I'm not with her."

"You'll say anything to get your money back."

"Starr, I love you."

"You love me or you love the money?"

"Hey, I left you the condo, and I paid the rent up for a year, what else did you expect me to do?"

"I expected you to be faithful." She laughed a wicked laugh and then said, "But you are not capable of that, are you?"

"Look, I need my goddamned money!"

"Who the fuck are you cursing at?"

Trey knew he was pissing her off. This was the last thing he wanted to do. "Look, I'm sorry for everything I've done to you. I really am."

"Whatever, Trey."

"What do you want me to say? What do you want me to do?"

"I don't want you to do anything."

"I'm coming to get my money."

"Trey, don't come over here. I swear to God I will call the police."

She terminated the call.

Seconds later, her father, Ace, called.

"Hey, Daddy."

"What's going on with you and Trey?"

"What do you mean?"

"He called me and told me to talk some sense into you."

"Trey has a problem with sleeping around. One thing I can't take is an unfaithful-ass man. I despise them." Soon as she said that she realized that she might have offended her father who had cheated on her mother on multiple occasions and even fathered a child outside of their marriage. She didn't intend to offend him but if she did, it was okay. Even though she was young when it happened, she remembered how devastated her mother had been when she learned that Ace got another woman pregnant.

"Look, baby! What Trey did was wrong, but you need to give that man his money back. That money don't belong to you."

"The hell it don't."

"Trey told me that he would give you some of the money. He agreed that you deserved something."

"Glad he agreed. I deserve what I have and I'm keeping it."

"Look, baby. You're going to get me in trouble because if this nigga comes after you for this money, I'm going to have to kill him and you know I will."

There was no doubt in Starr's mind that her father would kill Trey or any man that tried to harm her but she was going to make sure it didn't come to that. She was going to give Trey most of the money back. But not right now.

*   *   *

Craig had completed three procedures on Shamari and his face was bandaged. He was still asleep under the influence of the anesthesia. Craig said he needed to rest up for a few days.

Jada said, "We're going to need some pain pills. We need a prescription."

"I can't give a prescription in his name. I thought you said he was on the run."

"Make it in my name."

"I can't do that either. I don't want to lose my license to practice. They are so strict nowadays."

"So what the fuck is he supposed to do? Just suffer in pain?"

"Motrin."

"Motrin, my ass. What do you have around here?"

Craig gave her twenty Percocet's. "This is all I can give you."

Jada put them in her purse. Craig came back with a wheelchair and said, "Help me get him in the chair."

Jada said, "You're a grown man. You pick him up and put him in the chair. I gotta make sure you don't try no bullshit."

"What are you talking about? I've performed the surgeries. I just wanna go home to my wife and son. It's late."

Craig stood Shamari up. Shamari was still groggy. "What's going on?"

Jada said, "Baby, we need you to get in the wheelchair."

He walked to the wheelchair by himself and then passed out again.

"Why, Jada?"

"Why what?"

"Why do you love this man so much?"

Jada never realized that she loved Shamari. She didn't think that she loved him but there was no denying that though she shared her body with other men, he had her mind. He'd done so much for her and though their love was dysfunctional on so many levels it was true on so many other levels.

"Now is not the time for silly-ass questions."

Craig wheeled Shamari to Jada's car that was parked in the back of his office. He picked Shamari up over his shoulder and laid him in the backseat of the car. Jada drove away. She would take him to a Marriott in Sandy Springs. She had paid the bill for three weeks. She would stay with him for a few days, but she'd found a townhome that she liked in Marietta.

CHAPTER 19

Kyrie was now out of jail and he met Black over at Lani's house. Black gave him a hug as soon as he came into the house. "Damn! I'm glad to be out of that motherfucker, homie."

"I'm glad for you too," Black said.

"You sure as hell don't sound like you glad."

Black said, "Look, man, my goddamned son got kidnapped. I'm sorry I can't throw you no welcome home party, but I got other shit on my mind."

"Your son? Which one? Who did it?"

"Man-Man," Black said.

Kyrie entered Lani's living room and sat on a sectional.

Black said, "Chris's brother had something to do with it."

Lani entered the living room wearing some white shorts that were gripping her ass and highlighting a camel-toe. Ordinarily Kyrie wouldn't have paid any attention to Lani. She was Black's woman, but he'd just spent three days in jail and hadn't seen an attractive woman. He stole a couple of looks.

Kyrie said, "Chris's brother?"

"Yeah," Black said.

Lani stood at the bar in the kitchen providing Kyrie an excellent view of her ass. He was about to say something but he lost his train of thought.

Black said, "They want two hundred and fifty thousand dollars and they will return my son."

"You believe that shit?"

Lani turned and Kyrie eyes were now on the camel toe. "I'm going to get him in a few hours."

Kyrie turned to Black. "Why don't you go snatch up one of his relatives? Fuck! I wouldn't give him shit."

"Look, man, this is my son you're talking about. I ain't 'bout to make a situation worse."

"So you're gonna give this clown two hundred and fifty stacks?"

Black said, "I'll give up everything I got for one of my family members, nigga. We are all we have."

"Don't do it."

Black turned to Lani and said, "Show this motherfucker the door before I slap the fuck out him."

Kyrie said, "Look, Black, I'm sorry. I want Man-Man back too."

"Well shut the fuck up then. My mind is made up. I'm giving them the money."

*   *   *

Trey lay on the bed playing Ruzzle on his iPhone, trying not to think about everything that had happened to him in the last few weeks. First, his woman had left him, now she betrayed him by doubling back and taking his stash. Shantelle entered wearing a microscopic red-string and six inch stripper heels that made her long legs look amazing. Trey could smell that vanilla scent that always drove him wild.

She knew Trey loved her legs, but she knew that he really loved her mouthful of breasts. He'd said before that she had the "prettiest titties that he'd ever seen." They were natural, and though she was in her thirties, they still didn't have any sag. She noticed Trey still had not looked up from his phone when she entered. She made her way to the bed where he was lying and removed the phone from his hand. She placed Trey's hand on her ass and he grinned.

"Whatever you're doing on that phone can wait."

"You're right." He smiled, harsher than before.

There was an iPad lying on the lamp stand, she opened the Spotify app. Rihanna and Chris Brown's "*Birthday Cake*" played and she shook her ass. Cake- Cake -Cake came blaring though the Bluetooth speaker set that sat on the desk.

He sat up and his dick stood to attention. She moved closer and placed his hands on her cake. He snatched that tiny-ass g-string down with his teeth almost ripping it. Her pussy, usually bald, had just a hint of hair. She'd gotten a landing strip wax. He preferred bald, but he never complained about well groomed hair down there as long as it was fresh and clean and it was. Goddamn this woman looked fantastic.

She bit down on his ear and said, "Come and put your name on it, Trey." She mocked the song.

"Oh my name ain't already on it?"

"Maybe." She opened her legs just a little and she stood in front of him naked.

He pulled her into him and he began to lick her pussy gently. She grabbed the back of his head. He licked her clit slow and carefully and she was enjoying the hell out it.

"Suck my clit, Trey. You know I like my clit to be sucked," she cried.

He sucked it and this drove her crazy. She fell on the bed beside him and he lifted her legs until they were spread like a field goal post. He kept sucking and licking and finally she said, "Trey, what are you waiting on? I need you inside me. Put that big dick inside me, daddy."

Trey removed his boxer's and his dick was now limp. She reached for it and she could tell it was not hard. She frowned and said, "What's wrong, baby?"

"Nothing."

"Something is wrong, Trey. You're always hard. Even at your age you're hard all the goddamned time."

"My age?"

"Well, Trey, you are almost 40. I didn't mean it like that. I meant it to be a compliment. But what's wrong, Trey? What the fuck is going on? I don't turn you on no more?"

"Of course you do!"

"I don't believe it."

Trey got up and put his boxer's back on. With the remote lying on the nightstand, she lowered volume of the speakers.

"Well, I've had some problems lately."

"Let me guess. Starr?"

"Yeah."

Shantelle was now pissed the fuck off. The nerve of this motherfucker having the audacity to admit he was thinking about his ex and furthermore this was the reason that she couldn't get some good dick. She stood and disappeared into the bathroom showered, and returned wearing a pair of bikini panties. She'd wrapped her hair since there was no chance of her getting any dick. Trey had started playing Ruzzle on his phone again.

She tried not to talk about it but the silence in the room was just too much for her to deal with. "So you're not going to tell me what happened?"

"What do you want to know?"

"What happened with you and Starr."

Trey didn't want to tell Shantelle what Starr had done. He didn't feel comfortable telling anybody though he figured what Starr had done to him was really fucked up. He didn't feel like putting Shantelle in his business but he needed to talk to somebody.

"Talk to me, Trey."

Trey said, "You remember the house I took you to in Dunwoody?"

"The place where I offered the young girl the workout tips?"

"Yeah, that place."

"Well, that was a stash spot."

"Really?"

"Yeah." Trey turned away from her gaze. It was difficult for him to show Starr in a bad light even though, what she had done was so wrong."

"Somebody broke in?"

"Yes and no."

"Starr had someone rob the house?"

"Not exactly."

"Will you please tell me what the fuck happened?!"

Trey looked at her like she'd lost her goddamned mind. "First of all, I'm a grown-ass man!." He pointed his finger at her and said, "Don't fucking curse me because I don't curse you!"

Shantelle said, "You're right. I'm sorry."

Trey took several deep breaths to calm down. When he was calm he said, "Starr took some money from my stash house."

"What? Are you serious?"

"Yes. I wish I wasn't, but I am."

"How much did she take?"

"That's not important."

"Not important or you don't want me to know?"

"What difference does it make?"

"You're right. How do you know it was her?"

"She admitted it."

"I can't believe that bitch. I bet you them ghetto-ass friends of hers helped her. None of them chicks had any class. Decorated hood rats, that's all they are. You can have all the Gucci bags you want, but money can't buy class."

Trey wanted to tell her to shut the fuck up but he'd just told her not to curse him. So he would pay her the same respect. "I think she's going to give me the money back."

"Hmmph. You think so? I'm not so confident. Don't ever put your confidence in a hood rat."

"We got history together. She's going to give my money back."

"If she cared about history, she wouldn't have taken it in the first place."

"I don't want to talk about it anymore."

"Fine. I just wanted to know what was wrong with you."

"Well that's what's wrong."

"Are you broke?"

"No." Then Trey wanted to know why in hell she wanted to know if he was broke, but he wasn't stupid. He knew that if he didn't have money, there would be no way a woman like Shantelle would be with him. Just the fact that she wanted to know if he was broke screamed gold digger.

"That was just plain wrong what she did."

"Look, I don't wanna talk about her anymore. I told you that already."

She sat beside him and removed his dick from his underwear and licked the head of his cock before taking him deep inside her mouth.

CHAPTER 20

Mike's apartment was located in Buckhead. He'd told Lani to meet him at 7:30. It was 7.33 when Lani exited the elevator on the eleventh floor and wheeled a big suitcase to apartment 1109. She tapped lightly on the door. Kenny-Boo answered the door, looking uglier than she remembered.

One of his eyes was on her breast and the other was looking down at her feet. Not only were they crossed, they were red as a tomato. She thought he'd been drinking until she smelled the marijuana stench. He licked his lips, not in a flirtatious way, but because they were dry as fuck. God, she wanted to throw up.

"Where's Mike?"

Mike heard Lani's voice and said, "Let her in."

Kenny Boo stepped aside and Lani entered. She waved at Tater who was sitting on the sofa engaged in a conversation on his cell phone. Man-Man approached Lani and hugged her. "Hey, Miss Lani."

Lani was surprised that Man-Man remembered how she looked. She hadn't seen the kid in close to two years and she was almost certain he'd seen his father with multiple women. But she use to enjoy spending time with Man-Man and his sister Tierany. Out of all of Black's kids, they were the ones she had been the closest to because they would often be at Nana's place. Lani kissed Man-Man on the forehead. "Hey, baby!"

"Where is my Daddy?"

"I came to get you and take you back to your daddy."

Man-Man smiled and said, "Thank you, Miss Lani."

Mike said, "Go back in the room and play your video games. Me and Miss Lani gotta talk."

Man-Man looked at Lani as if he didn't want to do what Mike said.

Lani said, "How have they been treating you?"

Man-Man said, "First, I was having fun. You know, we played video games and ate pizza and stuff, but I miss Tierany."

Lani said, "Go back in the room and play. We'll be ready to go in a few minutes."

"Promise?"

"I promise."

Man-Man looked at Kenny-Boo and Mike before going to the room.

Lani said, "What have ya'll done to this child?"

Mike said, "You know me better than to harm a child."

"I know."

Kenny-Boo said, "Besides, he's the meal ticket."

Lani looked at Kenny-Boo but didn't say anything to him. She didn't have shit to say to him. She'd wish he would go somewhere else or at least shut the fuck up, but she couldn't tell him that, not right now."

"So where's the money?" Mike asked.

Lani presented him with the suitcase. Kenny-Boo scooped it up and carried it to the sofa. When Kenny unzipped the bag there were bundles of cash.

Mike stared at Lani. "Is it all there or are we going to have to count it?"

"It's there. I helped him count it."

"Zip the bag back up."

Kenny-Boo's bloodshot eyes danced, one stared at Mike and the other was on the cash. Then the eye that had been on the money was now on Lani's ass. He liked her ass but he hated her. Finally he said, "You trust her?"

Mike said, "Zip the goddamned suitcase up."

"Whatever, you're the boss."

"I know I'm the motherfuckin' boss," Mike said. Then he said to Lani, "We got a problem."

Lani looked confused. What kind of goddamn problem could he be talking about? She brought the money and expected to take Man-Man home. Kenny-Boo looked confused. He even managed to have both of his eyes beam in on Mike. Obviously whatever the problem was, Mike hadn't discussed it with him.

Lani said, "What's wrong?"

"Yeah, what's wrong?" Kenny-Boo asked.

"Tell Black that we're going to have to have 50 more stacks."

"Huh?"

"That wasn't the agreement. You told that man that you was going to give him his son back for two hundred and fifty stacks."

"Who's going to bring my goddamned brother back?!" Mike shouted.

Then Kenny-Boo said, "Who the fuck is going to bring his brother back?"

Mike said, "My brother's life is worth more than two hundred and fifty thousand dollars. Don't you think?"

Lani said, "I loved your brother."

"Really? Well if you loved my brother, you would help me get 50 grand more."

"Actually we should get a hundred stacks. For what them niggas did to me," said Kenny-Boo.

Lani said, "What is he talking about?"

Mike laughed and said, "They stripped him butt-naked and dropped him off on the interstate."

"Huh?" Maybe that's what Black meant by a run-in. Once again he'd proven he was a grown-ass boy that wanted to keep shit going.

Mike said, "This ain't about you, Kenny-Boo. This is about my brother. Tell Black I need 50 more G's and I'll let his son go with you."

CHAPTER 21

Starr had just gotten dressed and was about to make a quick dash to the mall, when her intercom buzzed. She pressed the button. "Who is it?"

"It's me, Troy."

"Who?"

"Troy, Trey's brother."

Troy was Trey's half-brother. What the fuck did he want? She hadn't seen him in years. Suddenly he pops up at her house. He probably wanted the money.

She would let him in, but she'd made up her mind that she wasn't giving that money back until she felt like giving it up.

She remembered him as being a bit corny. He'd graduated from Morehouse and was now a pharmacist. He was a very handsome guy but was not a street guy at all. Trey never cared too much for him because he thought his father left him and his mother to fend for themselves and did more for Troy and his mother.

Starr knew she could just tell him to get lost and he would. She let him in and seconds later, he stood in her doorway. Troy wore a very metrosexual looking light blue V-Neck sweater exposing his muscular frame and contrasted against his chocolate skin. He was tall with wavy hair and perfect teeth. Starr thought goddamned this man is fine. Too bad he was a cornball and she'd been fucking his brother. She invited him in.

Troy said, "This place is amazing. Who decorated it?"

"I did," said Starr.

"I don't believe you."

"I did. I swear to you."

Then Troy looked at his sweater and said. "This color scheme kind of matches my sweater."

"No it don't." Starr laughed. "A man wearing a Tiffany blue sweater."

"Kinda gay, huh?"

"Very gay."

Troy laughed and asked, "Do you mind if I have a seat?"

"Not at all."

Troy sat on the loveseat and Starr sat on the sofa across from him.

"So, Troy, what brings you over?"

"I spoke to Jessica and she told me that you and Trey had broken up."

"Yeah, well it was something that didn't work out. I still have love for him and always will."

"That's a shame."

"So, is that what you came over here for?"

"No."

"Why are you here?"

"I just came to say you deserve better."

Starr looked at Troy and wondered what the fuck was his angle. Was he trying to trick her into giving him the money back by being the nice guy? If they thought that shit was going to work, they were sadly mistaken.

"I do deserve better and that's why I left."

Troy licked his lips and said, "Trey didn't know what he had."

Starr looked at him like he was crazy as hell. "So what do you think Trey had?"

"Well, I don't know you like he knows you obviously, but I always found you to be loyal."

"You don't know me. I've only seen you a few times. Look, Troy, I got somewhere to be going." Starr stood and said, "So when are you going to ask me for the money?"

"What money?"

"Trey's money."

Troy looked confused as hell. He had no idea what she was talking about.

She walked toward the door and was hoping he took the hint. She could feel him staring at her ass and it made her very uncomfortable. She knew her ass looked amazing in those tights that she was wearing but it wasn't for Trey's brother eyes.

She turned to Troy who was licking his lips suggestively and said, "I'm about to leave. You need to go."

He stood up and made his way over to the door and handed her a business card. He said, "Keep in touch. I can send some business your way."

While Shamari was lying in the room recovering from his surgery, Jada had some business that she needed to handle. It was 4:30 in the morning and Jada was sitting at the Waffle House on Piedmont Avenue when Skyy and another dancer walked in.

Skyy didn't recognize Jada and as soon as she sat in the booth on the other side of the Waffle House, Jada removed her five inch wedges and slapped the fuck out of Skyy. When the other girl tried to stand up, Jada slapped the hell out of her too and then smacked her with the napkin holder.

The manager came running from behind the counter and said, "I'm calling the police."

Jada said, "Call the goddamned police!"

Skyy said, "Jada, I'm sorry for what I did to you."

Jada grabbed Skyy by the throat and began choking the fuck out her. "You thought I was through with you, didn't you, bitch?"

Then Jada turned to the other girl and said, "If you don't want the same, you better get the fuck out of here!"

The other girl that had been with Skyy eased away from the table like the coward that she was. Jada started banging Skyy's head against the table.

Skyy yelled, "Please, Jada! Please, let me go! Please!"

The manager and some waitresses separated Jada and Skyy. Skyy crawled out of the booth from underneath the table.

Jada jerked away from the manager and said, "Get yo' motherfuckin' hands off me!"

Skyy headed toward the door. Jada ran out behind her but Skyy and the coward got into a white BMW 535i and drove away.

Jada yelled, "Bitch, I'm gonna whip yo ass every time I see you!." Jada jumped into her Benz and drove away. She was sure that bitch-assed manager had called the police.

CHAPTER 22

It had been a couple of months since Trey had any product and he needed to make a move and make a move fast since he didn't know if or when Starr would give him his money back.

With Monte locked up, he would have to bring the drugs back himself, well him and Shantelle. He didn't want to bring her but she'd traveled with Monte and she knew the best route for returning to Atlanta safely.

They gassed up a Ford Fusion—one of several vehicles that he'd used to bring the product back from Houston. They had passed through Birmingham, Alabama when Shantelle said, "I can't believe you're actually doing this."

"Doing what?"

"Going on a run."

"We're in Alabama. Do you think I drove to Alabama to make a point?"

"I guess not."

Trey could sense her uneasiness. Maybe she didn't think he knew what he was doing. "I've done this plenty of times before. How do you think I got where I'm at?"

"But you don't have to do this now."

"Who else is going to do it?"

"Trey, you have money. You may not have what you used to have, but you have more than enough money."

It was true. Trey had a lot of money, but when Starr took that five hundred thousand he felt like he had to make it back up. He liked to be at a certain level and three million dollars was the number that he felt secure with and right now he didn't feel secure.

"You're either with me or against me."

Shantelle stared at Trey like he was out of his goddamned mind. "What do you mean I'm either with you or against you? You know I'm with you. Otherwise, I wouldn't even be here."

"True. Now would you shut the fuck up please?"

She got quiet and she looked sad. When Trey noticed he said, "Hey, I'm sorry."

Shantelle said, "I changed my mind. I don't want to go."

"What do you mean you changed your mind?"

"I don't want to go, Trey. We're only an hour and a half out of Atlanta. Take me back home or just drop me off at the bus station. I don't want to go."

Trey pulled over at a Shell gas station off Interstate 20.

She said, "Can you take me to the bus station?"

"I don't know where the bus station is here."

She used her iPhone to Google the location of the Greyhound bus station.

"It's on 19th street."

Trey knew he'd pissed her off when he told her to shut the fuck up. He knew he'd been disrespectful to her ever since that day Starr caught them at Atlantic Station.

He stared in her eyes and she was tearing up. He said, "Look, I'm sorry, baby."

She began to sob and she covered her face. She wasn't the one that had stolen his money and she damn sure didn't force him to have sex with her, but yet he was attacking her.

He unbuckled his seat belt and they embraced. She cried hard on his shoulder as he rubbed her back and he said, "I need you."

"I'm going to need you to quit talking to me like I'm a child."

"I'm sorry. I promise I will."

They stared at each for a while and finally he kissed her.

*   *   *

The showroom was in Buckhead and it was 3050 square feet and two levels. Mr. Stanson, the realtor, wanted $14,000 a month and Starr would need another thirty thousand dollars to renovate the place to make it the way she wanted. She felt foolish for paying so much on renovations for something that she didn't own. But the whole time she'd been with Trey she'd owned nothing, so what would be the difference.

She knew that once she'd committed to the contract that she would have to work hard to make it work. She would pay the rent up for a year and take another sixty grand for living and give Trey the rest of his money back. Her heels clacked as she walked across the showroom imagining the showroom filled with furniture showcasing her designs.

This would be the first time in her life that she would be on her own without the help of any male figure. She'd worked up until the time she met Trey, but even when she worked, she had her father, Ace, to support her. Even when Ace was away in prison, he had some of his lieutenants make sure she had what she wanted. She had always dated drug dealers and gangster-type men even before Trey but now she was almost 29. She needed to start looking for regular men because gangster guys just can't be faithful.

She walked outside and glanced up above the door imagining her sign above the doorway. What would she call her place? It would have to be something that reflected her new life. She felt like she is starting over and she felt she was much better than before because of her wisdom.

She glanced up over the door once more and that's when it came to her. A Starr is Born. The perfect name for what she would make into a perfect journey of self awareness. She knew she could get over Trey, but the thing that she knew she would struggle with was dating regular dudes. They just didn't do it for her. She would ask the Lord to help her in that area.

With first and last month's rent, the renovations and the money she would use for liying expenses, it would come close to one hundred and thirty thousand dollars. Trey would hit the roof, but fuck it—she deserved it. She was damn near married to that man and was faithful except for one time. But even then, it was early in their relationship and she was sure he was fucking multiple bitches. Almost ten years with one primary dick, she deserved everything that she got.

*　　*　　*

Later that evening Starr was carrying a box of business cards about to enter her building and someone yelled out her name. "Starr!"

She turned and it was Troy again. He was surely here for the money. If he didn't know about it before, she was sure he knew about it now.

Starr stopped and they were now face to face.

His hands were in his jeans pockets. He looked like a nervous little schoolboy.

"What do you want? Just say it."

"I don't know how. I mean it's kind of scandalous."

"What's scandalous? "

"I mean I feel kind of fucked up for even asking you this."

"Asking me what?"

"I wanna take you out on a date. You know, to let you know what you deserve."

"I can't do that. You know I was with your brother for a long time."

"Half brother. It doesn't matter. He didn't treat you like you deserved to be treated."

She couldn't argue with him about that, but she felt she owed Trey a certain level of loyalty, although she didn't know why?

Troy said, "Look I know you like money and I don't have any, but I can give you all of me."

"Wait a minute Troy you got the wrong idea about me, I'm not materialistic."

"I'm sorry. I didn't mean for you to take it that way."

"That's exactly how I took it."

Troy looked sad. He really didn't mean to hurt her feelings.

Troy said, "Why can't you go out with me?"

"I was with your brother. What part of that don't you understand?"

"Were you really with him? He had a baby on you, that nigga wasn't loyal to you. Even now he's living life, not giving a damn about nobody but Trey."

There was a long silence. This conversation had become uncomfortable. Troy had made a lot of good points but dating him would be absolutely scandalous.

Troy said, "Looks like you got a box of business cards.

Starr smiled and removed one from the box and passed it to Troy.

He read it: *A Starr is Born Interior Design.*

"Nice, but do people use business cards anymore?" He snapped a picture of the card with his phone and passed her the card back.

"You can keep it."

"It's stored in my phone."

"Oh."

"Look, Starr, think about what I said. I mean it's just a date. That's all I'm asking."

She said, "I'll give it some thought." Then she entered the building.

Chapter 23

Nana, Black, Asia, and Rashida sat in Nana's living room. Nana was still getting on Black's ass for what had happened to

Man-Man. Asia was braiding Tierany's hair. Lani stormed into Nana's house without Man-Man.

Black said, "Where the fuck is my son?"

Lani said, "Chris's brother still has him."

"What do you mean he still has him?"

Lani said, "He wants fifty grand more."

Black stood and began pacing. His mind raced. The pressure was surely on him to get his son back and that's what he intended to do.

"Fifty thousand dollars, my ass! I'm not giving this mother-fucker one more cent."

There was a small lamp sitting on the end table beside Nana. She picked it up and slung it at Black's head, barely missing him. "Stop all that cursing, Tyrann, and you better get that boy back, or I'm calling the police!"

Asia stopped braiding Tierany's hair and looked at Lani and said, "I knew this bitch had something to do with this."

Nana said, "One more person curse in here and I'm putting everybody out of my house."

Lani, with tears in her eyes, said to Asia, "I swear to you, I didn't have anything to do with this. I'm so sorry, I really am."

Asia charged Lani and slapped her with a comb. Lani grabbed her by her shirt and slung her to the floor and was about to smack the fuck out of her before Black grabbed her and said, "Quit dis-respecting my grandma's house."

Nana said, "It's all your fault!"

Asia stood and said, "I'm calling the police. Fuck this! I'm call-ing the police!"

The little girl passed her mother her purse and Asia removed her iPhone and was about to dial 911 when Black yanked it out her hand.

Black grabbed Asia by the arm. She was kicking and scream-ing, "Let me go! Let me go, motherfucker!"

Nana wanted to say stop cursing but she figured it was no use.

Tierany said, "Let my mama go, Daddy! Let my mama go!"

Black led her into another room against her will. Tierany followed.

Black released Asia and kneeled down to speak to his daughter. "Look, Princess, I'm not doing anything to hurt Mommy. Daddy wants to talk to Mommy. We are trying to get Man-Man back from the bad guys so we can go to the movies and I'm going to take y'all to Toys R US and get you anything you want."

Tierany smiled and said, "Okay, Daddy." She kissed Black on the jaw.

Though Black was a thug, he loved his kids and they loved him because he was more than just a provider to them.

Black said, "Go back in the other room with Nana."

"Okay."

When Tierany was gone, Black looked at Asia. "Now look, you can call the police if you want to, but if you do, you're going to get me fucked up." He looked her directly in the eyes. Her eyes were still watery. She'd been crying for the last two days. "I am going to get Man-Man back. You've got to trust me."

"I've trusted you and that stupid-ass bitch, and my son is still God knows where with God knows who."

Black said, "You've lived a pretty good goddamned life. You haven't worked in years."

"What does that have to do with anything?"

"It has everything to do with it. You've benefited from every bad thing I've done. So has everybody in this motherfuckin' house. Now all of a sudden you want to call the police."

Asia sat down on a chair that was in the corner of the den and was about to light a blunt when Black said, "Now, you know Nana is not going to allow that."

She put the blunt away and said, "I'm so fucked up right now. My baby is gone." She started crying again.

Black said, "I'm going to get him back or they are going to have to take my life. I swear to you."

Asia starred at Black for a long time. She believed him. She knew that either her son was coming back home or Black was going to get killed trying to get his son back. She knew that he could and would get ignorant if needed.

CHAPTER 24

Trey's connection was a dude named Q who was born and raised in Houston. He had gone to college in Brownville where he found his Mexican connection. The connection would give him as many kilos of coke as he wanted for thirteen thousand dollars apiece. The keys would even be delivered to Houston, where Q's base of operations was located.

Q was one of those smooth-ass niggas. He was tall and dark with short hair, but no facial hair and an athletic frame. He usually dressed in Athletic sweats and didn't wear any jewelry except for a nice watch. He would sell his product to out of towners for eighteen thousand a piece. Q had a condo in the Galleria area of Houston.

Trey and Q had a relationship that went back about eight years but they only got to hang out about twice a year. Usually when Q came to Atlanta, Monte would see Q for Trey. Q's condo was a penthouse with an amazing view of the Galleria area, the city lights dazzled through the floor to ceiling glass. Art Deco and beautiful artwork made it the ultimate bachelor pad. Q and Trey hugged when Q entered the condo.

Trey introduced Q to Shantelle. Q gave her a hug, which let Trey know that Monte had been truthful. Shantelle had never met the connect. Besides, Shantelle would have mentioned if she'd known Q.

Shantelle had a seat on the sectional before standing up. She turned to Q and said, "This view is spectacular. Do you mind if I go on the balcony?"

Q said, "Go right ahead. There's a bar out there. Help yourself to some liquor if you want."

Shantelle went to the bar and poured a Ciroc and Cranberry juice. She drank it slowly enjoying the Houston night air.

Trey closed the balcony door.

Q said, "How long have you known her?"

"A few months now."

"You fucking her?"

"What you think?"

Q laughed and said, "It's just a question, nigga. Don't get offended."

"Not offended. I came to get the work, and head back to the A. We can talk about that shit later."

"I'm just saying she fine. Nice legs and all, but she ain't Starr. I prefer my women thick, you know what I mean?"

"Yeah."

"What happened to Starr?"

"Nothing happened. Why you ask?"

"You haven't spoken about her in a while."

"We ain't together."

"You left Starr for her?" He pointed in the direction of the balcony and then shook his head and said, "You are losing, nigga."

"Do you have the work or not?"

"I got some bad news."

"What?"

"I only got half of the work."

"Half. What the fuck you mean half?"

"You wanted twenty keys, I got ten. I will have the other ten in a couple of days."

"Ah shit." Trey began to pace. "I can't wait a couple of days. I got shit I gotta do. I need it now."

"Get a room at the Derrick Hotel, I'll pay for it. Send Shantelle to the mall store and get her a nice handbag on me. But it'll still be a couple of days. Just wait and you can get the entire twenty."

"I can't wait," Trey said. "But damn, I don't wanna take this money back with me. I don't want to have money and product with me. You feel me."

"Just leave the money with me."

Trey knew he could trust Q with his money because he was sure Q didn't need it, but he still didn't want to leave it with him. With the money Starr had, his money would be scattered all over the place.

"I can't leave it."

"So, you're going to take the money back with you and the work?"

"Yeah, it will be okay."

Q said, "I wouldn't, just in case something happens."

"Nothing is going to happen as long as we conceal the work."

"I ain't worried about the work. You know damn well we the best at that."

"Still in the door?" In the past Q would have the doors of his customers' cars removed and the product stuffed in the panel of the door, but snitches had told cops about those methods.

"Hell no, that's old. We put it under the hood. Now, don't worry. The police will never find it.

Chapter 25

It was 7:30 pm when Lani entered Mike's apartment carrying a small black briefcase. She didn't know how this was going to go down. She'd hoped that Mike would do what he said he was going to do because if he didn't, there would be hell to pay. Kyrie was staked outside just in case Mike didn't release Man-Man. Black was prepared for war. He'd enlisted eight goons from his old hood; dudes that would die for him because he'd done so much for them in the past. Lani walked right pass Kenny-Boo without so much as acknowledging his ugly ass. Mike and Tater sat on the sofa watching TV. Man-Man was crying in a back room.

Lani sat on a loveseat across from the sofa where Tater sat. Man-Man was crying louder and louder and Lani finally said, "What the fuck have ya'll done to that baby.

"Nothing," Mike said.

Lani passed the briefcase to Mike and he passed it to Tater. Mike said, "The money you left earlier was a thousand dollars short, but I ain't gonna worry about it."

Lani pretended like she didn't hear him.

Kenny-Boo sat beside Lani on the love seat and she avoided eye contact with him.

Lani yelled, "Man-Man? Come here baby!"

Man-Man came running out of the back room and as soon as he saw Lani, he ran toward her and hugged her tightly. He avoided looking at Kenny Boo.

Lani said, "What's wrong with you, baby?"

"He was being mean to me." He pointed to Kenny-Boo.

Kenny-Boo made an ugly face as if that was possible with his already hideous face and said, "Quit acting like a baby."

"He is a baby."

"Whatever."

Mike said, "Is the money all there?"

Tater popped the briefcase and glanced in the suitcase. "It seems to be all there," he said.

"It is all there," Lani said. "Don't try any more bullshit."

Mike laughed and said, "Take the little rug rat with you. That little motherfucker eats too much."

Lani stood up and Kenny-Boo stood up as well. Lani was making her way over to the door when her cell phone rang. It was Black. "Hello? I got Man-Man and we're about to leave now."

"So you left already?"

"No. I'm about to walk out the door now."

"Put Mike on the phone"

"Why do you wanna speak to him?"

"Just put him on the phone."

Lani sighed and passed Mike the phone.

"Yo?," Mike said into the phone.

Black said, "I'm here with yo Mama and yo' cracker-ass step-daddy. Either you send all that money back with Lani or both of them die."

"Quit playing games! You don't know shit about my mama."

"I know she drives a Benz."

"That means nothing."

Black said, "Ms. Paulette. Get yo ass over here."

Seconds later Ms. Paulette was on the phone. "Mike, baby. There are six men here with me and Tom. I'm afraid, baby. I'm really afraid. Don't let us die."

*   *   *

Trey was on Interstate 110 right outside Baton Rouge. He was tired and he was seriously thinking about stopping to rest but he was behind schedule so he kept going. It was 9:00 p.m. and it was dark outside. He really hated riding dirty while it was dark. Shantelle was asleep, resting with noise cancellation headphones on while Trey blasted Rick Ross. He was playing the radio exceptionally loud to keep him awake. There was a sign on the highway that said twenty-five more miles, to Baton Rouge when he noticed a State Trooper behind him.

Trey told himself not to panic and held the wheel with a steady hand. Keep driving and keep your eyes on the road. Don't panic, Trey! Don't panic! You are legit. You have nothing to worry about. Just obey the law and don't swerve. If you keep calm, ain't a motherfuckin' thing they can say. All of this was self talk.

He glanced over at Shantelle, who was snoring. He didn't want to wake her. He knew she would panic and they would be fucked.

He thought about the product. It was hidden on the hood. Even he didn't know exactly where it was. He would have to call Q as soon as he got to Atlanta to get the instructions on how to uncover the work. He glanced in the mirror and the goddamned cop was still on his ass. Fuck!

He changed lanes and the trooper changed lanes and seconds later, Trey heard the siren. He pulled over to the side of the road. The trooper, a white man with a very red face and a handlebar mustache, approached the car.

"License and registration, please?

Trey reluctantly passed the man the proper paperwork. Shantelle woke up and she looked worried. So did he. They were fucked. It was just a matter of time.

Shamari was tired of the goddamned bandages. They draped his face and made him look like a mummy. He was frustrated from being in the hotel room day and night, waiting on Jada to bring him food and other things that he needed. His face needed to breathe. Plus he was very anxious to see how he looked once the bandages were removed.

He stood in the mirror and he removed some of the bandages that wrapped around his chin. The sutures had dissolved and his chin was slightly swollen. Jada told him it would be 4-6 weeks before they were fully dissolved and this was only the first week. And he knew his face was still very swollen. He would have to remove the bandages sooner than recommended. He needed to make some money and that would require him to take a trip to Cali to get some more heroin in the next few weeks.

T- Money, a friend and a former Crip, had a line on some pure Afghanistan heroin. He didn't want to go through T-Money, because he was black and he knew that going through another black dealer would almost assure that there would be a tax on the product. But he needed it. He needed the money to run.

Lying in the hotel room made him realize he'd be a complete fool to turn himself in. Earlier in the week he'd given Jada the remainder of the money to make the final payment to Joey Turch so if he was ever caught, at least he had a reputable attorney. That goddamned Tony was trying to put him away to save his own ass.

Shamari wrapped his face the best he knew how and made his way back over to the bed. He turned the television to the six o'clock news.

The anchorman said, "Breaking news. The police have stated that six people have overdosed in the Atlanta area. All six overdosed on heroin known by the trade name Obamacare. This heroin came to our attention a few weeks ago when a six year was found with 19 packets in his backpack at an area elementary school."

Shamari powered down the TV and called Jada.

"Hello."

"Please come to the room. I have to tell you something. I need you."

"I'm on my way."

Shamari lay on his bed staring at the ceiling, knowing that his situation had just gotten a thousand times worse. The last thing he needed was to be linked to that heroin. He'd made up his mind that there would be no more heroin dealing for him. He turned to his side and yelled, "FUCK!" Man, FUCK!"

bad

* * *

PART 7:

WHO DO YOU LOVE?

CHAPTER 1

Mike passed the phone back to Lani. There was an awkward silence.

Kenny-Boo saw the look on Mike face and asked, "What the hell is going on?"

Mike sat on the sofa in total shock. How in the hell did Black find out where his parents lived? Did Lani tell him? What was he going to do now? If he killed Lani and Man-Man, he would never see his mother and stepfather again. He would be without his parents and his brother.

Lani held Man-Man's hand. She spoke into the phone. "What the hell's going on?"

There was nobody on the other end of the phone, only a dial tone.

Mike ordered Kenny-Boo to get the money, count it, and give it back to Lani.

"For what?"

Mike barked, "Do what the fuck I say!"

Kenny-Boo dropped his head and made his way to the back room and re-emerged with the one hundred and ninety-nine thousand from earlier. Black had been a thousand dollars short with the payment.

Kenny-Boo passed the suitcase to Lani. Then he turned to Mike and said, "So you're not going to tell me why we're giving the money back?"

Mike ignored his silly ass and asked Lani to call Black.

She dialed the number and passed the phone back to Mike. "Lani has the money. How do I know you're going to let my mom go?"

"I could've snatched your mom a long time ago. I've known where she lived for a while now. I don't want your mom. I want my son and my motherfucking money. You give the money back and you won't have no problems."

"Put my mama on the phone."

Seconds later Mike's mother said, "Hello?"

"Ma. You okay?"

"I'm fine."

"Do you believe he'll let you go?"

"I think so, son. They haven't harmed us at all."

Black snatched the phone out of her hand and said, "Listen, nigga, give me the goddamned money back and you won't have any problems."

"Lani has the money."

Kenny-Boo said, "If it were me, I wouldn't give them a god-damned thing."

Man-Man said, "Quit cursing so much."

Kenny-Boo said to the kid, "Shut the hell up!"

Lani terminated the call. She could tell that Kenny-Boo wanted to slap the fuck out of her. He gave her back the fifty thousand dollars that she'd brought over today as well.

Mike said, "Call him back one more time and tell him you have all the money."

Lani dialed the number and said, "I have the money."

Lani was scared as hell. She wondered how in the hell Black found Mike's parents house and sure as hell hoped that Mike didn't think she let Black know where they resided. There was no way in hell she would do something like that, but she was almost certain that even if Mike didn't think that, Kenny-Boo damn sure did.

Black said, "Kyrie is outside. When he is in possession of the money, I'll release his parents."

Lani terminated the call and said, "He's going to release them when I'm outside, and Kyrie has the money."

Kenny-Boo with his limited comprehension had just figured out that Mike's parents were being held. "Don't believe him."

Mike said, "Shut the fuck up! Mama is all I got."

Lani stared at Mike, she could feel his pain. This whole ordeal had gotten completely out of hand, and it was time for this bullshit to stop. Lani walked toward the door with Man-Man in front of her and Kenny-Boo behind her. As she exited into the hallway, Kenny-Boo shoved the fuck out of her and she crashed into the wall before dropping the briefcase and stumbling over the suitcase. Man-Man looked frightened as Lani rose back to her feet.

Kenny-Boo said, "Bitch, your day is coming!"

He slammed the door as Lani made her way outside where Kyrie was waiting behind the wheels of a blue Honda Accord.

CHAPTER 2

Trey said, "Officer, can you tell me why you pulled me over?"

The man ignored Trey and said, "License and registration."

Shantelle was awake now, wondering what in the hell they were going to do. Hell, they couldn't run. Though she was in better shape than most girls, she was wearing sandals and Trey wasn't in the best condition. Even if they did run, the police would have the car. She'd gone through this with Monte. She didn't want to get arrested. It was time for her white-girl voice.

"Honey, just do what the man tell you. I'm sure whatever you did, the officer will let you know, write your ticket, and then we'll be on our way."

Trey passed the trooper his license and registration. The trooper walked back to his patrol car and when he was out of sight, Trey said, "Remain calm as possible. Whatever he stopped us for, it's going to be okay. Think positive. Think legit. Act legit."

"Got ya," Shantelle said. Though she was a smart girl, she knew she wasn't as street smart as Trey.

Seconds later the trooper returned.

Shantelle was nervous as hell. She'd been calm, she acted legit. This was not how this was supposed to go.

Trey removed his seatbelt and sprang from the car. The trooper waited for him by the rear of the car.

Trey asked, "What did I do?"

The trooper's face got a shade redder and he said, "I'm going to ask the questions. Not you. Got it?"

Trey wanted to smack the fuck out of the hillbilly cop but instead he said, "Yes sir."

"Where you coming from?"

"Texas."

"What part?"

"Houston"

"What were you doing in Houston?"

"Visiting."

"You got family down there?"

"Yeah, family and friends."

"What kind of work do you do?"

"Why you want to know that?"

"So you don't have a job?"

"I'm in the music business."

"Somehow I figured you were going to say that."

Shantelle heard the whole conversation. She scrolled through her phone looking for her friend Lori. Somebody had to know if she was going to get arrested. She spotted Trey's phone on the seat. She picked it up and decided to call Q. He picked up on the first ring.

"What's up?"

"Hey, this is Shantelle. Me and Trey just got pulled over."

"Oh yeah? Where is Trey?"

"He's outside talking to the trooper. "

"Where are ya'll?"

"About thirty minutes away from Baton Rouge."

Q hung up the phone and when Shantelle tried to call him back, she got his voicemail. Fuck! She dialed Lori from her phone and her phone went straight to voicemail as well. Fuck!

Trey said, "Why do you want to know what I do for a living? You can google me and my company if you want. I have my own record label."

The trooper laughed. "Let me guess the name of it. Hmm…
Dope house records?"

"Google me if you don't believe me."

"Google you?" The trooper laughed. "I'm not on Google,
Instagram, Facebook or none of that shit."

"Google is a search engine."

"A search engine? You know what else is a search engine? I'm
a search engine and I'll search this whole goddamned car, including the engine, if you don't tell me where the goddamned dope
is, Boy!"

"Boy?"

The man looked Trey straight in the eye and he said, "Yeah I
said 'Boy'. You got a problem with that?"

With ten kilos of cocaine in the car, Trey had absolutely no
problem with the redneck calling him boy, or nigga for that matter. He simply had to accept it.

"There's nothing in the car."

"So you're telling me if I search this car, I ain't going to
find nothing?"

"You don't have any right to search this car. Where is your
probable cause?"

"I don't need no probable cause but if you want it, you'll get it.
I'll just write the goddamned report up and say you were swerving
like you'd been drinking, and when I pulled you over, I smelled
marijuana, and that pretty little girlfriend of yours was drunk and
belligerent. Then you'll go to jail for six months while awaiting
trial by a jury of your peers. If you're lucky, you'll get one black
on your jury who is going to go along with the whites because he
has to live in this town of thirteen thousand residents. Who do
you think the courts are going to believe, a decorated officer of
the law or two goddamned niggas?"

The man looked Trey straight in his eyes and there was a long
silence. "You want to take your chances?"

Trey didn't respond.

"Now you can hand them drugs over and I can forget about this, or I can radio in the K9 unit. I'm trying to be nice and I'm asking you nicely."

"You call that being nice?"

"I could have cuffed your ass first then searched the car."

"What do you want from me?"

"I want the truth."

"There is nothing in here."

Trey popped his knuckles and kicked dirt.

The trooper said, "Somebody is nervous."

"Listen, I've told you the truth."

"I don't believe you," the trooper said, his handlebar mustache curled up further because he was visibly angry with Trey. "In fact, I know your lying. I've been a trooper for over twenty years. I can smell a slick-talking drug dealer from a mile away."

Trey laughed, not because the man was funny but to keep from crying. There was no way in the hell he wanted to go to prison for possession for ten kilos of coke.

The trooper said, "Hand over the drugs and I'll drive away. You'll never hear from me again."

"What?"

"Hand over the drugs or I'm calling K-9 and we'll find them."

Trey couldn't believe what the fuck he was hearing. Did the man say hand over the drugs and he would never hear from him again. "What if I give you money?"

"Even better, how much you got?"

"A hundred thousand, at least."

The trooper handed Trey his license and registration back and Trey retrieved the briefcase full of money from the car and passed it to the trooper.

The grinning-ass trooper said, "Have a nice day, Mr. Carter, and slow down." He winked.

CHAPTER 3

Jada removed the last of Shamari's bandages as he stood looking at his new face in the mirror. He barely recognized himself,
but that was the point. He didn't really notice a difference in his
nose. Jada had warned him that it would take a few years before
he'd notice a difference. He turned to Jada who stood beside him
with her mouth wide open.

"So what do you think, baby?"

Her mouth was still open and she was unable to speak.

"Do you like it or not?"

"It's okay."

"What do you mean, 'it's okay'?"

"I think he did a good job. He did what he was supposed
to do."

"But you don't like it?"

"I don't like it! Not at all!" She stormed out of the bathroom
and made her way to the bed. She buried her face in the pillow
and cried. She was not attracted to his face at all, even though it
was beautiful. She liked him looking a little more rugged. That's
what she was used to, not some perfect pretty boy.

Shamari came in seconds later and sat on the bed beside her.

Jada stared at Shamari, she recognized only his eyes. His chin
was hideous and those cheek implants made her feel like she
wanted to vomit. The tears rolled down her face and she wiped
them away with the palms of hands.

"Am I that ugly?"

"You're beautiful, but I don't like that look on you. I want the old Shamari back."

"I don't look that much different."

"I hate this new look."

Shamari removed her hands from her eyes and said, "It's not for you to like, baby. Remember, I did this to evade the police."

"But what about your ID?"

"Going to get a new one today, but we need to get the fuck up out of this hotel."

"I'm going to look at a town home today. If I like it, I'm going to give the man the money then I can move in next weekend."

Shamari noticed that she had said I instead of we so he asked, "So, I'm not welcome to your new home?"

"Of course you are, baby."

She sat up on the bed and he leaned into her and they kissed.

Shamari said, "Trust me, it's going to be okay."

"You think?"

"I sure as hell hope so."

"You're not going to turn yourself in?"

"I don't see a reason to. Do you?"

"No. Not at all. There is no way anybody is going to know it's you, I want the old Shamari back."

"You'll get used to me."

Jada kissed him again and said, "I don't think so."

*　　*　　*

Trey was on his way to Jessica's to see his son when he dialed Q's number and received a recording saying that the number was not in service. Trey hadn't heard from Q since the day he'd gotten pulled over. He tried to reach him with the three different phone numbers he had for him. He wished like hell Shantelle hadn't called him. Trey had dealt with Q for years and Trey knew that if Q thought he had gotten arrested, there was no way that he would ever do business with him again. Period. So he was in a really fucked up position. He would have to chill for now. Maybe this was God's way of showing him that he needed to slow down.

Jessica opened the door she said, "The world's greatest dad."

"Kill the sarcasm, Where is my son?"

"You mean my son."

Trey was annoyed with Jessica but he knew he would have to put up with her bullshit because she was his son's mother and there was no way he could see T. J. without dealing with her.

Jessica invited him in, and they made their way to the living room. Seconds later, T. J. appeared.

Trey said, "How is daddy's big boy doing?"

T. J. ignored him and took a seat beside Jessica on the love seat.

Trey was pissed the fuck off. How in the hell was his son going to ignore him?

"T. J., did you hear me?"

"I heard you."

"What's wrong?"

T. J. ignored Trey.

"Jessica, what have you done to my son?" Trey turned to Jessica.

"I haven't done anything. T. J. is a growing boy. He's old enough to know when someone cares about him or if they are full of shit."

"You been poisoning my son's goddamned mind?"

T. J. said, "Quit cursing my mommy."

"I'm your daddy!"

"You ain't my daddy!"

This made Trey furious and before he knew it, he'd said, "Boy, I will whip your lil ass in here! I brought you in this world, not the other way around!"

Jessica turned to T. J., "Trey is still your father. Go back in your room and play with your video games. Let me and your father talk for a minute."

When T. J. was gone, Trey said, "What's his god-damned problem?"

"You're his problem, Trey."

"You're turning that boy against me. I know what's happening."

"Oh my fucking god, Trey!" Jessica threw her hands up in disgust. "You really think I would do that?"

"You're capable of it."

"I don't have to. T. J. is just tired of you lying to him. You're always telling him that you're coming to pick him up and he gets his hopes up high, not only don't you show up, you don't call either."

"Well, I got things to do, money to make."

"Money is more important than your own son?"

"Never."

"Take him with you then."

Trey was hoping that she wouldn't ask that of him. Not that he didn't want to,-but he didn't have a place to take him besides his stash spots, his mother's house, or Shantelle's apartment. He knew Shantelle would be cool with it at first, but then she would get all emotional on him. He didn't want his son to stay at the stash house. It was too dangerous.

"Just as I thought." She laughed. "You have no idea what it's like to be a parent, Trey. How in the hell can you even call yourself a dad?"

"He can go with me."

Jessica called T. J. and he ran into the living room. He took hold of his mother's arm and stared at Trey and asked, "Are you being mean to my mom again?"

"Of course not, champ." Trey laughed.

"He acts just like you. That's the scary part," Jessica said

Trey made his way over to T. J. and said, "I'm going to take you to Cirque de Soleil."

"What's that?"

"It's like the circus but a hundred times better," Trey said.

T. J smiled but then remembered that he was supposed to be mad at his dad. He held his mother tight."

Jessica turned to T. J. and said, "Don't you want to go with your father?"

"No."

Trey said, "Why not?"

"Because you always lie to me!"

Trey said, "Give daddy a chance to make it up to you. I want to take you to see Cirque de Soleil and I'm going to take you to grandma's house. Grandma has been asking about you."

T. J.'s face lit up and said, "She called me yesterday."

Trey looked confused and Jessica said, "Yes, your mother keeps in touch, and I'm glad she does."

Trey had no idea that his mother kept in touch with them. He was barely in touch with his mom himself nowadays. He would have to do better with his priorities.

Jessica said, "Let's go to your room to pack some clothes." They disappeared into the bedroom.

Trey texted Starr.

Trey: *Hey.*

Starr: *Hey!*

Trey: *I really need my money. I had some bad luck.*

Starr: *Sorry to hear that.*

Trey: *Do you think you can meet me to give my money back?*

Starr: *Yes, I can meet you on Wed. Anytime after 7.*

Trey: *Cool. I'll meet you on Wed.*

Starr: *K.*

Jessica and T. J. entered the room carrying his backpack. T. J. said to Trey, "Can we go to grandma's first?"

"Of course."

Trey brushed T. J.'s hair as T. J. grinned.

Trey and T. J. had made their way to the door when Jessica said, "Trey, let me talk to you for a second alone. Take T. J. to the car and come back in."

"Leave him in the car alone?"

"Not with the keys, silly, and this is a nice neighborhood. He'll be okay," Jessica said. "Trey, just think how much it would mean to T. J. if I could come with you guys?"

"Huh?"

Jessica smiled and said, "We can be one big happy family. T. J. is always asking me why aren't we together."

"Yeah, I know every kid wants their parents to be together."

"T. J.'s no different."

"Bad idea. We don't get along."

Jessica said, "Look, Trey, I'm not trying to marry you. I just want a couple of days where T. J. can be with his parents. Is that too much to ask for?"

"I'm not with it."

"It's your new girlfriend, isn't it?"

"It's because you're going to be thinking that we're something that we're not."

She laughed. "I don't want to be with you."

"Okay, well let me spend time with my son."

There were tears rolling down Jessica's face. "You ruined my life!"

"How?"

"You got me pregnant and just left."

"You knew I had a woman, from day one."

"Now you're not with that woman, so why can't we be together? T. J. needs a family!"

"I knew that was what this is about."

"So what if I do want to be with you? What's wrong with me wanting to have a family for my son?"

"Leave T. J. the fuck out of it because you not going to get no sympathy from me, bitch!"

She lowered her voice. "Oh, I'll leave T. J. out of it. I love you, Trey."

"You tried to ruin my life. You ruined my relationship with the only woman that I ever loved."

"You never loved her. If you loved her, you wouldn't have fucked me and you damn sure wouldn't have fucked Shantelle."

"What did you say?"

"I said you wouldn't have fucked me or Shantelle."

"How do you know Shantelle's name?"

"I sent the pictures to Starr, remember?"

"I swear, you're the biggest stalker ever. I could never be with you."

Trey headed to the door and she took hold of his shirt and said, "Please! Don't leave! I wanna be one big happy family."

Trey shoved her and she stumbled to the floor. She took hold of his leg. He struggled to make it to the front door and she said, "Trey! Please don't go! Why can't we be one big happy family? I want a family, Trey."

When Trey made his way to the door, she was still locked on to his leg like a pit bull. Trey pried her fingers off his leg and slammed the door shut.

Jessica was still on the floor screaming, "All I want is a big happy family! All I want is my family to be together!"

CHAPTER 4

Black stared at the screen of the cell phone at a picture of a Blue pit bull that his daughter Tierany had sent him. He'd promised that he would get her and Man-Man a dog, but he didn't know if he wanted them to have a pit bull since they were so temperamental. He was quite surprised that Tierany wanted a pit bull since she was a girly-girl. He thought she would have wanted a Yorkie. Black was about to text her back when he noticed someone he didn't recognize creeping up his driveway. Black grabbed the Taurus nine millimeter from his waist, cocked it, and opened his front door.

"What's up, Partna!?" Black yelled out to the stranger.

"You can give me all your motherfucking money." The man smiled, but Black wasn't smiling.

"You better get the fuck away from here before I blast yo ass." Black brought up his gun.

"It's me. Mari."

"What?"

"It's Shamari."

Black looked closely and finally he recognized him. "What the fuck have you done to your face, man?"

"Changed my look, man."

"What the fuck?"

"Yeah, had to get some work done if I'm going to be on the run."

"Damn. I swear I didn't recognize you. Only a slight resemblance. I was 'bout to kill yo ass, asking for money."

Shamari laughed and Black asked, "Who did it?"

"Plastic surgeon that Jada knows."

"How much did it cost?"

"I ain't pay him shit."

"Huh?"

"It's a long story."

Black led Shamari inside the home and once they were sitting at the bar, Shamari asked, "Where's Kyrie?"

"I don't know? Why?"

"What ever happened with that case of his son taking the dope to school?"

"Nothing yet." Black eyed Shamari suspiciously, wondering why Shamari was asking all the goddamned questions about Kyrie. Black said, "Do you want something to drink?"

"What you got?"

"Henny, water or soda."

"Give me a soda. Got the taste for sugar."

Black came back with a can of Mountain Dew then he poured himself some Hennessey.

"Why all the questions about Kyrie?"

"When I was recovering from my surgery, I saw on the news that a few people had OD'd on-heroin."

"What does that got to do with us? You know how many heroin dealers in Atlanta?"

"How many of them have the name Obamacare?"

Black sipped his liquor said, "We stole that name, remember?"

"I know, but now don't you think it's time that we give it back?"

"Maybe."

Black stared at Shamari's face and said, "I'm going to have to get used to this face, man. It's tripping me out."

"Freaked Jada out too."

"I bet."

"We need a new name."

"We need more product first."

"I can find us some."

"Where?"

"L.A."

"Look, I ain't into trafficking shit all the way across the country, but you get it back, I'll help you."

"I have no choice. If I'm going to be running, I gotta make some money."

"You're going to chance it going through airports and shit when you're on the run."

"I'm driving. I got a new license." Shamari flashed a license Hunch's cousin had made for him. His new alias was Ricky Stevenson.

"Driving it back is a big risk."

"I ain't got shit to lose."

Black said, "You got a point." He then downed his liquor.

* * *

Lani had been watching Breaking Bad on Netflix when someone rang her doorbell. She figured that it had to be someone at the wrong house because nobody had used the building keypad to notify her. She looked through the peephole and saw that it was Black. Lani opened the door but blocked the entrance into her home.

"I'm sorry I didn't call before I came, but I figured you didn't want to see me," Black said.

"You're smarter than I thought you were."

"Can we talk?

"About?"

"Can I come in? I'll be quick."

"I don't have time for this bullshit."

She stepped aside and let him inside. He followed her to the kitchen. They sat side by side at her bar. She offered him a drink but he declined.

"What do you want?"

"I wanna say I'm sorry. I swear to god, I didn't want to get you involved."

His eyes were sincere and she wanted to believe him, but there was no way she could believe him. She always wanted to believe what he said, and that is what has gotten her into trouble before.

"Tyrann, cut the bullshit. You know there was no way that I wasn't going to be involved. No fucking way. I'm the common denominator between you and Chris. You've been in trouble with the law before. You knew that once you killed Chris, the police were going to come see me."

"Shh. Quit saying that."

"Saying what?"

"I killed Chris because I ain't killed nobody."

"Who pulled the trigger?"

Black attempted to frisk her. Why was she asking him all these goddamned questions?

"Get your goddamned hands off me. You know I ain't wearing no wire."

"Twan pulled the trigger if you must know."

"How did Twan know Chris?"

"He didn't."

Lani and Black locked eyes. "Chris's blood is on your hands, not Twan's."

"Says who?"

It was now clear to Lani that Black was delusional as hell. In his mind, he was innocent of murder since he didn't actually pull the trigger.

Black rubbed her back. He wanted to comfort her. He knew she'd been through a lot.

"You get your motherfucking hands off me!"

Black laughed and said, "All that I've done for you, this is how you treat me?"

Lani made her way to the fridge to get some Greek yogurt. As she stood at the fridge, Black examined her body. Her ass was poking out nicely. He wished she would remove that robe but didn't think that would happen.

Lani sat at the bar and ate a spoonful of yogurt. "Look, Tyrann, you've done a lot for me and I appreciate the hell out of you, but there is no way I can be with someone like you. You showed me a different side of you."

"Like what?"

"Motherfucker, have you forgot that you murdered Chris?"

He placed his finger over his lips. "Shh."

"You got me in the middle of a bunch of bullshit."

"You have an excellent lawyer. Nothing is going to happen to you."

"You don't know that."

"I know nothing can happen to you because you didn't know about it."

"I do now."

"But I'm the only person that knows for sure that you know about it."

"Mike kidnapped Man-Man for nothing, right?"

"Mike thinks he knows."

"Now, I'm almost certain he thinks that I told you where his mother lived."

"But you didn't."

"He doesn't know that."

"Don't worry about Mike. Fuck Mike! I can handle Mike!"

"Now you see, this whole vigilante lifestyle is what I can't deal with."

Black stood up from the bar and said, "Don't say shit about my lifestyle. This same vigilante lifestyle got you living good."

"So what do I owe you? Some pussy? This is what you do, Tyrann. Ever since I've known you, it's been the same thing. You made a lot of money and spoiled a lot of women and you think the money is going to allow you to do what you want to do. Can't you see that way of thinking is fucked up?"

"I might be fucked up in the head. Just a little. I'll be the first to admit, but if I'm fucked up then that means that you're fucked up too."

"Huh?"

"You broke up with me. You went to Chris. You thought he was legitimate, but he turned out to be nothing but a dope boy too. A has-been basketball player that was no better than me."

Tear rolled down her face. Not because of what he said, but because of how he'd said it. He mentioned Chris in the past tense. He was gone.

Black said, "I got issues, but you got issues too. You ain't no better than me."

Lani took another spoonful of her yogurt and said, "You're right. We're both broken. It's time to re-evaluate my life. I'm not a young girl anymore, and you're not young anymore either."

Black grinned. "I know."

"What do you want from me? What do you want me to say? You want me to accept your apology then you'll leave. Well, I accept your apology. Now leave."

"I want you to come live with me."

She laughed and said, "You're sick."

"Look, nothing is going to happen to you. I know you're worried, but I swear to you, ain't a goddamned thing going to happen to us."

She finished her yogurt. It made no sense to go back and forth with the fool.

Black made his way over to her. He started massaging her shoulders and she liked it. She liked the way he made her feel physically and she hadn't been touched in a while. She needed sex. She wanted him inside of her. She sat the empty yogurt container on the bar and he leaned into her to kiss her.

She stopped him and said, "Get the fuck out right now."

Black stood there with a silly-ass grin on his face. He said, "It's like that?"

"It's like that, motherfucker."

He made his way to the door and she followed him. Before he left he said, "I love you, Lani."

She closed the door. She believed Black loved her—the only way he knew how to love, and at the moment, it wasn't good enough to keep putting herself at risk with him.

*   *   *

Lani needed a drink, so she called Starr and Jada to meet her at the W for cocktails. They sat at a table in the back of the lounge. All three ladies had strawberry margaritas. Starr paid back Jada the money that Jada had given her earlier. She told the ladies about her new showroom and business.

Jada smiled, "I gotta check it out. I'm so proud of you."

"You need to send some of your rich friends to do business with me."

"I'll send Big Papa to you."

"Who?"

"My friend, Ty. I call him Big Papa because he's a big guy, but he's a teddy bear."

Lani said, "Teddy bear translation–he'll spend his money on you."

Jada laughed and said, "Well, why wouldn't he? Ain't I worth it?"

Starr wanted to say something to Jada about that kind of behavior but who was she to judge. Besides Jada was a grown woman.

Jada said to Lani, "So, what about your love life?"

"What love life? You know I'm not with anybody? Damn sure ain't with Black."

"What's wrong with Black?"

"What's not wrong with him? He's a big juvenile."

Lani didn't want to tell them about the kidnappings. She didn't want to scare the girls because she hadn't spoken to Mike and she was almost certain that he thought she was involved.

Jada turned back to Starr. "I've always wanted to start a business, but I don't know what I would do."

"Just think about whatever you're good at and whatever there's a need for."

Jada said, "I got a few ideas. I just gotta make sure I'm ready to put in the work."

Starr sipped her drink and said, "That's important for sure. Sometimes I ask myself, do I really have the work ethic to make this thing work? Well, I'm going to have to put in the work. Trey is not supporting me anymore."

"So I'm assuming he gave you the money to start the business." Lani said.

"No, I took it." She sipped her margarita.

"You took it?" Lani asked. "What do you mean, you took it?"

"I took what I felt was mine. I took the money for the showroom and I took some money for me to live off."

"I can't believe you did that," Lani said.

"Why not?" Jada said, "She deserved it."

"I sure as hell did. I was damn near married to that man and he thinks he can just kick me out with nothing."

"You kicked him out, tho," Lani said.

"Same damn thing." Jada sipped her drink and turned to Starr. "You did the right thing."

"I think so."

"What did Trey say?"

"I haven't seen Trey, but I'm going to give him back the money I didn't spend."

"How much did you take?"

"Five hundred thousand dollars."

"Black would kill me if I took his money," Lani said. "That's a fact."

"Does he know?" Jada asked.

"Yes." Starr sipped her drink and then said, "I thought he'd sent his brother over to try to talk me into giving it back, but can you believe Trey's brother tried to hit on me?"

"I didn't know Trey had a brother," Lani said.

"Half brother. His dad was a whore, well mine was too," Starr said as she thought about Ace's infidelities.

"Sounds like Black's daddy. That man got twenty-three kids spread across Georgia, South Carolina, and Alabama."

"Damn. So Trey's brother tried to holla," Jada said.

"Yeah, girl."

Lani said, "They're obviously not close."

Starr sipped her drink and said, "He's not like Trey. First he's younger and went to college and works as a pharmacist. He's a square."

Jada said, "I've fucked with a few squares in my day."

Starr said, "He's attractive, but I can't roll like that."

"Why not?"

"He's Trey's brother."

"Let me tell you something," Jada said. "When a man decides he wants to fuck something, he's going to fuck whoever and whomever he pleases."

"Not every man is like that," Lani said.

Jada said, "Not every man, but the men we deal with do. And that's all I can speak on."

Jada turned to Starr and said, "If you like him, go out with him. You don't have to fuck him."

CHAPTER 5

Starr lay naked on a set of 1500 thread count sheets. She wanted to be held, needed to be fucked, but her man was somewhere holding somebody else, fucking somebody else. She stood up, and walked to her dresser to retrieve her white rabbit. It wasn't a man that could hold her and tell her everything was going to be alright, but what it could do was aid her in getting off and right now she needed an orgasm more than anything. She rarely used toys. Most of the time when she did use them, it was with Trey. He used to love seeing her get herself off.

She dimmed the light and retrieved some lube from the bathroom, lit some candles and crawled back into the bed. She turned on the battery-operated rabbit and stimulated her clitoris as she imagined Trey's head between her legs. She loved how he would go down on her. She would often grab his head when he was down there even though he had hated it when she did that.

Her mind wandered. She thought about what she would do without Trey and what he was going to say when she handed him the money. Suddenly, Troy popped into her head. She hated to admit that she thought he was attractive, but she wondered what it would be like to be with him sexually. Would he fuck her or would he make love to her? Sometimes she liked to be held and romanced while being made loved to and sometimes she liked to be fucked. Her ass smacked. Hair pulled and just manhandled. She knew Troy could make love, but a woman like her needed to be fucked and she didn't know if she could find someone like Trey who was so in tune with her body.

The white rabbit stroked her kitty and it felt damn good, better than Trey's tongue. God she loved this. She was almost there, but she couldn't quite get there without some help from her imagination. She'd have to rely on her mental rolodex.

She remembered the time Trey had fucked her on the balcony in a Vegas hotel while the people in the suite above were looking at them. The memory was turning her the fuck on when Troy popped into her head again. In her mind, he was licking her kitty exactly how she liked it. She felt dirty for thinking about two men getting her off. Two brothers at the same time, but it was getting her off. Troy sucked her clit and now Trey bit her nipples. She exploded.

Starr was dressed up in a blue pinstriped business suit and three inch heeled Louboutins made for work, when Trey showed up at her place and though she was wearing a business suit, she looked damn good to Trey. Her three-inch heels elevated her ass and Trey smiled when he saw the pantsuit struggling to contain it. Damn he missed those hips and that tiny-ass waistline, but more importantly he missed a great woman.

"Why are you all dressed up?" Trey asked.

"Been working."

"Working?"

"Yeah, what regular people do, you know?"

"What is that supposed to mean? I'm a regular person too."

Trey sat on the sofa and Starr sat across from him. Trey said, "So what's been up? Did you miss me?"

"What do you think?"

"I think you do miss me."

"Maybe a little."

He smiled.

"You look nice."

"Just nice?"

"Well what do you want me to say? You're wearing a pantsuit. I can't say that you look sexy. I mean it's a business suit."

"You can say whatever you want—you do whatever it is you want."

"So you want to argue?"

"No, I don't, but I can't believe that you didn't ask me where I work. I tell you I've been working and you have nothing to say about it."

"That was my next question."

"I work for myself. Since you're so interested." She was very sarcastic.

"Doing what?" His tone was very demeaning, as if there was nothing she could possibly do to earn a living and needed to depend on him forever.

"Interior design."

"I didn't know that you liked doing that."

"Hmmph. That's the problem, Trey. You don't know me. Everybody that comes here talks about how I have an eye for design and how it comes natural to me, but my own man says he didn't know I like that."

He grinned and said, "So I'm your man?"

"You know what I mean."

He laughed and said, "I've always encouraged you. You forgot about the salon."

"My heart wasn't in that salon. That's why I never go and it's barely making money."

"I hate that you feel that way about me. I want the best for you."

"But you never encourage me. Even your brother complemented me on how nice the place looks."

"My brother has been here?"

"Yeah."

"What did he want?"

"Looking for you," Starr lied. She didn't know why she lied but she did. She wasn't ready to tell him that his brother had tried to hit on her. She wasn't sure it was her place to tell him since they were no longer involved.

"I wonder what he wanted."

"He didn't say."

"How did he know I lived here?"

Starr shrugged. "Maybe your baby's mother. I didn't ask."

"But he liked the place, huh?"

"Yeah."

"Look, baby, I like what you've done too."

Starr stood and they made eye contact briefly before she turned away. She had to admit that she missed him—him and his dick.

Finally, she said, "I'll go get your money."

She made her way to the bedroom where the rest of the money was as he stared at her wonderful ass. She turned and said, "Oh, there is something that I forgot to tell you."

"What?"

"I spent some."

"I figured you were going to spend some. How much did you spend?"

"Close to a hundred and forty thousand dollars."

"What did you spend that kind of money on?"

"My showroom."

"Showroom?"

"Yeah, for the business."

"Where is this place located? I mean I should at least know where my money went."

She disappeared into the bedroom and then reappeared with a gym bag containing the rest of the money. She passed it to him along with a business card.

"'A Starr is Born.' I like that play on words."

"Thanks."

He pulled her into him until she was on his lap. Trey stared at her for a moment before leaning into her and they locked lips.

They kissed passionately for five minutes; his mouth was warm and salty. Damn, she missed this man.

Finally, he said, "I missed the hell out of you."

"I missed you too."

He kissed her again and then removed her suit-jacket. He removed her shirt and bra and began sucking her tits. Her nipples sprang to life as he licked and kissed them. She was rubbing his hair as he tongue kissed her neck. Trey knew this made her hot, and this time was no different. She stood and removed her pants. She stood in front of him only wearing some pink boy shorts. Her ass was even more amazing in the flesh. Trey missed the hell out of her.

He stood and kicked off his shoes and his dick was now as hard as concrete. He dropped his pants, underwear and his dick was at full attention. The thickness and the veins were just beautiful to her. He sat back on the chair and she sat on his lap and stroked him. He continued to kiss her neck. She wanted him inside her. His hands were on her and she kept pushing him away.

"I want you," he said.

"I want you more."

"Why do you keep pushing me away?"

"I don't know."

"This is crazy. If you want me, let me have you."

"I want you, but I'm confused. I mean, this isn't right."

He kept trying to yank her boy-shorts down without results.

"What's not right about it?" Trey asked.

"You love her."

"I love you."

"Do you have a condom?"

"A what?"

"A condom."

"No."

"I can't do this. I can't fuck you knowing you been fucking somebody else. I can't take a chance with my life."

She stood and he said, "Are you fucking serious?"

She scooped her pants from the floor and he was focused on that ass and those tits. This was absolute bullshit to him.

He stood and picked up his pants and shoes. "So, you're serious?"

"Trey, I just can't trust you."

"I ain't got time for these silly-ass games," Trey said.

"I'm playing games? Motherfucker, as loyal as I was to you, and I'm the one playing games?"

He slid into his pants and he was now lacing up his sneakers. He grabbed the gym bag with the money and made his way to the door.

CHAPTER 6

It was nine p.m. and Black was at Sasha's house. She had one of those white Martinque headboards, the third woman that Black had slept with this year with a headboard like that. Her bedding was all light colored and too damn delicate looking for a roughneck-ass nigga like Black, but it was very inviting. The smell of lit vanilla scented candles filled the room. Black kicked off his Jordans and was about to sit on her bed.

"Don't sit on my bed with your jeans on," Sasha said.

Black sat on a chair in the corner of the bedroom. He said, "You women kill me with that 'don't sit on the bed with your jeans' shit. You complain, then be eating, doing your nails and all kinds of shit in a man's bed."

She smiled and said, "You're so right. I never thought about that, but I just think of my bed as a kind of sanctuary."

"A sanctuary. No way is this bed a sanctuary."

"There's more than one meaning of **the** word sanctuary, asshole. Sanctuary doesn't have to be like a sacred place. It can also be a place of safety."

"I'm sorry. I didn't go to college like you did."

"That's why you need a woman like me. You can be the muscle, and I can handle the money."

"What money?"

"Don't play dumb."

"So, you want me for my money?"

"No, I want you for that dick of yours, but I'm just saying that if you want someone to help you manage that money, I can invest it for you."

"How do you know if I have money?"

"Am I wrong?"

"I might have a few coins."

She stood from the bed and made her way into the bathroom. When she returned Beyonce's XO was playing through the surround sound speakers. She was wearing a yellow thong that looked amazing on her. Her waistline was almost non-existent. Six-inch stripper heels made her ass sit high and round. Black couldn't take his eyes off her.

She was smiling. "I want you to do something kinky to me tonight."

Black stood, kicked his shoes off, and removed his shirt. He stood there in a pair of blue boxers that was fighting hard to contain his pulsating dick.

She said, "How did you get the scars?"

"Gunshot wounds."

"Really?"

"Yeah."

Sasha didn't know why, but Black's gunshot wounds and tats were turning her on in a weird kind of way. She was a princess and he was a bad boy. She wanted him to fuck the hell out of her and treat her like a slut.

He made his way over to her and pulled her into him. His hands were now resting on her ass.

"What did you have in mind?"

"I wanna be spanked."

"You mean like when I'm hitting you from behind?"

She laughed and said, "Hell no. I'm going to lie across your lap and you're going to spank me."

"What the fuck?"

She laughed and said, "Just do it. You'll enjoy it. I promise you."

Black sat on the bed before he sprang back up. "Is it okay to sit on the bed? You know how you be tripping about your bed."

"Of course, silly."

He sat on the edge of the bed. She disappeared and came back with a small paddle and passed it to him.

"Use this or use your hands. I'd prefer your hands," she said.

"I don't know if I can do it."

She made a sad face. "Too weird for you?"

"I've never done nothing like this before."

She sat on his lap, wrapped her legs around his, and kissed him and bit his ear. She whispered, "I want you to manhandle this pussy."

She sang along with Beyonce. Black closed his eyes, his dick was throbbing. He wanted to be inside her. She lay across his lap and said, "Don't think about it. Just do it."

He smacked her ass.

"Keep going."

He kept spanking her and she was squirming and gyrating on his knee. "Keep spanking me, Daddy. I've been a bad girl."

He paddled her ass and she was getting off. She was actually getting off from a spanking. In a weird kind of way, this was turning Black the fuck on. He kept spanking her ass. He pulled her thong aside and began fingering her and spanking her at the same.

"Oh my god! You feel so goddamned good to me," she cried as her body began to convulse and she reached multiple orgasms.

He stopped spanking her and she lay across his lap for a moment, catching her breath. Finally she stood up and removed her thong.

"I want you inside me," she said.

Black stood and dropped his boxers. He made his way over to his pants to get his Magnum.

"What are you doing?" she asked.

"Getting a condom."

"I want you inside me bareback. I want to feel that dick inside me."

"No more kids for me, I'm sorry I can't do that." Black would fuck only one person raw nowadays, and that was Lani because they had history.

She made a sad face.

"I'm sorry, baby, but I'm through having kids." He removed the Magnum and slid it on. She propped herself on the bed and he entered her doggy-style.

Two hours later they were still cuddling. "I gotta admit, I like you."

Black didn't respond. He didn't know how to respond to that. He'd told her that he wasn't ready to be in a relationship and he was wondering about her alleged boyfriend.

She laughed and said, "You don't have to be quiet. I'm not trying to make you marry me."

"I know you said you have a boyfriend. Where is this mystery man?"

"Don't worry about him. I don't ever ask you about all your women."

"Whatever."

"But seriously, I think there are a lot of things I can help you with."

"Like what?"

"You ever think about not hustling. You know, making legitimate money."

"Who said I was a hustler?"

"Come on. You don't work. I can call you anytime of the day and you're doing absolutely nothing. Besides, you told me yourself you were a bad guy. Your words, not mine."

"I did say that, didn't I?" Black grinned.

"You absolutely told me that."

"But you don't have to be the bad guy? I can help you invest your money. Just give me a little at a time if you don't trust me."

"What do you call a little?"

"Well, there is this franchise opportunity that I'm interested in that requires about a hundred thousand dollars in capital. I can come up with the money myself, but I'd rather have a partner."

Black said, "Wait a minute. Your father is the mayor. He has money."

"That's a misconception. He doesn't make that much money as mayor. He has a little bit of money, but that's his money, not mine. I'm a grown woman, what would I look like going to him? Besides, he's done so much for me. He paid my tuition in full, so while most people my age are walking around here with student loans. I don't and I'm grateful."

Black said, "I can respect that. What kind of franchise?"

"Well, there are a few I'm interested in."

"Give me the details and I'll consider it."

She scooted her ass next to his dick that was now rock solid. She reached for his dick and tried to put it inside her, but he resisted and said, "No, No, No. Not without a condom."

She grinned. "Well, you can't knock a girl for trying."

CHAPTER 7

Detective Mike Williams had contacted Lani and asked her if she wanted to meet up and answer a few questions. She gave him the name of her attorney, and a few hours later, her attorney, Tom Gilliam, contacted her.

"Detective Mike Williams wants to meet and talk to you," he said.

"Do I have to talk to him?"

"You don't have to, but I think it's best."

"Why?"

"I just believe in being proactive. My job is to clear you and make sure nobody brings any charges against you. I spoke briefly with Joey Turch, and he told me the jist of what has been going on, but I can meet you at my office in a couple of hours and you can tell me your version of events. Then, I'll drive you to the detective's office."

Lani didn't want to meet with the attorney and she damn sure didn't want to meet with the police, but she kind of expected this. She knew that the police weren't just going to go away. "Okay. What's your address?"

"300 PeachTree Street NE."

Mike Williams eyeballed Lani's breasts and this brought back the memories of him rummaging through her underwear. She didn't like his perverted ass.

Thomas Kearns and Tom Gilliam exchanged pleasantries before Thomas Kearns said, "Good to see you again, Lani."

Tom Gilliam was a tall slender white man with a naturally red face and dark brown hair. He had a hook nose and wore horn-rimmed glasses. He had absolutely no sex appeal and a very matter of fact demeanor, but he was a very smart and capable attorney.

"Likewise." Lani didn't want to be there, but it was the right thing to say. She looked at Mike Williams but didn't say anything to him. Thomas Kearns sat behind his desk and Lani and her attorney sat across from him. Mike Williams stood behind Thomas Kearns occasionally stealing glances at Lani's erect nipples.

Thomas Kearns said, "Let's get down to business."

"Let's do it." Tom Gilliam said.

Mike Williams said, "We're going to take this case to the state grand jury and we're giving your client a chance to come clean about her involvement of the murder of Chris Jones."

Lani said, "Come clean? I haven't done anything."

"Do you think that the grand jury is going to believe that you had absolutely nothing to do with this man's murder? The common link between the murderer and the victim is you."

Tom Gilliam said, "So, who's been charged with this crime?"

"Kelvin Bryant."

He turned to Lani. "You know him?"

"No, I have no idea who that is."

Mike Williams said, "Her link is Tyrann Massey."

"But he hasn't been charged?"

"No, but he masterminded the whole thing."

"So you're operating off assumptions that he's going to be charged?"

"I'm almost certain that at some point he will."

"Almost is not absolute."

Mike Williams said, "Look, we wanted to give your client a chance to come clean with us. She seems like a nice girl."

Williams stared at Lani's lips wondering what it would be like to make love to a girl like her, but he could tell by her hair, expensive handbag and jewelry that it would take money to sleep with her.

Thomas Kearns said, "You know how these things go. I see it every day, young women covering up for their boyfriends. Then when we get the boyfriend, he spills the beans, tells everything, implicates the girl and then she gets more time than the boyfriend."

Lani said, "First of all, I'm nobody's girlfriend."

"But you were Chris Jones's."

"I was."

"And you were Black's."

Tom Gilliam looked confused.

"Black is Tyrann's nickname, Mr. Gilliam. Isn't that right, Lani?" Mike Williams said.

"I don't know. You tell me," Lani said.

Tom Gilliam said, "Can I have a moment alone with my client?"

Mike Williams and Thomas Kearns stepped out into the hallway.

When the door closed, Tom Gilliam said, "So you know nothing about the murder?"

Lani looked the man in the eye and said, "I didn't orchestrate the murder. I didn't order anybody to kill Chris."

"Sounds like they are trying their best to nail Tyrann and if they do, can he implicate you?"

"No." Lani felt bad because she knew about the murder, she felt like she was betraying Chris, but she knew that Black would never say that he admitted the murder to her. Hell, she knew Black wasn't going to admit shit to anybody. Besides if she cooperated with the police, there was no telling what Black would do to her.

"Well, if you are certain that you can't be implicated. We're going to end the interview."

When Mike Williams and Thomas Kearns came back into the room, Tom Gilliam said, "Gentleman, we have nothing to tell you. We'll see you in court." And they left the small office.

Lani said to Black, "So you ain't worried about getting picked up by the police?"

"Why should I worry? Whatever is going to happen, will happen. I'm not going to have a goddamned heart attack about something that may or may not happen. Besides, I'll let my lawyer worry about that bullshit. His job is to make shit go away. I pay him good."

"But the faster he makes shit go away, the more shit you get yourself into."

"Whatever, Lani. You're always so motherfuckin' negative. You know how I am, and I ain't about to change for nobody."

"Well, I can tell you right now. They're on your ass. They are trying their best to link you with the murder."

"Look, I know how the police work and what they were doing was trying to get you to flip on me. That's why I got you an attorney," Black said. "I'm a mastermind at this shit."

"That's exactly what they are calling your stupid ass— the mastermind."

"Well, they are just assuming I did some shit. How are they going to prove it?"

"Are you sure your boy is not going to flip?"

"He ain't going to say shit about me, and if he did, it will take me to implicate you and you know there is no way in the hell I'm going to say anything about you."

She believed him. She knew that if he didn't go to the police when his son was kidnapped, there was no way he would talk if he was arrested.

"I think they know for sure that you had something to do with it."

"Me too," Black smiled.

"How can you not be concerned?"

"Look, I know they know I had something to do with the murder, but proving it is different from knowing. How they hell are they going to prove it?"

Lani's phone rang. Jada was calling. "Hello?"

Her phone beeped, and she said, "My battery is dying. I'll call you back on Black's phone."

Black passed her is cell phone. "But you can't worry about that. I don't know for sure what's going to happen to me, but ain't shit going to happen to you." He put his arms around her waist and she moved away from him.

"Quit acting like that."

"Acting like what?"

"I already told you there will be no more you and me. We're friends. That's it." She took a deep breath and said, "I can't believe that I'm even your friend with as much shit as you have put me through. Yeah, I've dated hustlers most of my life and I've reaped some good benefits, but I never imagined being questioned by the police about a goddamned murder."

"You gotta take the good with the bad."

"That shit sounds comical to me. I gotta take the good with the bad."

"You're a pretty girl, Lani. You could have gotten a professional nigga, Hell, that pervert-ass police officer sniffed your goddamned panties. You could have had him too, but you know what? You chose dudes like me and Chris."

"Every time you see me, it's going to be about how flawed I am," Lani said.

"Hey, you keep telling me how fucked up I am. So I'm supposed to just sit here and put up with that?"

"I was just letting you know that there is no you and me."

"And I'm letting you know that you can't be with a regular motherfucker with a nine to five."

"What's your security code for your phone."

"1982."

When she punched in the code, a picture mail came though from a woman named Sasha. All Lani could see was a naked ass and heels propped on the edge of the bed.

"Somebody sent you a photo." She showed Black the picture of the naked-ass woman.

Black stood there with a silly ass grin.

"So you want to be with me, huh?" Lani asked.

Black shrugged and said, "What am I supposed to do? You ain't trying to give me no action."

She flung the phone at him and he ducked. It barely missed his head.

He picked up his phone and saw that the screen was shattered. "What the fuck was that all about?"

"Quit saying shit that you don't mean!"

"You just told me that we will never be together, but you get mad cuz somebody sent me a pic?"

Lani was trying to calm herself down. She said, "Look, I'm sorry."

"No, bipolar is what you are."

"Whatever."

"Seriously, why did you do that?"

"I got caught up in the moment. I'm sorry. Let me see the phone."

"The screen is cracked."

"Look, Black, I'm sorry."

"You love me, and I love you."

"I'll always love you. You'll always have my heart but not my mind, so I guess in that sense, I might be bipolar. My brain hates you, but my heart will always love you."

Black was staring at the cracked screen. Trying to decide if he could still use it to make calls.

Lani said, "Who is Sasha?"

"Why?"

"I've never heard you say anything about her."

"She's just somebody I know."

"You don't need any more baby mamas."

"Trust me, no more kids for me."

"Trust you?" Lani laughed. "You're a comedian."

"I think it's time for me to leave."

"I was thinking the same thing."

CHAPTER 8

Starr had hired Brooke, the girl who lived beside Trey's stash house. She was enjoying her second day on the job when an irate customer walked in. Mr. David Walker stormed in and demanded to see the manager. Seconds later, Starr appeared and said, "Mr. Walker, what seems to be the problem?"

"I want I full refund. I am very unsatisfied with the work you did to my home."

Starr was calm. She didn't want to get into a verbal sparring match with the man. He'd been her first customer when she opened up the showroom. She earned close to eight grand decorating his home. His wife had told her that she had another home in Florida that she wanted decorated and would give her an even bigger commission.

"What's wrong?"

"I want my money back."

"I'll give you a full refund, but first I want to know what didn't you like."

"The furniture in the den looks tacky and cheap, and I hate the artwork that you chose."

Starr said, "You're wife chose the artwork."

Troy entered the showroom. He stood a few feet away from Mr. Walker and listened to the whole conversation.

"My wife didn't choose that tasteless artwork."

Starr said, "Could you hold on for a second?" She disappeared into the office and returned with a consent form stating that all the artwork sales were final. Starr showed Mr. Walker his wife's signature on the paperwork.

David Walker scrutinized the form before admitting that it was his wife's signature. "Okay, I'll take the loss on the artwork, but that still doesn't excuse the piss-poor job you did."

Starr wanted to curse him the fuck out, but she kept telling herself she had to be professional.

Troy approached Mr. Walker. "Sir, is there any way we can make this right?"

Mr. Walker was startled and he turned to Troy. "Who the hell are you?"

"I'm her business partner, and we're just starting out and want to make sure you are satisfied. If you're not satisfied, we'll refund your money and even the money for the artwork." He winked at Starr.

Starr didn't know if she could survive a hit on the artwork if she gave Mr. Walker a full refund.

"I get this. You just don't want to give my money back," Mr. Walker said.

"That's not it at all. We're more concerned with our reputation than your money."

Mr. Walker was silent for a long time. "Can you put this in writing? That you will refund the money for the artwork if I'm not satisfied."

"We sure will, but only if you're going to give us your input. We got your wife's input the first time, and we assumed that she would be happy, but we never considered you."

"Not only will you get my input, but I'll be there while you're working."

The two men shook hands. Mr. Walker left without signing any paperwork.

When Mr. Walker was gone, Brooke said, "What an asshole."

Starr came from behind the counter and hugged Troy and said, "Thanks for handling that situation, I was about to curse his ass out." Then she turned to Brooke. "Will you fix me a cup of tea?"

"Sure," Brooke said then disappeared to the back.

When Brooke was gone, Troy said, "I'm glad you didn't curse him out. This is the business world. This is not easy money. You have to be patient with people. People are not going to just throw money away. They are going to scrutinize everything you do. This is not the drug business."

"I see. So what brings you here?" she asked.

"I wasn't doing anything, so I decided I would stop by. How is business going?" he asked.

"Mr. Walker has been my only client this far. I have another client this weekend and another the following weekend. I guess to answer your question. Very slow."

"It'll get better."

"I hope so."

He smiled and said, "Well, at least you stepped out on faith to pursue your dreams."

"But is faith going to pay the bills?"

Troy looked around the showroom. "This is a very nice place you got here."

"Thanks."

"What are you doing to market yourself?"

Starr shrugged. "It's just mostly word of mouth, but Brooke my assistant has been doing some social media stuff."

"That's what I was going to suggest and I have a couple of friends that are realtors and maybe you could pair with them, so they can give your business a boost."

"That's a good idea. If you could help me do that, I would be grateful."

"Can't believe Trey hasn't tried to help you."

"Please. Trey is only concerned with Trey. You know your brother."

Brooke reemerged with a cup of green tea and 3 packets of Stevia for Starr.

"Thanks for your help, Troy. If you will excuse me, Brooke and I need to do some organizing."

"Maybe we can meet up later for a drink. I'll text you."

"Okay, cool."

When Troy was gone, Brooke said, "I can see you have a type."

"What do you mean?"

"That man resembles Mr. Trey."

"He does, doesn't he?" Starr wanted to laugh.

Starr called Troy later that evening and they decided to meet at a little bar across from her building. She sat at a small table in the front, so she could spot Troy. She noticed him right away when he entered the room. He was wearing a blue plaid button down with a pink tie and Ray-Ban eyeglasses. His pants were a little tight but somehow he made it work. The outfit made his athletic body look even more amazing. Starr couldn't believe that she was even attracted to the metrosexual look, but maybe she was growing up. Troy sat at the table and he was smiling hard. When he sat at the table, the barmaid appeared and asked what they were going to have to drink.

"Water for me," Troy said.

"I thought you were a grown-ass man."

He laughed. "I am."

"Two Cirocs with cranberry juice."

When the barmaid returned, Starr slid one of the drinks to Troy's side.

"I'm not drinking."

"You are if you want to talk to me."

He laughed and sipped his drink. "I hope I can get up and go to work tomorrow."

"You will."

"I know I can't afford not to. Too many damn student loans."

Starr sipped her drink and said, "So, Troy, what's your deal?"

"What do you mean, 'what's my deal'?"

"Why do you want a girl like me?"

"I don't understand."

"You're a college boy, and you know I like street dudes."

Troy laughed and said, "So you're calling me a square?"

"No, I'm just trying to figure out what's your motive. Do you want to fuck me to get back at your brother or something? What is it that you want with me?"

Troy sipped his drink. "I see where you're coming from."

"Good, because I'm puzzled by this attention that you're giving me."

"Look, I'm not trying to get back at my brother, and it's not about sex. I'm not trying to press you for sex."

"If it's not about sex, tell me what is it about?"

"It's about knowing a good woman when I see one."

Starr laughed. "How do you know I'm a good woman?"

"I had a good woman before."

"What happened?"

"I wasn't ready."

"You cheated?"

"Well, not exactly."

"What the fuck does that mean?" Starr sipped her drink and said, "I'm sorry, but I'm not feeling cheaters these days, and just in case you didn't know, I have a foul mouth from time to time. You sure you want to deal with that?"

"Well, she wanted a title and I thought that was high school."

"How old were you when this happened?"

"Twenty-eight."

"Well, why wouldn't she want a title? You're the one that's high school."

"I know."

"But you cheated?"

"Well, she wanted to take a break from seeing each other. While we were away from each other, I slept with somebody else."

"Just like your brother."

"I'm nothing like him. Nothing. Ever-since then, I've been keeping it real with everybody I meet. If I want to be in a relationship, I say it, and if I don't want to be in one, I say it. I don't lead nobody on."

"You're a grown-ass man, huh?"

"Exactly." He sipped his drink and said, "You're loyal to my brother and he don't deserve it."

"You know, if I fuck with you, my reputation is going to take a hit."

"Look, that dude has fucked around on you so much, you wouldn't believe it."

"You sound like a hater."

"You're right."

"Let's talk about you and me. What do you want from me? You want pussy? What?"

"I want more than that."

"Really?" She licked her lips, not to be suggestive, but he took it as that and his dick jumped.

"I want you to give me an opportunity."

"Troy, I like you a lot, but I can't be with two brothers. No matter how hard I try, I would never be able to get over the fact that Trey is your brother."

The barmaid appeared and asked if there was anything else she could get them. "No," Starr said.

Troy dug into his wallet and removed twenty-five dollars then he stood, kissed Starr on the cheek, and made his way to the door.

CHAPTER 9

Black had been trying to contact Kyrie all morning. He started calling him at around 10 a.m. and it was now 1 p.m., and he still hadn't answered his phone. Black felt something was wrong. Kyrie always answered his phone. He dialed Kyrie's wife, Melody, but she didn't answer either. He was just about to make a drive out to their home when someone knocked on his door. Peering through the peephole, Black realized it was Kyrie.

"Where the fuck have you been?"

"I been talking to the cops all morning."

"The cops?"

"Calm down, bruh. You know I didn't give them shit."

Black led Kyrie to the den where Kyrie sat on an armchair and Black sat across from him.

"What the fuck happened?"

"They were talking about some heroin ODs."

"No shit."

"Yeah they been ODing off the Obamacare package."

"Damn." Black remembered what Shamari had told him days earlier. "We gotta put a new stamp on the package," he said.

"I know, and the fucked up thing about it is that it may not have even been our shit that people are ODing off of," Kyrie said.

"No. The fucked up part is we gotta get a new product out there and one that everybody knows again."

"I don't want to deal with this shit no more."

Black said, "Motherfucker, don't be such a pussy. Man, we're making three times as much as we did with coke."

"So I'm a pussy now because I don't want to go to jail for life? You weren't the motherfucker getting interrogated."

Black had never heard Kyrie talk like that before. Though he believed in his heart that Kyrie hadn't given the police any information, he detected a softness in Kyrie he'd never seen before. He'd have to distance himself from him. He could crack under enough pressure.

"You're right man, I'm going to chill," Black said.

"Listen, man, I didn't say we had to chill. I still want to make money, just not with heroin."

"Too much is going on. We'll take a break then we can get back to business in a month or so."

Kyrie studied Black's face wondering if he'd said something wrong. He was concerned with Black's change of heart.

Black said, "So what did the police ask you?"

"Wanted to know where I got the heroin from."

"And you said?"

"Mexicans, but they didn't believe me."

"Why?"

"They said it came from Pakistan."

"What else did they ask you?"

"Who were my customers."

"And you said what?"

"I told them I sold mostly to business people."

"Really?" Black was skeptical as hell.

"Yeah, I had to tell them something because they held up some pictures of two white teens saying that they'd overdosed."

"That don't mean that you were responsible."

"I know. Maybe I shouldn't have said nothing at all."

"You think?"

Kyrie sensed Black's sarcasm and said, "I know you probably thinking I said something about you."

"Now that's where you're wrong. Not for one minute did I believe that you would implicate me. You and I both know that you know better than that."

"You seem pissed.

"Cuz you shouldn't have said a motherfucking THANG!"

"You're right."

Rashida rushed to the door wearing a robe. She was surprised to see that it was her brother on her doorstep. They embraced and she invited him in. He was sweating and he looked very concerned.

"What brings you here?" she asked.

"I got a lot of shit on my mind, and you're the only person I can talk too. I need to use the restroom."

He walked in the direction of the hall bathroom before she said, "Use the one on the other side of the dining room."

Black stopped and he looked confused before she said, "I have company, Tyrann."

"My bad." Black didn't know why he had assumed his sister spent her nights alone. Hell, she was a grown woman with needs and she was a lot older than he was, but he still didn't like to think of some clown humping his sister. Even though she was damn near a genius, she wasn't that smart when it came to picking men. He used the restroom and met her at the kitchen table.

"Who is he?"

"A friend I knew since college."

"Not that married clown again."

Rashida laughed and said, "No, not him, and quit judging me."

"Not judging you. I'm judging him. That nigga is exactly like me, just with a college degree."

Rashida was laughing her ass off.

"What's going on?"

"I'm afraid, sis, and you're the only person I can tell this too. You're the only person that has ever seen me afraid."

"I can't remember ever seeing you being afraid."

"Remember when I was a kid and those twins, Donald and Darnell, tried to jump me? I ran home afraid and you made me kick both of their asses."

Rashida laughed. "But you were only eight years old."

"Doesn't matter, I was afraid."

"Don't understand your point, but what are you afraid of now?"

"There was no point to the story. It's just that I don't like everybody to see me vulnerable."

"What the fuck is going on?"

"I don't know where to begin."

She rubbed his hand and said, "You can tell me anything, lil brother. I won't judge."

"I been thinking about K.B. a lot lately and I don't know if he can hold up."

"K.B.? Who the hell is that? What are you talking about?"

"K.B. is the dude that they holding for murder."

"The one that you had something to do with?"

"Yeah."

"Why did you do it?"

"You just said you wouldn't judge, so I don't wanna hear all that coulda, woulda, shoulda bullshit. Besides, I wasn't the one that pulled the trigger."

"Is that what you like to tell yourself to justify shit? We all like to tell ourselves things to make us feel good about ourselves, but, Tyrann, the bottom line is you did wrong. Admit it. Get it out. I'm not going to judge you and I damn sure ain't going to tell anybody."

Black turned from his sister's gaze. "Yeah, I did wrong, sis, and I know that I'm going to have to answer for it one day."

"Why'd you do it?"

"The man tried to kill me."

"Why did he try to murder you?"

"He was Lani's boyfriend."

"This is about Lani?"

"Not exactly." He didn't want Rashida or anybody in his family to think badly of Lani because the fact of the matter was, Lani was a good person.

"So you're afraid K.B. might rat you out?"

Black stared his sister in the eyes and said, "If he does, I'm going away for a very long time."

Rashida felt herself tearing up. She didn't even want to think about the possibility of losing her brother.

"Don't cry, sis. Now that's the exact reason I didn't want to tell you anything. I knew that you wouldn't be able to take it."

"You're my baby brother, and when I see you in pain, I can't help but cry."

Rashida stood and ripped a paper towel from the roll in front of her and dabbed her eyes.

"I need a favor," Black said.

"Anything."

"Go see K.B."

"In jail?"

"Yeah, I think he's on Wright Street. I need you to find out where his head's at. I know you don't like to visit jails, but you're one of the only people I trust besides Lani and I can't send Lani down there because she's been questioned. The police think that she had something to do with it."

"I'll do anything that you want me to." She finished drying her eyes and he stood and hugged his sister before walking to the door.

"So I'll meet you the day after tomorrow."

"That's fine, preferably in the morning."

Before she opened the door to let him out, Black said, "You tell that nigga that he better treat you right or else I'll kill his ass."

She said, "You don't need to kill anybody else. You've done enough, boy. Please go somewhere and sit yo ass down."

He laughed and gave her another hug.

The next day at 11:45 p.m., Black was standing on Rashida doorstep again ringing the hell out of her doorbell. She frowned when she saw him and stood there with her hands on her hips. He sensed that she didn't want him to come in. She looked pissed off. Her hair was messy as hell and not wrapped. He sensed that his big sister was being a victim of a brutal doggy style when he started hammering on the door again.

"Why in the hell do you keep popping up at my house like this?"

"What did K.B. say?"

"I thought the deal was that we were supposed to meet in the morning?"

"That's what I said, but I needed to know what's going on now. There is no way I could get any sleep without knowing what the fuck is going on."

"Hold it down. I have company again tonight."

"I figured that was why you were looking pissed when you opened the door. Getting some dick, huh?"

"Boy, I'm not about to discuss my personal life with you. Just keep your voice down."

"Was I that loud?"

"You know how your voice carries."

"Promise not to wake your Boo."

"Will you shut up!" She knew he was teasing but she wasn't in the mood for it. She led him back into the kitchen and before they were seated, she got a Coke Zero from her fridge and handed it to him.

He popped the top and took a sip before asking, "So what'd you find out?"

"K.B. said he was offended that I'd come down there to see him."

"Why?"

"He said that he would never let anything bad happen to you. I took that as he wasn't going to talk to the police."

"But why was he offended?"

"Because two and two is four, Tyrann. He figured out that I'd come down to see if he was talking to the police. I'm your sister. I've never seen this man before, and all of a sudden, I show up to visit him. Don't have to be a genius to guess what that is all about."

Black laughed and said, "I see, but I gotta watch my ass now."

"He said to give his baby's mother some money for his attorney."

"I know I've been meaning to take her some money and also Twan's baby mother."

"Who the hell is Twan?"

"A friend of mine from Alabama."

"Is he locked up too?"

"No. He's dead."

"Was he in on the murder?"

"Yes."

Rashida stood up and made her way to the fridge to get a Coke Zero for herself. She said, "Jesus Christ, Tyrann. I don't even want to know what happened to him!"

"Good. But look, sis, don't worry. Everything is going to be fine. Don't worry about me."

"But you're worried. You told me so last night."

Black took a swig of his coke. He didn't respond because she was absolutely right.

"Look, Tyrann, I don't know what the fuck is happening. I just don't want anything to happen to Nana."

"Nothing is going to happen to Nana. Trust me, sis. I'm going to buy her a new house as soon as this blows over."

"Then what are you going to do with your life? Being a forty-year-old drug dealer is not cool."

"Forty? I'm nowhere near forty."

"You'll be surprised how fast time will creep up on you."

"I've got some things in the works."

Rashida laughed. "You've been saying that all your life."

"I know I have, but this time it's for real. I met a girl who wants to partner up with a couple of franchise opportunities."

"I hope so." Rashida stood and said, "Bro, I'd love to talk to you all night."

He finished is coke and said, "Your dick awaits you."

They both laughed their asses off.

CHAPTER 10

Shamari had just arrived from California. He scored some heroin from his connection, and it took his runner three days to drive the product back from Los Angeles to Atlanta. It was nine a.m. when Shamari rang Black's doorbell. He carried a blue backpack containing the product. Black laughed when he saw him.

"What's funny?" asked Shamari.

"I still gotta get used to that Caucasian-looking face." Black chuckled and said, "You know what I was just thinking? You look like a goddamned black-white man."

"What is that supposed to mean?"

"You ever see a black person that looks like a white person?"

Shamari was getting pissed and Black sensed it.

"Have a seat."

"What's in the backpack?

"Pure shit." He removed the product and tossed it on the table.

"Where'd you get it?"

"L.A. Remember, I told you I had a friend in Cali that could get it for me? He taxed me, but it's pure."

"Black dude?"

"Yeah."

"Well it ain't pure, I can guarantee you that."

"Looks good, but since I don't do it, I'll have to get somebody to test it." Shamari said.

"You trust your connect?"

"Yeah, I've been to his mom's house before."

"Look, like I said before, I doubt that it's pure, but I hope it's decent."

"We'll soon find out. So what are you going to call it?"

"Obamacare." Black replied.

"No way in hell! Are you crazy? That shit is killing people!"

"But it's what people want and it's in demand. It's the package that people want. We gotta give them what they want."

Shamari stood and paced. "You've lost your goddamned mind, man! White kids are dropping left and right because of this. I don't want to be the one that they associate with this shit. The mayor, police chief and the DEA were on T.V today talking about how they're going to find out who is pushing this poison. It was a huge press conference with a couple of white families holding pictures of their kids that OD'd."

"I understand all of that. But understand that you're already a wanted goddamned man that needs to make money!"

Shamari sat his ass back down.

Black said calmly, "There's a million motherfuckers out here selling hamburgers but you know who the big three are—McDonald's, Burger King, and Wendy's. You know why? Because motherfuckers recognize them, that's why."

Shamari smirked, thinking was this motherfucker serious with his analogy?

Black said, "Obamacare is a brand that people recognize and they want. I don't want to have to build up another brand."

"It's also a brand that's killing motherfuckers so quit comparing dope to hamburgers."

Black said, "Okay, you're the one that needs the money, not me."

Shamari sat there and thought about everything Black had said. He weighed the risk with the rewards and said, "You know that I'm in. I don't think it can get much worse than attempted murder on an informant."

Black gave him a pound.

"Where is your boy?"

"Who?"

"Kyrie."

"Man, police picked him up, but they let him go and he came over here all shook up."

"The police picked him up for what?"

"Questioned him about that heroin he'd gotten charged for, but we knew that was going to happen."

"What did he say?"

"He said he'd gotten it from some Mexican but they didn't believe him. Police said it came from Pakistan. I told you when I first saw it that I thought it was from Afghanistan or Columbia."

"So, did he tell them anything else?"

"No. But he was scared. Kind of like you were a few minutes ago," Black laughed.

"I wasn't scared. Just being careful."

"Okay, are we going to make this money or are we going to join the army?"

Shamari said, "You've got to be the craziest motherfucker I've ever known."

Black laughed then they embraced. Suddenly, there was a knock on the door.

Shamari said, "Who the fuck is that?"

There was a black nine millimeter on the end table. Black grabbed it and made his way over to the door. "Who is it?"

"It's me."

"Me who?"

"It's Kyrie. Open the door."

Black opened the door as Shamari stood behind him. Black stepped aside and let him in.

Kyrie said, "What's up, Shamari?" His eyes went straight to the product that was on the coffee table. "Just as I thought."

"What the fuck are you talking about?"

"I knew I scared you earlier. I knew you were bullshitting me about taking a break."

Black said, "Dude, you talked to the police and you come here all shook up, like you're afraid and shit. I don't like pussies. You know that."

Kyrie said, "I understand and I'm not afraid of shit. I just want to change the name and quit cutting the dope with rat poison. That shit is killing people, man."

Shamari said, "Cutting it with what?"

Black said, "Don't pay that nigga no mind."

Shamari said, "I know goddamned well you're not cutting the dope with rat poison! Please tell me that's a lie. Please tell me that you're not cutting this shit with rat poison?" Shamari glanced at Black.

Kyrie realizing that he'd said something that he shouldn't have and said, "No, we're not cutting it with rat poison. That was just a figure of speech, nigga."

Black stared at Shamari and could tell that he wasn't buying it. "You want to make your million dollars, don't you?"

"But I don't want to kill a bunch of motherfuckers in the process."

Black said, "Look, I'm not forcing them to use this shit. I've never forced nobody to snort anything. There is a risk in ODing off any drug. Quit worrying about that shit."

Kyrie said, "Black, you think I would tell on you? I've been knowing you since we were kids, nigga. I would never, ever, tell on you. I love you, man, but I'm with Shamari. I'm not feeling all these motherfuckers dying and we got to change the name of the dope."

Black stared at the two kilos of heroin and said, "I understand, but you know what happens when somebody ODs off Obamacare. It makes the news and gives us publicity. And guess what? The junkies hear about it and they want to try it. They know they can die, but they want to try it. I know it's the craziest shit you've ever heard but that's how it works."

"Change the name," Kyrie said.

"To what?"

"I don't know. Anything but Obamacare."

Black said, "Cool."

"No more rat poison," Kyrie said.

Black said, "Okay, Okay."

CHAPTER 11

Jada was headed to her mom's house to pick her up so they could run a few errands when her phone rang. Craig? What the fuck did he want? She didn't know if she could trust him after she and Shamari made him operate on Shamari's face. She doubted he'd call the police but she knew that he would probably try to get even with her. She decided not to answer but at the last moment changed her mind.

"Hello?"

"Can you talk?" Craig asked.

"No. Why?"

"I need a favor."

"What?"

"I need some blow. Just a couple of grams."

"For what?"

"Jada, you know I use."

"Quit calling me about goddamned drugs on my cell phone! What the fuck is your problem?"

"Nobody is trying to get you busted."

"Get me busted? I'm no drug dealer. Look, I'm going to hang up on your stupid ass."

"Do you really think if I had the police with me, I'd be asking for a couple of grams? Get real."

She thought about what he said. There would be no way the police in Atlanta would be worried about a couple of grams. They had the Big Papas and Treys and Blacks of the world to think about, even the Cartel.

"Look, I don't wanna talk on the phone about this."

"Let's meet up."

"I have to take my mom to a few places. I'll call you back and we can meet up."

"Look, can you get what I asked for or not? I mean if you can't, just say so. I'll see if I can get somebody else to do it."

"What about Skyy? Why don't you get Skyy to cop it for you?"

"I asked her already."

"So you're asking every black girl you've slept with to cop coke for you?"

"Jada, if you can't do it, just say you can't do it."

"I didn't say I couldn't do it. I said let's meet and talk about it."

She could hear him breathing heavy into the phone. Finally, he said, "I need it. Can you get it for me or not?"

"I'll see what I can do." She ended the call and dialed Big Papa.

"Hello?"

"Hey, baby," Jada said.

"You finally call me back?"

"Been super busy, trying to find a place to live."

"You still in that hotel?"

"No. I'm in another hotel, but I've found a place in Buckhead. I'll be moving in this weekend."

"So what's up, baby? You wanna see me?"

"Of course."

"When?"

"First, I gotta take my mom a few places then let's meet at the Atlanta Fish Market at one p.m."

"See you then."

Big Papa and Jada sat at a booth. Big Papa looked like he'd lost ten more pounds since the last time Jada had seen him. At least, he was able to fit comfortable in the booth. That was a feat in itself. She had to admit he was still big as hell but she admired his discipline and determination.

"Looking good, babe," Jada said.

"Not as good as you." Big Papa looked at her like he wanted to throw her on the table and eat her pussy right there in the restaurant. As thirsty as he looked, it actually made Jada feel good because it was a jeans and t-shirt kind of day and her hair was in a pony-tail. Nothing special, but she was sure that she looked better than every woman that he'd ever slept with.

"So what's going on, baby? Why did you want to see me?"

"I need a small favor."

He took a deep breath indicating that he was possibly tired of her using him.

"What do you need?"

"White girl"

"Huh?" Big Papa's dumb ass actually looked confused.

"Blow!" Jada said then she sniffled hoping he would get the hint.

"Coke? Who said I sold coke?" Big Papa said loudly.

"Well, why don't you just get on top of the goddamned table and yell it out and let everybody in this motherfucker know we are talking about drugs."

"You think I sell coke?" He lowered his voice.

"Nobody said you sold coke, and I'm still not saying you sell coke. Do you know where I can get some?"

"No."

Jada realized this clown was thinking that she was trying to set him up. She wanted to laugh. She knew he was no dummy, but she was no dummy either. She knew that his fat ass knew where to find coke.

"Look, I'm looking for a gram."

He laughed and said, "A gram? Who the hell wants a gram? Wait a minute, you snort?"

When he said that, the couple at the next table looked toward them.

"Will you shut the fuck up! No, I'm not a coke head."

"But, you do lines?"

"No. This is for a friend."

The waitress appeared and Jada ordered a chef salad and a margarita. Big Papa declined to order. When the waitress had gone, Big Papa said. "So you're looking for coke for your friend?"

"Yeah."

"A gram? Who is the friend?"

"You don't know everybody that I know."

"Atlanta is small."

"You don't know him."

"That dude that was at the hotel that day? That nigga told me to 'take a hike, Fat-Boy'. I've never been so humiliated in my goddamned life."

Jada reached over and massaged his hand, trying to repair his fragile little ego.

"Look, I'm sorry for that."

Papa tapped the table. "So you want a gram?"

"Look, it's for a friend of mine. A white professional man. Not a police officer. He likes to party and he doesn't know where to find it."

"I ain't gone lie. I was a little leery at first." Papa said.

Jada knew she'd read him right. She knew that his fat ass thought she was trying to set him up. Comical.

"So can you get it?"

"I can, but a gram is not going to be enough. Nobody that I know sells grams."

Jada stared at him. Now she would have to play his silly-ass game like she didn't know the coke was coming from him.

"So what is the least amount your people will sell?"

"An ounce."

"How much?"

"800 dollars."

"Are you kidding me?"

"Well if he gets a gram, they are going to tax."

"How much?"

"A hundred dollars."

Though Jada slept with her share of drug dealers, she really didn't know the ins and outs of the actual business, but she could tell that it would make more sense to buy the ounce. She just wasn't sure Craig wanted to spend 800 dollars for the ounce.

"I'll have to ask him."

The waitress dropped Jada's salad and when she was gone, Big Papa said, "I'll get you a gram for your friend."

Jada removed a hundred dollar bill from her purse and was about to pass it to Big Papa when he said, "Just keep it. Tell your friend, it's on me. Next time he's going to have to buy an ounce."

"I'll let him know."

Jada finished her salad real quick, and then she followed Big Papa to his condo. Thirty minutes later, one of Big Papa's friends arrived with the coke. He was tall, dark, and well-built with some very neat locks. Jada thought the nigga looked fine and she would definitely fuck him, but out of respect she'd have to pass. Besides, she knew from experience those kind of men didn't like to pay for shit. Big Papa sensed Jada staring at his friend and he led the man to the kitchen. Moments later, Big Papa let the man out and then he made his way back into the living room where he presented Jada with the coke.

"Thank you, baby."

"This is three grams."

"You treat me so well."

"I try my best, but I know you really don't like me."

She made a sad face. "Why do you say that?"

"I just get a sense that you don't like me."

"I love you."

"You love me? How can you love me? We've never been intimate except that one time."

"What time?" Jada was trying to jog her memory. Had she gotten drunk and fucked this disgusting motherfucker?

"You remember that time I went down on you."

"Oh yeah," Jada said, trying to block that shit out of her memory.

"But you said you loved me."

"I said I loved you, but I'm not in love with you."

He looked sad.

"Don't look like that, Daddy."

He shrugged and said, "What am I supposed to do?"

"About what?"

"My needs. You know I got needs too."

"What are you saying?"

"Just hold on a second." He disappeared into the bedroom and came back with five thousand dollars and tossed it on the table.

"What is that for?"

"It's yours?"

"You giving that to me?"

"On one condition."

"And that condition is?'

"Let me taste it again."

"You think I'm a ho?"

"No, baby."

"I'm insulted, motherfucker! I let you do that to me the last time cause I liked you and I was in need. But I wouldn't have done that if I didn't really like you."

Jada was playing on him. The last time she let him perform oral sex on her was because she needed the money. "No, I'm not saying that you a ho."

"I hope not." Jada started crying fake tears, and Big Papa ran over to her. She laid her head on his shoulders and he was rubbing her head.

Jada said, "I thought you really cared about me, like I care about you. You know it took me a lot to say that I love you and now you playing me like I'm some kind of two-dollar ho."

"I didn't mean to upset you."

"I had sex with you, I trusted you, and you treat me like a low-class stripper."

"No."

"You don't respect women." Jada pulled away from him and made her way over to the door. "I'm leaving and you can just delete my number."

Big Papa ran over to the door and blocked the exit. "Please don't be mad at me. I'm sorry."

"I'm just a sex object to you. I'm more than sex, you know?"

"I know."

"I shared my body with you. I don't do that with everybody. I thought you were one of the good men and you turned out to be just like the rest."

"I'm sorry. You know I'm not like that." He eased over to the table where the money was and scooped it up. He tossed it to her and said, "Go to Phipps and go shoe shopping."

She tossed the money into her bag and said, "I forgive you." She approached him and hugged him and said, "I gave myself to you, and like I said, I love you."

"I love you too."

"Text me later and I might just come over and let you get a taste."

"You don't have to."

She gave him a peck on the lips and walked toward the door. Before she opened it to let herself out, she glanced over her shoulder; he was staring at her ass.

Jada met Craig at Starbucks on Peachtree. They sat at a table near the front window. He didn't look well at all. He looked as if he hadn't slept in a few days. His hair was disheveled and he had a three-day growth of stubble on his face. She passed him the coke under the table.

"Thanks. How much do I owe you?"

"Well that's three grams and it's a hundred dollars a gram." Though Jada had gotten it free, he didn't have to know that.

"I only got two hundred in cash on me. You can follow me to the ATM."

"You give me the two hundred. Consider the last gram on me."

"Thanks." He slid the drugs into his pocket.

"You are turning into a coke head, man."

"Hey, I like to party a little bit."

"Whatever, man. You were begging like this shit was a matter of life and death."

"I got problems. Who doesn't have problems?"

"What kind of problems? You can talk to me. I care about you."

"You care about me?" He laughed and said, "You care about me, extort me and then practically abduct me and make me perform three procedures pro bono."

"Pro bono?"

"Well not pro bono because that would mean I volunteered."

"Tell me what's going on."

"My life is going to hell, that's what's going on."

"Be specific."

"My wife has basically kicked me out."

"For what?"

"Well I guess she suspected me of cheating and she had some goddamned software hooked up to my iPhone. She was somehow able to get all my text messages and pictures."

"Pictures of women, I'm assuming."

"Yeah, but surprisingly, there wasn't a picture of you."

"But you had my goddamned name in your phone, didn't you?"

"No. I simply had J. That could be anybody. She don't know shit about you."

"So she knows about Skyy?"

"Yes. And this girl was sending pictures every goddamned day."

"Wow."

"Okay, your wife knows you've been sleeping with a black stripper, that's still no reason to go on a coke binge."

"Look, I got more problems than you'll ever know."

"Well, how will I know unless you tell me?" She reached for his hand and held it.

"Got financial problems."

"I don't believe it. "

"Well, I gotta pay the mortgage for three homes, and the judge said I have to pay spousal support until we go to court."

"Then what?"

He looked away then made eye contact with her.

"Talk to me," she said.

A tear rolled down his cheek and she squeezed his hand. "You can tell me," Jada said again.

"You already know."

"You're an addict?"

"I have a problem." He wiped the tears from his face and said, "I know your saying, if I know I have a problem, why don't I just stop?"

"No. I'm not judging you. My sister has been battling addiction most of her adult life."

"I didn't know that."

"I never talk about her. I never see her. Though I hear she's been doing better."

"Well, that's good."

"Back to you, how can I help you?"

"Unless you've won the lottery and you want to give me a loan, there's not much you can do."

"I still have the money that you gave me. I can give it back to you."

"You mean extorted from me?"

"Whatever." Jada laughed.

"No. Keep it."

"I don't understand. Why don't you want the money?"

"If I need it, I'll ask for it back, but right now, I've been borrowing money from my business."

"How long do you think you can do that for?"

"I don't know."

She let go of his hand and said, "Well, the money will be here for you if you need it."

"Thanks."

CHAPTER 12

Trey entered Shantelle's apartment with a key she'd given him. She was startled when he barged into the bathroom. She was standing in front of the mirror, butt naked.

He kissed her and she said, "Hold on a minute, babe." She laid the hair curlers down beside her Sonicare toothbrush and applied some lip balm to her upper lip then puckered up.

He laughed and said, "All of that for a kiss."

"I'm a girly-girl."

"And you know that's what I like."

"You do, don't you, Daddy?" She tried to hug him and he moved away.

She frowned.

"I have a surprise," he said.

She smiled. "I love surprises."

Trey held onto something behind his back. She tried to see but he was concealing whatever it was very well.

"Guess?"

She thought hard, wondering what he could have behind his back, but she had no idea.

"I don't know, but please tell me." She tried to peek around his back again, but he kept moving."

"Take a guess?"

"Big or small?"

"Small."

"Jewelry."

"You're good."

She was smiling hard as hell. "A ring?"

"Not quite."

Trey brought the package to the front where she could see it. "David Yurman."

"Yes." Trey passed her the bag and she removed the two boxes. Inside she found two bracelets.

She placed the boxes in front of the Sonicare toothbrush and leaped into his arms. He struggled to hold her, not because she was heavy, but because she surprised him. She planted kisses all over his face.

When he released her, she embraced him again and said, "I love them."

"I'm glad"

"Why'd you do it?"

"I appreciate you."

"Awww."

She kissed him again and said, "So, are we official?"

"What do you mean official?"

"Are we a couple?"

There was an awkward silence. Trey didn't know how to answer her question but he could see how giving her gifts could relay that message.

"So, I guess that means no?"

"No...I mean that doesn't mean no."

"So it means yes?"

"No."

"What does it mean?"

"It means we are adults. Do we really have to have labels? As long as I love you and you love me, what difference does it make?"

"It means a lot. It means I'm in a relationship, and I will have certain boundaries that I don't cross."

"I was in a relationship with Starr and I crossed boundaries with you. So saying that you're in a relationship don't mean shit."

"Can we ever have a conversation without you bringing that bitch up?"

"Look, I'm sorry."

"No you're not. I'm not stupid, Trey. That's who you really want to be with."

Trey pulled Shantelle into his arms and said, "Don't feel like that, baby. I want to be with you."

They kissed and he held her for a long time.

CHAPTER 13

Black and Sasha met at the Atlanta Bread Company. She ordered clam chowder and a cup of water. Black had a coke and a turkey sandwich. Sasha was looking spectacular as usual. She was wearing a high-waisted pencil skirt that made her waist look extra skinny and it was shellacked on her showing her curvy figure. Her hair was in a do that highlighted her face.

Black watched her ass sway from side to side as he followed her, while carrying the food. Finally when they made it to the table pulled her chair out. After she was seated, he said, "You are fine as a motherfucker."

"Is that a compliment?"

"Damn right it is."

She laughed. "You are too funny." She stared at him and she could tell he wanted her. She felt a little horny too, but she was pressed for time; otherwise, it would be nothing to deep throat him in the backseat of her car.

"So what's up? How you been?" Black asked.

"I made a list of the companies that I would like to seek franchise opportunities with."

"What are they, and how much is it going to cost?"

She laughed and said, "The black man always wanting to know the bottom line."

"I don't know about other black men, only this black man, and I need to know how much I'm spending."

"I feel you on that one."

Her phone rang and she said, "Excuse me, I gotta take this call." She stood up and dipped into the ladies room. Five minutes later, she was back at the table.

"Sorry about that," she said.

"Was that your boo?"

"No actually it was my dad. Man, he's getting on my nerves. He's going to have another press conference and he wants me there to support him."

"A press conference?"

"Yeah. Supposedly there's some heroin on the street that's killing people, and he, the police commissioner and the DEA are having a press conference."

"But didn't they just have a press conference about that?"

"They did. Just a few days ago and it's really pissing me off because black people are dying off drugs and killing each other all the time; now, a few white people die, and it's like we gotta do something about this. But when you're in politics, you know how it goes. You move for the people with the money."

"He's a puppet," Black said.

"Huh? Did you say my dad was a puppet?"

Black sipped his coke and said, "Look, I'm sorry."

"No, it's okay, I never thought about it like that, but I guess you're right."

Black bit into the turkey sandwich. He knew damn well that this new heroin was not the same as before, but it carried the same name, and though it was killing people, the name was branded and that's what people wanted because they believed it was the best.

"What's wrong?"

"Oh, nothing. I was just thinking about what you said."

"What part?"

"Oh, the part about how now that white kids are OD'ing off heroin, all of a sudden, drugs are a priority for the city."

Sasha said, "Drugs are paradoxical for black people."

"Para what?"

"What I mean is, black people want drugs off the streets but when we give the dealers a lot of time, we scream that it ain't fair."

"True, but the time should fit the crime. I think that's all black people want. I mean, don't give me a hundred times more time than somebody else that does the same thing or worse."

"True."

"Let's talk about something else."

"Have you ever done time?"

Now this bitch was being nosey. He really didn't want to answer the question, but hell, he was who he was.

She was staring at him, waiting on him to answer.

"Yes, I've been to school a time a two."

"School?"

"People like you got schools like Spelman and Georgia Tech, and then there is people like me that attend other schools. You know the kind of schools where niggas don't know what paradoxical mean."

She was laughing her ass off. "You are one funny dude."

"Let's discuss business," Black said.

"I have a list of the franchises that we can decide on."

"What are they?"

"Smoothie King, ColdStone and Wingstop which I think would do great in the Atlanta area."

"Okay, what will I need to come up with?"

"I will let you know in a few days. Well, after we decide which one we're going to pursue."

"One more thing, my sister will be your partner. She's totally legit. Knows what paradoxical means and everything."

"Really?" Sasha eyed him like she didn't believe a goddamned word he said.

"Yes, she's a physician's assistant."

"A physician's assistant or a medical assistant? There is a difference, you know?"

Black laughed and said, "Man, you trying to play me. I know the difference. My sister is right under a family practitioner."

"So she'll be my partner on paper."

"Absolutely."

Sasha's phone rang. It was her dad again. She stood up from the table and said, "I gotta go get ready for this damn press conference."

CHAPTER 14

Craig: *Can you get me three more grams?*

Jada: *Are you kidding me?*

Craig: *I need them like yesterday. Can you help me or not?*

Jada called him and he picked up right away.

"Why are you texting me this bullshit over my phone. I've told you this over and over. Plus, you told me your wife had some kind of tracking device on your goddamned phone. I don't want to be dragged into your divorce proceedings. I don't want my mother-fucking name to come up. Is that clear?"

"Look Jada, I'm sorry, but I need to see you. Can we meet up?"

"No, I'm busy."

"Okay, you're too busy for me?"

"Look, I've just moved into my new place and I was getting everything situated. Unpacking and stuff."

"I can come over."

"No."

"Why? You don't want me to know where you live, huh?"

"Do I know where you and your wife live?"

"Look, she kicked me out of the house, so I'm living in a hotel. I told you that."

"I can't meet up with you."

"Well, you told me if I needed the money that I gave you, that you would give it back. Well, I need it back."

"Can it wait till in the morning?"

"No. I have a proposition."

"What kind of proposition? I'm not fucking you for money. I'm not a goddamned prostitute. You need to call Skyy for that."

"Not that kind of proposition."

"Why don't you just say it?"

"I would, but you get all weird-about cell phones."

Jada took a deep breath. She really didn't want to leave the house and she knew Shamari would be back soon. Even though they weren't officially together, she didn't want him to be giving her the side eye.

"Look, I can meet you for thirty minutes then I gotta go. Where are you?"

"I'm at the Days Inn on Spring Street. Can you come here?"

"No. Let's meet at Cheetah's."

"Perfect."

Janelle Monae's "*Prime Time*" played as they sat at a table next to the stage. A scrawny-ass black girl in a neon green thong and tits that looked like they belonged to a thirteen year old, danced on stage. Craig was admiring the woman and Jada said, "You like that?"

"No, I just like the way she's dancing."

"The girl looks like a fucking adolescent teenage boy. But you will fuck anything."

Craig smirked but didn't respond. There was no time to argue with her, he had more important matters.

"So, tell me, good doctor?"

"Tell you what?"

"Tell me what the fuck was so important that I had to run out of my house?"

"I need a fix."

"But you said you wanted the money back and by the way I didn't bring it."

"It's okay, but can you get me something to snort?" He sniffled and snot was now on his upper lip.

"Clean your nose."

He scooped a napkin from the table and dabbed his nose.

"I'm not going to get you any more coke. Fuck that! You can get high, but you're going to have to get high on your own. I'm not going to be the one that helps."

"Okay."

The scrawny girl stepped off the stage and approached the table and hugged Craig.

"Hey, handsome. You want a dance?" the girl asked.

"Not right now. Come back in a few moments."

When the woman was gone, Jada said, "Why didn't you get a dance? I saw you looking at her."

"With what?"

"You want coke. Where were you going to get the money from?"

"I was hoping you could get it for me."

"Are you fucking serious?"

"Very."

"Look, I cannot believe you're that broke."

"I have a little bit, but my wife is trying to take all of my goddamned money. Can you believe she just told the judge that she can't live off eleven thousand dollars a month? She wants sixteen thousand."

"What?"

"That bitch just wants to take everything I have. She wants to leave me with nothing."

"Damn."

"I'm selling two of my cars tomorrow. I need some money."

Jada flagged the waitress, and then asked for a Ciroc and Coke.

"So what did you want with me?"

"I don't know. I was thinking I could do some more work on your boyfriend's face. Give him a brow lift maybe some fillers. To make him even more un-recognizable."

"He's not going to go for that, and I don't like the way he looks now."

"You didn't think it was good work?"

"It was great work, but I don't like him looking like that. I liked him better when he looked rugged."

"But he's friggin hiding."

"I guess."

The waitress dropped the drink and Jada took a sip and said, "I'm sorry, but I don't think we can help you with that."

"What about the rhinoplasty you wanted?"

"I decided I don't need one," Jada said. "Wait a goddamned minute! What's going on with your business? Why are you trying to get side business?"

"Well, my partner is counting every goddamned coin that comes into the account."

"So, you want to do some work under the table?"

"Exactly."

"There is nothing I can do for you," Jada sipped her drink. "Did you ask Skyy to get some of her stripper friends?"

"Most strippers are broke, you know that."

"You ain't lying."

The scrawny bitch was eyeing them from across the room, looking desperate for a dance. Jada waved her over, handed her a twenty, and said, "Give him a dance, honey."

Jhene Aiko's *"Comfort Inn"* was playing. Jada's mind was racing, trying to think of someone who might need some under-the-table work. Lani's view on surgery was that she would have it after kids. Jada doubted Starr would want any surgery. She was stacked like a brick house, naturally. The skinny bitch finished dancing and asked Jada if she wanted a dance.

"Gain a few more pounds, sweetheart."

The woman frowned and thanked Craig.

Jada said, "I'm the one that paid for the dance, skinny bitch."

When the woman was gone, Jada said, "I've been thinking, and there is nobody I can think of that would need your services right now."

Craig's face got serious. "Can I help your boyfriend in some capacity?"

"Huh? What the fuck did you say?"

"Can I help Shamari?"

"Help him how? I already told you, he's not going to get any more surgery."

"No, I didn't mean like that."

"What did you have in mind?"

"I was thinking I could be a mule."

Jada spit her drink out thinking about him being a drug runner. "First of all, who uses those terms except the goddamn police?" She was laughing her ass off thinking of his corny ass trying to traffic drugs.

"No seriously, I could bring the drugs back. Look at me? Who would think of stopping me? I'm a middle aged, professional, white male. No cop is going to stop me."

She looked at him seriously and said, "This ain't Breaking Bad, white boy. This is serious and you will go directly to prison if you get caught. You need to reconsider it." She sipped her drink and said, "Actually, you need to find you a twelve-step program. Get your ass clean and then get back to being the top plastic surgeon in Atlanta." She looked at the snot crawling down his nose again. "You have fell way off."

"I hear you and I do want to get myself clean, but that doesn't take away the fact that I need some money now, Jada. I don't think I will get caught."

"But if you do?"

"It's not going to happen."

"But if it does?"

"If I get caught, I'll take my licks."

"This ain't grade school. There will be no licks. There will be time."

"I understand."

"But he's not going to go for it because you have a habit."

"What does that have to do with anything? And he doesn't have to know."

Jada passed him a napkin and said, "Wipe your nose again, please."

Craig cleaned his nose and said, "Are you saying that I would steal something from him?"

"Fuck no! I'm not saying that at all. Just saying you'll get pulled because your nose is running like a goddamn faucet."

"That's not going to happen."

"Look, I'm going to be honest with you. I don't think he's going to go for it. He don't like you. He don't trust you."

"I understand that, but he's a business man and as a business man you have to put your emotions aside."

"I'll ask him."

"That's all I'm asking. It's worth a try."

Jada stood up and was about to leave when he asked, "Can you bring me a gram back?"

Jada said, "You need to stop your nose from bleeding."

He dabbed his nose with the napkin as Jada made her way to the exit. When she looked back, the skinny bitch was on his lap rubbing his back.

Shamari had unpacked most of the boxes, set up the bed, and hung the bedroom TV when Jada arrived home. Jada sensed that Shamari thought he would be moving in. While she didn't mind him staying for a while, she would have to make it clear that this was not his home. She would do anything she could to help him, but he was wanted by the Feds. When she entered the bedroom, he looked up.

"Hey, baby," he said.

They kissed briefly.

Jada said, "Have a seat. I need to ask you something."

He looked at her and said, "I think I know what it is and I don't plan on being here long. I love you, Jada and I always will, but I know that the Feds are after me and that's not your problem. Even though I have a new face, my fingerprints are the same and I still have tattoos that they can identify me with."

Jada smiled and said, "Well, I'm glad to know you love me and that you're thinking about me."

"Is that what you wanted to talk about? Me leaving?"

"Well, I was going to have that talk eventually."

"Look, you don't have to explain. You've done enough for me."

"Thanks."

"Plus, I don't want you to get a harboring a fugitive charge on you. You were my girlfriend. It's just a matter of time before they come here."

"Ok, but that's not what I wanted to talk about."

He looked confused.

"I wanted to ask you how you were transporting your work."

"Huh?"

"I know you went to Cali a few weeks ago to pick up something. How did you get it back?"

"A girl name Erica, a friend of my sister's boyfriend, brought it back."

"Is she black or white?"

"Black. Why?"

"What if I tell you I could get a middle aged, white man to bring it back?"

"What are you talking about? How do you know him?"

"You know him too."

"Who is he?"

"The surgeon."

"No way."

"Yeah, he wants to do it."

"Why do he want to do it? I don't believe it. Why would a man like that want to be involved with something like this? He's making legitimate money."

"He has a problem," Jada said.

"What kind of problem?""

Though Jada was more loyal to Shamari, she still didn't feel good about telling him Craig's business. But she had to, if she expected him to want to help him out.

Shamari pressed, "What kind of problem?"

"A habit."

"What kind of habit?"

"Coke."

"He's a coke head?" Shamari laughed. "But he doesn't look like a coke head."

"I know."

"He needs money?"

"Well, things are going really bad for him. His wife is divorcing him and he has to pay her a lot of money per month."

"And he has to get the nose candy."

"Cut it out, Shamari."

"You defending this motherfucker?"

"Not defending anybody. He told me to ask if you can use him, and so I'm asking."

"Why should I help that motherfucker?" Then he thought about Craig fucking Jada, getting head from Jada, and fucking Jada in the ass. "Tell me why should I help this motherfucker, Jada?"

Jada sensed that Shamari was getting upset and she said, "Now would you really be helping him or would you be helping yourself?"

"What the fuck are you talking about?"

"It's a matter of perspective."

"Perspective?"

"It's all about how you look at shit, Shamari. You would really be helping yourself. I mean, look at this motherfucker? No cop is going to stop him."

"You're right." Shamari thought maybe this wasn't a bad idea after all.

"I mean, he's not going to go through all the bullshit a black male or female will go through."

"True. What does he want for doing this?"

"I don't know."

"He's gonna want a lot more money than what I'm willing to pay."

"Maybe. Maybe not."

Shamari said, "Think about it. You think this man is going to risk his personal life and freedom for three thousand dollars?"

"Three thousand dollars?"

"Yeah, that's the most I'm paying a runner."

"You're right. He's not going to want to do this for so little. It just won't make sense."

"Exactly!"

CHAPTER 15

Trey was lying on Shantelle's sofa about to doze when the phone rang. It was his son, T. J.

"T. J., my main man, what's going on?"

"Daddy, what are you doing?"

"I'm lying on the sofa. Why? What's up?"

"Can you come and play with me?"

"Sure," Trey said. There was nothing else he was doing, so there was no reason for him not to meet up and play with his son for a few hours.

"Can we go to the park and then to grandma's house?"

"We can do anything you want."

"I want a Mountain Dew too. Mommy won't let me drink sodas like you do."

"Where is your mother?"

"She's in the other room."

"Don't let her hear you say that."

"I know, Daddy. That's our secret. Remember we pinky promised."

"That's right." Trey sat up and looked at his watch. "I'll be there to pick you up in about an hour okay?"

"Ok. Yay!" T. J. yelled.

When Trey terminated the call, he glanced over his shoulder to see Shantelle staring at him with her hands on her hips.

"Who was that?"

"My son. I'm going to pick him up and play with him for awhile."

"That's nice."

"Yeah, I figured I wasn't doing anything else."

Shantelle sat on the edge of the sofa and said, "Baby, when am I going to get to meet your son and your baby's mother?"

"In due time."

"Why can't I meet them now?"

"Now is not the right time."

"When will be the right time?"

"I don't know."

"Trey, give me an answer instead of saying it's not the right time."

Trey looked her straight in the eye. He wanted to tell her to shut the fuck up, but he knew how super sensitive she was and he didn't like being verbally abusive. He never had to say anything to Starr. She just followed his lead, but she could hold her own. Damn he missed that woman.

"Why is this important to you?"

"T. J. is a part of you and I want to see him."

"I'll tell you what, I'll let you meet T. J. I'll bring him by, but now is not the time to meet his mother. She'll make it hard on me."

Shantelle smiled and said, "At some point, I'd like to meet your mother."

"Slow down. One thing at a time."

"Okay, baby."

Trey stood up from the sofa and made his way to the door. Shantelle's insecurities were beginning to get on his god-damned nerves.

Trey had spent the whole day with T. J. They had gone to the movies. He'd taken him to see his grandma. He played catch with him at the park and he had taken him shopping to buy him some new shoes. Then they met Shantelle, who had baked T. J.

some cookies. He was exhausted and though he liked spending time with his son, he was happy to be bringing him back home so he could go home and get some rest. When Trey approached Jessica's driveway, T. J. became sad.

Trey said, "What's wrong, champ?"

"I don't want you to go."

Trey said, "I'll come back and get you next weekend."

"I don't want to go in there. I don't like being home."

"Why not?"

"Because it's lonely in there. It's just me and mom all the time. I don't have any brothers or sisters like the other kids."

Trey knew exactly how T. J. felt. He grew up in a house where he was the only child. Although he had a half brother, he hardly ever saw him growing up and Trey knew it could be lonely. He didn't know what to do right now, he didn't want to try and gain custody of T. J. until he was through with the drug business. Right now was not a good time. Trey kissed his son's forehead and said, "I tell you what, champ, I'll come to your school to eat lunch with you tomorrow."

T. J. was smiling hard. "Would you?"

"I love you, son. Don't ever forget that. Be good and take care of your mother, okay?"

"Okay."

"You're the man of the house. Okay?"

"I know that, Dad. Mom tells me that all the time."

Trey and T. J. got out of the car and made their way to the front door. They stepped inside the house. Jessica was waiting for T. J. and she looked amazing. Her hair was down, she was wearing a black fitted dress, and her legs looked absolutely delicious. Trey noticed her right away.

T. J. said, "Mom, I had so much fun. Dad and I went and saw grandma and we went to the park, the movies and this nice lady, named Ms. Shantelle, baked me some cookies."

"Ms. Shantelle, huh?"

"Yeah, she's nice and pretty too. She's gonna be my girlfriend."

The fact that her son had said some other woman was pretty infuriated the hell out of Jessica.

"So she's going to be your girlfriend?"

T. J. smiled revealing the missing teeth that most six year olds have. "Yeah."

"I don't think your daddy would like that." Then she kissed T. J. again and said, "Go to your room. Let me talk to your daddy for a moment."

T. J. high-fived his father then disappeared into his bedroom. When he was gone, Jessica said, "So you have my son around women I've never met."

"It's not what you think."

"You know, Trey, the grownup thing to do would be to introduce me to your new girlfriend. But that's what a grownup would do and I'm giving you too much credit for being grown. You hid me and T. J. from Starr for years."

"Could you chill? Damn, you're getting on my nerves."

"Look, I'm not going to let you upset me, I'm in a good mood and I'm going on a date, so there is no way I'm letting you get me down."

"Look, can't we get along for T. J.'s sake?'"

"Of course."

"So where are you going? You're all dressed up."

"Catching a movie with a friend. Mom is going to watch T. J."

"Good, you need to get out more."

"I think so."

"You looking damn good."

"So, I was right."

"Right about what?"

"I thought I saw you admiring me."

Trey smiled. "I was checking you out a little bit"

She smiled and walked toward him. "You know you still want me."

"I never said you weren't fine as hell."

She leaned toward him and kissed him. He tried to resist for a moment but then he found himself kissing her back. His hand was on her ass then around her tiny-ass waist. She kneeled and placed her mouth on his dick through his jeans and his dick sprang to life. He wanted to fuck her badly but he knew that it would ultimately lead to destruction. He resisted and pulled away.

"What's wrong?"

"We don't need to go down that path."

"Why? I know you have a woman. I mean women."

"I need to be going."

"Whatever, Trey. You know you wanna fuck me."

Trey made his way to the door. He looked back at her and said, "Tell T. J. to remember I'm coming to his school tomorrow for lunch."

"Fuck you, Trey!"

CHAPTER 16

Two white men were knocking at Lani's door. There was a doorbell outside but they were knocking. How did they get into the building? They didn't know the code. They never buzzed her and she never let them in. They had to be the police on official business, not like those clowns, Williams and Kearns. They were wearing nice suits, clean shaven, and looked very serious. She did not want to let them in but she had a feeling they knew she was inside, and they were not going to leave until she answered. Besides, she didn't want the neighbors to be alarmed. She tip-toed over to the peephole so they knew that she was there.

One of them said, "Open the door, Ms. Miller."

"Who are you?"

"Department of Homeland Security."

"What?"

"Homeland Security."

"Just a second," she called out.

Lani disappeared into the back room thinking this was some bullshit. What the fuck did the Department of Homeland Security want with her? She hadn't done anything and as far as she knew, Black didn't do anything to warrant the Department of Homeland Security to want him. He wasn't a terrorist. The Department of Homeland Security went after motherfuckers like Bin Laden. Motherfuckers who are trying to take over the country, overthrow the government and hijackers who ran planes into buildings, not an Atlanta D-Boy that rides around listening to Trap music.

She knew that they had better shit to do than to fuck with her and Black. She slipped on a pair of tight jeans. She wasn't concerned about either of them lusting after her ass. They seemed to be more professional than that Williams clown who'd been in her house before.

She opened the door and the two men presented their badges. They looked to be in their mid-thirties. They were very handsome white men. One was kind of short. He had dark hair and was clean shaven. The other man had movie star good looks. Tall, blonde and very well built. The type of guy she would fuck if she were into white men.

The movie star said, "Scott Chandler."

The brunette said, "I'm agent David Carroll."

"What do you want with me?"

"Can we come in?"

"Please do."

She led them into the living room.

Once they were seated, David Carroll said, "I know you have no idea why we are here."

"I don't."

"You're part of an ongoing investigation."

"Me? Wait a minute, you're homeland security, I'm no terrorist."

The men laughed and said, "That's a common misconception that all we investigate is terrorism."

"Okay, what do you want from me?"

"Not here to ask you anything. We know you had an interview with the APD about a week ago."

"Yeah, I did."

"I'm here to tell you that this case is bigger than you think, bigger than even what the APD thinks."

"What case? And what do I have to do with it?

"You have a lot to do with it, but you don't have to."

"What are you saying?" Lani was racking her brain. Wondering what the fuck they were talking about and what the hell did they want from her? She'd never killed anyone or sold drugs. This had to be a mistake.

"I'm saying Tyrann is a major drug trafficker and has been for a long time. We know you haven't been with him for a long time."

"So why are you here?"

"Because when he first came to our attention, you were together. Remember the House at 2121 Alpine Circle?"

"Yeah. That house was in my name."

"But financed by Tyrann."

"Wait a minute, I was working at the time."

The movie star said, "So we're supposed to believe that you paid the rent with a hotel front desk salary?"

Lani realized that they had been investigating her thoroughly because she had been a front desk clerk at the Marriott at the time. "What do you want with me?"

"We're here to give you an opportunity."

"What kind of opportunity?"

"To walk away from all of this unscathed."

"In exchange for information, right?"

"Right."

Lani looked at the two white men. Both of them were very serious and devoid of any personality. She knew they weren't playing and they were in fact on Black's ass. As much as she hated that son of a bitch Black, she loved his black ass at the same time. He'd done too much for her and her family for her to say anything about him to the authorities.

"Am I being charged?" she asked.

"No, not right now."

"Listen, I would like for you to leave my house right now."

The two men stood up and made their way to the door. They didn't argue or try to persuade her. They left without saying another word.

Lani drove to Black's home in Alpharetta. Black was surprised to see her. He attempted to hug her and invited her in when he noticed that she looked worried.

"What the fuck is wrong, babe?" he asked.

"I had some visitors today."

"Visitors? What kind of visitors?"

"Department of Homeland Security."

"What? What did they want with you?" He laughed and said, "So, you're a part of the Taliban?"

"No, they came to my house asking about your black ass."

"What?"

"Yeah it was two white men with the Department of Homeland Security asking for information about you!"

"What did they ask, and why in the fuck did you talk to them?"

Lani looked puzzled and confused. "That's just it. They didn't ask anything."

Black stood up and made his way to the bar. He poured himself a glass of Hennessy.

"And you didn't tell them anything?"

"Are you listening, motherfucker? They didn't ask me anything."

Black sipped his drink and said, "But you said they were looking for me."

"They said they were there because of an ongoing investigation that I was a part of along with you."

Black was laughing his ass off. "Wait a minute, so you trying to tell me the same people that are trying to stop terrorism are investigating me? Yeah, right. What the fuck is wrong with you, Lani? Who put you up to this bullshit? Is this some kind of sick joke? Nobody is looking for me. I went to my lawyer's office. He checked to see if I had any warrants and I didn't."

"Look, I'm not here to argue with you. I'm just telling you what happened at my house. Two white men showed up and said they had been investigating us since we lived on Alpine Circle."

Black finished his liquor.

Lani said, "I know this sounds crazy, and it sounded crazy to me to. I thought it would have been the DEA or ATF, not the goddamned Department of Homeland Security. I thought it was a joke too."

Black's face got serious and he said, "So what did they want with you?"

"They said they wanted to give me an opportunity."

"What kind of opportunity?"

"To walk away unscathed."

"And what did you say?"

"I asked them to leave my house."

Black said, "I don't believe it."

"I can tell you don't believe it."

"What in the fuck would they want with me?"

"Have I ever lied to you?"

"No." He was now quiet and reflective.

"Haven't I always been loyal to you?"

"Even when I didn't deserve it."

"You don't believe me."

"I just don't want to believe it, I guess."

CHAPTER 17

Big Papa called Jada and asked to meet up for drinks. She asked him to bring one of his friends with him for Lani.

"As a matter of fact, bring that fine-ass nigga that came over to your house the other day." Jada said, then realized that she just called one of his friends attractive.

"You like my boy?"

"Well he's good looking, but you baby—you have substance. You are a man of character. I couldn't date a man like that. He probably spends more time in the mirror than I do, but he'd be perfect for Lani."

"Ok I'll call Shakur and we can meet at the W on 16th Street at eight o'clock."

"Perfect."

Lani and Jada sat at a table in the middle of the lounge and they'd already started a tab that Big Papa would have to pick up. The ladies drank mojitos while they waited on the men.

Jada said, "I'm telling you, this man is drop dead gorgeous."

Lani was smiling but she said, "You know I'm not into pretty boys."

"I'm not into pretty boys either, but when you see this man, you're going to be like 'that motherfucker is perfection'. I mean tall with long, well maintained locs, perfect skin, and perfect teeth. Gorgeous, I'm telling you."

"What does he do?"

"What do you think he do?"

"Another D boy?"

"Quit being concerned about that. All you need to know is that the motherfucker has money."

"I'm so tired of this lifestyle."

Jada looked at Lani like she'd lost her motherfucking mind. "So what are you going to do? Date a regular nigga with a nine to five?"

"What's so bad about that?"

"Just do it and you'll see. Dudes out there now be wanting to go Dutch with you on a damn forty dollar meal. I ain't got time for that."

Big Papa and Shakur approached the table and Jada introduced Big Papa to Lani. They shook hands and Big Papa said, "Everybody, this is Shakur."

Lani thought this was the finest goddamned man she'd seen in her life as she marveled at his beautiful locs, his wide shoulders, and tiny waist. And that goddamned 'I will fuck you to death' smile made her pussy wet. Those damn teeth were sparkling white and just perfect. The genetic gods had been good to him.

"How are you, Lani?"

Lani thought she'd be fine once he put his dick inside her, but she had to act like a lady. "I'm doing okay."

Shakur sat beside her and he was wearing Aventis by Creed. It was mesmerizing. Everything about him was on point. Hair? Check. Teeth? Check. Body? Check. Style? Check. He was the complete package until she spotted a beaded necklace around his neck. That shit was gay but she'd give him the benefit of the doubt for now.

He sat beside her, still smiling like he'd fuck her into a coma and then eat her out of it.

The waitress came and Lani and Jada order two more mojitos. Shakur ordered a Red Bull, and Big Papa ordered a diet coke.

Lani said to Shakur, "You don't drink?"

"I do. Been up since five a.m. so I'm a little tired."

Jada said, "And this nigga ordered a diet coke. How are ya'll going to ask us out for drinks and not even drink?"

Big Papa was grinning with his yellow ass teeth. "Gotta get this weight off me. Liquor equals calories."

Jada rubbed his back. "I'm so proud of you, baby. You've really been doing a good job."

Lani said to Shakur, "Why don't you have a woman?"

Shakur said, "Who said I didn't?"

Lani laughed and said, "My bad. So why are you here?"

Shakur said, "I don't have a woman. I was just fucking with you."

"You look like a player."

"I've heard that all my life."

"Are you?"

"I've played women but I've also been played. That's life, but right now you looking at a grown man. If I died today, I've had my share of pussy."

Lani sipped her drink thinking he must have gotten a lot of pussy with those sexy-ass lips.

Shakur said, "What about you? Who is the lucky man?"

"No man. He was murdered a few months ago."

"Sorry to hear that."

"It's okay."

"What happened? I mean, if you want to talk about it."

"I don't know exactly what happened, but his body was found in the trunk of a Lincoln…."

"Chris Jones?"

"You knew Chris?"

"Didn't really know him, but I know Mike."

Lani shook her head and said, "It's a small world."

Shakur called out to Big Papa, "Ty, this is Mike's brother's girlfriend."

Big Papa said, "No way."

"Yep," Lani said.

Shakur said to Lani, "That just happened. Are you ready to move on?"

"Depends."

"On what?"

"If I meet somebody that is good to me. Not just financially and sexually, but faithfully. God knows I dealt with my share of dogs."

He laughed and said, "I want to take your mind off all those losers."

"You do?"

"It's my mission."

"Is that so?"

"If you let me in."

With that body and that pussy-eating grin, she wanted to let him in. Damn did she want to let him in.

Later that night Lani followed Shakur to his home in Riverdale, Georgia. It was a very modest two-story home, very surprising for a big drug dealer. Once they were inside and seated in the den, Shakur made them drinks. He handed one to Lani.

"No thanks."

"So, you're not drinking now?"

"I would but I have to drive and besides I didn't see you fix the drink."

He laughed and said, "Oh, so you think I would spike your drink?"

"I'm not saying you would or you wouldn't. I just said I didn't see you fix it."

"You didn't see them fix the drinks at the hotel."

"You didn't drink at the hotel."

"Now that I'm home, I want to have a drink."

"But you said that you had to be up early in the morning."

Shakur laughed. "Look, we're arguing about nothing. You don't have to have the drink." He set her drink on the table then sat beside her. He put his arm around her shoulder and said, "I like you a lot. What do you think of me?"

Was he seriously asking her what she thought of him? She thought his tall chocolate ass was delicious, but she couldn't say that since it wasn't appropriate. "I think you're a nice guy."

"Nice guys finish last. I don't want to be a nice guy."

She blushed and said, "So what do you want me to say?"

"Say what you want to say."

She was blushing hard as hell. She would not say what she wanted to say and she would try her damndest not to do what she wanted to do.

"I like you."

"I don't think you trust me."

"We just met."

"But I let you come to my house."

"I guess that means you trust me."

"Of course. Why would you be here?"

Lani saw where this was going. Not only was Shakur fine, but he was an arrogant-ass motherfucker and in a weird way it was turning her the fuck on.

He rubbed her knee and said, "I can tell you ain't been touched in a while."

She avoided looking at those sexy-ass lips of his. She didn't want this night to end up with her face down and her ass in the air. He was making it hard as fuck.

He stood with the drink in hand and walked over and dimmed the lights then turned on his surround sound. Kanye West singing "Say You Will" came through the speakers. He removed his shirt and she couldn't keep her eyes off the tats decorating that sexy, wide-ass back or his eight pack, but damn why did he still have that gay ass beaded necklace on? Yuck!! But she wanted him inside her.

He sat beside her and placed his hands on her legs. Then he sipped his drink and leaned forward and kissed her. Before she knew it, they were tongue wrestling. His hand was now on her ass and her left hand was on his dick. He tried to remove her jeans but she resisted.

"What's wrong?"

"Nothing's wrong."

He leaned into her and kissed her again. His hands gripped her ass and he tried to remove her jeans again but she still resisted.

"Come on, you know you want to do it," he said.

"I do."

'Well what's wrong?"

"I'm a little too old for this bullshit. What happens when you don't call me and I'm somewhere pissed the fuck off at myself because I allowed it to happen?"

"I like you a lot, Lani." He made his way over and scooped up his shirt and put it back on. "I don't think you like me."

"So 'like' for you, is me face down and ass up?"

"I thought we were feeling each other."

"Me too."

Shakur said, "I get it. You think I'm going to tell Mike if we have sex?"

"Actually that hadn't crossed my mind until now. You're a grown man. I would hope you wouldn't do something like that."

"I get good vibes about you, Lani. Regardless of what people have been saying about you in the street, I think you're a good person."

"Lani said, "What did you just say?"

"About what?"

"What have people been saying about me in the street?"

"Mike and his friends are saying that you set his brother up to get killed and then had some niggas come to his parents' house and hold them hostage."

"What?"

"I'm just telling you what they are saying."

"Nobody is saying that."

"I don't know you. Why would I make some shit up like that? I don't believe them, so what difference does it make?"

"The reason why you don't believe them is because it never happened." Lani stood up, gathered her things and said, "I gotta go."

"I'll walk you out to the car."

When they were in his driveway, he gave her a kiss on the cheek and said, "I'll be in touch."

When Lani drove away from Shakur's home, she dialed Mike's number. He didn't pick up. She dialed it again and again until finally he picked up.

"Hello?"

"Mike, I need to talk to you."

"I'm listening."

"People are telling me that you think that I set your brother up, and I had your parents held hostage."

"Oh, really?"

"Mike, tell me you don't think that?"

"Look, Lani. All I know is those motherfuckers were at my parents house and you're the only person that knows where my mom lives."

"Mike, you don't believe that. You know I wouldn't do nothing like that."

"I don't know, Lani."

"Mike, that's not the part that even hurt me the most. The part that really hurts me is that you're saying I had Chris set up. I loved your brother."

"Whatever."

"Look, you don't have to believe me."

"Good because I don't believe you." He ended the call.

CHAPTER 18

Jada met Craig in the parking deck of his office after work. She sat in the passenger side of a rental car. She said, "You're looking well."

"Thanks."

"Have you been using?"

"No, not in a few days. Why?"

"Oh, I can just tell."

"So are we here for you to tell me how much of a junkie I am, or do you have some news about what I asked you?"

"He doesn't want to do it."

"Why?"

"He's only paying three thousand dollars for drug runs."

"Three thousand dollars? Not worth the risk."

"I know."

He took a deep breath. "Does he need any partners?"

"What do you mean, partners?"

"Well I've sold the two Maseratis. I have cash."

"You want to be a drug dealer?"

"No. You know I don't know the first thing about drug dealing. But I can invest some money."

Jada laughed and said, "You want to invest some money? Like what kind of money."

"I need to know the return first. Ask him if I invest a hundred thousand dollars. How much can I get back? I would want you to be in charge of it, of course."

"If you have money from selling your cars, why do you need to sell drugs? It doesn't make sense."

"Jada, I'm not selling, I'm investing."

"But it's not making sense."

"I have a lot going on. I told you, my wife is trying to take everything."

"Okay, but you know you can go to prison?"

"I don't have a choice."

"You do."

He turned away and said, "Look, I'm embarrassed to tell you this but I have a few malpractice suits and my insurance is going through the roof. I need money."

"Malpractice? You're the best."

"Hey, it happens to the best of us."

"I don't think Shamari wants any partners."

"Ask him."

"Okay."

She was about to get out of the car and he stopped her. They stared into each other eyes for a long time and he said, "Thank you."

Later that night she texted him.

Jada: *For a hundred thousand, he said you'll get a fifty thousand dollar return in a month but you're going to have to bring it back for him.*

Craig: *No Problem.*

The rooftop pool at the SLS hotel in Beverly Hills was just fabulous. And Jada's body looked just as spectacular as she wore a white thong and a very fitting bathing suit top that was struggling very hard to contain her tits. She'd thought about a yellow conservative one piece but decided at the last moment to wear the thong, after all this was Beverly Hills so she figured what the hell. Jada and Shamari stood next to the pool sipping drinks. Shamari was drinking a Hennessy and Coke and Jada had a white wine when Craig approached with a woman that looked like a black Barbie doll. The woman introduced herself as Imani. Imani had a very long weave and Jada could tell she'd had several nose jobs as well as cheek implants, chin implants, an eyebrow raise, veneers, and a breast augmentation.

Shamari whispered to Jada, "This woman looks like a god-damn robot."

Jada said, "Hell, I hope I don't look like that. Everything on this bitch is artificial."

Craig and Shamari shook hands without smiling and Jada suggested they go to the hotel room to discuss business. Though she loved the ambiance, she knew that nosey-ass people could still overhear their conversation.

Once they were in their room, Jada said, "So why did you bring her?" Jada pointed to Imani.

"She's going to help me get it back to Atlanta."

"How is she going to get back to Atlanta?"

"Drive." Craig said.

Shamari looked at her. She looked so goddamned fake, he fig-ured she didn't have the brains to get back to Atlanta. Could she read a map? Hell, could she even follow a GPS navigation system.

Craig said, "Relax. I'm going to take care of her. Don't worry, I'll handle her."

Shamari said, "What do you want for doing this?"

Jada said, "Yeah, what's in it for you?"

Craig said, "I'll take care of her. We worked out a deal."

"I just want the perfect nose," replied Imani.

"This is crazy. I've never heard of anything like this in my life," Jada said. She wanted to tell Imani she looked like a goddamned cat already. This woman did not need any more surgery.

Shamari said, "Who the fuck are we to judge anybody as long as she gets what she wants?"

Jada said, "Imani does not need any more surgery. She looks…"

Imani smiled and said, "I look fake. I know. You can say it. I won't be offended. When people say I look fake, it's a compliment."

Shamari just stared at the crazy-ass bitch. What the fuck? He wondered how this happened. What had taken place in her life to get her to this point?

Jada wanted to say something, but clearly the bitch was delusional and they were there for business, not to give this ho a psychological evaluation.

Shamari said, "Where's the money?"

Craig presented him with a briefcase.

"You'll get your profit back in a month."

"Don't worry about it. I'll handle it," Craig said.

"Okay, meet us back in the hotel lobby at seven. I'll have the product."

The two men shook hands.

Shamari tossed the two kilos on Black's table and Black said, "What the fuck? Why is the dope in these balloons? This shit has probably been cut a thousand goddamned times."

"No. I gave it to the courier and he thought that it was a good idea to take it out of the original wrapping."

"He? What the fuck do you mean he?"

"Yeah, bruh, it's a white dude. I'm talking about a nerd-looking motherfucker who the police will never suspect."

Black was visibly upset. His eyes were red and he stared at Shamari and then back at the balloons on the table. "And what make you think this motherfucker won't run his goddamned mouth, man?"

Shamari turned from Black's gaze and said, "He's not just a runner. He invested with us."

"Who? We don't need no investor."

"Look, all we gotta give him is fifty thousand dollars for a hundred thousand dollars."

"Motherfucker, that's a fifty percent return. No wonder you ain't got no goddamned money."

"It's a fifty percent return if we give him the money right after we use the hundred thousand but I told him I would see him in a month. But you know how the game goes. That month might turn into two months. By the time I pay his ass, we'll have made about three hundred thousand off his hundred."

"We don't need him."

"He is the reason we got the heroin back to Atlanta. What's the goddamned big deal? We are talking about pure heroin. We can afford to give him fifty thousand dollars."

"I don't know why you keep saying pure. If you get it from niggas, it is not pure."

"Okay, but the last product was a good product right."

"It was, but why do we need him?"

"Transportation."

"Fifty thousand dollars for transportation?"

"No, he invested a hundred thousand. What part of that don't you understand?"

"I don't want to meet him."

"I never said you had to meet him. I will deal with him."

Black scooped up the packages of dope off the table and examined them.

"My contact said it's better than before."

"Perfect."

Shamari said, "One thing, before I leave we need to change the goddamn name. This is getting out of hand. I don't want to be associated with that Obamacare name. Its killing people and I don't care if it's not our package that's killing people. I don't want that name."

"Look, Shamari, I handle distribution, you handle everything else."

Shamari snatched the product from the table and said, "I will take this somewhere else. I don't want you to use that name."

Black stepped in front of Shamari. "You want to take a step back! I sent money with you, so this is partly mine."

Shamari said, "I'll give you your goddamned money back, but I'm not going to let you use that name."

"Let me use? I'm confused. You are talking to me like you are my goddamned daddy! I'm a grown-ass man. I will do what the fuck I want to do."

"Look, Black." Shamari lowered his tone. "I want to keep working with you. I really do. I think we make a good team. Can't you see motherfuckers are dying off that Obamacare heroin?"

"But it's not our package."

"You don't know if it's ours. I didn't know you were cutting our shit with rat poison."

"Look, everybody cuts their shit with deadly shit."

"I guess you're right. It doesn't matter what you name the shit if it's deadly."

"All heroin is deadly—if they OD."

"But why rat poison?"

"Look, man, when we started this shit, I didn't know shit about this business, just like you didn't. This is what the OGs said to cut it with and they showed me how to do it. I had to cut it, otherwise I wouldn't have made shit."

"What are you talking about? You gave me a hundred and fifty thousand dollars. I know you made at least that much."

"I don't know what world you living in, but you cannot make three hundred thousand dollars off a kilo of heroin."

"Really?"

"Who told you that dumb shit? Like I said, I gave you damn near all the profits the first time because you needed the money more than I did. Did I make money? Yes. But the first one was pure, but we still didn't make three hundred thousand dollars. That isn't possible. Notice the second time we made about seventy-five thousand each."

"I thought that was because it wasn't as pure as the first."

"You are right. It wasn't as pure as the first kilo and guess what? If it wasn't for the goddamned rat poison, we wouldn't have made what we made."

"Well, why do it then? Why don't we just get some coke, something that we both know about?"

"Because coke is not going to sell this goddamned fast. These heroin junkies, they need this shit, man, and I'm going to give them what they need."

"We gotta change the name."

"I've been giving it some thought. I think I got a new name even better than Obamacare."

"And that name is?"

"Pretty Hurts."

"Like Beyonce's song?"

"Exactly. I mean who don't like Beyonce? Whites. Blacks. Mexicans. Asians. Hispanics."

Shamari wanted to tell Black that Mexicans were Hispanics but he knew Black didn't give a fuck. Shamari laughed. As crazy as Black was, he was a shrewd-ass businessman.

"I actually like the name," Shamari said.

He hugged Black and Black whispered into Shamari's ear, "This partner of yours better not run his motherfuckin' mouth."

"I'll handle him."

"If he runs his goddamn mouth, I'll handle him."

CHAPTER 19

Black changed the name of the product and it was a hit in the streets. The two kilos were gone in a week's time and Shamari and Jada met Craig in California again. This time, Shamari purchased three kilos of heroin. Craig called Jada as soon as they made it back to Atlanta. It was a little after six p.m. and he told her to meet him at his office. The other surgeon and receptionist and all the assistants were gone for the day. As soon as Jada stepped in the office, Jada saw a woman that she recognized, but she didn't know from where. A really cute, skinny, black girl.

"Hi, I'm Jada."

The girl said, "Hi." But she didn't offer her name.

Craig said to Jada, "Just wait out here in the reception area."

Jada said, "Can you just give me what I came for so I can go see Shamari?"

"It will be just a few minutes." Craig disappeared into the back.

Jada skimmed through a People magazine but then turned to the black girl who was sitting in the lobby holding her breasts. Maybe she'd just gotten implants and they were bothering her, Jada thought. She looked really uncomfortable.

Jada said, "Where do I know you from?"

The woman said, "I don't know. Do you dance?"

"Hell no," Jada said. "Not that I have anything against dancers, but it's just not my thing." Jada sat the magazine down and said, "You dance?"

"Yeah."

"Where?"

"Mostly Cheetah's. I dance at the white clubs."

Then it occurred to Jada that the girl was the skinny bitch that had been dancing for Craig that night that he'd asked her to buy him some coke.

Jada said, "Oh yeah, I remember you. I was with him at Cheetah's the night that he met you."

"Oh yeah, I remember," the woman said.

"You got a name?"

"Rain."

"So you fuckin' for tits, Rain?"

"Excuse me?"

"Never mind," Jada said, as she scooped up a Time magazine and skimmed through it. She thought that not only was Craig addicted to coke, he was a sex addict as well. Fucking all these low-class, black, stripper girls, but that wasn't her problem. She was over his trifling ass.

Jada said, "How long have you been waiting for him, Rain?"

Rain was still holding her chest like she was in excruciating pain and Jada noticed that her boobs were leaking blood. She had a gauze that she was using to try and slow the blood."

"I was out here an hour before you came."

Jada glanced at her watch and said, "Well, this is getting ridiculous."

Jada set the magazine down and marched to the back and burst into the operating room. Craig stood over Imani who was lying naked on the operating table. When he realized Jada was standing over him, he turned to her and said, "Get the hell out of here!"

"Can you give me the dope, so I can go? I don't have time to wait for you to perform surgery on this bitch."

Craig held Imani's hand. He said, "Jada, get out of here!

Jada was about to shut the door when she noticed two blood drenched balloons on the counter. She stepped back inside the operating room and said, "What the fuck is that, Craig?"

"Nothing. Get out of here!"

"No, I ain't going no motherfucking where! What the fuck? I can't believe you, Craig!"

Craig let go of Imani's hand and made eye contact with Jada.

"Are you out of your mind? You implanted the heroin in this woman's body? What the fuck were you thinking?" Jada yelled.

"It's not like that."

Imani looked very faint. She said, "Daddy, am I going to be alright?"

Craig said, "Jada, please get out of here."

He turned to the woman and said, "Yes, you're going to be okay."

Imani smiled and said, "Good. I want to be perfect for you, Daddy, and when I get rhinoplasty, I'll be perfect."

Her breasts were leaking blood and it was disgusting as fuck to Jada. It suddenly occurred to Jada why Rain's breasts were leaking. She'd been transporting heroin in hers as well.

"I feel so tired, Daddy."

Jada said, "What happened? What the fuck happened in here?"

"Relax. Everything is going to be okay," Craig said.

Imani faded in and out of consciousness.

"What the fuck is going on in here?"

"Everything is going to be fine, Jada," Craig assured her.

Jada grabbed Craig by his scrubs. "There's dope in this woman's blood isn't there?"

"No."

"You're a goddamn liar!" Jada said. She stared at the two blood drenched balloons. One of them was ruptured and dope leaked from it. "We gotta get her to a hospital."

Craig said, "We're going to go to prison if we do. It's going to be okay."

"Hold my hand, Daddy."

Craig held Imani's hand and she said, "I love you, and I want to be perfect for you." She took a breath and closed her eyes.

He held her hand, his thumb on her wrist and he felt her pulse getting weaker.

She looked up at him again, smiled and said, "I'm going to be perfect for you." She closed her eyes again and her pulse stopped.

He placed his lips on hers and breathed into her mouth three times then with the heel of his hands between her bloody breasts he began to apply pressure expecting her heart to jumpstart. There was no result.

"Goddamn it!" Craig said.

Jada said, "What the fuck is going on, Craig?"

Craig smacked Imani on the face three times. "Open your eyes, damn it! Open your eyes! Goddamn it, don't you die on me! No you can't go! Don't go! You can't die on me!"

He placed his mouth over hers again and tried to resuscitate her but he couldn't.

"No. No. No," he whispered, tears cascading his face.

Jada said, "I fucking hate you! I hate you so goddamned much!" She called Shamari.

"Hey, babe," Shamari answered.

"Get over here right away!" She was crying and screaming into the phone.

"Over where?"

"The surgeon's office!"

"Why? What's going on?"

"Just come and come fast!"

Twenty minutes later, Shamari was banging on the office door. Rain opened the door and Jada was sitting in the lobby with her head between her legs crying like hell.

Shamari said, "Jada, what's wrong with you?"

She looked up at Shamari and hugged him, but kept crying

Shamari had to calm her ass down. "What's wrong, babe?"

She kept sniffling, trying to talk but couldn't get her words out.

Shamari looked at Rain. "Who the fuck are you? And what is going on?"

"Imani is dead," Jada said.

"What? How did this happen?"

Jada stood and led him to the operating room where he found Craig wearing latex gloves as he mopped up a small pool of blood. Then Shamari saw Imani's corpse on the operating table. There were speckles of blood on Craig's scrubs and his surgeon's mask.

"What the fuck happened?"

Jada said, "This goddamned clown placed the dope in this woman's implants and the heroin leaked into her blood and killed her."

Shamari grabbed him by his scrubs. "Motherfucker, I will kill your bitch ass in here! Now you got me in more bullshit!"

Shamari punched Craig in his goddamned mouth. He stumbled over the body and his head crashed into the counter.

"What the fuck have you done, you dumb motherfucker?" said Shamari.

There was a scalpel lying on the counter. Shamari picked it up and was about to stick Craig in his goddamned throat when Jada grabbed him.

"Don't kill him. He ain't worth it, Bae."

"You defending this motherfucking idiot?"

"No. Not at all, babe. You are in all kinds of shit. You don't need to kill him. If you kill him, you're fucked for real."

"I'm fucked anyway."

Jada tried to pry the scalpel from Shamari's hands. "Gimme the knife, babe."

Shamari released it. Craig rose to his feet and Shamari punched him in his motherfucking mouth again, and knocked out one of his front teeth.

Craig nursed his mouth.

Shamari said, "I can't go down for this."

"What are we doing to do?" Jada asked.

"Where is the dope?"

Jada pointed to the four medical balloons on the table. There had been only two before. Jada realized that Craig must have removed the other two balloons from Imani's chest.

"Who is the other chick?" Shamari asked Craig.

"The other courier," Craig said.

Shamari turned to Jada. "Did you know about her? Tell her to bring her skinny ass in here."

When Rain entered the operating room, Shamari said, "We're all going to have to take this secret to our grave."

Everybody nodded except Rain, and Shamari said, "Do you understand, skinny bitch?"

"Yeah."

"What are we going to do?" asked Jada.

"We got to get rid of the body," Shamari said. "That's the only thing that we can do." He turned to Craig. "Does her family know she was with you?"

"She was raised in an orphanage."

Shamari slapped the fuck out of Craig for taking advantage of the clearly emotionally damaged woman.

CHAPTER 20

Trey sat in the parking deck, his car parked directly across from Starr's BMW.

Trey had found out from Brooke that Starr usually went home about six o'clock in the evening. He'd wanted to surprise her and show up at the showroom, but he'd peeked inside earlier to find her talking to a white gentlemen. It looked as if they were discussing business and he didn't want to impose. He decided he'd let her handle her business and then speak to her later.

Trey glanced at his watch. It was 7:45 p.m. He'd watch Brooke leave five minutes ago so he decided now was the perfect time to surprise her. He'd observed Starr through the window of the showroom talking to someone. A black man seated in one of the sofas on display. He couldn't see the man's face since his back was turned. Trey wondered if he was an employee or a customer. If it was a customer, he'd soon be leaving. He entered the showroom. A bell rang indicating that someone was entering the building. Starr was behind the counter organizing a desk while talking to the man who was seated with his back turned. When she heard the bell ring, her eyes darted toward the door.

"Trey. What are you doing here?"

"I thought I would come by and check you out."

The man stood up and turned toward Trey. Trey recognized him immediately. His brother, Troy. What the fuck was he doing here?

Troy said. "Bruh, what's up?"

"You tell me what's up?"

Troy stood and was making his way toward Trey smiling. "Good to see you."

"Really?" Trey said.

Trey glanced at Starr. Trey was trying to figure out what the fuck was going on between the two. Troy was standing there in some tight-ass pin stripped suit with a pink shirt.

Now Trey knew goddamned well Starr was not trying to fuck with this corny-ass dude. But why was he here and why hadn't he been in touch with him? This was the second time he'd been around her without checking in with him. Well, the second time that he knew of.

Troy offered Trey his hand but Trey refused. He stared at Starr.

"Somebody tell me what the fuck is going on? Why is he here? Sitting down all relaxed and shit."

Starr said, "He was just visiting."

Trey turned to Troy. "Why are you visiting my girl, brother?"

Starr said, "Trey, we are not together."

Trey said, "We are together until I say we are not together."

Starr said, "See, that's why we aren't together. Because of an attitude like that. You think you can do whatever the fuck you want to do and I have to obey you. Really, Trey, is that how this works? You go out and fuck whoever you want to fuck but I can't talk to anyone?"

Starr made her way from behind the counter and was walking toward Trey.

"You tell me how it works! You get to fuck my brother?" Trey said.

Starr made her way to Trey and slapped the fuck out of him.

"You think I'm that kind of woman," she said.

"You may not be that kind of woman, but I know my brother and I know how dudes are. This nigga wants to fuck you."

Troy said, "I'm going to leave now."

He tried to make his way past Trey and Starr but Trey stopped him. His hand now on Troy's chest.

"It's like that, huh, bruh?" Trey said.

"What are you talking about, man?"

"Look me in my eye and tell me that you ain't trying to fuck my girl?"

"I gotta go, man."

Trey took hold of his arm and Starr said, "Trey, don't start no bullshit up in here."

"I just want this nigga to tell me why the fuck he hanging around you."

Troy said, "Look, you got a good woman. You need to learn how to treat—"

Before he could finish talking, Trey punched him in his god-damned mouth. Blood shot from his lip and he broke two teeth before falling onto one of the living room display tables.

Starr tried to get in between the two of them but Trey shoved her out of the way.

Troy tried to stand up but Trey kicked him in his ribs then pinned his arms to the floor. Though Troy was younger, Trey was stronger and had more experience with fighting. He held Troy down as blood spilled from Troy's mouth.

Trey said, "Motherfucker, I will kill you over this woman! The only reason I don't shoot your punk ass is because of our daddy!"

Trey kicked Troy in his ribs once more and said, "You get the fuck out of here, and don't never come back in here!"

Starr said, "You can't tell who to come in here."

Troy made his way to the door and let himself out.

Trey said, "I need you to answer me truthfully. Did you fuck my brother?"

*   *   *

Shamari called Black but he didn't answer. He called him three more times back to back. Finally Black answered.

"What's up, bruh? Why are you blowing up my god-damned phone?"

"We got big problems, bruh. Big motherfucking problems."

"Is somebody in jail?"

"No."

"Okay, that's all I wanted to know."

"Can we meet somewhere?"

"Meet me at my house in about an hour."

*   *   *

To be continued